WICKED!

Volume 2

At B[...], an independent school crammed with the children of the rich and famous, charismatic headmaster, Hengist Brett-Taylor, hatches a plan to share his well-funded facilities with Larkminster comprehensive. His reasons for doing so are purely financial, but he is also encouraged by the opportunities the scheme gives him for frequent meetings with Janna Curtis, the dynamic new head of Larks, who has been drafted in to save the fast-sinking school from closure.

Janna is young, pretty, enthusiastic and vastly brave—and she will do anything to rescue her demoralized, run-down and cash-strapped school. Neither parents nor staff of either school are too keen on this radical move. For the students, however, it offers great opportunities for further joyous mayhem.

Janna, meanwhile, finds herself fatally drawn to Hengist. Will she emerge with her heart and her school intact?

WICKED!

Volume 2

Jilly Cooper

WINDSOR
PARAGON

First published 2006
by
Bantam Press
This Large Print edition published 2007
by
BBC Audiobooks Ltd by arrangement with
Transworld Publishers

Hardcover ISBN: 978 1 405 61650 8
Softcover   ISBN: 978 1 405 61651 5

The author and publishers are grateful for permission to quote
from 'Three Little Birds', Words and music by Bob Marley. ©
Copyright 1977 Blue Mountain Music Limited. Used by
permission of Music Sales Limited. All Rights Reserved.
International Copyright Secured.

British Library Cataloguing in Publication Data available

Printed and bound in Great Britain by
Antony Rowe Ltd., Chippenham, Wiltshire

This book is dedicated with love and admiration to two great headmistresses, Virginia Frayer and Katherine Eckersley, and also in loving memory of the Angel School, Islington, and Village High School, Derby

CAST OF CHARACTERS

ADELE	Single mother who teaches geography at Larkminster Comprehensive (otherwise known as Larks).
PARIS ALVASTON	Larks pupil and icon. Founder member of the notorious Wolf Pack.
ANATOLE	Bagley Hall pupil and beguiling son of the Russian Minister of Affaires.
RUFUS ANDERSON	Brilliant and eccentric head of geography at Bagley Hall. Henpecked father of two, liable to leave coursework on trains.
SHEENA ANDERSON	Rufus's concupiscent careerist wife—the main reason Rufus hasn't been given a house at Bagley Hall.
MRS AXFORD	Chief caterer at Bagley Hall.
MISS BASKET	A menopausal misfit who teaches geography at Larks.

BEA FROM THE BEEB	A researcher at the Teaching Awards.
DORA BELVEDON	Bagley Hall new girl. Determined to support her pony and her chocolate Labrador by flogging school scandal to the tabloids.
DICKY BELVEDON	Dora's equally resourceful twin brother who runs his own school shop at Bagley Hall selling booze and fags.
LADY BELVEDON (ANTHEA)	Dicky and Dora's young, very pretty, very spoilt mother. A Violet Elizabeth Bottox, drastically impoverished by widowhood, and determined to hunt for a rich new husband, unobserved by her beady son and daughter.
JUPITER BELVEDON	Dora and Dicky's machiavellian eldest brother, chairman of the governors at Bagley Hall, Tory MP for Larkminster, and tipped to take over the party leadership.

HANNA BELVEDON	Jupiter's lovely and loving wife, a painter.
SOPHY BELVEDON	An English teacher of splendid proportions and great charm. Ian and Patience Cartwright's daughter, and wife of Jupiter Belvedon's younger brother, Alizarin.
DULCIE BELVEDON	Adorable and self-willed daughter of Sophy and Alizarin.
SIR HUGO BETTS	Governor of Larks who sleeps through most meetings.
JAMES BENSON	An extremely smooth private doctor.
THE BISHOP OF LARKMINSTER	A governor of Bagley Hall.
GORDON BLENCHLEY	The unsavoury care manager of Oaktree Court, Paris Alvaston's children's home.
HENGIST BRETT-TAYLOR	Hugely charismatic headmaster of Bagley Hall.
SALLY BRETT-TAYLOR	Hengist's wife, classic beauty and jolly good sort, hugely

	contributory towards Hengist's success.
ORIANA BRETT-TAYLOR	Hengist and Sally's daughter, a much admired BBC foreign correspondent.
WALLY BRISTOW	Stalwart site manager at Larks.
GENERAL BROADSTAIRS	Lord Lieutenant of Larkshire and governor of Bagley Hall.
'BOFFIN' BROOKS	The cleverest boy at Bagley Hall, a humourless prig.
SIR GORDON BROOKS	Boffin's father, a thrusting captain of industry.
ALEX BRUCE	Deputy head of Bagley Hall, nicknamed Mr Fussy.
POPPET BRUCE	His dreadful wife, who teaches RE. An acronymphomaniac, determined to impose total political correctness on Bagley Hall.
CHARISMA BRUCE	Alex and Poppet's severely gifted daughter.
MARIA CAMBOLA	Larks's splendidly flamboyant head of music.

RUPERT CAMPBELL-BLACK	Former showjumping champion and Tory Minister for Sport. Now leading owner/trainer, and director of Venturer, the local ITV station. Despite being as bloody-minded as he is beautiful, Rupert is still Nirvana for most women.
TAGGIE CAMPBELL-BLACK	His adored wife—an angel.
XAVIER CAMPBELL-BLACK	Bagley Hall pupil and Rupert and Taggie's adopted Colombian son, who has hit moody adolescence head-on.
BIANCA CAMPBELL-BLACK	Xavier's ravishingly pretty, sunny-natured younger sister, also adopted and Colombian.
IAN CARTWRIGHT	Former commanding officer of a tank regiment, now bursar at Bagley Hall.
PATIENCE CARTWRIGHT	Ian's loyal wife—a trooper who teaches riding and runs the stables at Bagley.
MRS CHALFORD	Head of history at Larks. A

self-important bossy boots who likes to be referred to as 'Chally'.

TARQUIN COURTNEY   Charismatic captain of rugger at Bagley Hall.

ALISON COX   Sally Brett-Taylor's housekeeper, known as 'Coxie'.

JANNA CURTIS   Larks's very young, Yorkshire-born headmistress.

P.C. CUTHBERT   A zero-tolerant police constable, determined to impose order on Larks.

DANIJELA   Larks pupil from Bosnia.

DANNY   Larks pupil from Ireland.

EMLYN DAVIES   A former Welsh rugby international, known as Attila the Hunk, who teaches history at Bagley Hall and coaches the rugger fifteens to serial victory.

DEBBIE   Ace cook at Larks.

ARTIE DEVERELL   Head of modern languages at Bagley Hall.

ASHTON DOUGLAS   The sinister, lisping Chief
                        Executive Officer of S and C
                        Services, the private
                        company brought in by the
                        Government to supervise
                        education in Larkshire.

ENID   Lachrymose librarian at
                        Larks.

PRIMROSE DUDDON   Earnest, noble-browed,
                        ample-breasted form prefect
                        at Bagley Hall.

VICKY FAIRCHILD   Two-faced but both of them
                        extremely pretty. Cures
                        truancy at Larks overnight
                        when Janna Curtis appoints
                        her as head of drama.

JASON FENTON   Larks's deputy head of
                        drama, known as Goldilocks.

PIERS FLEMING   Wayward head of English at
                        Bagley Hall.

JOHNNIE FOWLER   Good-looking Larks
                        hellraiser; BNP supporter;
                        persistent truant.

LANDO
FRANCE-LYNCH   Master of the Bagley
                        Beagles, whose sparse
                        intellect is compensated for
                        by dazzling all-round athletic

and equestrian ability.

DAISY FRANCE-LYNCH   His sweet mother, a painter, wife of Ricky France-Lynch, former England polo captain.

FREDDIE   A waiter at La Perdrix d'Or restaurant.

CHIEF INSPECTOR TIMOTHY GABLECROSS   A wise, kind and extremely clever policeman.

MAGS GABLECROSS   The wise, kind wife of the Chief Inspector, part-time modern languages teacher at Larks.

GLORIA   PE teacher at Larks not given to hiding her physical lights under bushels.

THEO GRAHAM   Head of classics at Bagley Hall, an outwardly crusty old bachelor with a heart of gold. Takes out his hearing aid on Speech Day.

GILLIAN GRIMSTON   Head of Searston Abbey, an extremely successful Larkminster grant-maintained school for girls.

LILY HAMILTON — Aunt of Jupiter, Dicky and Dora Belvedon. A merry, very youthful octogenarian and Janna Curtis's next-door neighbour in the village of Wilmington.

DAME HERMIONE HAREFIELD — World famous diva, seriously tiresome, brings out the Crippen in all.

WADE HARGREAVES — An unexpectedly humane Ofsted Inspector.

DENZIL HARPER — Head of PE at Bagley Hall.

UNCLE HARLEY — Jamaican drugs dealer, lives on and off with Feral Jackson's mother.

SIR DAVID 'HATCHET' HAWKLEY — Headmaster of Fleetley, illustrious classical scholar. Later Lord Hawkley.

LADY HAWKLEY (HELEN) — A nervy beauty. Having numbered Rupert Campbell-Black and Roberto Rannaldini among her former husbands, Helen hopes marriage to David

Hawkley means calmer waters.

ROD HYDE — An awful autocrat, headmaster of St James's, a highly successful Larkminster grant-maintained school, known as St Jimmy's.

'SKUNK' ILLINGWORTH — Deputy head of science at Larks.

'FERAL' JACKSON — Larks's leading truant, Paris Alvaston's best friend and founder member of the Wolf Pack. Afro-Caribbean, beautiful beyond belief, seriously dyslexic, and a natural athlete.

NANCY JACKSON — Feral's mother, a heroin addict.

JESSAMY — A teaching assistant at Larks.

JESSICA — Hengist Brett-Taylor's stunning second secretary, a typomaniac.

JOAN JOHNSON — Head of science at Bagley Hall, also in charge of Boudicca, the only girls' house. Nicknamed 'No-Joke

Joan' because of a total lack of humour.

MRS KAMANI | Long-suffering owner of Larks's nearest newsagent's.

KATA | Larks pupil and wistful asylum-seeker from Kosovo.

AYSHA KHAN | One of Larks's few achievers. Destined for an arranged marriage in Pakistan.

RASCHID KHAN | Aysha's bullying father.

MRS KHAN | Aysha's bullied but surprisingly brave mother.

RUSSELL LAMBERT | Ponderous chairman both of Larks's governors and Larkminster planning committee.

LANCE | An understandably terrified newly qualified Larks history teacher.

AMBER LLOYD-FOXE | Minxy founder member of the 'Bagley Babes', otherwise known as the 'Three Disgraces'.

BILLY LLOYD-FOXE | Amber's father, an ex-Olympic showjumper, now a presenter for the BBC.

TEDDY MURRAY	Randal Stancombe's foreman.
NADINE	Paris Alvaston's social worker.
MARTIN 'MONSTER' NORMAN	Larks pupil. Overweight bully and coward.
'STORMIN'' NORMAN	Larks parent governor and Monster's mother, given to storming into Larks and punching anyone who crosses her ewe lamb.
MISS PAINSWICK	Hengist Brett-Taylor's besotted and ferociously efficient secretary.
CINDY PAYNE	Deceptively cosy New Labour county councillor in charge of education.
KYLIE ROSE PECK	Sweet-natured Larks pupil and member of the Wolf Pack. So eternally up the duff, she'll soon qualify for a free tower block.
CHANTAL PECK	Kylie Rose's mother and also a parent governor at Larks.
CAMERON PECK	Kylie Rose's baby son.

GANYMEDE	Another baby son of Kylie Rose.
COLIN 'COL' PETERS	Editor of the *Larkminster Gazette*. A big, nasty toad in a small pond.
PHIL PIERCE	Head of science at Larks, loved by the children and a great supporter of Janna Curtis.
MIKE PITTS	Larks's deputy head, furious the head's job has been given to Janna Curtis.
COSMO RANNALDINI	Dame Hermione's son and Bagley Hall warlord, with a pop group called the Cosmonaughties and the same lethal sex appeal as his father, the great conductor Roberto Rannaldini.
DESMOND REYNOLDS	Smooth Larkminster estate agent known as 'Des Res'.
ROCKY	Larks pupil and ungentle giant until the Ritalin kicks in.
BIFFO RUDGE	Head of maths at Bagley Hall, ex-rowing Blue, who frequently rides his bike into

the River Fleet while coaching the school eight.

ROBBIE RUSHTON — Larks's incurably lazy, left-wing head of geography.

CARA SHARPE — Larks's fearsome head of English and drama.

'SATAN' SIMMONS — Larks bully and best friend of Monster Norman.

SMART — Stalwart Bagley Hall rugger player.

PEARL SMITH — Another Larks hell-cat, member of the Wolf Pack.

MISS SPICER — An unfazed member of Ofsted.

SAM SPINK — Bossy-boots union representative at Larks.

SOLLY THE UNDERTAKER — Governor at Larks.

RANDAL STANCOMBE — Handsome Randal, definitely Mr Dicey rather than Mr Darcy, a wildly successful property developer. One of his private estates of desirable residences, Cavendish Plaza, sits uncomfortably close to

Larks.

JADE STANCOMBE   Randal's daughter, sharp-clawed glamourpuss and Bagley Babe.

MISS SWEET   Beleaguered under-matron at Boudicca, reluctantly put in charge of Bagley's sex education.

CRISPIN THOMAS   Incurably greedy deputy director of S and C Services.

TRAFFORD   An unspeakably scrofulous but highly successful artist.

GRANT TYLER   An electronics giant.

MISS UGLOW   Larks RE teacher.

PETE WAINWRIGHT   Genial under-manager at Larkminster Rovers, the local second division football club.

BERTIE WALLACE   Raffish co-owner of Gafellyn Castle in Wales.

RUTH WALTON   A ravishing adventuress, voted on to Bagley Hall's board of governors to ensure full houses at meetings.

MILLY WALTON   The third Bagley Babe,

charming and emollient but overshadowed by her gorgeous mother.

THE HON.
JACK WATERLANE

Bagley Hall thicko, captain of the Chinless Wanderers.

LORD WATERLANE

Jack's father, who shares his son's fondness for rough trade.

STEWART
'STEW' WILBY

Powerful and visionary headmaster of Redfords, Janna Curtis's former school in the West Riding. Also Janna's former lover.

SPOTTY WILKINS

Bagley Hall pupil.

DAFYDD WILLIAMS

Sometime builder and piss artist.

'GRAFFI' WILLIAMS

Dafydd's son, and captivating, conniving fifth member of the Wolf Pack. Nicknamed 'Graffi' for his skill at spraying luminous paint on buildings.

BRIGADIER
CHRISTIAN
WOODFORD

A delightful octogenarian, hugely interested in matters

military and his beautiful neighbour, Lily Hamilton.

MISS WORMLEY	English mistress at Bagley Hall—poor thing.

THE ANIMALS

CADBURY   Dora Belvedon's chocolate Labrador.

LOOFAH   Dora Belvedon's delinquent pony.

PARTNER   Janna Curtis's ginger and white mongrel.

NORTHCLIFFE   Patience Cartwright's golden retriever.

ELAINE   Hengist Brett-Taylor's white greyhound.

GENERAL   Lily Hamilton's white and black Persian cat.

VERLAINE AND RIMBAUD   Artie Deverell's Jack Russells.

BOGOTA   Xavier Campbell-Black's black Labrador.

HINDSIGHT   Theo Graham's marmalade cat.

FAST	One of Rupert Campbell-Black's horses. Aptly named.
PENSCOMBE PETERKIN	Another of Rupert Campbell-Black's star horses.
BELUGA	An extremely kind horse who teaches Paris Alvaston to ride.
PLOVER	Patience Cartwright's grey mare, doted on by Beluga.

Continued from Volume 1

68

The week before Larks faced Ofsted, as if deliberately to derail Janna, Ashton and Crispin had finally summoned her to S and C headquarters for the intended pep talk.

A lovely Hockney of a kingfisher-blue swimming pool brightened the beiges of the Evil Office, no doubt reminding the pair of the fortnight they'd just enjoyed in Tangier. Both were tanned, although Ashton must have plastered himself in factor 100 to stop his pink and white skin burning. Crispin was fatter than ever, his primrose-yellow shirt straining at the buttons to reveal his waxed chest. A new goatee beard failed to hide an extra chin. The sun had bleached both goatee and his hair a rather startling orange. The room reeked of Ashton's chloroform scent as he launched straight into the attack.

'S and C were bwought in to waise educational standards in Larkshire but we have just had to pay a massive three-hundred-and-ninety-thousand-pound fine out of our annual management fee purely because you and a handful of rural schools failed to reach their targets. Your GCSE figures were among the lowest in Larkshire.'

'Much higher than last year. We rose six per cent.'

'Not enough. You've let us down.'

'Are you aware'—Crispin glanced at his typed

notes—'your governors called an unofficial meeting because the parents were in such despair over the results and the lack of information provided?'

'Only a few parents,' said Janna, thinking of the pile of cards at the end of the summer term. 'How dare the governors hold secret meetings? It's illegal.'

'A measure of their fwustration,' sighed Ashton.

He's getting a real buzz out of this, thought Janna, looking at his hateful soft features and unblinking serpent's eyes. Putting out a delicately manicured hand, Ashton helped himself to a white chocolate from a shiny mauve box. Crispin's piggy lips watered.

'Your projected intake is also disastwous,' went on Ashton.

'The county council sabotaged that by changing the bus routes,' said Janna quickly. 'No parent is going to allow their eleven-year-olds to walk three-quarters of a mile from the school gates—particularly in winter. We were just getting known as a rapidly improving school then crap press ruins it. A lot of parents changed their minds about coming to Larks after the hopelessly biased reports on the geography field trip.'

'Oh my dear, I was coming to that.' Ashton nibbled another chocolate and finding it lime-centred, lobbed it, to Crispin's distress, into the bin. 'That disaster was of your own making. In this vewy office we warned you not to bond with Hengist B-T. Carried away by his glamour, you flew too near the sun. You were the only head in charge that fatal night. If Alex Bwuce hadn't arrived and taken control, you'd all have lost your

2

jobs. You're lucky Wandal Stancombe didn't have Paris and Xavier Campbell-Black up on a wape charge. Jade Stancombe was evidently so traumatized she couldn't bear to go through the experience again in court.'

'Jade's been going through the same experience since she was twelve. She's a slut.'

'Dear, dear, your language! And after all Wandal's done for you. I hope you're making enough use of that minibus.'

Janna decided to go on the attack.

'I'll never improve my school until you give me more money. We must have more teachers. We must have the roof repaired: reception was flooded last week. We must have more books and more computers—'

'Must, must, must,' interrupted Ashton smoothly: 'I'm amazed you can ask when you've just lost us nearly four hundred thousand pounds. I'd concentwate on pulling yourself together as much as possible before Ofsted next week.'

'The new refuge for asylum-seekers hasn't helped either,' protested Janna, getting to her feet. 'They're great kids, but we're getting six and seven a week, most of them with no English. You just settle them in and find them friends, so they don't totally destabilize established classes, then they move on again. Many of them come from war zones and are used to carrying guns.'

'Then they must feel thoroughly at home at Larks,' said Crispin nastily, 'and at least they're easing your surplus-places situation, so don't knock it.'

'I bet Rod Hyde hasn't been lumbered with them.'

'That's because Wod's school is overflowing, and if you're going to use words like "lumbered" '—Ashton pretended to look shocked—'you shouldn't be in teaching. What was Larks's mission statement about cultivating every child's special excellence?'

'Oh eff off,' screamed Janna and stormed out.

'Good luck with Ofsted,' a highly satisfied Ashton called after her.

Janna's determination to conquer Ofsted was not helped by the panicking of her entire staff. At breaktime the day before, even an old hand like Skunk Illingworth was grumbling that he'd stayed up until four in the morning typing out the three-term development plan of the entire science department.

'I didn't,' scoffed Red Robbie, who was ringing jobs in the *TES*. 'All inspectors are failed teachers.'

'Takes one to know one,' muttered Wally who seemed to have painted the entire school, even the bird table, a brighter canary yellow.

During the same breaktime, Enid the librarian had fallen asleep on the sofa clutching a cup of coffee, which dripped on to her fawn flares. She had worked the entire weekend rolling back the date stamp, slapping it on every book in sight to indicate extensive borrowing, even bringing in her own rampageous children to rough up unread volumes. If only Paris were still here: he'd never stopped reading.

The pupils, on the other hand, were gleeful at the prospect of seeing their teachers going through the hoop, particularly silly old Basket who was one long panic attack. Dr Boon, the appropriately named local GP, was getting writer's cramp scribbling sick notes and prescriptions for tranquillizers.

'It may seem obvious,' said Janna as she gave the remaining staff a last-minute briefing, 'but I trust by now you've all familiarized yourselves with the files of every child in your class or tutor group. Please emphasize our positive use of the whiteboard and IT, even if most of our computers need updating. Show the inspectors the children's best work. Tell them the good things about our school. Dress attractively but conservatively—no minis or cleavages.' She looked pointedly at Gloria. 'Be friendly; they're not ogres.'

By which time most of the staff had gone into Red Robbie mode, folding their arms and gazing truculently up at the tobacco-stained staffroom ceiling.

'And when you go to the toilet'—Janna addressed their thrust-out chins—'for God's sake check, before slagging anyone off, that an inspector isn't lurking in the next-door booth. Finally, the inspectors will be based in the interview room, so if any of the more volatile parents roll up, head them off and ask them to come back later.' Janna forced a smile. 'Frankly you're a terrific bunch so just be yourselves and good luck to you all.'

As well as pupils, teachers and parents, the inspectors would be interviewing the governors, who were sharpening their claws, particularly after Janna had ticked them off at the last meeting for caballing behind her back.

'And please don't badmouth the school,' she had added, 'when we're trying so hard to save it.'

'Could have fooled me,' muttered Stormin' Norman, who was marshalling disaffected parents to put in the boot.

'We just hope you'll keep your students under control,' had been Russell's last word. 'It's we who have to carry the can.'

At least Janna's friends hadn't let her down.

Mags Gablecross and Year Nine had produced a marvellous Spanish display of sombreros, tambourines and brave bulls tossing terrified matadors.

Cambola was magicking celestial sounds out of the choir and an orchestra which she'd started. ' "If the trumpet gives an uncertain sound",' she exhorted them, ' "how shall he prepare himself to the battle?"

'Every child matters. Our ethos is to cultivate each child's special excellence and bolster their self-esteem so they confront the future with confidence,' intoned Lydia, Lance and Gloria. 'Every child matters, our ethos is to . . .'

'Please let me not let Larks down,' prayed pretty, very plump Sophy Belvedon, Patience and Ian's daughter, who had taken Vicky's place as head of English and drama and who had proved a huge success.

Mike Pitts, meanwhile, was overdosing on Gold Spot, scurf drifting on his shiny blazered shoulders. Skunk Illingworth ponged so dreadfully, Janna engaged in stench warfare and placed on his desk a deodorant, which he merely returned to her desk.

'This must be yours, headmistress.'

I'm a head's mistress, thought Janna wearily, or would be if I ever got a chance to see him.

Determined not to look like a school-marm, she had invested in a lovely ivy-green suit and a pretty frilled shirt in wild rose pink, which she had laid out with new tights last thing, before falling to her knees: 'Oh dear God, look after my school tomorrow.'

After a restless night, she arrived at Larks at half past seven. Partner, sporting a crimson bow, his red winter coat thickening, bounced ahead, happy to find Debbie, whom he loved and who meant titbits, had already put on a slow cooking goat curry, and was now in reception watering a jungle of potted plants forming the background of the Save the Tiger project. In and out of them drifted gaudy parrots, howler monkeys, sly snakes and splendid amber-eyed tigers. Graffi, who had drawn and cut them out of cardboard for Year Seven to colour, was touching up the tigers' stripes with black gloss.

'That looks grand,' sighed Janna. 'Bless you, Graffi.'

To add authenticity to the tiger display, the schizoid central heating had opted for tropical. Graffi had already removed his crimson sweatshirt. Noticing a big purple bruise on his arm, Janna hoped his father wasn't drinking again.

Reception had also been brightened by flags representing the nationalities of every child in the school. Two more had been added after yet another influx of asylum-seekers on Friday.

Beside the main desk like a welcome committee was a second display entitled 'Movers and Shakers', which included life-size cut-outs of Kennedy, Martin Luther King and Margaret Thatcher.

'Here's hassle,' hissed Graffi as Chally bustled in, her dark brown suit topped with a yellow autumn-leaf-patterned scarf, which Janna found herself sycophantically admiring.

'Yes, everyone likes it,' replied Chally smugly. Having sniffed Debbie's goat curry approvingly— 'a caring gesture to our Afro-Caribbean brethren'—she predictably bristled at 'Movers and

8

Shakers'.

'Black women are deplorably under-represented.'

'Not any more they ain't,' grinned Graffi, splashing black gloss over the faces of Margaret Thatcher, Germaine Greer and Florence Nightingale. 'Florence was a lesbian as well, which makes her even more PC. Silly old bitch getting her effnics in a twist,' he murmured as an apoplectic Chally was fortunately distracted by one of Johnnie Fowler's BNP posters and made a fearful fuss about breaking a nail when she ripped it off the wall.

The young teachers, Lance, Lydia and Sophy Belvedon, yawned as they straightened displays, checked spelling, jazzed up lesson plans and prayed the children would be in a good mood.

'It all looks lovely,' repeated Janna.

In her office the sun had shrugged off its polar-bear coat of dirty white cloud and was shining on the new yellow paint. She was touched to receive good-luck cards from all the Bagley children who'd been on the geography field trip except Paris, and from Sally Brett-Taylor, but worried that the central heating was growing increasingly tropical. She longed to take off her jacket but before the inspector arrived at nine she had to take assembly.

' "Every little thing gonna be all right," ' sang Bob Marley over the public-address system.

'We won't bother with a hymn or a talk today,' she told the packed hall, 'but I'd just like you all to put your hands together, shut your eyes and ask God to look after our school.

'On the other hand,' she continued thirty seconds later, 'God will need your help. The inspectors will be with us for several days, so please be nice to them. Try not to shove or shout, or swear, or drop litter, or your gum.' Glancing around at their anxious faces: 'And try to look happy.'

'How can I look happy when I'm trying to remember all these fings,' grumbled Rocky.

'Above all,' urged Janna, 'be yourselves.'

On cue she received a text from Hengist: 'Above all, *don't* be yourself,' she read, 'or you'll duff up any inspector who criticizes your beloved children. Good luck. When am I going to see you? H'.

Laughing, Janna looked up at the children and said, 'As you file out, I'd like all teachers to double-check the appearance of their classes. Do up your shirt buttons, Kitten, and pull down your skirt. Tuck in your shirt, Johnnie; pull up your socks, Martin. Have you all brushed your hair and cleaned your nails? Miss Basket isn't in? OK, I'll check Nine A.'

She was just working her way down the row of black, yellow, brown, pink and freckled hands, all with commendably clean nails, when she felt Partner's tail bashing her legs, heard whoops of laughter and found herself examining a huge hand, whitened by scars from rugby studs, and with big square nails and fingers.

Looking up, she found Emlyn grinning down at her.

'Oh Emlyn, you are daft.'

' 'Lo, Mr Davies, 'lo Mr Davies.' The children swarmed joyfully around him. 'When are we going to Bagley again?'

'When you learn to behave.' Emlyn produced a big bunch of reddy-brown chrysanthemums from behind his back, 'For your office, lovely, and to match your hair. And these are for your inspectors.' From his pockets he produced packets of herbal, peppermint and fruit tea and a jar of decaffeinated coffee. 'If you don't have any, they're sure to want it.'

'You are so dear,' gasped Janna.

'And you look so pretty in your green suit, just smile and wow them. I must go.' As he kissed Janna on the cheek, all the children whooped again.

'Now, you be particularly good, Miss Curtis has worked her heart out for you lot.'

He was so reassuring and made everything seem so normal, Janna longed for him to stay.

'You're blushing, miss,' accused Pearl.

'It's the central heating,' said Janna hastily. 'Now hurry back to your classrooms, they'll be here in a minute.'

Dear Emlyn, thought Janna, then groaned as her head of PE approached in patent-leather thigh boots, leather shorts and a see-through black shirt.

'You told me to cover up,' protested Gloria. 'That Emlyn's right hunky, isn't he?'

Gloria, it seemed, had, out of nerves, gone out clubbing, and hadn't had time to go home and change.

'Well, for God's sake,' said an exasperated Janna, 'nip down to New Look and get a less transparent top.'

'It's nearly nine,' warned Rowan. 'You're a disgrace, Gloria.'

'You'd better take my shirt,' snarled Janna, dragging Gloria into her office. 'I'll just have to keep my jacket on.'

'I'm ever so sorry. Such a pretty blouse, are you

11

sure?'

'No, I'm bloody not. Put it on.'

In fact Janna's wild rose pink shirt straining over Gloria's thrusting thirty-eight-inch boobs looked even more flagrantly provocative than the see-through black.

Bugger, thought Janna buttoning her wool suit, the temperature was rising by the second.

As Wally gave her brown boots a last polish, there was an enraged banging on the door and Chally barged in.

'Oh, there you are, Wally. Everyone is so stressed, the women's toilet smells like a sewage farm. Can you please put more air freshener in there?'

'And in Skunk Illingworth's classroom,' snapped Janna.

'And I don't know'—Chally's lips tightened—'who put all those Penhaligon's toiletries in there, the inspector will think we're rolling in money.'

'I did.' Janna was fed up with Chally. 'They were a present. Do you want me to put up a sign saying "Gifted Toiletries"?'

'They're here, they're here.'

Rowan rushed in removing her suit jacket to show off a charming cream linen shirt, straightening Janna's papers, shoving her buckling in-tray under the sofa, then, like a teenager's mum before a dance, straightening Partner's bow tie, before he rushed off sending cardboard, black-faced Margaret Thatcher flying in his haste to welcome the visitors.

As Bob Marley was replaced by Schubert's *Marche Militaire*, such a brisk jaunty tune, Janna found herself marching down the corridor. In

12

reception, the inspector was crouched down admiring the largest of Graffi's tigers.

'This is a very fine beast,' he said. Rising to his feet, he took Janna's trembling hand. 'Wade Hargreaves, and, from your photographs, you must be Janna Curtis.'

Janna had expected an ogre but the man smiling down at her was tall, slim, in his late thirties and with the genial friendliness of a yellow Labrador.

'Welcome to Larks,' said Janna in relief.

'Oh Christ,' muttered Mike Pitts, going green and reversing into his office, 'it's Wade Hargreaves. I sacked him when I was head of maths at Rutminster Comp.'

Wade Hargreaves was accompanied by, amongst others, a spinster called Miss Spicer, who had one of Chalford's draped scarves, short spiky hair, a lantern jaw, disapproving coffee-bean brown eyes and who, having demanded a cup of peppermint tea, seemed disappointed when it was provided. Well done, Emlyn.

From then onwards Janna felt the sharp constant pain of a steel toothcomb being plunged into the scalp and tugged through tangled hair as Wade Hargreaves's team went everywhere, talked to everyone and asked for every lesson plan, file and balance sheet to be taken into the interview room. Brandishing clipboards they moved around devouring timetables, schemes of work, attendance figures, the first tentative coursework of Year Ten, and listening to Sam Spink in her Hogwarts' character socks, her massive thighs spilling over her chair like suet as she charted the inadequacies of Larks's workload agreement.

Mike Pitts, unable to face Wade Hargreaves,

13

disappeared home with stress. By contrast Mags Gablecross was everywhere, guiding, supporting, comforting staff who felt they had cocked up.

'I could have done it so much better,' sobbed Lydia. 'I made a tape about Simon Armitage to nudge my memory but Johnnie Fowler got hold of it and played it back to the class and Miss Spicer.'

'I got Ten C too revved up about Billy the Kid,' said Lance dolefully. 'One of the asylum-seekers pulled out a gun and Miss Spicer said I must remember that the Indians not the cowboys were the heroes.'

But there were good moments.

'Until Miss came, I had no grown-ups to talk to,' Pearl told Wade Hargreaves. 'No one respected me. Now school remembers my birthday, I get a card and a Mars bar and a song in assembly. She's going to help me take a make-up course.'

'Miss is there for the mums,' said Kylie. 'She helps them fill in forms for the social and the courts. She listens when their partners leave them or they can't pay their rent. She filled in my brovver's driving licence for him, and she remembered Cameron's birfday. Lots of teachers don't know all our names. Miss even knows all our babies' names.'

'We get letters to take home in Urdu,' said Aysha, 'so Mum and Dad can understand what's going on. Mum came to parents' day for the first time; there was cake and orange juice and she talked to other mums.'

70

Assembly the following morning was a great success. Kylie Rose lifted the hair on the back of everyone's neck singing 'It's a Wonderful World'. Aysha in her headscarf read from the Koran, Graffi from the New Testament—'Judge not that ye be not judged'—which made Wade and even Miss Spicer smile. Danijela, one of the new asylum-seekers, read a Bosnian prayer, then the choir sang 'How Lovely are Thy Dwellings' so beautifully as the morning sun streamed through the stained-glass St Michael that even Miss Spicer wiped away a tear and Wade grinned across at Janna.

He was a terrific listener, as still as a wildlife cameraman who knows the only way to score is to move quietly. He and Miss Spicer were unfazed when Graffi's father, who'd been in the pub all day, dropped into the interview room for a quiet kip before going home. Or when Pearl's boxer father, just out of gaol, rolled up to get even with one of the pushers outside the school gates and try and catch a glimpse of his wife and her toyboy friend.

Debbie had been thrilled yesterday when the inspectors lunched in the canteen and had second helpings both of goat curry and rhubarb crumble and were constantly requesting more flapjacks for the interview room.

Things were dicey when they caught up with Feral, sulky because he was having a one-to-one lesson with Sophy Belvedon in the individual learning unit, which had once been the changing rooms before the football pitch was sold off.

Sophy, realizing Feral would only attempt to read if he were interested, had blown up both Sunday's football reports on Arsenal and pages from a biography of Sol Campbell.

'You're not thick, Feral,' Sophy was telling him. 'People are stupidly characterized these days as gifted, able or with needs.'

'I've got needs all right. I need a fag and a shag,' said Feral, grabbing Sophy and burying his sleek face in her splendid breasts.

'I don't think my husband Alizarin would like that.' Sophy edged away her legs and hips, leaving her bosom in Feral's strong grip. 'He's six foot four and built like an oak tree.' Then, as Feral reluctantly released her: 'Not that you're not utterly gorgeous.'

'Wiv needs.' Feral batted his long eyelashes. He liked Sophy but he found it humiliating to be taught on his own. It was all Paris's fault for deserting him.

Wade and Miss Spicer asked Feral a little about work and then about the other teachers.

'Miss went to court with me in August; her evidence got me off. She got me a job working for two coffin-dodgers, mowing, chopping logs and fings; later me and Lily got wasted on sloe gin.

'Most of the teachers are shit here,' Feral went on. 'Chalford's shit, so're Robbie and Skunk, Miss Basket's crap too, she ought to be able to control us. Mrs Gablecross is nice, we can talk to her about anyfing. I need a fag.' Feral shook an empty pack in irritation. 'That no-good mother-fucking nigger-basher Monster Norman pinched my last one.'

'You can't call him that,' said Miss Spicer faintly.

'*You* can't call him that,' corrected Feral mockingly, 'but I can, 'cos I'm black and underprivileged. As a representative of an underprivileged effnic minority, I can call him anyfing I like.'

Sophy tried not to laugh, particularly when Miss Spicer rallied and asked Feral if he felt underprivileged.

'People call you "black shit".' Feral tipped back his chair, testing their reaction through narrowed speculative eyes. 'But if you play football well enough, you earn eighty grand a week and in a few seasons go from being "black shit" to God. That's why I'm gonna become a footballer. Put a recommendation in your report'—he tapped Miss Spicer's clipboard—'that Larks needs a football pitch.'

'Thank you, Feral and Mrs Belvedon,' said Wade.

Checking the dining room at lunchtime on the second day, Janna's heart sank to see Miss Spicer and a jolly blond member of the team called Mrs Mills tucking into toad in the hole and deep in conversation with Rocky. Did he know that Larkshire had one of the highest rates of teenage pregnancies in the country?'

'Sure,' replied Rocky. 'That's 'cos Kylie Rose lives here.'

'I don't think that's quite right,' said Mrs Mills, who was dieting and reluctantly setting aside a piece of gold, utterly delicious, batter. 'Do you find sex education enlightening, Rocky?'

'Sex education is wicked, man.' Rocky bit suggestively on a sausage. 'They never stop banging on about STDs but they tell you lotsa ways to have sex—blow jobs, going down and fings, anal sex—without getting girls up the duff.'

'That's enough, Rocky,' said Janna firmly. 'Go and get yourself some dessert, you know you like jam roly-poly.'

'Sorry about that,' said Janna, 'Rocky gets carried away. Can I get you some sweet?'

Both Miss Spicer and Mrs Mills felt they'd had enough.

'Would you like to hear my poem about a skylark?' asked Rocky, returning.

'That sounds nice,' said Mrs Mills bravely.

'I heard a skylark singing so sweetly in the sky,' began Rocky, seeing relief dawning on the faces of his listeners, 'but when I looked to find him, he dumped right in my eye.'

'I think I'd like to see the D and T department now,' said Mrs Mills.

'I'll take you there,' said Janna and was just expounding on the splendid work being done when they heard screams. Rounding the corner they nearly fell over Pearl, who was lying on top of Kitten Meadows, holding clumps of her hair in order to smash her head on the stone floor.

'Take it back.'

'No,' squealed Kitten.

'Take it fucking back.' Smash.

'No.' Clawing at Pearl's face with long silver nails, Kitten drew blood. 'You always look fucking crap.'

'Fucking don't.' Pearl smashed her fist into Kitten's face, whereupon Kitten hit Pearl on her left breast.

'Ow,' screamed Pearl.

'Please stop,' called out Basket faintly from the

safety of her classroom.

As a crowd gathered—'C'mon, Pearl, c'mon, Kitten'—Wade Hargreaves emerged from a history lesson, so Janna dived in on the right, ducking blows, trying to prise the contestants apart.

A second later, Sophy Belvedon had rushed up and dived in on the left. As Kitten tried to elbow her in the ribs, she said: 'Won't work, I'm much too fat to feel anything.'

'Stop it, both of you,' yelled Janna.

At that moment Wally arrived and with his superior strength dragged off a spitting, wriggling Pearl.

'Take her to my office,' panted Janna. 'You can go to the gym,' she told Kitten, 'and both of you will have detentions tonight and tomorrow.' Then, when they furiously protested, continuing trying to kick out at each other: 'That's final, now get out of my sight.'

Having administered smelling salts to Basket, Janna, aware that a button had been ripped off her suit and her neatly piled-up hair had come down, retreated to the Ladies where she met Sophy coming out, and said, 'Thanks so much for your help.'

'That Basket's a wet hen.'

'Hush.' Janna put her finger to her lips. Seeing an engaged sign on one of the doors she crept into the next-door booth. Climbing on to the seat and peering over the partition she discovered Miss Spicer knitting and reading *Good Housekeeping* and was so startled she fell back into the lavatory bowl with a shriek.

'Checking for spies?' asked Miss Spicer dryly.

'Sort of.'

19

'One needs a break from inspection.'

'And from being a head,' sighed Janna.

'Hello,' added Miss Spicer as Partner's snout appeared under her door. 'That is a delightful dog, he seems to know instinctively when a child is sad. He was trailing that pretty fair-haired Bosnian girl this morning.'

Shaking her wet boot Janna climbed down.

'That's probably because we made Danijela our bird girl. Every morning she takes out a tin of scraps which contains rich pickings from the kitchen. We couldn't think why the birds were standing indignantly round with their wings on their hips until we discovered'—Janna's voice quivered—'Danijela was emptying the tin into her school bag for her friends in the refuge.'

'Can't take on everyone's burdens,' said Miss Spicer briskly, but her coffee-bean eyes were kind as she washed her hands vigorously before applying Bluebell hand cream. Then, painting her small mouth bright orange and rearranging the folds of her scarf, she announced she was off to the Appletree annexe to monitor some science lessons.

Miss Spicer had an eventful day. She was observing one of Mr Mates's experiments when the roof of Appletree finally caved in on her and Year Ten E, who emerged unhurt but much aged by grey, dust-filled hair.

'It worked with the other division,' bleated a shaken Mr Mates, who had to be reassured that the collapsing roof had nothing to do with his experiment.

'How lousy are thy dwellings, oh S and C,' sang Cambola, whose music department next door had also been submerged.

'They'll have to give us a new roof now,' said Mags Gablecross.

*   *   *

Next day Pearl gave Wade Hargreaves even more pressing reasons.

'I spend half an hour straightening my hair every morning, then the rain pours through the roof and it goes all kinky; that's why Kitten Meadows said my hair was crap and that's why I hit her. If we had new roofs this wouldn't happen.

'My dad's a boxer,' she went on, 'so it's in my genes to land punches. Fights isn't Miss's fault. She's great, and so's Mrs Belvedon, the new English teacher.'

'I'm just going to watch Mrs Belvedon giving Year Eight a lesson on *The Tempest*,' said Wade.

*   *   *

'Oh bugger,' grumbled Sophy, retrieving some dropped folders, then, as Year Eight giggled: 'You'll have to move your table, Stefan and Josef, I'm much too fat to get through that gap.'

'You do sound posh, miss.'

'If you think I'm posh you should hear my mother.'

'Paris is living with her?' asked Kata from Kosovo longingly. 'How's he getting on?'

'Fine.' Sophy was amazed by Larks's ongoing obsession with their lost leader. 'Now to Caliban. My husband Alizarin has done a painting of him.' On the whiteboard appeared a picture of a ferocious-looking beast, half wild boar, half gorilla,

21

but with the saddest eyes.

'See his long nails for digging up pig nuts for his master. Caliban is a really sympathetic character,' Sophy went on, 'he's a bit ugly, but he longs to help and be loved and he says beautiful poetic things. Some horrid sailors are shipwrecked on his island and get poor Caliban drunk, so he makes a fool of himself. He adores Miranda, his boss's daughter.'

A picture of a pretty blonde in a ruff and long Elizabethan dress appeared on the whiteboard. 'But she's in love with someone else, and I'm sure you all know how it hurts when you love someone who doesn't love you.'

Wade Hargreaves couldn't imagine anyone not loving Sophy.

'And I bet lots of you boys when you go to parties feel shy of chatting up girls, so you drink too much and fall over—well, that's Caliban.'

'He's gentle giant like King Kong,' piped up Kata.

'Exactly.'

'And Monster Norman, except he's horrible.'

'No, no.' Sophy looked round nervously. 'Anyway, this is Alizarin's picture, and now I want you all to produce your own idea of Caliban. You've got paints on each table and plasticene and paper. Try not to paint each other. Anyone who comes up with an interesting idea can have one or two of these.' She waved a tin of Quality Street. 'Now: ready, steady, go.'

Sitting at the back of the class Wade and Miss Spicer made notes on their clipboards and watched Sophy advising, praising, laughing, screaming with joy—'That is so good!'—and occasionally remonstrating: 'Don't put that blue

22

brush back in the white pot, Jasper.'

The children, particularly the ones who couldn't speak English, were having a ball. As they slapped on paint or modelled in plasticene or clay, a wonderful zoo emerged.

'I can't do his nails,' wailed Kata.

On cue in pattered Partner and obligingly held up a paw so they could see his claws.

'Good boy.' Sophy hugged him and rewarded him with the Quality Street green-wrapped triangle which was all chocolate.

'That is really cool, Anwar,' she cried, pausing beside a Pakistani boy's desk. 'You've made Caliban look happy because he's asleep. That's in the text: he was so hurt by humans, only in dreams did he find happiness, and when he woke he cried to dream again. This is so good. Brilliant colours too. Lay it out on that chair to dry.'

What a lovely young woman, thought Wade wistfully. Shortly afterwards he was so impressed by another painting of Caliban he sat down on Anwar's picture to study it and was left with red, blue, green and purple splodges all over the seat of his elegant beige suit.

The children screamed with laughter.

'Oh, goodness,' wailed Sophy, 'you look more like a mandrill than a nimble marmoset. I'm so sorry. I'll get it dry cleaned or take it home and wash it for you.'

'Don't give it a thought, I might start a fashion.'

Janna, who'd just been forced into giving Monster a detention for cheeking some other member of the inspection team, was vastly cheered when she peered into Sophy's classroom and saw even Miss Spicer laughing.

As the bell rang for break, Year Eight bore Wade off to the playground to show him the bird table.

'That's a robin.'

'No, stupid, it's a bullfinch.'

'This is the pond,' said Kata, leading him out into the garden. 'We're going to clean it to encourage wild lives. Wally's made a ladder so anything drowning can climb out. And he's going to build a duck house and a bridge to the island.'

'Perhaps Miss Curtis will get you some fish.'

How nice he is, thought Janna, watching from the window, but we mustn't be lulled into a false security.

'Would you like a cup of tea?' she asked as he returned from his tour to her office.

She'd just put on the kettle, when Stormin' Norman roared in. 'You know Martin don't do detentions on a Thursday. You're depriving him of his liberty.'

She was about to punch Janna, who was protesting that surely it was Wednesdays, when Wade stepped out from behind the door, where he'd been admiring some stills from *Romeo and Juliet*.

'I wouldn't.'

'And 'oo the fuck are you?' yelled Stormin' Norman. 'Another of 'er fucking fancy men?' But at least her fist stopped in mid-air.

They were interrupted by the arrival of Chally, bright red in the face.

'One of the Croatians has exposed himself to Year Seven. I said, "We don't do things like that here, Roman, put it away," but he laughed in my face so I called back-up.'

'Front-up, more likely,' said Janna, trying not to

24

laugh.

'This is serious, Senior Team Leader.'

They were distracted yet again by a yell and the crash of plasterboard. Pearl's boxer father had rolled up drunk again and discovered Graffi's father, whom he suspected of once pleasuring his wife, fast asleep in the interview room.

'I told you it was in my genes,' said Pearl smugly as the police arrived to remove both her father and Stormin' Norman.

71

On Friday afternoon Wade called a meeting after school to report on his team's findings. Russell, Ashton and Crispin arrived early. As the interview room had been temporarily totalled by Pearl's boxer dad, they were ushered into Janna's office, where they drank tea, guzzled Debbie's chocolate cake and rubbed their hands in anticipation of a serious drubbing for little Miss Curtis.

Crispin, who was perched on the sofa beside Ashton, murmured that Debbie was an excellent cook.

'She'll be looking for a job tomorrow,' murmured back Ashton. 'I'll put in a good word at County Hall. Perhaps she could come and do for me.'

As Mike Pitts was still off with stress, Mags had been asked by Janna to stand in for him. Pacing up and down outside, Mags had never felt so tired. She was so worried for Janna, who never failed to wear her generous heart on her sleeve.

'Any room for a little one?' said Cindy Payne, the Larkshire county councillor in charge of education, parking her red-trouser-suited bottom on the sofa between Crispin and Ashton. Both men would have liked to edge away but were too firmly wedged.

Russell had commandeered a big upright chair. In his hand was another letter of complaint from Miss Miserden about Larks hooligans swearing and kicking balls into her garden.

'Thought you might like to see this, Inspector.'

Wade, sitting at an imported table shifting papers

and flanked by Miss Spicer and Mrs Mills, hardly glanced at the letter before handing it back.

'Sorry to keep you.' Janna rushed in followed by Partner. She settled down at her desk, ramming her hands between her thighs to conceal their trembling. So many things had gone wrong; so many bricks dropped; so many children out of control. Mags, sliding into a little red armchair beside her, squeezed her arm.

Through the window they could see the children running home through the pouring rain, their coats over their heads. After the row at the last governors' meeting, Russell's eyes refused to meet Janna's.

'Hope you survived,' he said heartily to the three inspectors.

'Extremely well,' said Wade, then turning to Janna, 'thank you for your hospitality. We have been made most welcome and given every assistance in forming our opinions.'

Then he unleashed both barrels. Larks in a word was being used by S and C and the county council as a pupil referral unit, or rather a dumping ground for all the rubbish kids with behaviour problems that were expelled from other schools.

'After four days, however, my team and I were delighted to see what efforts are being made by the staff to tackle attendance, unauthorized absence and deplorable behaviour. Support for vulnerable pupils is excellent, as is mentoring. Despite standards being constantly eroded by the behaviour of certain parents and a very disruptive band of children, bad behaviour is dealt with swiftly. Special needs are catered for well within very limited resources. Overall adherence to the curriculum has also been observed.'

Slowly, slowly, Janna felt her foot leaving the bottom of the sea as she drifted upwards towards the sunlight.

Wade consulted his notes. 'The teaching of the older staff is less than satisfactory. Their lessons are often dull, their marking unhelpful.' He pinpointed Chally, Mike Pitts, who had once sacked him, Skunk, Basket, Sam Spink and Robbie. Janna bit her lip: all her *bêtes noires*.

'On the other hand, language teaching was excellent.' Wade smiled at Mags. 'So was Miss Cambola's music and Mr Mates's science.' He then praised Janna's appointments: the new deputy head of history and the head of D and T, and in particular Sophy Belvedon. 'Quite excellent, we much enjoyed her English lesson bringing in both art and drama disciplines.

'Despite the appallingly deprived lives of so many of the children, this is a happy school, a haven which makes many of their lives bearable.'

Russell was rotating his signet ring; Cindy's little dark eyes were like those of an angry swan; Crispin, swelling like a balloon about to pop, seized the last piece of chocolate cake. Janna put her burning face in her hands. She must be dreaming.

'Janna Curtis'—Wade smiled at Janna's bowed head—'is clearly very popular with pupils and parents for whom she appears to act as a Citizens' Advice Bureau, and by all the staff except the reactionary and the work-shy. She has also had considerable success winning over the community.'

He also praised the excellent displays in reception and on the walls and particularly the hard work and cheerful contribution of Wally and Debbie.

'I shall miss her flapjacks. The beautiful grounds are in good order,' he went on, 'although the children need a playing field.'

Everyone jumped as a football smacked the window.

Much of Wade's disapproval was reserved for the state of the buildings—one of which had collapsed on a member of the inspection team—the atrocious damp, erratic central heating and leaking roofs.

'Which leads me back to the appalling poverty of resources,' he said bleakly. 'We get the impression that both S and C Services and the county council, for some reason, have been deliberately withholding money. From the minutes, the governors appear to have been totally unsupportive to Janna Curtis'—Wade glared at Russell—'ganging up and scapegoating her. In this they have been hugely aided by a local press so unrelentingly damaging that one might imagine conspiracy.'

As Partner gnawed on an old beef bone given him by Debbie, Ashton lost it.

'Get that bloody dog out of here.' He aimed a kick at Partner, who yelped.

Wade raised an eyebrow. 'If Larks fails,' he concluded, 'it will not be Janna Curtis's fault. As I've said, like its name, Larks is a happy place.'

Janna sat stunned, then, leaping to her feet, ran round and shook hands with a smiling Miss Spicer and Mrs Mills. She turned to Wade and, unable to stop herself, flung her arms round his neck and kissed him, leaving pink lipstick marks on both cheeks.

'Oh, thank you all, thank you, thank you,' she cried tearfully.

'Janna kissed me when we met, Jumping from the chair she sat in,' sighed Wade and then beamed. 'I'm sure you want to pass on the good news to your staff,' he told her. 'I'll be sending you a full report.'

'Thanks so much.' Janna bolted, unable to face the rage of the Gang of Four, who retreated to the Evil Office to lick terrible wounds.

'Curtis clearly dropped her knickers,' said Crispin pouring four large brandies.

'I've never been so insulted in my life,' spluttered Cindy Payne. 'Can we sue?'

'I can only resign,' said Russell. 'Scapegoated indeed. That trollop.'

'You stay put,' ordered Ashton. 'We've got work to do.'

*   *   *

Hengist brought round two bottles of Veuve Clicquot, lit Lily of the Valley scented candles and to the accompaniment of *Capriccio* on Radio 3 gave Janna a bath.

Slowly, lingeringly, he ran soap over her breasts and up between her legs, groping and fingering, then slapped her lightly on the bottom. 'Are you going to be good tonight?'

After he'd dried her, they collapsed in front of the sitting-room fire, made all the more cosy by the relentless patter of the rain outside.

'I cannot believe it,' sighed Janna. 'Wade's looks went everywhere and he seemed to like what e'er he looked on.'

'Your Ofsteady boyfriend, clearly a man of discernment,' said Hengist.

'He virtually accused S and C of malpractice. Cindy looked so pained, Crispin misery-ate most of Debbie's chocolate cake and Ashton went totally silent, but his eyes . . .' Janna shuddered. 'Then he kicked Partner. Spicer was so nice in the end and Wade—well!'

'You bewitched him,' said Hengist.

Pushing her back on the fluffy rug, he ran his tongue along the tender undersides of her breasts, but Janna couldn't get into the mood for sex.

'He loved me for the dangers I had passed,' she murmured, echoing Othello. 'And I loved him that he did pity me. This is the only witchcraft I have used. He realized I'd been scapegoated.'

'I wish you wouldn't butcher a perfectly good noun,' sighed Hengist. 'Scapegoated is worse than showcase.'

'It was the scapegoat curry wot did it,' giggled Janna, 'and probably Sally's good-luck card. I feel so guilty.'

'No you don't,' said Hengist, who was bored with Ofsted. He was due at dinner five minutes ago, was getting a reputation for lateness, and wanted sex now. As if in sympathy, the rain was drumming its fingers on the window. Throwing a log on the fire, which put up a shower of orange sparks, he took Janna's ankles and parted them like scissors, then kissed his way up her warm, scented, freckled thighs.

He loved it when she went quiet, but, surprised by her lack of response—by now she should be writhing, gasping and growing damp—he looked up. She'd fallen asleep.

72

The rage and humiliation of Ashton and Crispin knew no bounds. Ashton, despite his soft features, his lisp and his pretty hands, was a thug who bullied Crispin as relentlessly as everyone else.

'I want evidence to get wid of Janna Curtis,' he ordered his deputy the following morning. 'I don't want her or Larks bouncing back.'

Janna's and Larks's euphoria over Ofsted had been sharply terminated the following week by a couple of knifings in the Shakespeare Estate and a horrific sex murder just over the border in nearby Rutminster. Bethany Watson, the sweetest ten-year-old, had been raped, strangled, then chucked under a pile of rotting hay in a cow byre, leaving a devastated and terrified community. Police were conducting house-to-house searches. Hordes of media hung around, scathingly referring to Larks as 'the Shakespeare Estate sink school'.

Larks mothers were increasingly jittery about their children having to walk home on increasingly dark evenings, because the bus stop had been moved. There were sightings of prowlers everywhere.

Chief Inspector Gablecross had been seconded to Rutminster to lead the investigation. Earlier in the term he had instructed one of his junior officers, PC Cuthbert, to keep an eye on Larks and to break up fights in the playground or at going-home time, when tensions grew high.

PC Cuthbert, despite his blond curls and fresh face, was tough, ambitious, zero-tolerant and determined to rid the town of crime. Influenced by Tim Gablecross and his wife Mags, he was unusual among his colleagues in that he liked Larks kids and felt they had a raw deal. His presence had been a definite plus.

Another plus of the term had been Lily's lectures to the newly formed Wildlife Club. Frantic not to let S and C sell off any part of Larks's beautiful land, Janna had been determined to establish them as a wildlife sanctuary and had been much heartened by Wade Hargreaves's approval.

Lily would arrive with a bootful of plum jam doughnuts and ancient binoculars weighed down with Ascot, Kempton and Goodwood labels and bear the Wildlife Club off on rambles round the grounds, identifying coloured leaves falling from the trees and birds that flocked to the bird table.

They had also sighted roe deer, muntjac, squirrels, rabbits, several foxes and, on a very mild afternoon, an adder asleep on a sunlit pile of leaves, which provoked screams of terror from the children and Monster into picking up a branch.

'Don't hurt him,' Lily had cried. 'Adders are a protected species.'

'His parents must've had unprotected sex to produce him,' observed Feral. 'Nasty killing machine.'

'They ought to practise safe sex,' said Kylie, 'then they wouldn't produce any more babies.'

'Unlike you,' said Johnnie Fowler.

The adder had retreated into the blond grasses.

The pond had also become a focus of interest. The children loved swaying across Wally's narrow bridge to the island on which stood a pale blue duck house, surrounded by willows and white

34

poplars garlanded with brambles and wild roses.

Here, to Lily's great excitement, they sighted a greyish-brown creature covered in red warts, which turned out to be a very rare natterjack toad.

'Looks like somefing the witches'd cook wiv in *Macbeth*,' said Pearl.

'They probably did.' Lily bent down to admire the toad's bright green eyes. 'Natterjacks weren't protected in those days. You must take a photograph, Graffi. Thank you,' she added, as Feral hoisted her to her feet.

Partner, who was devoted to Lily, always accompanied them on these jaunts. The Wildlife Club adored them because Lily was easily distracted into telling them stories about her days in the Wrens, the exotic places she'd visited with her late husband the ambassador and about her wild nieces and nephews who were mostly artists.

The children had instantly taken to Lily because of her genuine kindness, sense of fun and her friendship with Feral who, now her lawn no longer needed mowing, was chopping logs, bringing in coal and sharing spliffs and a passion for Arsenal.

Feral would call her on one of his stolen mobiles: ' 'Lo, Lily, how yer doin', man?' and chat for hours about Sol and Thierry's latest exploits. Lily had started a scrapbook of Arsenal cuttings and encouraged Feral to practise and play as much as possible. Both were secretly very proud of this friendship.

It was Sam Spink, discovering Lily was being paid forty pounds in cash per nature ramble out of the school tin, who predictably sneaked to Ashton Douglas that Lily was entering the school when she hadn't been cleared by the Criminal Records

Bureau to work with children.

Ashton promptly banned Lily from Larks on the very November day when a contingent from Bagley Hall was coming over to take part in a ramble. With the honour of Larks at stake, Lily had done a huge amount of cooking, and was understandably upset.

'Hardly likely at my age to jump on children in broad daylight.'

'Quite right,' agreed Johnnie Fowler. 'Lily's too old to be a kiddy-fiddler.'

'We want Lily,' chorused the Wildlife Club.

But S and C were adamant.

'When it's a question of children's safety . . .' Ashton told an enraged Janna. 'Can't think how it's gone on so long.'

'Can't be too careful,' said Sam Spink sanctimoniously.

'Sneak,' hissed Janna.

As a result No-Joke Joan stepped in to lead the ramble.

'Gratifying to have a committed professional,' enthused Chally. 'Joan is a formidable biologist.'

Joan, who'd been regaled with horror stories and instructed to spy by Alex Bruce, was curious to have a look at Larks.

Janna would have fought harder for Lily if she hadn't been besieged by parents frantic about the Rutshire prowler. Yesterday morning Chantal had rung in to report that Kylie Rose was too stressed to come in having caught sight of a suspicious bearded character in a flat cap and dark glasses photographing girls in the playground. Later in the day, three of Year Seven complained they'd seen a bearded prowler lurking between the pond and the

36

car park. Two of the asylum-seekers from Year Eight claimed with graphic mime the same prowler had been flashing on Smokers' Bank.

Today, sightings were coming in thick and fast. What was Janna doing to safeguard the kids, demanded Kitten's mother. Chantal Peck rang to say that, like the little soldier she was, Kylie would be coming in because she didn't want to miss lessons. Or Jack Waterlane due from Bagley, thought Janna sourly.

Stormin' Norman made the next call. Did Janna realize kiddy-fiddlers went both ways and what provision had she made to protect Martin. Janna had just put the phone down when a sobbing Pearl barged in in a bloodstained shirt, having cut herself.

'My mum must be the only mum at Larks so unconcerned about her kid she hasn't phoned in to make a fuss.'

'Oh Pearl,' sighed Janna, getting out her first-aid kit.

It would need more than Dettol and plaster to heal Pearl.

*   *   *

In assembly, Janna tried to calm everyone's fears. 'When you're terrified, you sometimes see people who aren't there.'

'I saw him, miss, I saw his knife,' came cries from all over the hall.

'He's got a beard and a big red willy wiv a purple knob on.'

'That's enough, Kitten. Make sure you go round in groups of three or four, and never walk home

37

alone.'

'No one wants to walk with me any more,' sobbed Pearl.

'Oh, shut up,' snapped Kitten, throwing a hymn book at her.

Pearl was about to leap on Kitten, but, distracted by Janna's news that good-looking PC Cuthbert would be along soon, she belted off to do her face.

*   *   *

It was a damp, cheerless day. Trees wrapped thick grey mist round their shoulders to protect their last leaves; crows cawed morosely; any minute Dracula's carriage would rumble up the drive.

Joan, as if warding off the powers of darkness, rolled up in a calf-length Barbour, lace-up khaki gumboots and a sombrero worn over a headscarf, so only the lower half of her disapproving brick-red face was visible.

'Like a rubber fetishist's daydream,' muttered Wally.

Joan was accompanied by a giggling Amber, Milly and Jade, a sneering Boffin, a very nervous Primrose Duddon, quivering like a nun entering a brothel, the Chinless Wanderers, armed with hipflasks, and the Cosmonaughties, who had all brought wads of greenbacks to purchase drugs from the pushers who only deserted the gates if PC Cuthbert hove in sight.

'Why hasn't Paris come?' wailed Larks.

'He had double Latin,' explained Amber.

'Oh, did he now,' mocked Monster. 'How fritefly posh.'

'Watch it.' Feral bounced his football fractionally

38

faster, then, turning to Amber: 'You're looking good.'

'Almost as good as you,' murmured Amber.

'Why, you're hunkier than ever,' said Milly, hugging Graffi.

'Make sure the students keep away from the bushes,' Chally advised Joan.

Aysha, who had been worried Xav would think her ugly because she had circles under her eyes from not being able to sleep for excitement about seeing him, was devastated when he didn't turn up, although she'd probably have been too shy to speak to him.

'I want some of Lily's fruit cake,' grumbled Rocky.

'You've just had lunch, young man,' reproved Joan bossily, then, blowing her whistle, set off into the mist.

Noticing Cosmo was as fatally glamorous as ever in his astrakhan coat, Pearl couldn't resist trying to attract his attention.

'I saw the prowler yesterday. I was having a quick tinkle in the bushes, and looking round saw his long lens pointing up my bum.'

'Good thing it were only his lens,' leered Monster.

'He was horrible with a flat cap and a perv's beard and shades.' Pearl was famous for exaggeration, but as the mist thickened, everyone shivered and her words gave Milly the excuse to edge near Graffi, and Amber to sidle up to Feral, and Jack to put an arm round Kylie's shoulders. After a cold night, leaves were falling in their thousands, descending without a fight to mould and enrich the earth below.

Joan strode ahead, pointing out different species.

'Look at *Hedera helix*, commonly known as ivy, its little yellow flowers a last feast for the insects. Listen to them humming: hummmm,' she went.

'I want a doughnut,' grumbled Monster. 'Lily brings doughnuts 'n' fudge 'n' chocolate cake.'

Joan turned on him disapprovingly, 'If you want to avoid obesity, young man, you should stop eating between meals.'

'That's an affront to my human dignity,' spluttered Monster, reaching for his mobile. 'I'm telling my mum.'

On Wildlife Club days, feeding the birds was always saved until the rambling party reached the bird table.

Aysha opened the tin, tipping out stale cake, pastry crusts, bacon and birdseed, as the others filled up the nets with nuts.

'Christ, I'm starved,' grumbled Feral, whipping a piece of sponge cake. 'I missed lunch, 'spectin' Lily's doughnuts.' He glared at Joan.

As the rambling party retreated, sharing Lily's binoculars, the birds began to fly in.

'That's a fieldfare,' called out Joan. 'Listen to his cry.' She went into a series of jerky, nervous whistles. 'And here's the redwing, tirra lira, tirra lira, whit, whit. Redwings come south from colder climes. At this time chaffinches and lapwings go round in flocks, you can recognize the lapwing, tirra lira, whoop whoop. There's no need to laugh, Feral Jackson, must you mock everything?'

'Cockadoodle do,' murmured Graffi, sliding his hands inside Milly's fleece.

'Robin's still singing his rich little song.' Putting on a special face, Joan went into another frenzy of whistling and trilling, which had everyone holding their own or each other's sides. Jack and Kylie vanished into the bushes.

'I want a doughnut,' moaned Rocky.

'This is the mating call of the Feral Jackson.' Amber gave three wolf whistles.

'Don't be silly, Amber. Robin will fight over his little bit of garden.'

'Like I'd fight over you,' whispered Graffi. 'You are so beautiful,' he added as he drew Milly into a clump of laurels.

As Joan peered into some long grass, Lando offered Pearl a slug of brandy.

'How's Paris?' she asked.

'Better,' drawled Lando, 'although he can still be moody and aggressive.'

'Note the beech leaves shrivelling.' Joan was pointing in all directions. 'And evergreens in their dark dress like winter furniture: yews, bay trees and over there a Lawson cypress.'

'Joan's getting quite carried away,' muttered Amber from behind a blackthorn copse.

'So am I,' said Feral, sliding his long fingers inside her knickers.

'All animals are preparing for winter. Snails retreat into their shells, squirrels into the trees, even this dear little dog'—Joan patted Partner, who was hanging around for Lily's fudge—'is developing his thick winter coat.'

As they reached the pond, Joan put a big red finger to her lips:

'We might see the reedling. You can identify him by his brown back and grey and black head, and sometimes orange and lavender feathers. Reedlings are often known as bearded tits.'

41

'Plenty of those at Larks,' quipped Johnnie Fowler.

In front of the island, a blasted tree had collapsed, half in, half out of the water, its reflection like the strong limbs, torso and thrown-back head of a sleeping god. Above it rose poplar saplings and the whiskery grey ghosts of willowherb.

'I can see a bearded tit,' shouted Rocky.

'That's a moorhen,' reproached Joan.

'Not a hen, I know hens.'

'Note the beautiful yellow and crimson leaves of the bramble.'

'I can see a bearded tit.'

Practically garrotting Rocky, Anatole grabbed Lily's binoculars. Through the willowherb, black disks encountered black disks. Despite the lack of wind, the poplar saplings were shivering to the right of the pale blue duck house, as Anatole caught sight of a bearded figure in a flat cap.

'There is bearded tit on island,' he confirmed in his deep voice.

'It's the prowler!' screamed Pearl. 'He was looking up my panties yesterday. No one believed me.'

'Perv, perv, filthy perv!' chorused the remaining children, who were soon joined by the rest of the party spilling out of the undergrowth in various states of undress and intoxication, yelling: 'Nonce, filthy perving nonce.'

As they searched the water's edge for pebbles to hurl at him, Partner rushed forward barking furiously.

'It's the prowler, miss,' repeated Pearl.

Reluctantly, Joan moved her binoculars from the

water. 'Could have sworn I saw a natterjack.' Then, focusing on the island: 'Good God, there is a bloke there.' She blew her whistle. 'Calm down, students. If need be I shall make a citizen's arrest.'

Cheered on, she strode forward. But PC Cuthbert, hell-bent on promotion, who'd been hovering behind a vast cedar, was too quick for her. Racing round the pond, swaying precariously across Wally's bridge, he caught the prowler attempting to escape the same way.

The prowler was indeed wearing a flat cap and dark glasses and sporting a bushy grey beard. Hanging from his neck, binoculars and digital camera clashed against each other. Turning, nearly falling into the pond, he regained the island, calling out:

'Good afternoon, officer, I can explain everything. I've been photographing wildlife for a book I'm writing.' He had a snuffling voice that reminded PC Cuthbert of his aunt's pekingese. Probably an asthmatic.

'May I have a look at your camera, sir?'

The prowler then tried to make a run for it, and in other circumstances would have wondered if he'd gone to heaven when this forceful young constable flung him against the duck house to rousing cheers from the bank and slapped him into handcuffs. In the struggle his beard came off to reveal an orange goatee and several chins.

'I can explain everything, officer,' repeated the prowler. 'My name is in fact Crispin Thomas, Deputy Director of S and C Services, responsible for the education of Larkshire's children.'

'Funny way of showing it, sir.'

'I am actually doing undercover research into

43

challenging behaviour and whether the curriculum is being adhered to in Larkshire's schools. Mike Pitts and Janna Curtis can certainly confirm my identity.' His voice rose as PC Cuthbert dragged him across the bridge.

'Janna's away this afternoon,' shouted Graffi, 'and she don't owe you no favours, and if it's past dinnertime, Pittsy wouldn't know you from his Aunty Vera.'

On disembarking, PC Cuthbert removed the camera from around Crispin's neck, dislodging his flat cap and grey wig to reveal startlingly orange hair.

'That's my property,' screamed Crispin, as PC Cuthbert began looking at the camera's screen.

Clicking through, he found many shots of a questionable nature, namely Pearl urinating and displaying a lot of naked bottom; of sweet little Year Seven photographed from a low angle, their skirts flying as they leapt for a ball; of Kitten Meadows giving Johnnie Fowler a blow job; of Jack Waterlane unhooking Kylie's bra; of Monster sniffing glue; of Graffi and Feral hurling tiles off the roof last Friday and Partner trying to shag Miss Miserden's cat.

An everyday story of Larks Comp—but enough to convince PC Cuthbert he had done the right thing. He wasted no time in summoning back-up in the form of a second officer to ride in the back seat of the car with the prowler.

'I am arresting you on suspicion of taking indecent photographs of children,' he told Crispin and proceeded to caution him.

When Crispin screamed that he was a friend of PC Cuthbert's Chief Constable and would get him

44

sacked and, despite his handcuffs, attempted to run away, Partner rushed forward and nipped him sharply on the ankle.

'Ouch,' screamed Crispin.

'Do any of you recognize this gentleman?' demanded PC Cuthbert.

'Never seen the dirty nonce before in our lives,' lied the children. 'Lock him up.'

Puce, spluttering, swearing he'd sue for wrongful arrest, Crispin was borne off to the station. Joan thought he looked vaguely familiar but it was probably only his identikit photo in the paper. He looked a thoroughly depraved individual. How splendid if he were the Rutshire prowler.

After a very unpleasant session both in a police cell and under interrogation, Crispin was released when a furious Ashton rolled up to identify and bail him.

Chief Inspector Gablecross, who'd been working on poor little Bethany's murder all day, was also able to identify him. But Crispin still had the photographs and the false identity to explain. He was not sure the police believed his excuse about an undercover operation. Ashton was incandescent with rage. How could Crispin screw up so monumentally?

Janna was even angrier when she and Cambola got back from a meeting with the cathedral choirmaster and learnt what had happened, particularly when Hengist rang, having heard the news, and treated the whole thing as a huge joke.

'So perfect for a self-confessed wildlife photographer to cut his teeth on Larks Year Ten and Bagley Middle Fifth. Joan is thoroughly over-excited and longing to go to court.'

'Crispin was lurking on the island to give himself ammunition against us,' stormed Janna.

'I know and he could easily have caught you and me. We must be careful. See you later, darling, and don't wear any knickers.'

73

To Larks's disappointment, the *Gazette* failed to report Crispin's arrest and subsequent release; they were too busy leading on a forthcoming review of Larkshire's secondary schools. According to inside information leaked to them, Larkminster Comp was the preferred option for closure.

Janna was on to Col Peters in a trice.

'What inside information?' she yelled.

'We cannot reveal our sources,' said Col primly.

'You bloody well should when they're libellous and vindictive. You're just putting people off sending children to Larks and utterly demoralizing my parents, teachers and children.'

'Your kids can read our newspaper? They *must* be improving.'

'Bastard!' howled Janna.

As a result Larks pupils were mocked in the street by St Jimmy's, Searston Abbey and even the choir school.

'Sink school, stink school, you're closing down, you'll soon be gone.'

After Ofsted's recommendations, Janna had hoped for more funding or at least that Appletree would be rebuilt. Instead, at the end of the month, Ashton and Crispin, in a fit of spite, ordered Appletree to be boarded up and its science, D and T and music departments to be relocated to the main building. This not only devastated the teachers—Mr Mates had had his labs in Appletree for nearly forty years—but also the pupils, who felt less valued than ever.

When Janna complained, Ashton merely replied bitchily that with so many surplus places, Larks pupils couldn't even be filling the main building.

Hostile and bewildered, the children slipped back into their old, bad ways, particularly the Wolf Pack. Pearl was disrupting every class; Kylie was miserable and doing no work beause she'd just lost a baby. Feral and Graffi were truanting and acting up. The only chemistry the latter two did for the rest of the term was to make up a paste with an ammonium triodide base. This they spread thinly over the platform in the school hall the morning Rod Hyde rolled up on a fault-finding mission and insisted on taking assembly. His pacings up and down the platform triggered off such a series of explosions that, fearing a terrorist attack, there was a stampede out of the hall. Rod, punching pupils out of the way, was at the forefront. On learning the truth, he fired off a furious email to a gratified S and C: 'This school is so dreadful, it must be closed down.'

*　　　*　　　*

'My Rod and staff don't comfort me,' moaned Janna as she and Hengist lay in her double bed that evening, so sated with sex they could hardly lift glasses of Hengist's Veuve Clicquot to their lips.

'I had to give Graffi and Feral a detention,' she went on, 'but I had great difficulty not laughing. Pity it didn't blow Rod up. Where are you supposed to be?' she asked.

'Dining with some prep-school heads. The things I do to fill up my school.'

Tomorrow he and Sally were taking Randal and Mrs Walton to the ballet in Paris and a party at the British Embassy afterwards. Clinton and Hillary and a host of luminaries were expected.

'I have to ensure Randal meets everyone, he is such a star-fucker. He won't shut up until I nail down the poor dear Queen to open his bloody science block.'

'I'm the one who needs a science block. How's he getting on with Mrs Walton?'

'Moved her into a penthouse flat and picking up her bills, so her spirits will be lifted as well as her body.'

'Improving on previous bust,' giggled Janna.

'God, I'm going to miss you,' groaned Hengist as Janna crawled down, trickling champagne over his cock before sucking it off.

Janna was ashamed how her love affaire with Hengist insulated her at least momentarily against the horrors of Larks. Nor, she comforted herself, was any school with such a glowing Ofsted report likely to be closed down.

The morning after Hengist had left for Paris, she was horrified to see Alex Bruce, in a tracksuit, jogging up the drive on a courtesy visit.

'Thought your Year Ten bods might profit from some chemistry coaching'—Alex vigorously polished his spectacles—'now they've started their GCSE syllabus.'

But when he insisted Year Ten remove their coats and baseball caps, spit out their chewing gum and sit at their desks rather than on top of them, they started pelting him with rulers, rubbers and pencil boxes. Then Johnnie Fowler picked up a brick and, pretending it was a grenade, lobbed it at

49

Alex.

'Sending him belting down the drive,' Janna told Hengist when he rang that evening.

'Already training for the next steeplechase,' sighed Hengist.

'The children can't stand him.'

Nor could Alex stand them and wrote an even more damning report to S and C than Rod Hyde.

*   *   *

After that they were into the Christmas frenzy of reports, school plays, end-of-term parties, carol concerts and, apart from an official Christmas card, Janna didn't hear from S and C until January.

It was during mocks, whilst she was appreciating the vast amount of work needed to be put in by Year Eleven before May in order to boost Larks's place in the league tables, that a very amicable letter arrived from Ashton.

In it he wished her a very happy New Year and asked if, after school on 4 February, he could visit Larks.

'At last,' Janna told a staff meeting joyfully, 'S and C have responded to our Ofsted and are going to give us some funding.'

Exhorted by Janna, most of the children stopped trashing and vandalizing and pitched in to make the school look as attractive as possible. As a jokey reminder about the leaking roof, Year Eight had created a rainforest in reception. Janna also aimed to nudge Ashton about rebuilding Appletree and the labs.

*   *   *

The fourth of February dawned bitterly cold, with an east wind howling through every ill-fitting window.

'Pity we can't light a fire with all those DfES directives,' grumbled Rowan as she turned on the storage heater, which Emlyn had dropped in to keep Janna warm on long, late evenings. On a low table, she arranged the pansy-patterned tea set that the children had given Janna for Christmas.

Are pansies quite the right message for Ashton and Crispin? wondered Janna.

On her desk was a copy of the latest Review of Secondary Schools, packed with faulty statistics about Larks's results, attendance, surplus places and future intake. When confronted, smiley-faced Cindy Payne from the county council had airily dismissed them as typing errors, but had made no attempt to correct this publicly. Nor had the review made any mention of Larks's successful Ofsted.

'I must discuss it rationally with Ashton,' Janna told herself. 'I must not lose my temper.'

Thank God the children would be out of the building before he rolled up. There had been far too many fights recently. Many of the kids looked up at her window and waved as they set out for home. She mustn't let them down. Partner, knowing teacups led to biscuits, bustled in wagging ingratiatingly.

'You are *not* to bite Crispin,' said Janna sternly.

'They're here,' shouted Rowan. 'Are you sure you don't mind my sloping off? I must get Scarlet to the doctor.'

'I'll be fine.' Janna ran towards reception, proudly thinking what a contrast the riot of colour

51

in every classroom made to the chill, grey, dying day outside. This was a good and thriving school.

Her first shock was that Ashton had brought Cindy Payne. Her second that they totally ignored all the effort that had been made, even the Indians, cowboys and big toothy horses Graffi had designed for Year Ten's American Wild West display, as they marched along the corridor to Janna's office.

'They've been working so hard,' she said lamely, then after a pause: 'Where's Crispin?'

'He's moved on,' said Ashton, discarding his former deputy as casually as he whipped off an exquisite dark blue cashmere overcoat and palest pink scarf, dropping them over a chair. A pink silk bow tie enlivened a waisted pale grey suit and silver-grey shirt. As usual, he'd drenched himself in sweet, suffocating scent as if to ward off the fetid air of Larks.

Cindy today had matched a red nose and woolly flowerpot hat to the inevitable scarlet trouser suit. But the effect was not one of cheer. Her round face had the relentless jollity of a sister in a ward of terminally ill geriatrics, but her little eyes, like Ashton's, were as cold as the day.

'Those storage heaters are very dear to run,' she said disapprovingly.

'They keep me warm at night when the central heating goes off,' snapped Janna. 'Remembering how saunaed you are at S and C, I didn't want you to catch cold.'

Stop bitching, Janna, she told herself.

Cindy's smile became more fixed, then her face really lit up as Debbie arrived with tea, which included egg sandwiches and a newly baked batch of shortbread:

'Hello, Debs! You do spoil us, what a wonderful spread.'

'What a feast,' said Ashton heartily.

'Shall I be mother?' asked Cindy, flopping on to the sofa, narrowly missing Partner who retreated sourly to Janna's knee. 'I still haven't taken off that half-stone I put on over the festive season, but I won't be able to resist Debs's legendary shortbread.'

Ashton, with an equally greedy expression on his face, was gazing at a blow-up of Paris playing Romeo.

'He got into twouble knocking out a wef last term. Old habits die hard, I suppose.'

'He's playing regularly for the Colts,' said Janna sharply.

'Don't be so defensive,' teased Cindy, hiding the pansies on hers and Ashton's plates with sandwiches. 'A sarnie for you, Janna?'

'I'm OK, thanks.'

Picking up his plate, Ashton moved on to last summer's photograph of the whole school (except for Paris, he noticed, who had probably gone off joy-riding on trains by then). But there was Paris's alter ego, Feral Jackson, another beauty, clutching his football. All the children and teachers were laughing with Janna in the middle with that blasted dog on her knee.

'Nice one of Debs,' he said idly. 'Excellent sandwiches. She's one person who won't have any difficulty getting another job.' Then, as Janna looked up, startled: 'There's weally no easy way to say this, but I'm afwaid Larks is scheduled for closure at the end of the summer term.'

Partner squeaked as Janna's stroking hand

53

clenched on his shoulder. She felt as though she'd stepped back off a cliff with a bullet straight between her eyes.

'But you haven't even seen over it,' she whispered. 'We've spent days making it look lovely.'

'We don't need to see over a school to close it down.'

'But why?' stammered Janna.

'Do you really need us to tell you?' Ashton idly added sweetener to his tea and joined Cindy on the sofa. 'The figures speak for themselves.'

'We had a wonderful Ofsted.'

'The most wonderful Ofsted in the world can't change the fact that you have four hundred and fifty, probably four hundred by now, students wattling around in a building meant for twelve hundred. Your wesults are dreadful, truancy and vandalism are sky high.'

'The latest Review of Secondary Schools was rigged.' Janna could hardly speak through her stiff lips. 'All the figures were wrong and you averaged them over four years, so of course no improvement was discernible. You said they were typing errors, but you never publicly corrected them. We were doing fine until you changed the bus routes and leaked that rumour about Larks being targeted for closure back in November. Why didn't you hang a plague sign over the school gates?'

'You'll have a chance to appeal,' said Cindy cosily, helping herself to two pieces of shortbread. 'My word, these are good; Debbie really is a treasure. We always put our decisions for closure up for public consultation.' At Janna's blank look she added, 'We give people a chance to express

54

their views—public meetings, letters of support, etc.—then in May, the council cabinet will meet to examine these views and put forward recommendations to the Larkshire Schools Organization Committee.'

'If any of their five members vote against closure,' said Ashton, also helping himself to shortbread, 'it'll go to adjudication in the autumn.'

'Unlikely, as you've no doubt got the committee sewn up,' accused Janna.

She looked at the trees outside, disappearing into the twilight, like her school. She was shaking so violently that Partner jumped down and, unnoticed, took refuge on Ashton's navy blue coat.

'Ever since I've been here,' she said bleakly, 'I've battled against a disaffected governing body, a totally uncooperative privatized LEA and a county council who won't give me a penny and who are in league with a vindictive local press.'

'You're making dangerous accusations,' said Ashton sharply.

'Ofsted said exactly the same thing. They knew we were capable of improving if we were given the chance. What about my children?' Janna had a sudden vision of every one of them drowning before her eyes. 'You can't close Larks down. How could anyone in S and C understand? You don't give a toss about continuity. You all move on, like Crispin, if things get rough. What about my teachers? They've made such sacrifices and worked so hard.'

'They'll be wing-fenced,' said Ashton. 'So many have left already; if any jobs are advertised in the county, they'll get first option.'

'Doesn't mean they'll get the job, now they've

been tarnished with working at Larks.'

'Is it your career you're worried about?' asked Cindy as if she were dictating to a half-wit secretary. 'You're not old, you'll get plenty of job offers.'

Ashton, who'd been examining his nails, stretched out and selected a nail file from Janna's blue mug crammed with pens.

'Do drink up your tea,' urged Cindy.

Picking up the sugar bowl, Janna emptied it into her cup, then, realizing what she'd done, let the bowl slip from her fingers, so it crashed down on to her cup, smashing them both, spilling tea everywhere.

'Years Ten and Eleven gave me this tea set for Christmas,' she said in a strange, high voice. 'Oh, fuck off, Partner,' she screamed as he leapt off Ashton's coat and tried to lick up the tea.

'There, there,' said Cindy, 'I'm sure that bowl can be mended.'

'But my school can't,' yelled Janna, bursting into tears.

'I know it's a shock when a school closes down.' Cindy struggled to her feet. 'Have you got a friend to come and be with you?'

'Don't fucking patronize me. If you think I'm giving up Larks without a fight . . .' Dropping to the floor, Janna grabbed Ashton's scarf to mop up the tea.

'Give me that.' Ashton seized it back. He was even less pleased to see his coat covered in Partner's hairs. 'Twy not to be gwatuitously unpleasant, Janna,' he continued smoothly, 'you're suffering from hurt pride. I can only advise you to go gwacefully.'

56

Seeing the murderous expression on Janna's face as her hand grabbed the handle of the teapot, Cindy said hastily:

'We can show ourselves out. Don't get too stressed. I can recommend an excellent counsellor.'

'Anything's better than a county councillor, you fat cow,' shrieked Janna, 'they kill schools.'

*   *   *

'Dear, dear, dear,' said Ashton as they hastened out into the drizzle, 'how did that malevolent hysteric ever get a job running a school? Nothing has ever convinced me more of the rightness of our decision.'

'Thank goodness Alex Bruce and Rod Hyde put in such negative reports.' Cindy tugged her red wool hat over her ears. 'I don't anticipate much opposition, do you?'

'I hope not. Hengist Brett-Taylor might act up; he always had a *tendresse* for little Miss Curtis.'

'But he's so tied up in politics. At least Cavendish Plaza and Haut Larkminster will be on our side. Closing down schools causes such a rumpus. We must rush it through as soon as possible.'

After all, one didn't want to lose one's seat on the county council or all that kudos and fat expenses.

They jumped as a window was flung open.

'You won't get away with this, you murderers!'

Two minutes later Janna ran out to a deserted car park, crying uncontrollably: 'My teachers, my children.'

A hundred yards beyond the school gate, she had

to leap out of her car and throw up, mostly bile, on the pavement outside the Ghost and Castle.

'Drunk at this hour . . .' chuntered a couple disappearing into the saloon bar.

Only then did Janna realize she'd left Partner locked in her office.

'I'm so sorry,' she sobbed as she recovered him.

But as he snuggled across her thighs, attempting to be the seatbelt she had forgotten to fasten, all she could think was: My career is over. In Yorkshire, they'll say I failed, failed, failed.

She was overwhelmed by a stench of burning wax. Like Icarus, she had flown too near the sun.

74

By contrast, Brigadier Woodford had had such a wonderful piece of news, he had splashed out on two bottles of champagne (Lily's favourite drink, which she could no longer afford), two large cartons of potted shrimps, a beef and ale pie, strawberries and an even larger carton of double cream, and taken them over to Lily's to celebrate.

Lily had lit a fire and they were sitting comfortably on Lily's shabby sofa with the vast fluffy black and white General between them, accidentally brushing hands as they both simultaneously stroked him. Lily had rescued some poor crocuses trampled on the verge outside and, in a white vase in the warmth of the room, they had expanded like purple striped umbrellas with little orange handles. The Brigadier felt his heart expanding like the crocuses.

'God I miss champagne, this is such a treat,' said Lily happily. 'Now, what are we celebrating?'

'Rupert's offered me my own programme. It's going to be called *Buffers*. Each week we'll take a war or campaign in history and get four so-called experts or "old buffers", retired generals and admirals, to sit round a table having frightful rows about strategy and blame. I've got to chair it.'

The genuine delight on Lily's face nearly gave the Brigadier the courage to kiss her.

'How clever of Rupert! You're going to be a star, Christian.'

'Rupert wants to start with twelve programmes. We have to do something called a pilot first, which sounds more like the RAF. You'll have to come on it to add some glamour and talk about the Wrens.' He emptied the bottle into their glasses.

'D'you think we can manage a second?'

'Certainly, with a celebration like this.' As Lily leant across General and gave the Brigadier a peck on the cheek, he had a longing to kiss her passionately on the lips, but was worried it might dislodge his bridge. It was such a long time since he'd made a pass.

'If the pilot works, Rupert wants his father Eddie, who was in the Blues, to be one of the regulars. Said it might stop Eddie tapping him for money if he got an income from television. Frightfully amusing chap, Eddie, thought the programme was going to be called *Buggers*.'

'Probably be even more successful,' said Lily dryly.

Christian guffawed; then, because he didn't feel it was boasting with Lily, 'The Tories have asked me to open their Easter Fair. GMTV want me to go up to London to talk about the possibility of war in the Gulf and Larkminster Rovers wrote asking me to go on their board. I don't know much about soccer.'

'Feral and I will teach you,' said Lily. 'When you score a goal you have to slide to the ground and bare your breast by lifting up and shaking the front of your shirt.'

'Much more excitin' if you did,' snorted the Brigadier. As he heaved himself up to fetch another bottle, he noticed how empty the fridge was except for the strawberries and cream, and also that that dear little watercolour of the church at Limesbridge where Lily grew up was missing. He hated Lily having to sell things. What heaven if they could be together like this every night. Lily could have an 'old age serene and bright, And lovely as a Lapland night'.

General the cat opened a disapproving yellow eye but didn't shift as the cork flew across the room to the accompaniment of a hammering on the front door.

'Oh hell,' said Lily, 'let's pretend we're out.'

But there was no escape as Janna barged in, followed by Partner; nor was there any word of apology as she collapsed on to the dark blue velvet chair by the fire, shaking uncontrollably, her reddened eyes wide and staring.

'Oh Lily, oh Lily.'

'You poor child, whatever's the matter? Give her a drink, Christian.'

'They're closing my school down.'

'They can't do that.'

'They can, they can! What's going to happen to my children and my teachers and Wally?'

'That's rotten luck,' said the Brigadier, handing her a glass. 'You must fight it.'

'I know, but I don't know how to. I've been fighting since I took over.' Janna gulped down half the champagne and carried on talking.

Lily, of course, insisted she stay to supper, and divided the potted shrimps and the beef and ale pie for two into three, and buttered a lot of brown bread.

Christian tried not to feel irritated when Janna drank most of the remaining champagne but, incapable of eating, fed all her pie to Partner.

'I forgot to get him any food on the way home, and I left him shut in my office, I'm coming apart

61

at the seams, I've got to be strong for the children. Larks is the only security they know.' She started to cry again. Partner, his front paws on her knees, tried to stem her tears with a beef-flavoured tongue.

'We'll all fight,' promised Lily. 'Hengist will kick up a hell of a rumpus, and so will Rupert. And while my nephew Jupiter isn't my favourite person, he's excellent at putting the jackboot in—anything to discredit Cindy Payne and New Labour.'

'I called her a fat cow.' Janna was twisting a thread hanging out of Lily's green velvet chair cover so violently it broke off and a mass of kapok billowed out. 'Oh God, I'm sorry.'

Whatever happened to stiff upper lips, thought the Brigadier as Janna helped herself to the last of the champagne.

'I've let so many people down.' She sobbed. 'People like Sophy Belvedon and the new head of D and T who've got children and massive mortgages because they've specially bought houses in the area. I feel like a captain who's steered his great battleship on to the rocks.'

Lily patted Janna's shoulder. 'No one could have fought harder.'

The Brigadier felt ashamed. It was only because he'd so wanted to be alone with Lily.

'Oh God, I must tell Russell,' exclaimed Janna. 'So many people to tell—the children are going to be the worst. Can I use your phone?'

Her shaking hand kept misdialling Russell's number. She got the vicar and the local greengrocer before she finally reached him.

'I heard, and I'm not surprised,' he said heavily. 'I gather you were extremely offensive to Cindy when

62

she tried to be supportive. Why must you always construe help as criticism?'

'Their help is like snake venom,' shouted Janna and hung up.

'He knew,' she said flatly. 'Ashton and Cindy must have been straight on to him.'

'I smell collusion,' said Lily. 'First, you must appoint Dora as your press officer.'

*   *   *

Next morning Janna had the nightmare of breaking the news to the staff, taking an extended lunch hour, gathering them into the staffroom, feeling utterly sick at the sight of their stunned faces.

'It can't be true,' muttered Lydia.

Basket burst into tears. 'I'll never get another job.'

'We're going to fight it, of course,' said Janna quickly. 'We've got two months to register protest.'

'It wasn't unexpected,' said Mike Pitts. 'When will the axe fall?'

'Ashton said the end of the summer term, but that's only a few months away.' Janna looked bewildered. 'He must mean summer two thousand and four, and that's only if the Schools Organization Committee are all in favour.'

But when she dialled Ashton to check, he assured her if the Schools Organization Committee were unanimous, Larks would close in summer 2003.

'You can't close it so soon. You particularly can't do that to Year Ten,' whispered Janna in horror, remembering how she'd walked out on her GCSE classes at Redfords. 'Year Eleven will be OK.

They'll take their exams in May and we'll be able to see them through before we close down.'

Outside she could see the children in the playground. Graffi and Feral were idly kicking a ball around; Pearl and Kylie were reading the same magazine, stamping their feet to keep warm. All of them were perplexed by their extended lunch hour and, aware some storm was brewing, gathering in edgy little groups, glancing constantly up at her window. Are we in more trouble?

'We can't abandon Year Ten,' she told Ashton firmly. 'What about Aysha and Graffi and Kitten and Johnnie and Feral and Monster, they'll never get a job and out of this hell if they don't get any qualifications.'

'Your beloved Wolf Pack,' drawled Ashton.

'And at least fifty others.'

'Hardly the A team.'

'They bloody are!' yelled Janna, turning and catching Chally raising an eyebrow at Mike Pitts.

'They've been totally disrupted by all the rumour and speculation about closure,' she went on furiously, 'and the incessant bitching of other schools. They haven't completed any coursework, and they'll be chucked out at the end of the summer term into an unfamiliar school for the second year of their course. It's not bloody fair.'

'If their last SATs were anything to go by,' snapped Ashton, 'they're not likely to get any gwades anyway. Straight Us, I'd say.'

'They've got to be given a chance.'

'And you'll have a chance to air your views at the public meeting.'

'I'm afraid it's summer 2003,' she told the staff grimly, 'so we've really got a fight on our hands.'

*　　　*　　　*

If anything convinced her of the need to fight it was the anguish and terror of the children. Pearl, sobbing that she'd thought they'd have five terms more; an inconsolable grey-faced Danijela: 'I is only happy with you, this is my home.' 'Who will write our CVs and sign our driving licences,' wailed Year Eleven.

The boys reacted with violence, hurling more tiles off the roof, tearing off door handles, kicking over desks, trashing classrooms; soon they wouldn't have a school to close down. The *Gazette* and the television cameras were soon outside the door. The staff, panicking about lost jobs, gathered in corners, whispering and afraid, many of them blaming Janna.

But even the darkest cloud has a silver lining.

'Can I have a word?' demanded Chally later in the day, shutting Janna's door behind her and rearranging a crimson-leafed scarf before announcing she was off to take up a deputy head's post at St Jimmy's.

'Congratulations.' Janna tried not to display her delight. 'I'm really pleased for you. You'll find it inspirational working with Rod Hyde. Is one of his Senior Management Team leaving?'

'Not that I know of. They need an extra pair of capable hands. St Jimmy's is so over-subscribed.'

Probably soon with an influx of the brightest children from Larks, thought Janna in outrage, but at least I won't have to suck up to you any more, you old bat.

'Every Chally shall be exalted,' sang Cambola

when Janna pulled her and Mags into her office to tell them.

'Do you think there's any hope she'll be one of those high fliers who whisks all her key people away with her?' asked Mags.

'What bliss if she took Spink, Skunk, Pittsy, Robbie and Basket,' sighed Janna.

Next moment, a red-eyed Rowan put her dark head round the door. 'Hengist Brett-Taylor on the line, Janna.'

'That should cheer up the poor little duck,' whispered Mags as she and Cambola made themselves scarce.

'Darling, darling!' Hengist was ringing from Brussels. 'I only just heard from Jupiter. Lily Hamilton rang him. She must feel really strongly; first time she's spoken to him since he threw her out of her house. God, I'm sorry, are you OK?'

'Fine.' Janna battled not to cry. 'At least Chalford's just announced she's leaving to be deputy head at St Jimmy's.'

'Two wrongs have certainly made a right there.'

'And when I called Russell last night, an hour after I knew, he'd already been told.'

'Sounds like conspiracy,' Hengist echoed Lily, 'what fun we're going to have exposing them. Don't worry, darling.'

'How can I not? What will happen to my children?'

'I'm sure Bagley can accommodate any of your Year Tens in with a shout. I'd love to have Graffi and Feral and Aysha and mouthy Pearl.' Then, when Janna didn't react: 'You could join Bagley and keep an eye on them. You're always saying how you miss teaching, and I could see more of you.' His voice had grown softer, more husky.

'How can you trivialize such a terrible thing, I'd never teach in an independent,' yelled Janna. 'You've already stolen my teachers, my brightest pupil and my heart, you're not taking anything else,' and she slammed down the receiver.

To her dismay, Hengist didn't ring back. Was she misconstruing genuine help as criticism again?

Two days later she got a letter from Sally.

'Hengist has told me. What a dreadful thing to happen. I'm so sorry. We must save Larks. Hengist has got something up his sleeve.'

Affection had grown so strongly between Bagley and Larks that when news of the closure hit the press, mostly via Dora, both schools joined forces to create an uproar.

Graffi's poignant design of a lark escaping from a vicious black cat, with the slogan 'Larks will survive', was soon appearing on balloons, stickers, posters, waving placards and, indeed, scrawled on walls all over Larkminster.

Hengist, to Alex Bruce's fury, blithely encouraged his pupils to join the public protests and marches against both the closure of Larks and the imminent war in Iraq, so they seemed hardly ever in school.

'We bonded with Larks in good times, sir, we're not going to desert them in bad times,' Lando told Alex sanctimoniously.

'But you've got double maths.'

'I don't care,' said Lando, and he raced off to join Graffi and Johnnie on the picket line.

Save our school, boom, boom, boom, save our school, boom, boom, boom, it was so much more fun than lessons.

Tarquin Courtney was only too happy ferrying pickets around in his Porsche. Ashton was demented, particularly when someone spray-painted ascending larks all over his pretty Regency house in the Close.

Lily and the Brigadier were also in the thick of things. In March, to the horror of her nephew Jupiter, Lily whacked a Lib Dem councillor over the head with her placard. Luckily the officer poised to arrest her was PC Cuthbert, who promptly let her off.

Together, she and the Brigadier distracted themselves from the horrors of the war and the stock market by going on marches. Save our school, boom, boom, boom. 'Why does my heart go boom, boom, boom,' sang the Brigadier. The pilot of *Buffers* had been such a resounding success, his presence at Larks demos added considerable gravitas.

Emlyn added physical weight. With Attila the Hunk on the picket line, S and C heavies melted away. With war in Iraq seemingly inevitable, Emlyn was worried sick about Oriana in Baghdad, but he hid it well. He made all his history pupils write letters of protest to County Hall praising Larks, saying how much they'd enjoyed *Romeo and Juliet*, the field trip and the nature ramble in which an S and C executive, hell-bent on closing down Larks, was found in disguise spying in the bushes.

Only Boffin Brooks got under the wire, writing and sealing his own letter, claiming Larks was the most dreadful school he'd ever encountered.

Miss Cambola led every protest, playing 'Hark, Hark! the Lark' on her trumpet. Even Cosmo surprised everyone by proposing a concert in the water meadows near the cathedral. His mother, Dame Hermione, was a friend of the Bishop.

'What could be more lovely, my lord, than classical melodies on a warm summer evening?'

When it leaked out that Cosmo was planning to feature himself and the Cosmonaughties, belting out 'Cocks and Rubbers', among their cleaner lyrics, the Bishop's secretary slipped Cosmo a thousand pounds to go away, half of which Cosmo handed over to Larks.

Poor Feral, who never thought beyond tomorrow, which he thought would be spent at Larks, was terrified. Even incessant Arsenal victories didn't cheer him. He laboriously made his own poster: 'Saive are Skool', which the *Gazette* photographed him nailing up outside Larks. The photograph appeared on the front page, with 'sp' signs in the margin and a caption: 'Another reason why Larks should close'.

Stormin' Norman started a Parents' Action Group, but as most of the action consisted of thumping other parents, it soon fizzled out.

Dora was in her element with the press ringing her every day. In addition, she bravely went from house to house collecting signatures and even organizing a car-boot sale, to which she gave many favourite toys and several of her mother's best dresses.

Paris, pretending not to be interested, read every paper and watched every bulletin. If Larks closed, Janna would leave the area and he'd never see her again. She looked so thin, pale and tense in her photographs. He ached to comfort her.

*   *   *

Ashton and Cindy were getting increasingly rattled. If only the Americans could bomb Larks, but with their track record, they'd probably miss and take out Cavendish Plaza and the Close instead.

As a counter measure, S and C deliberately held their first public meeting to debate Larks's fate on the far side of town on a night when Larkminster Rovers were playing at home. As a result hardly any Larks supporters showed up and instead of pleading her case quietly and reasonably, as she'd intended, a riled Janna lost her cool and a lot of support as she heckled the speakers. A dreadfully dismissive report in the *Gazette* followed.

Meanwhile, Wally with a son, Emlyn with a hoped-for future wife and Hengist and Sally with a daughter were increasingly worried that Bush and Blair would raise two fingers to the UN and plunge into war.

'It's all oil. They don't want the Russians and the French to get their hands on it,' said Hengist.

Wandering across the dry cracked pitches to the Family Tree, he fingered Oriana's carved initials on its trunk. Was she going to be taken from him like Mungo? He longed to ring Janna and find solace in her freckled arms, but he was nervous that any transgression might invoke the anger of the gods, so he walked home to Sally.

*   *   *

Before the second public meeting, which was to take place in late March, Hengist met Rupert and Jupiter at Jupiter's flat in Duke Street, St James's, which had a lovely view over the park lit up by white daffodils and young green willows. A pink moon on its side like a rugby ball hung above Big Ben and the Houses of Parliament. Would they suffer the same fate as the Twin Towers if Britain got into bed with the Americans? wondered Hengist.

The charming flat had once belonged to Jupiter's

father, Raymond, a highly successful art dealer. Consequently, the walls were covered with wonderful pictures. On a side table was a photograph of Jupiter, his beautiful sweet-natured wife Hanna and their adorable two-and-a-half-year-old son Viridian.

'That should come in useful when we're electioneering,' said Hengist.

Jupiter, who was as pale as Rupert and Hengist were dark brown from skiing, smiled coolly.

'When are we going to war?' asked Hengist.

'Any minute, pushed as much by the unqualified encouragement of IDS as by Blair's ambition.' Jupiter glanced at his watch. 'I've got to be back in the House in an hour. Would you like a drink?'

'I'd like several,' said Hengist. 'Christ, what a day.'

Rupert looked up from the sofa and the racing pages of the *Evening Standard*. 'Oriana's fantastic on the box.'

'Isn't she? I see her face on every bulletin—so frustrating to touch the screen not her.' For a second Hengist betrayed his desolation, then, reverting to his usual flippancy: 'I was so depressed by my own company, I made the mistake of taking Randal Stancombe for a walk down the pitches this afternoon. He showed an unhealthy interest in Badger's Retreat, but failed to notice leaves leaping out of the wild cherry, breathtaking against a navy blue sky, or the sweeps of primroses and violets. Only sees land as a way of making money.'

'I wouldn't argue with that,' said Rupert.

'Can we skip the nature notes and get on with the meeting?' said Jupiter, pouring Hengist a large whisky.

72

Hengist turned back from the window where he could see cranes like malignant vultures preying on the city, destroying and rebuilding everywhere.

'We've got to save Larks Comp.'

'Whatever for?' Jupiter looked amazed. 'We can't anyway, once a school's targeted for closure, it's doomed. Only point of public meetings is for the county council and S and C to pretend they've listened to people's views. Anyway,' he went on, shooting soda into his own glass, 'do we really want to antagonize Stancombe, who's good for a massive donation, in order to save a small, pretty awful school? We've also got to work with S and C.'

'You have no heart,' drawled Rupert, getting out a pen to do the quick crossword. 'Janna Curtis was rather pretty, I remember.'

'I can afford to antagonize Stancombe even less,' admitted Hengist, 'he's giving me a six-million-pound science block. But you could take him on, Rupert.'

'I don't mind. His daughter's foul to both Xav and Bianca. What's he got against Larks?'

'He wants it and the entire Shakespeare Estate razed to the ground so they don't lower the tone of his absurdly overpriced Cavendish Plaza.'

'It's the Casey Andrews sculpture in the forecourt that should be razed,' Rupert said. 'Who was the brother of Romulus, five letters?'

'Remus,' said Hengist. 'I suspect Randal's after Larks's land. Whoever buys it, S and C and the county council will make a killing. So this meeting's the ideal opportunity to discredit both Lib Dem and Labour and make them look like heartless, unprincipled shits.'

73

'I like a good fight,' mused Rupert. 'Taggie and I got together when we were rushing round Gloucestershire, pitching for the Venturer franchise.'

'And Janna Curtis has been very shabbily treated,' pleaded Hengist.

Rupert glanced up, white teeth lighting his dark brown face.

'So you did get into her knickers.'

'Certainly not,' snapped Hengist. 'Caesar has to be above suspicion as well as his wife these days.'

The gods appeared to be on S and C's side. On the night of the second public meeting, which was held in a WI hall five miles south of Larkminster, the weeks of dry weather ended in a torrential rainstorm, which halted windscreen wipers in their tracks and turned country lanes into raging rivers.

'Larks parents and teachers'll never turn out in this,' gloated Ashton. '*EastEnders* and the war in its twelfth day will keep them safe in front of the TV. It'll be a walkover.'

He was therefore appalled on arrival to discover chairs being frantically unstacked to accommodate the crowd, a foyer reeking of drying macs and anoraks, and steaming umbrellas huddled together like coloured mushrooms at the back of the hall. The bar was already crowded out.

Emlyn and Wally, desperate to be distracted from the war, had all evening been bussing in parents from the Shakespeare Estate, bribing them with beer, wine, Dawn's hot sausage rolls on the way, and the prospect of a lift home, so they could drink themselves insensible. Stormin' Norman and Pearl's boxer dad were already well away.

They were soon joined by friends and fellow tipplers from the protest marches; Lily, the Brigadier, Ian and Patience Cartwright, whose daughter, Sophy, would be out of work if Larks were shut down.

The Brigadier was rather shyly autographing anti-closure leaflets.

'Love your programme, Brig.'

'All that matters is that every student achieves his or her potential,' intoned Cindy Payne as she hung up her soaking wet cape. One had to have nerves of steel to close down a school.

Having heard rumours that both Randal Stancombe and Rupert Campbell-Black were expected, Cavendish Plaza wives, with streaked hair, gold jewellery and beauty department make-up, were out in force. They'd all vote for closure, as would their drenched husbands, who'd nervously left their Mercs and Porsches in the car park before scuttling through the downpour, as would a bristling posse from the Close and the older Larkminster houses.

But there was a dangerously large anti-closure contingent from Bagley: including Dora and Dicky, Bianca, Amber and Milly and the Chinless Wanderers, who, changing allegiance on another front, had become thoroughly excited at the prospect of war in Iraq and kept marching about saluting each other.

'Why aren't you in school doing your prep?' asked Cindy disapprovingly.

'Part of our citizenship course is understanding how local government works,' said Amber piously. 'Mr Brett-Taylor was very anxious we should be present.'

Fuck Hengist, thought Alex, who never swore, even mentally, except in extremis and who had just rolled up with Chally and Poppet, plus her latest baby.

Alex was stressed. Over the weekend Poppet had insisted he look after the kids while she lay outside RAF Fairford protesting against the war. Tonight she had insisted on bringing Little Gandhi and

76

would later breastfeed him. Nothing wrong with that, but this simple act of motherhood seemed to engender such misogyny in his Bagley colleagues.

In the foyer and his father's astrakhan coat, Cosmo examined notices about singing workshops and evenings of circle dancing, as he played 'The Lark Ascending' on his violin. Not missing a trick, he watched the Great and not-so-Good: Ashton, Cindy, Russell, Chally and now Alex and Rod and their wives, drinking cheap red or white in an ante-room. Talk about a witch's coven. And what had happened to Ashton's Sancho Pansy, Crispin?

Cosmo had exchanged a soulful eye-meet with Ashton when he arrived. In front of him, on the floor, he had also placed a dark blue butcher-boy's cap to swell the fund to save Larks. He had already raised two hundred pounds, half of which he intended to keep. His mother, despite her millions, was tight with money.

Inside the hall, Cambola was cheering everyone up playing golden oldies on the tinny upright piano.

' "Night And Day",' sang the Brigadier, sweeping Lily into a quickstep.

'Who's chairing this meeting?' she asked.

'Col Peters.'

'That's totally loaded against Larks for a start; you ought to chair it, Christian. Talk of the devil.'

A hiss went round the hall as Col Peters, more toad-like than ever, put his crinkly black hair and bulging eyes round the door, then retreated to the ante-room.

Dora, meanwhile, was in her element talking on three mobiles.

'Great turnout. I'll ring you the moment it's over,

Mr Dacre.'

The rain was growing more frantic, scrabbling against the windows, begging to be let in out of the storm. A shudder and hiss went through those present from the Shakespeare Estate as Uncle Harley walked in in a black fur-lined suede jacket and more jewellery than all the Cav Plaza wives put together.

'Useful if there's a power cut,' giggled Amber.

Having clocked who was present, Uncle Harley took up his position against a side wall where he could watch both platform, hall and gallery, which was also nearly full up.

There was an equal hiss from Cav Plaza, remembering too many broken windows and missing car radios, as Feral slid in bouncing his football. He was absolutely soaked, his black curls flattened, raindrops leaping off his black lashes and running down his shining face. He had just exchanged a damp high five with Lily and the Brigadier, when Bianca, who'd specially worn a new crimson ra-ra skirt and a shocking pink fake-fur coat, leapt up and waved. It was a year since they'd danced together in *Romeo and Juliet*.

'Over here, Feral, I've kept a seat for you.'

Feral had no option; nor did he want one. Padding up the aisle, drenching people as he wriggled along the row, he dropped into the chair next to heaven.

'You're frozen,' wailed Bianca and, putting his ball under her seat, she whipped off her pink coat and wrapped it round him and everyone whooped and whistled. 'No, keep it on,' she cried, doing up the buttons.

Feral beamed.

'Suits you. Wolf in sheep's clothing,' shouted Johnnie Fowler.

Feral rolled his eyes, flung back his head and howled three times. Then he turned to Bianca. 'How yer doin'?' And he couldn't say any more, she was so adorable and gazing at him with such joy, her little shoulders hunched in ecstasy.

'When are we going to dance again?'

'Soon,' said Feral, tapping his feet as Cambola broke into a jazzed-up version of 'Hark, Hark! the Lark', because Janna was trying to slink in unobserved, aware she looked rough, ducking to avoid the exploding of flashes. Larks was about to break up for the Easter holidays and there'd been so many loose ends to tie up with children and teachers leaving, she'd had no time to wash her hair, which, lank and out of condition, she'd pulled back off her pale, pinched, face. She was wearing a silk dress the colour of faded bracken and an amber necklace, both of which Hengist had given her.

But he's not coming, she thought, glancing round the hall in despair and shame that she could think of him when her school was falling round her ears.

'No comment, for the moment,' she told the reporters.

'Miss! Miss!' Pearl shot out and, dragging Janna into the Ladies, applied coral lipstick and blusher to her blanched cheeks. 'That fluorescent light really drains you.'

'It's my Jane Eyre look.'

'Triffic turnout,' said Pearl proudly. 'My boxer dad's come; he's getting pissed with Lily and the Brig.'

'Thank you, dear Pearl.' Hitching up her smile

79

two minutes later, Janna braved the hall, moving from parents to teacher to pupil thanking, cheering, encouraging, only accepting a Perrier water so she didn't lose her rag as she had at the last meeting, before taking her seat in the second row, between Mags and Sophy Belvedon.

As the clock struck half past seven Col Peters, reluctant to wait any longer, trooped on to the platform followed by Cindy, Ashton, Russell Lambert, leading Labour and Lib Dem councillors, and the Bishop of Larkminster, whose window Feral's football had cracked. To accommodate them all, the Prussian-blue curtains on either side of the platform had to be drawn back even further.

Col was then prevented from starting by an avalanche of latecomers, starting off with Sally Brett-Taylor, who ran in wafting Jardin des Bagatelles and looking absolutely stunning in a dark blue velvet cloak over a lilac silk dress and with a rakish lilac sequinned butterfly in her gold hair.

'Looking good, Mrs B-T,' yelled Jack Waterlane to howls of laughter.

Sally smiled, then called up to Col Peters:

'So sorry for being late. Hengist'll be here in a moment.'

'Doesn't Sally look smart? Ah good, here comes Randal,' agreed the Cav Plaza wives in excitement.

They had been admired through Randal's telescope when they sunbathed topless in their gardens. Some of them had been summoned to romp in his Jacuzzi. Randal didn't want that dreadful school nearby; he'd fight their corner.

Here's Stancombe, thought the Shakespeare

80

Estate, better not get too pissed or we might deck him.

Both factions waved sycophantically as Stancombe sauntered in flanked by heavies. He was wearing a dark brown leather jacket, black polo shirt and black cords and looked more attractive than usual, Janna decided. The flash jewellery had gone and his hair had been more becomingly cut with ragged gypsy tendrils softening his predatory face. Was this Mrs Walton's influence? Janna blushed as he caught her staring, particularly when he smiled and waved.

'Don't frat with the enemy,' hissed Mags.

'Daddy, Daddy,' shouted Jade, clambering over the seats to sit with him.

'Hi, princess.' Stancombe kissed her on the mouth.

'Yuk,' said Dora.

Col Peters had just tapped the microphone, hammer poised, when another batch of Larks parents, dug out by Emlyn and Wally, poured into the hall and were reluctantly split up into the remaining single seats.

'There's my da, hope he's sober,' prayed Graffi.

'And my mum,' said Pearl, 'hope she doesn't deck my dad, and Chantal with Kylie and Cameron an' Aysha's mum in a headscarf.'

'That's brave,' murmured Janna to Mags, 'with so much anti-Muslim feeling about.'

Hall and gallery were completely packed out; people were standing among the umbrellas at the back.

'Feral's so vain, we're going to have to gaze at his profile all evening,' Amber, who was sitting just behind him, said acidly.

For Feral was gone. He couldn't take his eyes off Bianca. As if it had a mind of its own, his hand slid into hers; he tried to retrieve it in case he was being forward, but she hung on, gripping it with a surprising strength, gently stroking his palm with little, pink-nailed fingers.

I'm dreaming, he thought, sent reeling by the sweetness of her breath, the faint tang of lily of the valley, the huge, laughing eyes with lashes even longer than his, her pink coat caressing his chin.

'I'm out of luck there,' sighed Amber. 'I'll have to revert to my unrequited passion for Attila.'

Boffin was ostentatiously reading a biography of Marie Curie.

Randal was on his mobile. He'd love to have had Ruth on his arm, but he concentrated better without her. One never knew from where trouble was coming. Rising in his seat, he located Dora taking a photograph of the Bishop. Good, she still had her untidy plaits. He couldn't see if her breasts had begun to bud, but his cock stiffened beneath the *Evening Standard*. He must ask her mother out to dinner next time Ruth was in town. Bloody hell, he'd never expected such a turnout.

Nor had Col Peters, who was prepared to wait no longer. He needed a report of the meeting in tomorrow's *Gazette*, which would be picked up by the nationals.

But in the foyer, Cosmo had launched into 'Hello, Dolly!' as Taggie Campbell-Black ran in, wide-eyed, long-legged as a colt. The fuchsia-pink cashmere shawl she'd flung over her black sequinned dress was already drenched.

That's one woman I'd like even better than Bianca, decided Cosmo.

82

'Thank you,' he purred as Taggie fumbled in her bag for a fiver. He'd frame it. If he landed Bianca, he could have Taggie as well.

Seeing her husband, not his greatest fan, and Hengist approaching, both in dinner jackets, Cosmo slid into a side kitchen. 'To adjust the temperature in the hall,' he read, 'turn the boiler on or off at the control panel.'

Take more than a switch to control this lot.

Rupert and Hengist were followed by Jupiter. Why's he here? wondered Cosmo. He jumped as Hengist tapped him on the shoulder and handed him a tenner. 'Can you get Mr Campbell-Black a very large whisky?'

Everyone was excited by the latest arrivals, particularly by Jupiter: that really put the evening up a rung. Whose side would he be on? He was already proving a very effective MP.

Furiously, Col Peters raised his hammer, but Hengist was lingering in the doorway, talking intently to the press, asking, no doubt, for any news on Iraq. Janna was shocked how tired he looked. But as he wandered into the hall, he seemed to shrug off his concerns and his face broke into a wicked smile.

'So sorry to hold you up, Col, Ashton, Cindy, Russell, my lord Bishop.' Mockingly Hengist nodded to each in turn. 'Evil night. Fleet's about to burst its banks and sweep S and C away. Hope you've brought your lifebelt, Ashton, you're going to need it before the evening's out. Do kick on, Col,' and, turning his broad, dinner-jacketed back, he edged along the row, shaking hands, hailing Bagley and Larks children, blowing kisses to friends, stopping to grin at Janna—'Lovely dress, darling'—spying Poppet—'How's little Gandhi, hope you're resting enough?'—then in a stage whisper to Jupiter, who was following him: 'She's had plenty of rest, lying down in the road to stop the B52s leaving.'

'For Christ sake, sit down,' hissed Jupiter, 'why must you deliberately wind people up?'

Bringing up the rear was Rupert, who stopped to congratulate the Brigadier on the pilot of *Buffers*: 'We got bloody good ratings. I'll ring you tomorrow.'

'Col Peters is going to have a coronary,' observed Mags.

'With any luck,' said Janna. 'Isn't it wonderful Hengist and Co. have showed up?'

Christ, that Campbell-Black/Brett-Taylor/Belvedon faction was hell, thought Emlyn. Only way to shut them up was to cut off their heads—preferably with a guillotine. Hengist was insufferable in this apparatchik-baiting mood. Bloody Hoorays, aren't we wonderful, we all know each other.

Actually the most hip Hooray was Rupert, Emlyn decided, not just because of the beauty of his still, cold toff's face or the casual elegance of his lounging body, but his total indifference to the impact he had on everyone in the room as he devoured printouts, a large whisky in one hand, the other idly caressing his wife's sweet face as they compared notes on the day. Taggie had removed her soaked shawl and was wearing his dinner jacket round her shoulders.

Even if Oriana came home safely from Baghdad, wondered Emlyn wistfully, would she ever look up at him with a quarter of Taggie's tenderness, or in

84

the adoring way their daughter was gazing at young Feral, still wrapped in her pink fur coat.

Brought up to loathe the Tories, it confused Emlyn that, for some ulterior motive, it was Tories who were coming to Janna's aid and New Labour in their sharp suits, quite unrecognizable from his dad's beloved cloth-cap party, who'd palled up with the beige, open-toed-sandalled Lib Dems to grind the faces of the poor.

Oh God, here was Vicky, putting down her flower-festooned umbrella, rushing towards the platform:

'Col, I am so sorry, I couldn't find anywhere to park. Emlyn dear, could you find me a chair? Oh, Poppet's kept a seat for me.' As she ran along the gap between platform and audience, pausing in front of Janna: 'Jannie, I am *so* sorry it's come to this. Hello, Magsy, hello Cambola, you poor dears.' Vicky was beginning to sound just like Sally. 'I'm so guilty I haven't called,' then, lowering her voice only a fraction: 'And so guilty getting out in time. What a blow too, losing darling Chally. I must find her later.'

'Bitch,' exploded Sophy Belvedon, 'thank God she left before I arrived.'

'What an appalling number of beards,' grumbled Rupert, and jumped out of his skin as Poppet Bruce suddenly cried out, 'Rupert, Roopert.' Thrusting up baby Gandhi, she made him wave: 'Hello, Uncle Rupert.' As Rupert cringed behind Ian Cartwright, Poppet went on: 'And there's Auntie Taggie. Hello, Auntie Taggie.'

Taggie, who'd been hopefully looking round for Xav, waved weakly. As if reading her mind, Poppet yelled out, 'Xav's got another detention, so we couldn't let him out. Sorry. Let's have a word later.'

Seeing her mother red-faced and furious, Bianca whispered to Feral, 'Xav's been caught drinking again. He seems to be pissed all the time.'

'I thought he was mates with Paris,' murmured Feral. Somehow with Bianca's hand in his it didn't hurt so much.

'They used to be really close, but Paris is so taken up with his rugby friends and his extra lessons with Theo, he hardly notices Xav exists any more. Why didn't you ring me?' she asked.

'I wanted to. It's complicated.'

If only Paris held my hand like that, thought Dora.

'Don't worry,' Ashton whispered to Col, 'let them mess around for as long as they like, it'll give them less time to air their non-existent grievances.'

At last everyone was settled and Col Peters bashed the table so hard, he spilt all the glasses of water.

'Good evening,' he said. He had a thick, oily voice that seemed drenched in chicken fat. 'Good evening, everyone. We're running behind schedule and as some of you'—he glared at Rupert and Hengist—'clearly have other engagements, we'd better kick on. We have come together to discuss the proposed closure of Larkminster Comprehensive'—loud boos and cheers—'and we know you've all got lots to say. We want as many people as possible to air their views, so it'll be easier if you don't interrupt.'

'Save our school,' yelled Johnnie Fowler.

'And show some manners,' snapped Col. 'Not the best way to convince people that your school is worth saving, Master Fowler. I shall now hand over to our county councillor in charge of education, Miss Cindy Payne.'

Hearty cheers from Bruces, Hydes, the Close and Cavendish Plaza.

Cindy, anxious to project a cosy, earth-mother image, had for once abandoned her red trouser suit for a flowing dark brown caftan. Above this her round, ruddy, determinedly smiling face, from which rayed out her light brown hair, bobbed like a setting sun on the horizon.

'I have prayed and prayed for guidance on this issue,' she began, 'and must admit that closing a school is a very painful process.'

'Not for them what's going to make a fat profit,'

yelled Pearl's boxer dad to roars of applause. Stancombe's heavies squared their shoulders.

'I didn't hear that,' twinkled Cindy. 'Our aim is to give first-class education to each and every secondary student, which I am afraid Larks Comprehensive is not providing.'

'Who says so?' yelled Monster Norman. 'We isn't complaining.'

'Well said, son,' bellowed Stormin'.

'Closing a school is a painful experience,' Cindy ploughed on, her twinkle becoming fixed, 'but we are convinced this is a democratic decision because the vast majority of local parents have made it quite clear they don't want their children to go to Larks in that they have voted with their feet.' Then, as if taking a run at a fence, she added quickly, 'We've had many, many letters supporting closure, but during this formal consultation period, I'm so sorry, we've only received fifty letters of protest.'

'That's because Larks parents and pupils can't write,' yelled Brute Stevens, the rugger bugger from St Jimmy's.

'Hush, that's unkind,' reproved Cindy fondly.

'It's also fucking out of order,' shouted Johnnie Fowler, jumping on Brute and pummelling the hell out of him. As Johnnie was smaller than Pearl's boxer dad, Stancombe's guards were about to move in when Emlyn pre-empted them.

'Pack it in, for God's sake,' he snarled, peeling Johnnie off like a Polaroid.

'Thank you, Mr Davies,' said Cindy archly. 'Only fifty letters of protest,' she repeated, 'which included ten from a Miss Dora Belvedon, who doesn't even live in the area.'

Screams of laughter and bellows of 'Good on yer, Dora' were interspersed with shouts of 'Shame' and 'Cheat'.

An oblivious Dora was muttering into a tape recorder.

Mags Gablecross then leapt to her feet and introduced herself in a quiet, clear voice. Seeing her approaching the platform clutching a bulging box file, the platform recoiled in horror as if she were a suicide bomber.

'I thought people might be interested in the five hundred and fifty letters we received that were against Larks closing down and our petition signed by more than fifteen thousand people. I didn't want to hand these over before the meeting,' she added politely as she gave the box to a boot-faced Col, 'in case the figures were doctored as they were in your Review of Secondary Schools.' She smiled sweetly at Ashton. 'Please note I've taken a photostat of the petition, Mr Douglas.'

'That is a gwatuitously offensive remark,' snapped Ashton.

'We too have had overwhelming support for closure,' chipped in Cindy. 'Take this excellent letter from a Mr Bernard Brooks.' She waved a piece of paper: ' "Having observed both teachers and pupils at Larks Comp over the last eighteen months, I can honestly say it's the worst school I've ever encountered. I recommend closure instantly." '

There was a roar from the gallery as Graffi stopped snogging Milly and dropped into the hall, slithering across the umbrellas.

'That's Boffin Brooks, you snotty bastard.' Racing up the aisle, Graffi reached into the row,

89

seizing Boffin by his Alex Bruce house tie. 'Don't you dare slag off our school.' Egged on by a roar of Larks approval, he was about to ram his fist into Boffin's face when Johnnie Fowler tugged him off.

'Let me do the honours.'

'Don't touch me,' screamed Boffin.

'Put Boffin in a coffin, boom, boom, boom,' yelled Bagley and Larks in delighted unison.

As Johnnie raised his fist, Emlyn once more shot across the room, prising Johnnie and Graffi off by their collars.

'Stop it,' he bellowed, then, lowering his voice: 'You're not helping Larks.'

'Nor's Boffin, dissing us like that.'

Trying to wriggle free, Graffi made another lunge, but Emlyn hung on, tightening his grip.

'Stop it, both of you.'

'You's choking me.'

Fortunately a nasty scrap was averted by Amber Lloyd-Foxe crying out, 'Oh, why don't you manhandle us, Mr Davies, it's so sexist to pick on boys every time.'

'Why are we being discriminated against?' chorused Kitten, Milly and even Primrose from the gallery. 'We all want to be manhandled by Mr Davies.'

The hall rumbled with laughter.

Blushing furiously, Emlyn dragged Johnnie and Graffi outside and shoved their heads under the kitchen tap.

A scented, blond jangle of jewellery had meanwhile risen to her feet.

'That kaind of behaviour says it all, reely.'

'Oh shut up,' said Pearl, glancing up from the dress she was designing.

'I won't shut up,' said the blonde shrilly. 'As a resident of Cavendish Plaza, Larks kids make our lives a misery. They graffiti our walls, key our cars, carpet our pavements with chewing gum, beat up and spit at our kids. Why should we fork out for security guards to protect us? This isn't the inner city.'

'Larks should be closed down,' shouted a Cavendish Plaza husband in broad pinstripe. 'It's a breeding ground for thugs and drugs. If you live in a pleasant private estate, you don't expect a sink school that is almost a pupil referral unit on the doorstep.'

The platform was nodding in delight as an old biddy knitting in the front took up the cudgel.

'I don't have the privilege of security guards,' squawked Miss Miserden, 'I live next to Larks and I never feel safe in my bed.'

'You'd be quite safe in anyone else's bed, darling,' yelled Graffi, who'd somehow found his way back to the gallery, 'no one's going to jump on you.'

This was followed by more cheers and cries of 'Shame' and 'Disgusting, insulting a pensioner'.

'Who's she?' asked Dora, who was furiously making notes.

'She's the one who brings letters of complaint in every day,' said Junior, who'd been doing work experience on the *Gazette*. 'She's called Name and Address Supplied.'

And so the slanging went on, with the closure brigade attacking Larks and its record and Larks supporters defending it.

When a rather flushed Milly Walton shouted from the gallery:

'We at Bagley love meeting young people from a different background and Larks kids are great, we've had so much fun together,' Randal Stancombe made a note to alert Ruth, who didn't at all approve of her daughter's liaison with Graffi.

Sophy Belvedon then made an impassioned plea for the children and particularly Year Ten, who mustn't be abandoned in mid GCSE course.

'Year Ten will be accommodated and taught much better in other schools,' said Ashton, rising to his feet. It was time this meeting was wrapped up. 'My name's Ashton Douglas,' he told the assembled company smoothly, 'S and C Services Diwector of Opewations.'

'Operations performed without the use of anaesthetics,' shouted Hengist. 'No wonder your collaborator is called Payne. As she keeps informing us: "Closing a school is a Payne-full experience."'

As the audience cheered, Ashton's soft, bland features set into a cement of hatred.

'It is also an unnecessary and dishonest operation,' went on Hengist, rising to his feet, his deep, husky, bitchy voice carrying to every corner. Again he seemed to have shaken off his tiredness and worry. 'This discussion is about surplus places. The education department, we have been told, are very worried about the one thousand six hundred surplus places in Larkshire schools, which will evidently double by two thousand and ten.

'Why then,' he asked coolly, 'if our child population is ebbing away, does the housing department predict that two thousand five hundred extra houses will be built—no doubt roughshod over Larkshire's loveliest green belt—

in the next three years? Will all these houses be inhabited by childless couples?' He paused for effect. 'Clearly not, and even more interestingly, that one-off contributions from developers will be put towards new and temporary classrooms to accommodate extra pupils.

'Tut, tut, Ashton, Cindy and Russell, have you enlisted the health department to doctor your figures?

He paused again to allow a roar of approval from Larks supporters.

'It seems that S and C and the county council use figures selectively—just as they rigged the Review of Secondary Schools and, when challenged, blamed the falsely poor figures for Larkminster Comprehensive on typing errors. But did anyone have the decency to admit this publicly?'

'No,' roared at least half the hall.

'I don't know what you're talking about,' spluttered Cindy.

'As a Larkminster county councillor, you don't seem to know what *anyone's* talking about,' cracked back Hengist to more cheers. His dark eyes had recaptured all their old sparkle. 'It's absolutely typical of a Lab/Lib Dim council to have no idea what other departments are up to, or to pretend they don't to achieve their ends. This is a corrupt hung council which ought to be hung out to dry because the only thing that matters to them is selling off Larks's ten acres of prime land and putting millions of pounds into their own and S and C Services' pockets.'

'Save our school!' Stamp, stamp, stamp went a thunder of feet on the parquet as Emlyn grinned across at a flabbergasted Janna.

93

'Can you tell us'—Rupert had taken up the baton, his light, clipped, contemptuous drawl carrying just as easily round the hall—'why Randal Stancombe is putting up a large building for Rod Hyde to accommodate extra pupils? This building was commissioned in autumn 2002, at exactly the same time as the Review of Secondary Schools, with rigged figures, was sent out and a report, targeting Larks as the proposed choice for closure, leaked to the *Gazette*.'

'I must protest,' spluttered Rod Hyde.

'Feel free,' said Rupert sarcastically, 'but first, tell us why Larks, particularly after such a good Ofsted report, was chosen to be closed down.'

'Because it's the pits,' yelled Brute Stevens.

As Emlyn grabbed Johnnie Fowler's collar, Cindy saw a chance to dive in:

'As I keep saying, because the people of Larkshire preferred to send their children to other local schools or, failing that, go private or out of county, rather than Larks.'

'Rubbish,' snapped Rupert. 'Plenty of schools in Larkshire have empty desks. The difference is that Larks is sitting on twenty-two million pounds' worth of prime land, with Gap and Borders and Waitrose nearby. S and C have had a catastrophic year; shares in all their other companies have fallen. Selling off Larks would put them nicely in the black.'

Randal Stancombe was by now looking even less amused than Queen Victoria's portrait, which hung on the wall at the end of his row.

'How dare you make these slandewous accusations,' squawked Ashton.

'Because they're true. You've targeted not the

94

most failing school but the one that would bring in the most money. Janna Curtis has been dealt a marked card,' said Rupert chillingly. 'Her only crime was to succeed too well against all the odds, so her character and her school had to be repeatedly blackened by reports in your papers, Col, demoralizing pupils and staff and, in particular, changing the minds of parents intending to send their children there.'

'Oh, well done, Rupert. Col the toad will soon explode,' giggled Dora. 'I am a poet and I do not know it.'

'This is disgraceful,' thundered Russell.

'Disgraceful for Janna and Larks,' shouted the Brigadier.

Janna's face was in her hands, she couldn't believe such incredible support.

Feral gazed at Bianca.

'What are they going on about?'

'I've no idea.'

'This is totally out of order.' Col Peters crashed down his hammer. 'I hope Hengist Brett-Taylor can substantiate these accusations.'

'Only too easily.' Most of the platform, despite the heat, lost colour as, out of his inside pocket, Hengist produced a sheet of paper covered in writing and waved it at the audience. 'This is a list of people likely to profit from the sale of Larks. The wages of Cindy, for example, will be considerably enhanced.'

'How dare you?' squawked Cindy Payne.

'Shall I read it out?'

'Mr Fussy doesn't look too happy either,' whispered Amber.

'Perhaps little Gandhi needs changing,'

95

whispered back Dora.

'Save our school!' Stamp, stamp, stamp, thundered Larks supporters.

'Well?' taunted Hengist.

The big hand of the hall clock was pointing directly upwards: nine o'clock. Saved by the hour and just managing to contain his fury, Col Peters gathered up his papers.

'I'm afraid we've run out of time,' he said.

'Cop out, cop out, read the list, read the list,' roared the hall.

'I have a paper to get to bed with a report of this meeting,' Col said firmly, 'and we mustn't keep Sally and Hengist or Mr and Mrs Campbell-Black from their dinner party.'

'Read out the list,' shouted the *Western Daily Press*.

Hengist laughed and shook his head.

'Not yet. Unlike the editor of the *Gazette*, I feel it more honourable to substantiate rumours before spreading them.'

'Where are you off to?' asked the *Stroud News* as Sally and Taggie hurried towards the exit.

'Highgrove,' piped up Bianca proudly. 'Have a lovely time, Mummy.' Turning to Feral, she handed him three pieces of paper. 'Here's my number, put it in both pockets and in the pocket of your jacket, then there's no excuse.'

Danijela meanwhile had risen trembling to her feet.

'Before we go, I am an asylum-seeker from Bosnia, we love going to Miss Curtis's school, it is our home and best of England.'

Janna's eyes filled with tears.

'Exactly,' called out Jupiter who, having let

Rupert and Hengist do his dirty work, totally distancing himself all evening, now moved in for the kill. 'If Larks closes, all its children will have to find new schools, the teachers, cleaners and support staff new jobs. What will happen to the Shakespeare Estate without their school? Larkshire's other schools and several greedy individuals will profit. That's how private business works: targets must be met, so you sell off your best asset.' The whole room had gone silent. 'And so a whole community will be destroyed.'

There was a long pause.

'Save our school,' croaked Rocky.

'Janna Curtis has been dealt a marked card,' murmured Dora to the *Independent*.

'Let's have a quick show of hands,' said Cindy hastily.

'Those in favour of closure?' called out Col Peters, glancing round the hall as a lot of Rolexes and braceleted hands were held up and a County Hall minion did some cursory counting. 'And those in favour of retaining Larks?' Then as a forest of hands sprung up: 'I think that gives closure a clear majority. I will convey the feeling of the hall to the appropriate authorities,' he added and fled the hall to deafening boos.

The place was in uproar. Hengist fighting his way towards the door met Emlyn coming back in.

'Any news?'

'Definitely not Oriana,' said Emlyn, 'it was a British soldier in a car crash, poor sod.'

'Thank Christ.' Throwing back his head, Hengist took in a great breath of relief. 'And for you too. But, oh God, the poor man and his family. I must go and reassure Sally. See you in the morning.

97

Thanks for everything.'

Running through the deluge, Janna caught up with Hengist on the edge of the car park.

'Thank you all ever so much,' she stammered, 'you were wonderful. I must have made you so late for dinner. Where did you get all that amazing info?' Then, when Hengist laughed: 'At least let me see that list of names.'

'You can have it.' He handed her the piece of paper. 'It's Dora Belvedon's essay on why fox hunting shouldn't be abolished. She got an A star.'

'There were no names?'

'Not before I began counting the people who turned green this evening. Rather a good bluff, don't you think? I must go, darling. Just coming,' he called to the others, waiting in Rupert's revving up BMW.

Desire made Janna ungracious. 'You know how I disapprove of hunting,' she said furiously.

'Don't look gift hunters in the mouth, you chippy child. I'll come and see you over the weekend.'

78

Seeing a drenched Janna returning to the hall, Emlyn assumed her air of desolation stemmed from the likely loss of her school and suggested they go and have supper.

He swept away Janna's protests that she had so many people to thank.

'I've got to ferry several busloads of parents back to the Shakespeare Estate. I'll meet you in the Dog and Duck at ten. And put something warm on.'

The pub was packed when Janna arrived. Emlyn had already found a corner table and ordered a bottle of red and two and a half steaks for himself, Janna and Partner.

At the next table sat a group of students from the local agricultural college and their pretty, Sloaney girlfriends, who all had long, clean streaked hair, endless jean-clad legs and were equally excited by Emlyn and Partner. 'What a sweet little dog.'

The men hardly gave Janna a second glance. She must make more effort. She hadn't even bothered to comb her hair.

'So exciting, this war,' cried one of the Sloanes as the pub television was turned up for *News at Ten*, 'one needn't bother to get out a video any more.'

'I feel so sorry for those poor Baghdad dogs,' said a second, 'that terrible howl going up just before the bombing started.'

'Pretty amazing,' said her boyfriend, 'the way you can see the B52s leaving Fairford on television and, unlike British Rail, arriving on time in Baghdad.'

'You feel so guilty sitting in a warm pub when all

this is going on,' shivered the first Sloane. 'I'm crazy about Rageh Omar.'

'Not nearly as crazy as I am about Oriana Taylor,' said her boyfriend.

Janna glanced at Emlyn, who put a finger to his lips.

According to Breaking News, as it was now known, the Americans were pushing on towards Baghdad and a British soldier had been killed in a car crash. His parents, the sadness already carved into their faces, showed great fortitude.

'He was such a wonderful young man,' said the mother, 'he'd been ten years in the army and knew it would never happen to him because he was invincible.'

There were clips of the soldier's divine baby and lovely blonde wife, now a widow, but so brave.

Janna blew her nose noisily; even the Sloanes were hushed. Then it was Oriana reporting from Baghdad, her face growing thinner, paler, more shadowed by the minute and looking so beautiful—as if the stars and rockets and coloured smoke behind her were purely backdrop to enhance her fragility and the suffering and outrage in the same dark eyes as Hengist's. Predictably her sympathies were entirely with the beleaguered Iraqis.

'She's awfully left wing,' protested a Sloane.

Emlyn never took his eyes off Oriana's face.

'You must be so proud,' whispered Janna.

Their steaks had arrived. Janna cut up Partner's on a side plate and put it on the floor.

'Oh how sweet,' said the Sloanes, smiling at Emlyn.

Janna, who hadn't eaten all day, found she was

100

starving.

Emlyn, for once, poured his heart out, expressing his doubts that Oriana would ever settle down. 'It'd be like caging a song bird.'

' "We think caged birds sing, when indeed they cry," ' quoted Janna. Seeing Emlyn wince, she asked quickly, 'How did you become an item?'

'More an out-of-sightem, these days,' said Emlyn bitterly. 'I used to glimpse her from afar at Oxford. She broke men's hearts like Zuleika and had the added lustre of having a legendary rugby player as a father. Then, some years later, we actually met at a party, the night Tony Blair won his first election. Both euphoric; suddenly there was hope. We got hammered and ended up in bed. I couldn't believe my luck. The first months were miraculous, but in retrospect I always made the running.'

Janna let him bang on but finally, fed up with hearing about Oriana and having nearly finished her steak because Emlyn was doing the talking, she said, 'That meeting was wonderful,' and, having thanked Emlyn profusely for all his hard work, added, 'And Hengist and Rupert really turned things round.'

When Emlyn didn't say anything, she glanced up and to her horror saw only pity in his eyes.

'You don't think I'm going to save Larks?'

'I don't guess so, lovely.'

'But Hengist ripped them to pieces.'

'Hengist is a fox, he kills for the hell of it. Tonight he got what he wanted: publicly discrediting the Lib Dems and Labour.'

'You think he was only making political capital?' Janna's voice was rising.

'No, no, he's fond of Larks and devoted to you.

But at the moment, he's out of it. He lost Mungo, and he's overwhelmed with terror he's going to lose Oriana.'

'But he proved S and C are crooks and in bed with the county council.'

'I know, but despite the bribes they'll dole out and the cut they'll take for themselves, they'll still hand over such a hefty whack to Larkshire's schools. By not saving your school, they'll help everyone else's.'

'Torture the one to save the half-million? Why in hell did you waste your time ferrying all those parents over?' Realizing she was shouting she lowered her voice. 'I'm sorry.'

'Because I couldn't live with myself if we hadn't tried every avenue. I'm truly sorry. I just think S and C's minds are made up and all the protests, placards and petitions are piffle in the wind. They're not going to change anything.'

'I can't give up.' Janna thumped the table in real anguish. 'I'll sell my house or get a second mortgage. At least I must save Year Ten.'

'Hush, hush.' Emlyn came round and sat down beside her, engulfing her with a huge arm. 'I may be wrong.'

'Don't humour me. I only need a hundred and twenty thousand to pay for a handful of staff and for a building to teach them in, just for a year. Jubilee Cottage is too tiny. Just to give them a chance of getting some GCSEs.'

'Don't be unrealistic, lovely. Have another drink.'

'To hell with you, you're so bloody defeatist!' All Janna's Yorkshire vowels spilt out so loudly and angrily that Partner shot off to observe battle from the knees of one of the Sloanes, who were all listening, shocked and fascinated, to every word. 'I'm going to save Year Ten.' Janna wriggled out from under Emlyn's arm and, slapping thirty pounds on the table, gathered up Partner and fled into the night.

The rain had stopped. Climbing the sky was a sad orange half-moon. With a headscarf of black cloud lining her face, she looked like an Iraqi.

'Don't bug me either,' shouted Janna, 'I've got my own war to fight.'

Tomorrow she would seek out Randal Stancombe, who had smiled at her this evening, and ask him for help.

She was so shattered, she didn't check her messages until morning. The first of many was from Mags. Feral had been arrested for pulling a gun on Brute Stevens and, when grabbed by a Stancombe heavy, had misfired, taking an eye out of Queen Victoria's portrait.

As Feral was only fifteen he was later bailed by the Brigadier and the case adjourned.

'How could you, Feral?' stormed Janna. 'Everything was going Larks's way.'

'Brute stole my football and he dissed Bianca,' said Feral. 'He called her a posh black bitch. He showed no respect.'

'None of that'll emerge till the case comes up, which'll be too late for Larks.'

Brigadier Woodford wasn't pleased either.

'If you don't pull yourself together, Feral, and stop carrying guns, you'll be in and out of prison for the rest of your life.'

Feral chucked his jacket and jeans into the washing machine at the launderette deliberately blurring all Bianca's numbers.

The *Gazette* predictably ignored any reference to skulduggery and led on Feral being arrested in front of the Bishop and Ashton Douglas, confirming everyone's worst fears of Larks. They also reported a show of hands in favour of closure and drew attention to Larks's normally vocal headmistress, Janna Curtis, having no words to say in her school's defence.

It was not until well into the holidays that Janna screwed up courage to ring Randal Stancombe, who couldn't have been more charming.

'Come and have a drink this evening, any time after seven. I'll warn the guy on the gate.'

How did one dress for a man whom one wanted to convince one was worth a loan or, better still, a gift of £120,000? Peanuts to Stancombe, but the rich got rich by watching the pennies. A hundred and twenty thousand might buy another Ferrari, or a diamond necklace for Mrs Walton, both of which could be sold. You couldn't sell Year Ten.

At least she'd got some sleep and soaked her hair in coconut oil for twenty-four hours so it gleamed glossier than the coat of any Crufts red setter.

She wore a brown velvet pencil skirt and a cotton jersey twin set in the same soft apricot pink as the glow which ringed the horizon as she drove towards Cavendish Plaza.

'One, two, three, four, five, once I caught a big fish alive,' sang Janna.

Despite the deluge on the day of the public meeting, drought and late frosts, as if in sympathy with the war, had bleached the fields khaki. Hungry horses had stripped trees blown down in the gales of their dark bark, leaving pale bone below.

On the car radio she learnt that five Americans taken prisoner had been paraded on television and that, after bashing hell out of the Iraqis for nearly three weeks, the Americans were having the temerity to bang on about the Geneva Convention. She was so ashamed it was Labour who'd taken Britain to war. Great unpatriotic cheers had gone up in the staffroom every time the Iraqis were reported as fighting back bravely.

Stancombe, on the other hand, who was rumoured to be, among other things, an arms dealer, would probably be madly pro-war. She must keep her trap shut.

Janna didn't know which was more beautiful: Larkminster, gold in the setting sun, seen through Stancombe's telescope, which was so powerful she could pick out primroses on Smokers' and even the crumbs Wally, to distract himself from the war, was putting on the bird table, or Stancombe's apartment itself, which was a soothing symphony of sands and terracottas with soft suede sofas, fake fur cushions and fluffy rugs. Two walls of the vast lounge were window, the other two were crammed with wonderful pictures: Rothko, Chagall, Tracey Emin, Sam Taylor-Wood, CDs largely classical and admittedly many of them still in their cellophane wrappings and surprisingly interesting books: biographies of Alan Sugar, Bill Gates and Philip Green rubbing shoulders with Louis de Bernières, Sebastian Faulks, Donna Tartt, a first edition of *Lolita* and even some poetry.

Chopin's Second Piano Concerto rippled through speakers as though Marcus Campbell-Black and the BBC Symphony Orchestra were actually in the room.

'Whatever my feelings for his toffee-nosed father, I cannot get enough of Marcus,' announced Stancombe as, like Venus hot from some exciting, foaming jacuzzi, he welcomed her. His hair was damp and curling on his strong, suntanned neck. He was wearing just a dark blue, crew-necked cashmere sweater and white chinos, which clung to his sleek, still damp body. He smelt of toothpaste and Lynx, his favourite aftershave, as he padded round in beautifully pedicured bare feet.

Janna was flattered he'd glammed up for her, even if he was probably going out later.

'What a gorgeous apartment.'

Stancombe smiled. 'I used to think books and CDs ruined the look, but I've mellowed.'

On a glass side table in an art deco frame was a beautiful photograph of Jade, taken by Lichfield.

'How pretty she is,' sighed Janna.

'Takes after her dad,' joked Stancombe, handing Janna a long, slim glass of champagne; then, suddenly serious: 'She's a bit lost actually. Bloody Cosmo Rannaldini's messed her about.'

Ushering Janna on to a pale brown leather sofa, so vast Janna's little feet only just reached the edge, he sat down beside her.

'Hard being first-generation public school. You pick up the posh accent and the clothes, even the education, but not the roots. People laugh at me because I'm flash and vulgar. They laugh at Jade when she doesn't know things or people or pronounces them wrong. It makes her flare up, easily on the defensive.'

'Like me,' sighed Janna. 'If only I could keep my temper and learn some tact.'

Stancombe clinked his glass against hers. 'To the flash and the vulgar, may we inherit the earth. Problem with education, you've only got one chance. I often think Jade would have been happier at a state school. Nice if she could have

107

been taught by you. You'd have understood her.'

Janna had never felt so flattered or warm inside, particularly when he refilled her glass.

'People like Rupert, Hengist and Jupiter take your money, even ask you to their homes,' he went on bitterly, 'but they never really accept you and they laugh at us behind our backs—even Sally.'

'They were wonderful at the meeting,' protested Janna. 'They came out on a vile night to save me.'

'With respect, they saw it as a chance to rattle the other parties.'

'Oh,' wailed Janna, 'Emlyn said the same thing.'

'Emlyn's one of us.'

'You truly don't think I can save Larks?'

Stancombe shook his head.

Wriggling off the edge of the sofa, which was like falling off the edge of the world, overwhelmed with despair, Janna was tempted to walk straight through the big glass window and splatter on Casey Andrews's sculpture in the forecourt miles below.

On a side table was a *Telegraph* colour magazine open at an interview with Stancombe, photographed in this same flat with Mrs Walton.

'Lovely picture,' she said dully.

'Even with Ruth,' she realized Stancombe was saying a minute later, 'I have to watch myself. She gives me a lot of advice. I thought "mangy" was pronounced like "man".'

'Isn't it? She's so beautiful.'

'Works hard enough at it.'

'And succeeds.'

'She'd get an A star in leisure and tourism. She's in Rome with Milly as we speak.'

Janna could see La Perdrix d'Or, where she and Hengist had had their first lunch, and Larks,

108

appearing at a distance innocent and unscathed with the green blur of spring on its trees—as if for a last time.

'I like a woman who works,' said Stancombe joining her, then, glancing sideways: 'Why are you crying?'

'For Larks.' A great shuddering breath racked Janna's small frame. 'If I can't save it, would you help me to save Year Ten? Only about forty of them. Imagine if your Jade had to leave halfway through her GCSE course. Rod Hyde loathes my children; he'd bully them into the ground. Rutminster Comp's a jungle; they'd just give up.

'I only need a hundred and twenty thousand for some teachers and a new building or to rebuild Appletree. Would you lend me it? You can have my house as security.'

'How much did you pay for it?'

'One hundred and seventy-five thousand; three-quarters of that mortgage. I could sell it.' She wiped her eyes with her sleeve.

'How would you pay your staff?'

'That's why I need a hundred and twenty. Please, please help me.'

Stancombe retreated to get the bottle.

Janna put her hand over her glass. 'I'm driving.'

'A very hard bargain. I need time to think. I'll do all I can. I'll lean on Ashton to keep the school open a bit longer.'

Janna was overwhelmed with weariness. 'I think it'd be too difficult to rebuild now. So many teachers and children have left.'

'If I get you the money . . .' Stretching out a hand, Stancombe caressed the back of her neck . . . 'you've got to promise to sleep with me.'

109

Janna opened her mouth and shut it again, feeling herself growing very hot and wet as if she were fantasizing about something of which she was ashamed.

Stancombe laughed. 'OK, you need time to think, like me.'

'I must go.' As she jumped away, his hand closed on the scruff of her twinset.

'Why must you?'

'I just ought.'

'The first time I saw you, through this telescope on your first day, you were so bonny with your flaming red hair, like a beacon waiting to light up the town. Next time at Hengist and Sally's, you were so upset, because you'd found that little dog blown up, I still thought you were very tasty, but I'd just met Ruth—the road not taken.'

'I love that poem,' said Janna in surprise.

'Now you're patronizing me and my yob culture, too busy scrabbling his way to the top to read poetry. Then I saw you at the public meeting, I thought how tired and diminished you looked and how cheap your clothes were.'

Janna longed to protest that the dress was pure silk and from Hengist.

'And I wanted to take you under my wing and make your life happier and easier.' Stancombe dropped a kiss on the top of her head and let a leisurely hand move down over her bottom, exciting her unbearably.

'I must go, I've got the same little dog in the car,' she stammered. 'Thank you for seeing me.'

'It's good to talk,' said Stancombe, almost spoiling things.

As she ran to the lift in utter confusion, he

110

caught up with her and pressed the button.

'D'you know the sexiest thing in the world?'

'What?'

'Courage—and you've got it in spades. I'd like to help with your school and I'd like you to help me with Jade, she's so unhappy. Ruth's not the ideal prospective stepmother.'

As he drew her towards him, she felt his wonderfully fit body burning through the blue cashmere, his rock-hard cock practically raping her belly button. So much taller, he had to bend his head to kiss her. Janna gasped and resisted, then her mouth melted beneath his mouth as he sucked and his tongue caressed her lips with such tenderness and delicacy. He was so sexy.

'I want you to look bonny and happy again,' he whispered. 'I want to take those dark circles away and put them back for a different reason, "the lineaments of gratified desire".'

Recognizing the quote, Janna thought: This is ridiculous, he's appealing to my intellectual snobbery.

As the lift opened directly into the flat, she leapt into it.

'That was lovely, thanks ever so much.'

All the way down, she expected him to press a button from above and imprison her deep down in the hellish bowels of the building, for treating with the devil of whom Hengist, Mags and Emlyn so disapproved and yet who had just been so disturbingly adorable.

'One, two, three, four, five, once I caught a big fish alive,' sang Janna to Partner all the way home.

80

'One of the privileges of the great', wrote Giraudoux, 'is to witness catastrophes from a terrace', or, in Randal Stancombe's case, from the air. Flying off to the Far East, he never got back in touch, leaving Janna to her fate. Nor, after their Titanic support at the public meeting, did Hengist, Jupiter or Rupert return to fight her corner.

The war in Iraq, therefore, ended much less decisively than Larkminster Comprehensive when in the middle of May, the School's Organization Committee voted unanimously and conclusively to close it down.

This, although expected, came as a devastating death blow. On the steps of County Hall, a stunned Janna defiantly announced that even if the guillotine had fallen, she would still battle on to save her school. Inside, she knew this was impossible. There was no more money in the kitty.

The following morning, however, she was sitting in the kitchen drinking very strong tea and wondering how to stagger mortally wounded through the rest of her life, when she heard Partner barking at his very good friend the postman. Next moment he had rushed in carrying a blue envelope in his mouth, leaping on to Janna's knee to deliver it. The letter inside was on plain blue paper.

'Dear Janna,' she read, 'I'm sorry about your school. I thought you might need this in your battle to save Year Ten. A banker's draft for £120,000 should now be in your account. Best of luck.'

Janna gave a gasp of disbelief; it must be some cruel joke. There was no address, no signature, only a Royal Mail postmark; nothing to identify who'd given it her. But when she rang her bank in Larkminster, the manager, markedly more friendly and deferential, confirmed the money was indeed in her account, but that the donor had insisted on remaining anonymous.

It couldn't be Hengist, thought Janna, nor Rupert, nor Jupiter, unless Emlyn had told them of her desperate concerns about Year Ten. So she rang Stancombe, gibbering her thanks. After several moments of evasion, there was such a long pause that she thought he had hung up, then he said ruefully:

'I wanted it to be a secret.'

'I cannot believe such kindness. I'll pay you back somehow, I promise.'

'No, no, it's a gift. Lovely ladies deserve a leg-up.' Stancombe laughed softly. 'Just remember our bargain.'

And again Janna felt the warm quiver between her legs.

'I'm off to the States with Ruth on Monday,' Stancombe went on. 'I'll be back in June and we'll find you a building to accommodate your tearaways and get some decent funding from Ashton.'

'I won't accept a penny from him.'

'Don't be stupid. You'll need his help. See you in June.'

'He hasn't failed me, he hasn't failed me.' Gathering up Partner, Janna waltzed him round the room. 'You'll have another year with your friends, darling.'

113

Then she collapsed back on her chair, unable to comprehend such golden benison after the darkness of yesterday, reeling at the prospect of how much battling would still be needed to get the project off the ground. After she'd worked out the figures, she also realized she would need a lot more money to pay salaries, feed the children and heat and light the building, not to mention exam fees.

*   *   *

Janna remembered very little of the remaining summer term. As dogs moult in hot weather, Larks shed teachers and pupils. Many of the latter returned tearfully from their new schools: 'They called us Larks scum, miss, and put chewing gum in our hair.'

Ashton showed no desire to help Janna find a home for Year Ten. Instead, in early June, he offered her a headship turning round a failing Larkshire school.

'It's a challenge, Janna, restore your sense of self-worth.'

Janna refused; she'd no desire to kill off another school. She continued to refuse jobs and endured the humiliation of all the other schools in the area descending like vultures and slapping different coloured stickers on desks, books, computers and laboratory equipment, which they would collect after Larks finally closed down on 12 July. Enid, who'd built up the library over six years, was in perpetual floods. The choir school was the greediest and earmarked the most.

'The nearer the pulpit, the further from God,'

observed Cambola sourly.

Janna felt particularly guilty about teachers like Sophy Belvedon, who'd refused to abandon ship and so heroically carried on helping Year Eleven through their GCSEs that Janna was amazed the vultures didn't slap a coloured sticker on them as well.

Jupiter and Rupert returned to the attack and continued to hassle S and C and the county council, not just on the dodgy ethics of 'closing down' Larks, but also accusing them of diverting the education budget to other areas. Who, for example, had paid for Ashton's Hockney?

S and C and the county council denied everything, but they were rattled, particularly when, after Russell Lambert's resignation as chairman of Larks governors, Brigadier Woodford took over as temporary chairman and asked for the minutes of meetings over the past five years.

They were also fed up to the back teeth with Janna ringing every day demanding a building for Year Ten. Who would rid them of this turbulent priestess? Despite falling S and C shares, even if it would mean a year's delay before getting the big money from the sale of Larks, they decided it might be prudent, and in the end cheaper, to allow Janna to remain on site.

'We must snatch the moral high ground from the Tories,' insisted Cindy Payne. 'Let's go and look at Larks.'

There had been a hosepipe ban and all the little saplings planted by Wally in the autumn had died in the drought. Leaves were falling out of the trees, even though it was only June, as Ashton and Cindy arrived. Janna utterly jolted them by taking them

115

first over the main building. Like an elephant left to die in the jungle, all the flesh had fallen off its bones. Apart from the damp and the boarded-up windows, not a ceiling or a roof tile was in place. Doors had been ripped from their hinges, plugs and lavatory chains torn out, every classroom trashed. Wally had lost heart.

'I wouldn't educate a dog in here,' said Ashton faintly. 'How could this have happened?'

'The children did it. They were so hurt and angry you closed their school.'

Through gritted teeth and because the main building was beyond redemption, Ashton and Cindy agreed two weeks later to rebuild the annexe, Appletree. They then revealed to Janna that Randal had very, very generously offered to do the job at cost. After all, he was donating a science block to Bagley and a so-called vocational studies unit to St Jimmy's. Appletree would be another example of his wonderful philanthropy.

In the first week in July, therefore, S and C and the county council called a press conference.

'In view of the closure of Larks Compwehensive,' Ashton, in a new mauve striped shirt, told his large audience, 'it has been decided not to diswupt Year Ten in the middle of their GCSE course. S and C Services have therefore decided to pwovide a building in which they can be taught and to put funds towards their education for a further year, until June 2004.'

These funds were of course hugely bolstered by the £120,000 Randal had given to Janna—but he wished this donation to remain anonymous. Ashton, however, did go on to say the rebuilding of Appletree would be supervised by Janna Curtis

116

and carried out, on very generous terms, by Randal Stancombe Properties. Janna was to be given an extended contract until the end of August 2004, to close the school down finally.

'Mercy has a human face,' announced the *Gazette*, alongside a soppy picture of Ashton, which everyone graffitied.

Stormin' Norman appeared on television punching the air instead of anyone else and shouting 'Yes' when the news broke.

*   *   *

'Why isn't Janna Curtis more grateful?' grumbled Cindy Payne.

This was because saving Year Ten was small comfort compared with the anguish of saying goodbye to the other years.

'Why didn't you save us as well?' sobbed the little ones.

'Why didn't you march for us on Drowning Street?'

It was like working in a slaughterhouse, or a vivisection clinic, making their last moments as comfortable as possible. Janna tried heroically to remain cheerful, but on the last day, when the media poured in to photograph the death of a school, she lost it and screamed at them all to booger off.

'Why couldn't I have saved them?' she sobbed to Mags and Cambola as her children set off on their last journey down the drive to St Jimmy's or Searston Abbey or pupil referral units or to uncertain futures and no likelihood of a decent job, unless, in Year Eleven's case, they had

117

notched up a few GCSEs.

Janna felt more and more grateful to Stancombe who was planning to extend Appletree to include a dining room, a big hall, a gym and new labs.

'I'd like to rename it Stancombe House,' she told him when he dropped in with a bottle of champagne after the first day of work.

Stancombe shook his head. 'That'll tell everyone who funded it. It was a gift, remember?'

Although they were alone in the roofless, windowless building and could see a new moon scything its way through the soft blue twilight, Stancombe made no attempt to extract payment. At first Janna thought he was sensitively appreciating her mood of utter desolation, then he shyly confided that he and Ruth were off to Italy and that he was thinking very seriously of asking her to marry him.

When Janna hugged him in delight and urged him to go for it, he assured her that Teddy Murray, his foreman, would keep an eye on everything and told her to ring him on his mobile if she needed help.

*   *   *

Janna was heartbroken to lose Lance and Lydia, who both needed to work full time. She was, however, touched by the teachers who wanted to stay on: Mags, Cambola, Mr Mates, even Basket and Skunk, who she prayed would rise to the challenge. They were all taking early retirement, but were allowed to work two and a half days a week which was all that would be needed to cover the new Year Eleven's GCSE syllabus. This suited

Mags who had been only doing two and a half days a week anyway.

Among the younger teachers, sweet Sophy Belvedon had opted to stay. Wally and Debbie would both remain full time and, to the delight of the children, the Brigadier and Lily, who'd both been cleared by the Criminal Records Bureau, would respectively teach history and help Mags out with French, Spanish and German.

One of the nicest compliments came from Rowan who, having signed on for an advanced course in the summer holidays, offered to come in and teach IT.

'I know we've had our differences,' she told Janna, 'but I want to see Larks through to the end and, frankly, anything's better than looking after children full time.'

Gloria was staying on to take PE, so apart from maths and food technology, everything was sorted.

Everyone was being so kind; Janna couldn't think why she couldn't stop crying. There was the afternoon at Appletree when she was dickering over what colour to paint the new hall, when Partner shot off into the park. Janna only just had time to hide her swollen eyes behind dark glasses before he proudly led in Cadbury and Dora.

Dora was delivering a card which said: 'Sorry about your school, good luck, Paris', which nearly set Janna off again.

Dora was also in low spirits. She'd had to spend a lot of time recently counselling her brother, Dicky, because his hero David Beckham had moved to Real Madrid. She had continued to put sweets in Paris's locker but he hardly noticed her. He had been so gorgeous as Jack Tanner in the end-of-term play, *Man and Superman*, it had fanned the flames of her hopeless love for him. But life must go on. Dora cleared her throat.

'I feel one must put something back into the community,' she told Janna gravely, 'so I'd like to offer my services teaching media studies at Larks next term.'

Janna started to laugh and found she couldn't stop. Dora got quite huffy until Janna began to cry, whereupon Dora rushed off to the Ghost and Castle and bought her a quadruple vodka and tonic. When she assured the landlord: 'I'm not a binge drinker, it's for Miss Curtis, whose school has closed down,' he quite understood.

81

Bianca Campbell-Black was so dazzled that Feral had defended her with a real gun at the public meeting, she sent him a new violet and Day-Glo yellow football, a diamond cross and ear studs, did no work through the summer term dreaming of him and throughout the holidays bombarded him with cards inviting him home.

Feral longed to accept. Time and again he hitched a lift or 'borrowed' a car to drive over to Penscombe. On his first visit, he mistook the dear little lodge at the bottom of the drive for Bianca's home and thought how cosily he and she could live there. But when he knocked and was told by an ancient retainer that Bianca lived in the big house at the end of an avenue of chestnuts, whose trunk shadows striped the drive like an endless old-school tie, he turned round and went home.

On subsequent visits through the baking summer, he had borrowed Lily's binoculars and paused on the road out of Penscombe village. Here he had gazed longingly across the valley at fields filled with horses and the long lake squirming in the sunshine beneath Rupert's big, golden house, in the hope of catching a glimpse of Bianca, but knowing there was no way of him ever affording her, particularly as he had a court case pending, and if it was held in September he would be sixteen and named in the paper.

*　　　*　　　*

Nor had life in the big golden house during the holidays been peaceful. Xavier had got an even worse report than Bianca, indicating that he hadn't a hope of a single GCSE unless he did four or five hours' work every day in the holidays.

Shut away in his bedroom, ostensibly wrestling with *Macbeth* and the Russian Revolution one stifling mid-August afternoon, Xav looked up at the posters of Colombian beauty spots and fine-looking Colombian Indians, which his mother had had specially framed to make him proud of his origins.

Xav was very aware of the blood of his Indian ancestors flowing through his veins, blood tainted by an excess of drink and drugs, both of which he was now illicitly indulging in. Drunk or stoned, he felt capable of anything; the sadness and terror ebbed away. He forgot he was thick, friendless and had grown fat and spotty by stuffing himself with cake and chocolate when he was coming down.

On the wall hung a little wooden Madonna hollowed out inside to smuggle cocaine. These had been on sale in the Bogotá convent from which he and Bianca had been adopted by Rupert and Taggie. Rupert had nicked one as a souvenir and later given it to Xav, little realizing that Xav was putting it to its original use and, because Rupert himself indulged so rarely, that Xav had been regularly helping himself to his father's stash of cocaine.

At first, Xav had assumed people disliked him at Bagley because he was black, but seeing everyone swooning over Bianca when she arrived, he realized it was just him they didn't like. This was reinforced when Feral, who was much blacker than

122

Bianca, had rolled up, so agile, beautiful and larky that girls fell for him in droves, so Xav could no longer blame his colour for his not getting a girlfriend.

Formerly his great passion and bond with Rupert had been horses, but after a horrible hunting fall in the Easter holidays, when he had smashed his elbow, he had lost his nerve and the one way he could always win his father's respect. If he mounted a horse now, he trembled and poured with sweat. After a few abortive attempts to take him out on a lead rein, Rupert had given up and left him at home.

Finally, Xav's beloved, endlessly wagging, black Labrador, Bogotá, was on his rickety last legs. Rupert had never had any problem with adopting black children. Xav and Bianca were his son and daughter and that was that. Chided in the nineties by a social worker that Xav wasn't making enough black friends, Rupert had insolently bought the boy a black Labrador puppy and called it Bogotá, after Xav's birthplace. The puppy had ironically grown up into the best and truest friend Xav had ever had. Now Bogotá, temporarily oblivious of the arthritis that plagued him, lay snoring at Xavier's feet.

Rupert had been frantically busy all summer running the yard, politicking with Jupiter and Hengist and fighting off takeover bids for Venturer, the television company which he ran with his father-in-law, Declan O'Hara. Venturer was still very successful, but like all independent TV stations, was having an increasing battle attracting advertising.

Nor did the bloodstock market ever sleep, as

emails poured in from Tokyo, Dubai and Kentucky. Despite his legendary energy, chronic lack of sleep was making Rupert increasingly ratty and preoccupied, otherwise he might have attributed his son's mood swings to more than adolescent angst.

Hearing a terrific bang and the frenzied barking of dogs, Xav raced out on to the landing with Bogotá hobbling after him. Down the stairwell he could see his mother running white-faced out of the kitchen to be confronted by an outraged Bianca:

'Daddy's shot the television because Mr Blair's on it. I'll just have to go and watch Sky with the lads,' and stormed off.

Taggie clutched her head. She was desperately low both about Xav's deteriorating relationship with the entire family and because she was quite incapable of helping either child with its holiday work. Her agonizing was interrupted by the telephone.

'Helloo, helloo.'

Recognizing the strangulated Adam's apple whine of Alex Bruce, which instantly recalled her own disastrous school days, Taggie started to shake.

'Just checking you're on for our fundraiser for the new science block next week.'

Oh God, she'd forgotten.

'What date is it?'

'Twenty-first of August.'

Taggie went cold. That was Xav's birthday; he went berserk if it weren't celebrated in style. Alex Bruce had caught her on the hop when, back in June, he'd issued the invitation, implying that

124

Xavier's behaviour wouldn't be so 'challenging' or his learning difficulties so excessive if the parental back-up were more committed.

Riddled with shame and guilt, Taggie had weakly accepted but failed to tell Rupert, who was allergic to being gazed at by mothers and forced to put one's hand in one's pocket, when one was already bankrupted by bloody fees.

'Helloo, helloo?' Alex was still on the line. Taggie shuddered at the thought of his pursed red lips framed by beard pressed against the receiver.

'We'll be there,' she bleated.

'Randal Stancombe's agreed to host our promises auction. How about your spouse donating a helicopter trip to the Arc, complete with hospitality, or a peep behind the scenes at Venturer Television? Some of our parents might bid quite high for a chance to appear on *Buffers*.'

'You'll have to ask Rupert,' gasped Taggie and rang off.

Rupert, as she predicted, was insane with rage.

'I'll be in France—there's no way I can get there before nine.'

Taggie said she'd go on ahead, which made Rupert even crosser. He loathed his beautiful wife being out on the toot without him: predators were everywhere.

But his rage was nothing to the sullen fury of Xav that they were abandoning him on his birthday.

'I'm so sorry, darling, I muddled the dates.'

'You should have known it was my birthday from the date. Not that it's my real birthday—that's why you don't care.'

'Don't be bloody to Mummy,' protested Bianca, thinking how unattractively white-tongued and

125

covered in zits her brother looked.

'You can fuck off,' spat Xav, then, swinging back to Taggie: 'Can I have a party at home that night?'

Taggie quailed. 'Of course you can, darling.'

What the hell was Rupert going to say? Mrs Bodkin, their ancient housekeeper, was far too doddery to keep order.

'Will you ask Feral?' pleaded Bianca. 'And Paris? If you ask Paris, Feral might easily come. Oh per-lease.'

'I might.' Xav stormed upstairs, slamming his bedroom door.

Talk about an own goal. Pushing aside a rug and raising a floor board, he lifted out a half-empty bottle of vodka and having filled a tooth mug, hid it again.

He had been so endlessly sulky and difficult at Bagley he had no friends to ask. Girls were repelled by him. Sweet Aysha would never be allowed out by her bullying father. The only reason boys might turn up was to have a crack at Bianca or because the mothers delivering the girls wanted to gawp at the house and his father. He could try the children of his parents' friends: Junior, Amber, Lando and Jack Waterlane. Milly, Dicky and Dora might come. As a brown-nosing gesture, he could ask the hateful Cosmo, but they were probably all away.

Why did his father increasingly hate leaving his dogs and horses and not take them on holidays abroad, so they could row in the Caribbean or Mauritius like everyone else's families? Then he wouldn't have to have a party.

Xav took a slug of vodka, then jumped out of his skin as the door opened, but it was only Bogotá,

126

entirely white face smiling, pink tongue hanging down like a tie, black legs going everywhere.

'You can be guest of honour,' said Xav, giving him a piece of KitKat.

He'd better text people with invitations. He was too shy to telephone. If only Paris were still his friend, then everyone would have come.

*   *   *

Over the next week no one accepted.

'No one answers invitations these days,' Bianca consoled him. Not wanting her brother to be humiliated, she wrote to Feral: 'Xav is having a party on Thursday. Please come, he has asked Paris who would love to see you, so would I. Love, Bianca'.

*   *   *

As the party approached, the spats grew worse.

'How many yobs from Larks are coming?' demanded a departing Rupert.

'I'm not sure,' stammered Taggie.

'They'll chuck all your quiches at each other. For Christ's sake, lock up the silver and bolt all the yard doors.'

Taggie had racked her brains what to give Xav. Before his fall, it had been anything horsey, even on occasion a horse, or a drawing by Lionel Edwards or Munnings. Soon, but not yet, it might be a puppy. Xav didn't want clothes until he'd lost weight. Desperate to placate him, she spent far too much on DVD portables and computer games and mobiles which became cameras. As Rupert was

127

abroad on the day of his birthday, Xav felt free to play up and hardly opened anything, which resulted in a blazing row when Bianca accused him of being an ungrateful pig.

'Mummy's spent days making yummy food and mixing this gorgeous drink.' Bianca pointed to the Pimm's cup floating with exotic fruit in the big blue bowl on the terrace table.

'I wanted people to have Snakebite or Black Russians, not piddling fruit salad,' snapped Xav, who'd been smoking and drinking all day to cushion himself against the nightmare ahead.

At least it was a beautiful evening, with air balloons drifting up the valley out of a soft rose glow in the west and flocks of birds returning home from scavenging in the fields. Beyond the stables, turning poplars soared like paintbrushes dipped in gold.

Taggie had tied scarlet and blue balloons saying 'Happy Birthday, Xav' on the gate and the balustrade running along the terrace, on which panted Rupert's pack of dogs, grateful that the cruel heat of the day was subsiding.

Rupert's horses were still inside to protect them from the flies and because he didn't want them galloping about, laming themselves on the rock-hard ground. From the rim of brown rush on the water's edge, the lake could be seen to have dropped a couple of feet. Eminem on the CD player battled with the roar of combines.

People had been invited for eight. At five minutes to, Taggie hurtled downstairs. Insufficiently dried, her dark hair fluffed out like Struwwelpeter. Her big, silver-grey eyes were red and tired. Never had her and Rupert's huge four-poster seemed more inviting.

'You look lovely,' lied Bianca, her hands shaking as she fastened a double row of pearls round her mother's slender neck.

'And you look heavenly,' said Taggie, very aware that her daughter was showing too much flesh in a pale pink crop-top and ice-blue shorts and wearing far too much make-up. Bianca had ironed her black curls straight, so a long lock fell over one eye. Jewelled flip-flops showed off ruby toenails and Taggie recognized her own Arpège on Bianca's hot, excited body and her own rubies in Bianca's ears. Rupert would have gone ballistic.

Xav was smouldering in the doorway to the terrace.

'Have a lovely evening.' Taggie tried to kiss him, but Xav, humiliated that, in her high heels, his mother was about seven inches taller than he, shoved her away. Although longing to bury his face in her lovely, scented bosom and beg her to make the party disappear, he couldn't thaw out.

'Don't expect we'll be late, Daddy'll have had a long day.' Then when Xav mumbled about olds not spoiling the fun: 'Don't worry, we'll creep in.'

The moment his mother had left, Xav chucked a bottle of gin into the Pimm's cup.

82

Over at Bagley, the Mansion, square-walled and square-windowed like a great doll's house, was softened by floodlights. Someone had tied pink balloons to the bay trees on either side of the front door and left an empty champagne bottle in one of the dark blue tubs. From the open ground-floor windows came the yelping roar of suntanned parents being force-fed drink to elicit more generous promises later in the evening.

On the way in Taggie bumped into dear Patience Cartwright, who, when he'd kept a pony at Bagley, had been one of the few people Xav had liked and talked to.

'Summer has been rather wearying,' Patience now confessed in her raucous voice.

Ian had let the school to a football academy, who'd trashed the kitchens on their last night, and a youth orchestra rehearsing for a prom, which had entailed non-stop Stockhausen and Hindemith. 'If only it'd been a nice Haydn symphony.'

'How's Paris getting on?' asked Taggie, wincing at her gaunt reflection in the hall mirror.

'All right.' Patience touched wood, then, lowering her voice: 'Could we have lunch and compare notes sometime?'

'Oh, do let's.'

'Paris has been a bit up and down. We love him,' Patience went on firmly, 'but we're not quite sure how much he loves us.'

'I know the feeling,' sighed Taggie. Crossing her fingers, she asked: 'Is he coming to Xav's party?'

'Oh dear, didn't he answer? I'm so sorry. He's going to Jack Waterlane's. A whole crowd: Amber, Milly, Junior, Lando, Kylie, Pearl and Graffi have hired a minibus and taken sleeping bags. That's why David Waterlane isn't coming tonight. He won't pay fees, let alone for promises, and he wants to keep an eye on the Canalettos.'

Oh God, thought Taggie in horror. That lot were the core of Xav's party.

The next moment Daisy France-Lynch had hugged her. 'I've got a message from Lando. Will you apologize profusely to Xav, but he'd already accepted Jack's party which is only a couple of miles down the road. Cosmo and Jade are going there too.'

Next moment Dora was offering Taggie a trayful of brimming champagne glasses. 'Can you tell Bianca and Xav I'm terribly sorry I had to work. Mummy gives me no pocket money. Anyway, if Feral turns up, Bianca won't have eyes for anyone else. Paris has gone to Jack Waterlane's,' Dora added wistfully.

Taggie grabbed a drink, gulping down half of it. Poor, deserted Xav. She wanted to rush home to Penscombe but she had to wait for Rupert.

Creeping into the General Bagley Room, which had just been repainted in a glowing scarlet called Firestone, appropriately since so many of the mothers had acquired spare tyres cooking three meals a day for their offspring and visiting friends all summer. Most of them hid these bulges beneath floating flower prints or white caftans to show off suntanned breasts and shoulders.

Led by the frightful Anthea Belvedon, one mother after another charged up saying: 'No

131

Rupert?' in aggrieved tones, as though Taggie'd pushed him over a cliff. Fleeing to avoid No-Joke Joan, who was obviously going to lecture her on Bianca's lack of application, Taggie went slap into Poppet Bruce, beaming like a lighthouse and clutching a hideous baby sucking on a pink dummy.

'Just off to give the babe his supper. Do let's exchange views,' cried Poppet and next moment Taggie found herself perched on a sofa in a side room as Poppet plunged a dishcloth-grey boob into goldfish-mouthing Gandhi.

Oh God, she hoped someone had arrived at Xav's party.

As if reading her thoughts, Poppet said, 'We must encourage Xavier in social skills, he's very troubled.'

'He's very shy,' protested Taggie.

'Last term his behaviour was distinctly challenging. I know parents of adopted children often blame themselves for disasters that happen in any normal families, but you and Rupert lead such full lives, I sometimes wonder if anyone is listening to Xavier.'

'I haven't left the house all summer,' squeaked Taggie, 'and it's difficult listening to someone who won't talk.'

Poppet's bright, cheery eyes were boring into her like diamond cutters. 'Are you able to help him with his maths?'

'I can't do them at all,' gasped Taggie. If only she could ram a dummy into Poppet's mouth.

'Then I advise you to have some coaching. We have a good friend, Mike Pitts, who could come to the house three or four times a week.'

'I don't have the time,' stammered Taggie, which

was quite the wrong answer, as Poppet frowned and suggested Taggie made time.

'Nor do I feel Rupert is a supportive father.'

'He absolutely adores Xav.'

'Maybe, but the lad must miss his birth parents. The wound never heals.' Smugly Poppet unplugged baby Gandhi and hooked him on to another dishcloth-grey tit. 'I cannot advise you too strongly'—her tone grew more bullying—'to take Xav to birth-mother groups. He could then witness grieving mothers coming to terms with giving up their babes and might achieve closure. Have you told Xav everything about his background?'

'I couldn't,' yelped Taggie.

'Have you wondered if your longing for your own children makes you reject Xav in some way?'

'No, no.'

Out of the window, Taggie could see General Bagley gleaming in the moonlight and longed to climb on to the back of his charger so he could gallop her home to Penscombe.

Rescue instead appeared as Hengist, resplendent in a dark blue velvet smoking jacket, appeared in the doorway.

'Taggie, darling, I've been looking for you. Your drink's empty, unlike little Gandhi's.' He and Poppet exchanged smiles of radiant insincerity. 'Come and talk to me.' He pulled Taggie to her feet, sliding his arm round her narrow waist and stubbing his thumb on her protruding ribs. 'You're losing too much weight. Has that bloody Milk Marketing Board been hassling you? I fear the geeks when they come baring breasts.'

Taggie didn't laugh. She was adorable but not very bright. Not that Rupert was the Brain of

Britain.

As the gong went, Taggie pulled herself together. 'It was so sweet of Sally and you to send Xav a birthday card.'

'Sweet of Sally—she remembers everyone. She's the light of my life, as you are of Rupert's. I'm terribly sorry Alex has dragged you along to this grisly jaunt in the holidays. It was also Alex's grisly idea for parents to sit at their children's housemasters' tables. Afraid you're lumbered with Poppet and Alex again.'

Next moment Janey Lloyd-Foxe had buttonholed Taggie. 'How are you, darling? I can't wait for Amber and Junior to go back. We'll starve if I don't get some work done soon.'

Janey unnerved Taggie. She was married to Rupert's best friend, Billy Lloyd-Foxe, and was a well-known journalist who always seemed to know more and worse about you than you did yourself.

'Billy always complains he never gets any sex in the summer holidays because I'm so exhausted,' Janey went on. 'Amber and Junior's friends have been pouring through the house all summer.'

Which was more than Xav's had. Retreating to the Ladies, Taggie rang home. 'Are you OK?'

'Fine,' said Bianca. Dropping her voice: 'No one's arrived yet. Hang on, there's the doorbell. We're OK, bye.'

As she belted in from the terrace, Bianca passed Xav downing another mug of fruit cup and Mrs Bodkin in the study, sleeping peacefully through *The Two Ronnies*.

Followed by two striped lurchers, three Labradors and a couple of Jack Russells, Bianca opened the front door. There was no one outside, but the dogs carried on barking.

'Who's there? They're noisy but harmless,' shouted Bianca.

Very slowly, blacker than the shadows from which he emerged, long, lean and relaxed in a soft leather jacket, with the peak of his Arsenal baseball cap over one ear, a diamond cross gleaming at the neck of his black shirt, black jeans glued to his long legs, was Feral.

'Oh Feral!' Joy spread over Bianca's face like the glow in the west returning. 'You found us.'

'I did.' Feral couldn't believe how pretty she looked—and older, with her sleek, black hair and pale pink lipstick and dark liner emphasizing her ravishing mouth and eyes. He no longer felt avuncular, just lustful. 'Not sure about those dogs.'

'They're as dopey as anything.' Terrified he might run away, Bianca grabbed Feral's hand and led him into the hall, which was hung with pictures of horses and more dogs, and past rooms filled with beautiful battered furniture and splendid portraits.

'Who's that old git?'

'Our grandfather. He's been married five times.'

'Must like wedding cake. Looks familiar.'

'He's in *Buffers*.'

'So he is, friend of the Brig.' Then, peering into the library: 'Who reads those books?'

'No one. Mummy can't read; Daddy only reads Dick Francis and the racing pages.'

Out on the terrace, they found Xav, eyes crossed and slumped against the balustrade, just sober enough to say 'Hi' to Feral.

'This cup is cool,' said Bianca, 'I've eaten most of the fruit out of it. I'll get you a glass.'

As she went off to find one, Xav, who admired and envied Feral, offered him a line of coke.

Feral shook his head. 'Don't do drugs. Don't drink much.'

'This'll kick-start you.' Xav plunged the ladle into the Pimm's, picked up Bianca's glass and missed it.

Behind them the house reared up watchfully, ordering them to behave. A lawn to the right was almost as big as a football pitch.

'Paris coming?' asked Feral.

'Not yet,' mumbled Xav, 'evening's young.'

Bianca came back with a glass and filled it. Feral took a cautious sip, then a gulp.

'It is cool, man.' He took another gulp, then, putting down the glass, edged a box out of his tight jeans and handed it to Xav. 'Happy birthday.'

'Thanks.' Xav put it on the table.

'Open it,' nagged Bianca, 'Feral brought it all this way.'

It was a bracelet, consisting of two black straps attached, instead of to a watch, to two silver skull and crossbones flanking the word FUCK in diamanté letters.

Xav's face lifted, showing for a second how good-looking he could be. 'That is wicked, man, really wicked.' He was worried he'd got too fat, but it did up easily.

'Thank Feral,' chided Bianca.

'I was about to, you stupid bitch.'

Feral, who'd been admiring the lake in the moonlight, swung round to defend Bianca, but she shook her head and his fists unclenched.

'It's great,' mumbled Xav. 'Can't wait to wave it at Poppet and Alex,' and he wheeled off into the house.

136

Justin Timberlake, fortissimo and blaring out over the valley, obliterated the need to talk.

'Don't people complain about the noise?' asked Feral, thinking of the fuss Miss Miserden made at Larks.

'Not really, Daddy owns the land,' said Bianca simply. 'What have you been doing all summer?'

'Working here and there, mostly for Lily and the Brig. He's been doing a series of *Buffers*; I've helped him dress—cufflinks and fings.'

'Daddy says it's going to be a huge hit, the network's taking it. Grandpa's booked for the next series. So naughty, he forgets I'm his granddaughter sometimes and pinches my bottom.'

'Not surprised in those shorts.' Feral drained his glass.

'They ought to do a programme about me called *Duffers*,' said Bianca, filling it up.

'And me.' Feral collapsed on a bench. He wanted to kiss Bianca's ruby toenails in those jewelled flip-flops. 'Can your mum really not read?'

'Hardly at all, she's dyslexic. Suits me, she can't read my diary. Dora's mother's always reading hers.'

'What does yours say?'

'Feral didn't come and see me today. Boo hoo.' Bianca was on the bench beside him, edging up like a kitten. She had no wiles, no defence mechanism; he knew she was dying to be in his arms just as he was to be in hers.

'Are you hungry?' asked Bianca.

'Kind of.' It wasn't cool to say he'd been too nervous to eat all day. 'This drink's strong. Perhaps I should.'

'It'd be nice if you could. Mummy's worked so

137

hard. Poor Xav, I don't think anyone else is coming.'

'Bad for him, suits us.'

There is a limit to the inroads three people, two of them dottily in love, can make on supper for twenty. Feral ate some chicken pie and some chocolate roulade and Bianca toyed with a piece of quiche. Xav had another line of cocaine and another glass of Pimm's and passed out on the sofa.

'Shall we go upstairs?' murmured Bianca, taking Feral's hand, 'Daddy and Mummy have gone to some dinner.'

Drunk with love and fruit cup, Feral had to cling on to the crimson cord to pull himself up the splendid oak staircase.

He would never have followed Bianca upstairs, or even turned up, if he hadn't been boosted by the prospect of a trial with the Rovers on Monday. A contributory factor had also been that this week (earlier than expected) his court case had come up. The Brigadier had accompanied him to court and vouched for his good character. Luckily the magistrates were all fans of *Buffers* and had let him off, and because he was still just fifteen, none of this had been reported in the papers.

Inside Bianca's bedroom, someone appeared to have shredded a rainbow, as clothes she'd rejected littered bed, chair and carpet. As she gathered them up, chucking them on a blue and white striped sofa, Feral admired the daffodil-yellow curtains and the pink and violet quilt on the little four-poster. On the powder-blue walls, framed photographs of Colombian beauty spots—sweeps of orchids, giant water lilies, the lake where the legendary El Dorado was hidden—rubbed shoulders with posters of Michael Owen and Justin Timberlake, which he wanted to tear down. When he was striker for Larkminster Rovers, he'd have his own posters.

'This used to be the nicest spare room, but Daddy hates having people to stay so much, he let me have it.'

Feral leapt for the wardrobe in terror as he heard what he imagined as frantic hammering on the door, but it was only the hooves of Rupert's horses being let out into the fields in the cool of the evening.

'It's like a zoo here,' he grumbled, peering out of the window. 'Graffi'd be in heaven with all these horses and pictures.'

'Bring him tomorrow,' begged Bianca.

Feral had had so many girls, taking what he wanted without compunction, but none had touched him like Bianca, nor been as beautiful. Her clear, pale, coffee-coloured complexion was flushed with rose, her slim, supple body quivering to be entwined with his. He longed to bury his lips in her belly button and progress downward, to caress the delectable curve of buttock emerging from her blue shorts, to feel against his thighs the fluttering caress of her sooty eyelashes. Grown-up things.

But this was a child's room. On the shelves Harry Potter and Jacqueline Wilson fought for space with Barbie dolls, rows and rows of lipsticks and coloured nail polish. She was only thirteen—where the hell could it lead?

Above the bookcase hung a glass plate engraved with the words: 'Welcome to Penscombe, Bianca

139

Maud Campbell-Black. May 1990'.

'I don't remember arriving here, I was only three months old, but Xav does and there were flags and balloons all the way up the drive. Mummy and Daddy crossed the world to find us,' Bianca added proudly. 'They were sad they couldn't have children but so pleased to have us. Our mother is the sweetest woman in the world.'

Feral edged towards her. 'Makes two of you.'

Bianca shrugged. 'Daddy's tricky, I used to be jealous of how much he adored Xav, but now they fight all the time.' She crossed the room, peering out at the empty terrace and the stars nearing their full brightness. 'I'm really sorry, it doesn't look as though Paris is coming.'

'Don't matter.' On her return from the window, Feral reached out for her, realizing she was trembling as much as he was.

'Why didn't you ring me? I gave you my number on three pieces of paper.'

'They ran in the washing machine. I tried once and got your Dad and bottled out. I watched your house across the valley for hours like a stalker.'

'Promise?'

'Promise, promise.'

Grabbing her tiny waist, encountering goose flesh, he caressed the edges of her springy, surprisingly full breasts, then he bent his head to kiss her arched-back throat, then her closed eyelids, the tip of her tiny nose, behind each ear, breathing in the deliciously heady Arpège. Finally he kissed her soft, sweet, pink lips, which parted shyly, her darting tongue touching his, flickering then retreating like a dancer, drawing him into heaven.

140

As her little hands closed on his head, his hair felt so thick, vigorous and right, compared with the floppy silken tresses of other boys she had snogged, that she clung on. Their first, magic kiss seemed to last for ever.

'Oh Bee-unca,' murmured Feral, collapsing back on to the bed, 'I have dreamt of you.'

'Why, uncle, it isn't a shame at all,' giggled Bianca, collapsing beside him. 'Xav's passed out, Mrs Bodkin's asleep and Mummy won't be back for centuries.'

83

Mrs Axford and her fleet of waitresses were clearing away the main course of chicken supreme with tagliatelle and wild mushrooms when Rupert stalked in. He could have murdered a quadruple whisky, but couldn't drink as he had to fly home. A ripple of excitement ran through the hall as mothers readjusted their cleavages and checked their reflections in little gold compacts. The only man in the room not in a dinner jacket (except Alex Bruce, who'd refused to wear one on principle), Rupert in a crumpled off-white suit and cornflower-blue shirt suddenly made everyone else look overdressed.

Hengist leapt to his feet. 'You've made it, well done, you're over here.'

Rupert had already clocked his wife looking utterly dejected between the appalling Alex Bruce and the just as appalling old queen Biffo Rudge. Serve her right for dragging him along to such a ghastly evening.

'OK?' he asked as he kissed her rigid cheek.

'No one's come to Xav's party,' whispered Taggie in anguish, 'they've all gone to Jack Waterlane's.'

'Might teach him to be nicer to people,' snapped Rupert.

Nemesis descended swiftly with a jangle of ethnic bracelets as a voice cried, 'Rupert, Rupert, you're here,' and Poppet Bruce patted the chair beside her. 'You've got Joan Johnson on your left, so we can enjoy an exchange of views about Xavier and Bianca. You know Alex and Biffo, of course, and

Boffin's parents Gordon and Susan Brooks, and Anthea Belvedon.'

'Oh, Rupert and I are old friends,' said Anthea, delighted with an opportunity to captivate. She'd always thought Rupert was gorgeous and wasted on Taggie. How infuriating Dora, watching her every move, was waiting at table and had now rushed over and dumped a large piece of venison pâté in front of Rupert.

'Poor thing, you must be starving. Toast's on the way. How's Penscombe Peterkin?' That was Rupert's star horse, much fancied in the St Leger.

'Awesome, but we need rain, he loathes hard going.'

'Then he wouldn't like sitting between Joan and Poppet,' whispered Dora.

Seeing amusement in Rupert's eyes, Anthea said icily, 'You're supposed to be working, Dora. Had a good day's horse racing, lots of winners?' she called across the table.

'None,' said Rupert.

'Are Meridian going to take over Venturer?' asked Gordon Brooks.

'Not if I can help it.'

Out of the corner of his eye, Rupert caught sight of Hengist, Ruth Walton and his friend Billy Lloyd-Foxe at the next table, laughing their heads off at his plight.

'Trapped between Silly and Charybdis,' sighed Hengist, 'poor Rupert.'

As compensation, Rupert had a direct view of Mrs Walton, golden brown and replete in a beautiful Lindka Cierach dress in old rose silk, with a tiny pink cardigan knotted under her glorious boobs. She smiled lazily at Rupert, who smiled back, an exchange instantly registered by Randal Stancombe. At least he was at the head's table and not Rupert, who made no effort and called him Randolph (if he deigned to recognize him).

Gordon Brooks was now discussing some chemical formula with Joan, so Rupert turned to Poppet. 'How's the new baby?'

'Flourishing, flourishing. His siblings are so supportive. They relish developing their parenting skills. Parenting could be a good GCSE for Bianca.'

'Bit premature, she's only thirteen. Might qualify her for a free house, I suppose.'

'Now you're deliberately misunderstanding me.' Poppet laughed merrily. 'And we need to discuss Xav.'

'He's fine.'

'He has very few friends.' Poppet sipped her cranberry juice reflectively. 'If it's any consolation, Charisma, our eldest daughter, was dreadfully bullied for being severely gifted.'

'Not Xav's problem.'

'They accused Charisma of being "posh".'

'Posh? Your daughter?' said Rupert in genuine amazement.

'Because she always gets A stars. Charisma, of course, is a workaholic.'

'Neither of my children's problem,' snapped Rupert. 'Thanks, darling,' as a grinning Dora exchanged his venison plate for a plate of chicken.

'I've given you lots of mushrooms, they're really good.'

Greedily shovelling up butterscotch ice cream, Poppet trundled on: 'Xav yearns for acceptance by his peers.'

'Peers live in the House of Lords,' said Rupert coldly, 'or they did before Blair gelded the place.'

He glanced across at Taggie. Accustomed to being married to the prettiest woman in the room, he noticed her red, swollen eyes and unbecoming, unruly hair and felt outraged that Alex Bruce was wrapped in conversation with Boffin's mother and Biffo had gone off table-hopping, leaving her stranded. A second later, Biffo's seat had been taken by Sally B-T.

'How's Xav's birthday going? Such a super chap.'

'Are you sure we're talking about the same child?' Rupert answered for Taggie. 'Six weeks into the school holidays, he's emerging as the devil incarnate.'

'Rupert,' gasped Taggie in horror.

Rupert crashed his knife and fork together, chicken hardly touched, fingers drumming, and turning to No-Joke Joan for heavy relief, learnt she'd been giving a paper on the evolution of the potato.

'Does Bianca lack social skills?' he asked finally.

'Quite the contrary. She and Dora Belvedon never stop chattering. I shudder to think of their phone bills. I'm afraid there's little likelihood of Bianca getting any GCSEs unless she buckles down.'

'It's a first step of the most evil tyrants,' Alex Bruce was droning on to Boffin's mother, 'destroying the teaching profession. In the seventies, teachers and academics arrested by Idi Amin never re-emerged because he tortured, then murdered them.'

'What a sensible man.' Rupert took a swig out of

a nearby Perrier bottle.

As Alex went purple and stormed off, Poppet renewed her attack.

'There's a wonderful government initiative called Dads and Lads, Rupert. Fathers reading with their sons and helping them with their homework. I'm sure you could give your Colombian lad a lift.'

'Dads and Lads?' said Rupert softly.

'If you and Taggie struggle with the homework,' joined in Joan, 'I think Bianca's only salvation is to board.'

'She will not,' said Rupert, so sharply everyone looked round and Randal Stancombe decided to join the table, taking Alex's chair. He made a great show of kissing first Taggie's, then Anthea's hands, before expressing hope that they were all going to make promises he could auction later in the evening.

'What's on offer already?' asked Poppet.

'Lord Waterlane's offered lunch at the House of Lords,' Stancombe consulted his clipboard. 'Ricky France-Lynch has pledged polo lessons; Daisy his wife has offered to do a free pastel of the person of your choice. Billy Lloyd-Foxe'—he raised his voice so Billy and everyone at the next table stopped talking and laughing—'has promised a tour round Television Centre, lunch in the canteen and tickets to his programme *Sport and Starboard*.'

'Good old Billy!' everyone cheered.

'What have you offered us, Randal?' simpered Anthea.

'Two weeks in a Caribbean villa and a free flight,' said Randal modestly to more cheers. 'Dame Hermione—' he began.

'Christ, is she here?' Rupert was about to dive

under the table.

'Dame Hermione is at a gig this evening,' reproved Joan. 'She has pledged tickets for Covent Garden and supper afterwards. We're still looking for more bumper prizes.'

'How about a night at the Ritz with Rupert Campbell-Black?' yelled Billy.

'Yes, Rupert,' asked Poppet archly, 'what are you going to pledge?'

'A day at the Arc in your private box?' suggested Stancombe. 'And a ride back and forth in your chopper?'

'Or on your chopper,' shouted Janey Lloyd-Foxe to shouts of laughter.

'That would be an exciting pledge,' dimpled Anthea.

'For whom?' snapped Rupert.

'Oh, come on, Rupert, that's not going to break the bank,' chided Stancombe.

'Racing's work. I can't concentrate if I have to spend the day being charming.'

'You'll just have to try harder,' teased Poppet.

'Poor Rupert,' murmured Mrs Walton, 'he does look fed up. Is he ever unfaithful to that sweet, stupid wife?'

'Certainly not,' said Billy with rare sharpness, 'and she's not stupid, Penscombe would crumble without her holding it together.'

'Let's go and cheer him up,' whispered Mrs Walton to Hengist.

Leaving Billy, filling up everyone's glasses with a fresh bottle of red and pulling up two chairs beside Rupert, Hengist muttered:

'Are you OK?'

'Not until you find me a red-hot poker to ram up

147

Mrs Bruce's ass.'

'Hush,' giggled Mrs Walton.

'Those emeralds are stunning,' said Rupert, unthawing slightly, 'and they couldn't have a better setting.'

'Randal brought them back for me from Bogotá.'

What was Stancombe doing there? wondered Rupert. Drug centre of the world; Xav's birthplace. Remembering the happiness and excitement when they'd brought him and Bianca home, he vowed to make things better.

Glancing across at Taggie he saw she was shaking with terror. Toothy Susan Brooks, whose favourite subject was Boffin, had got on to GCSEs and whether it would be too taxing for her G and T son to take fourteen.

'How many did you take, Poppet?'

'Ten, but they were O levels.'

'And you, Anthea?'

'Nine.'

'And you, Ruth?'

'Eight.'

'And you, Hengist?'

'About twenty-five. That's enough of that.' Hengist, who'd also noticed Taggie's twitching face, drained his glass and announced it was time for a pee break before the auction.

But Poppet refused to leave it. 'How many GCSEs did you get, Taggie?' she asked loudly.

'None,' whispered Taggie, colour suffusing her grey cheeks.

'Really?' said Anthea in amazement. 'None at all?'

'I didn't get any either,' said Rupert quickly. 'Never took any.'

148

'How the hell did you get into the Blues?' asked Hengist.

'I took a civil service exam, which was the equivalent, then went before a selection board at Westbury. I was only in for a year or two before going back to showjumping.'

'No O levels between either you or Taggie,' mocked Poppet.

'One wonders if you could achieve a GCSE today?' Alex quizzed Rupert as he returned to the table.

'Course I could. They're so bloody easy. You can take in calculators and history notes and poetry books. I'd walk it.'

'What a wonderful idea.' Poppet clapped her hands with another mad jangle of bracelets. 'You and Xav must take a GCSE together. English literature. You can read the books he's working on and exchange views at mealtimes.'

'Don't be fucking stupid, I haven't got the time,' snarled Rupert.

'You mean you haven't got the bottle,' taunted Stancombe. 'You wouldn't risk it, knowing you'd fail.'

'I bloody wouldn't.' Rupert had risen to his feet, shaking with rage, about to leap across the bottles and glasses and strangle him.

'Kindly don't swear in front of our spouses,' said Alex querulously.

'Oh fuck off.' Rupert turned back to Stancombe. 'I have got the bottle.'

'Prove it,' taunted Stancombe softly. 'I bet you a hundred grand, which I'll pledge to the Bagley Fund, you can't pass Eng. lit.'

'I'll sponsor you for ten thousand, Rupert,' said

Gordon Brooks, 'but only if you get a C grade or above.'

'My newspaper would sponsor you for at least fifty thousand, Rupe,' shouted Janey Lloyd-Foxe leaping up and down in excitement, 'as long as we can have the story. Make a fantastic diary: Rupert takes a GCSE.' She was now scribbling on her wrist.

Offers of sponsorship were coming in from eager mothers all over the room.

'I'll give you twenty-three pounds,' said Dora.

'We'll have paid for the new science block in one night,' murmured Theo Graham.

'Then it's a done deal.' Stancombe jumped on to a chair, shouting, 'Rupert Campbell-Black has agreed to take an English lit. GCSE and has already been sponsored to the tune of two hundred and fifty thousand pounds if he gets a C grade or above.'

Rage no longer robbed Rupert of speech.

'I fucking haven't,' he howled. 'I've got a yard and a television station to run and there is no way I'm taking any exam,' and he stalked out of the hall.

Table Ten were very slow in getting coffee, petits fours and their ordered liqueurs, because Dora, their waitress, had retreated to the sixth-form common room.

'Wicked!' she was whispering into her mobile. 'Rupert Campbell-Black is going to take a GCSE. Yes? I swear. At a promises auction at Bagley. Parents have sponsored him to over a quarter of a million already. It happened after a row with horrible Randal Stancombe, who was taunting Taggie and Rupert for not having any O levels. English lit., I think, although according to his daughter Bianca, Rupert only reads Dick Francis and the racing pages.'

There was no way Dora was going to let that old tart Janey Lloyd-Foxe pip her to the post.

84

Taggie raced after Rupert as he strode towards his helicopter.

'I'm so sorry, I'm so sorry. You were so kind to defend me, it was all my fault.'

As he waited for clearance to fly, Rupert rang Lysander, his assistant, who said everything was as quiet as a mouse.

'Most of the horses are out, except Peterkin and the ones racing on Monday. No sound from the house, hardly any lights on and no music for ages. Party must be over, frankly I didn't see anyone arrive.'

Flying into Penscombe, Rupert looked down at the empire he had created without a single O level. There was the ancient blond house with its billowing woods and venerable oaks skirting a fast emptying lake, more than a hundred horses out in the fields, all weather gallops, indoor school, tennis court, swimming pool, animals' graveyard, and the moonlit ribbon of the Frogsmoor stream, like a white parting down the valley. An empire built up by his own hard work. There was no way he was going to take any fucking GCSE.

He was so angry he ignored the fact his wife was crying. On landing, he went straight to the yard. Penscombe Peterkin whickered at his master's approach, hopeful of being let out to join his friends. The son of Rupert's Derby winner, Peppy Koala, Peterkin had been born and brought up at Penscombe, where everyone loved him. When one of Rupert's jockeys used a whip on him in a race for the first time, the little colt was so outraged, he stopped in his tracks and was never whipped again. Since then, he'd never lost a race. A huge amount was already on him for the St Leger. Rupert patted and gave him a handful of pony nuts and wandered back to the house to find chaos and his wife frantically wiping up pools of sick in the hall.

The dogs had obviously raided Taggie's supper. Stalker, Rupert's favourite Jack Russell, was polishing off a chicken pie abandoned on the terrace table, from time to time dropping pieces on to the flagstones for a patiently waiting Bogotá to hoover up.

Mrs Bodkin was still asleep in front of some X-rated film. Xav's presents were still unopened, little beast.

'I told you not to give him a party,' growled Rupert, avoiding another pile of sick, then catching sight of a black leather jacket over the banister.

*   *   *

Feral had had so many girls before, but this was the real one. The problem was keeping Bianca's love in check. She was so anxious to give him everything. He had removed her bra and stroked her sweet, tip-tilted breasts; he had buried his face in her scented shoulders, stroked her hair and kissed her on and on. They were too preoccupied with one another to hear anyone arriving.

Suddenly the door burst open.

'What the fuck d'you think you're doing? Get away from her, you black bastard,' howled Rupert.

Only when Feral reared up, shaking off the duvet, did Rupert realize Bianca was only naked to

153

the waist and Feral still wearing his black jeans. Standing, he was almost as tall as Rupert.

'I ain't no black bastard, man,' he said with quiet dignity. 'Back in the dark ages, my dad was married to my mum.'

Next moment he had leapt on to the blue striped sofa and jumped out of the window, falling on a yew hedge. But as he dropped down on to the lawn, landing awkwardly, a sharp pain gripped the right ankle of his shooting foot. He gave a groan as he limped away, keeping to the shadows.

'Daddy, how could you?' screamed Bianca. 'We were just snogging. How dare you call Feral a black bastard? I made all the running.'

'You shouldn't bloody be in bed with him,' said Rupert, slightly shaken. 'I suppose your brother's passed out?'

But Xav, sobering up and lurking on the landing, had overheard the row.

'Black bastard?' he yelled. 'Black fucking bastard? I'm black and I'm a bastard. Now I know what you really think of me.'

'Oh, for Christ's sake, it's just a figure of speech.'

'How dare you insult Feral?' sobbed Bianca. 'We were only kissing.'

'Go to bed,' shouted Rupert.

But Xav was fired up.

'My birthday was the day I was wrenched from my mother and chucked out on the streets to die. If only I had died. I've always had shit birthdays.'

'Xav,' pleaded Taggie, running up the stairs, 'that's not true.'

Xav turned on her. 'Shut up! I never wanted you as a mother, I hate you, *hate* you. You never loved me either, because I'm fat, ugly and useless.'

154

He ran sobbing out of the house, slamming the door in poor limping Bogotá's white face, heading out for the yard. Peterkin was delighted to see Xav, who had been the first person on his back and had often slept in his box. Both horse and boy had moped when Xav went away to Bagley. Xav led Peterkin into the yard by his head collar, jumped on to his back and set off across the fields, flat out towards the main road. Moonlight, more silvery light than day, sculpted dark grey trees and pale grey walls.

'Black bastard, black bastard,' yelled Xav in time to Peterkin's galloping hooves. Cocaine and booze had cushioned him against fear. He wasn't frightened of anything, not even his father. I hate him, I hate him, I hate him.

Rupert had poured himself a quadruple whisky and was just telling himself Xav would come home as soon as he sobered up, when the best horse he'd ever owned and trained passed the window, hurtling towards the main road on rock-hard ground. Rushing out to the yard, Rupert leapt on a mare who was racing on Monday. He'd have to head Xav off.

Xav by this time had turned Peterkin round and, rejoicing he'd got his nerve back, was riding quietly home across the fields, when Rupert thundered up and whacked Xav across the face, yelling:

'Get off that horse, you can bloody well walk home.'

As Xav slid to the ground, he felt all his fuses blow. He watched Rupert pull off his tie and slot it through Peterkin's head collar, then began almost conversationally:

'I know all about you.'

155

As Rupert paused, he went on:

'I know how much you drugged and boozed. I know you beat up your horses and your first wife. I know you bullied Jake Lovell witless on the showjumping circuit. You're an utterly crap role model. I don't belong to you any more, I want a divorce.' Xav's quiet voice had risen to a scream of pain.

'I dug out my secret files in the cellar. I know I was battered and left for dead as a baby because they thought my birthmark was the sign of the devil. Well, now I'm older, your fingermarks on my face are worse than any birthmark. They're the sign of a devil.' He spat at his appalled father's feet. 'The curse of being your son and a Campbell-Black.'

*   *   *

Hearing screams and shouts, fearful it might be Rupert after him, Feral hobbled faster. Glancing back, he saw Rupert's drive stretched out in the moonlight like a bandage to bind up his broken heart or his totally fucked ankle. No trial, no Bianca.

Next morning, Peterkin was as crippled lame as Feral. All the late editions of the papers picked up the *Independent*'s story about Rupert taking a GCSE.

85

For the first time in her life, Bianca Campbell-Black was utterly miserable. She had always been so proud of her parents, but now her father had revealed himself as a foul racist—and after all her coaxing, Feral had shot back into the jungle again. She kept imagining his cat's eyes shining out of the beech wood behind the house.

The Saturday after Xav's party, she and Dora went into Larkminster to see *I Capture the Castle*, a film Dora loved because she identified with the diary-writing heroine and her large eccentric family. Afterwards, she and Bianca went on to a Chinese restaurant where, as they rolled duck, sliced cucumber and dark sweet crimson sauce in pancakes and harpooned sweet and sour prawns, Bianca relayed the events of the last few days and Dora's eyes grew bigger and bigger.

'Your father was horribly hassled before he left Bagley,' she said in mitigation. 'He'd been trapped by Joan, Mrs Fussy and my mother all evening, then he was manoeuvred into that GCSE which he's been forced to agree to take.'

'That was shocking. Someone must have leaked it to the papers that very night.'

'Shocking,' agreed Dora. 'Some people have no principles.' Then, hastily changing the subject—after all, dinner tonight was being paid for by the *Independent*'s cheque: 'Do you think Feral would be caught in bed with me if I paid him? How ballistic would Mummy go? OK, OK, only joking.'

Dora vowed on this occasion not to ring any

newspapers, Bianca was so desolate. She'd eaten nothing. Dora had to finish the spring rolls and prawns and bag up Bianca's duck for Cadbury. Unable to bear seeing her happy friend cast down, she suggested they call on Feral.

It was getting dark. The Shakespeare Estate was only 750 yards away, but they might have been plunging thousands of miles into the depths of hell. Rasta music fortissimo, football commentary, shouts and screams poured out of graffitied buildings. Jeering gangs of youths roamed the streets. Tarts screamed abuse. Addicts, like corpses dug up from the grave, hung stinking and unwashed over broken fences.

'If only Cadbury was here to defend us,' quavered Dora as a snarling Dobermann hurled itself against a gate. 'Shall we try another day?'

'We'll be safe when we find him,' pleaded Bianca. 'Here we are. Macbeth Street, number twelve.'

All Feral's windows were boarded up, as though he no longer allowed himself to look out on the world. The garden was full of burnt-out cars, fridges and wheelless bikes. Running up the path, Bianca hammered on the front door, which was answered by a fat man in a filthy vest, clearly off his face with drugs. Leering, swaying, he beckoned them inside, where Uncle Harley, immaculate as ever in black leather, Feral's diamond cross gleaming at his neck, was watching a revolting film in which a man and a woman were clearly enjoying sex with a little girl.

'Not something you'd show the vicar,' mocked the fat man.

Nearly asphyxiated by a stench of sweat, puke and fags, ready to bolt, but hearing the front door bang behind them, Dora bravely announced they'd come to see Feral.

The fat man jerked his head. 'Next door.'

In the kitchen they found glasses and plates piled high in the sink and a woman, presumably Feral's mother, lying moaning on the floor in a drug-induced stupor, surrounded by playing children.

Then Bianca gasped as she caught sight of Feral, stripped to the waist, shiningly beautiful in this midden of squalor, masculinity in no way diminished by the fact he was working his way through a pile of ironing and trying to feed a yelling baby in a high chair.

Bianca was still speechless, but over the lecherous cajoling of the man in the porn film, Dora yelled:

'It's us, Feral.'

Feral looked up in horror. Hissing like a cornered wild cat, he screamed at them to get the fuck out.

'I wanted to say sorry for Daddy,' sobbed Bianca, 'and see if you were all right.' Then, when Feral said nothing: 'I love you.'

'Well, I don't love you. Get out.' As he hobbled towards them, brandishing the iron in their faces like a riot shield, Dora caught sight of a bandage on his ankle.

Next moment, Uncle Harley had lurched into the room and made a grab at Bianca who, catching him off balance, shoved him crashing against the sink, smashing several glasses. Dora meanwhile had clouted the fat man with her bag and unchained the door, enabling them to flee out of hell. Seeing their terrified faces, a prostitute screeched, 'Taught you a lesson, did it? Don't mess with Uncle Harley.'

Dora and Bianca didn't stop until they reached the bridge. Leaning against it, gasping for breath, Dora couldn't stop shaking.

'What an utterly disgusting, revolting place.'

Bianca couldn't stop crying; her only emotion was sympathy for Feral living with those crackheads.

'That's why he's so poor,' she wailed, 'and why he wouldn't go on the geography field trip, or take up that games scholarship at Bagley. There'd be no one to look after those children. What are we going to do? I daren't tell Mummy and Daddy where I've been.'

'I'll just call Dicky and check Cadbury's OK. I expect they're both watching disgusting porn on the internet too. Then let's take a taxi to Janna's.' Dora put an arm round Bianca. 'Don't cry. She'll know what to do.'

*   *   *

Music louder than any on the Shakespeare Estate poured out of Jubilee Cottage. The Brigadier had been sent a crate of red by a fan and he and Lily were teaching Janna and Emlyn the Charleston. They were all hammered.

'I'm terribly sorry, we haven't got enough for the taxi,' were Dora's first words.

After Emlyn had paid it, Bianca gazed into space shuddering whilst Dora, one hand on her hip, the other gesticulating wildly, described their adventures.

'Poor Feral,' she said indignantly. 'Rupert called him a "black bastard" and chucked him out of

160

Penscombe, although he and Bianca were only snogging, or as Mummy calls it "heavy petting". Mind you, there are plenty of pets at Penscombe.'

Meeting the Brigadier's eye, Lily tried not to laugh.

No one was laughing by the time Dora had finished.

'Oh poor, poor Feral,' whispered Janna.

'We must rescue him,' wept Bianca.

'I think we've all drunk too much to do anything tonight,' said Emlyn. 'Janna and I'll go round in the morning and sort it out.'

'Feral's got a soccer trial on Monday. Should cheer him up,' volunteered the Brigadier.

'I don't think so,' sighed Dora, 'he was lame as a cat.'

'That's from escaping out of my bedroom window,' wailed Bianca. 'It's all bloody Daddy's fault.'

'Better stay the night,' Lily told Dora and Bianca to the Brigadier's regret.

*   *   *

'Shall I come with you?' asked the Brigadier next morning, as he tried to keep down a Fernet-Branca.

'Fewer of us the better, less ostentatious,' answered Emlyn as he coiled his long length into Janna's green Polo.

'Something rotten in the state of Larkminster,' he observed as Janna drove past smashed-up playgrounds, shuttered shops, shells of houses, front gardens full of junk instead of flowers, and parked at the end of Macbeth Street. Emlyn edged

161

her inwards so he could walk on the outside of the pavement.

'Although this is the sort of hell-hole where I should walk on both sides of you.'

At first Feral wouldn't open the door.

'If you're from the social,' observed an old biddy scuttling past, 'they've gone.'

Hearing a baby crying, Emlyn continued thumping.

When Feral finally let them in, they found him alone with three young children and the howling baby, whose nappy he'd just changed. From the mop in a bucket of suds, he'd obviously been cleaning up the floor. There was no fridge. Flies were everywhere.

After a lot of coaxing and a cigarette from Emlyn, he admitted that Uncle Harley and his mother had pushed off abroad to punish him. Gradually, eyes cast down, stammering out the sentences, occasionally returning to his former hauteur, he explained how he'd stolen to feed his brothers and sisters and carried a gun to protect them.

'Harley used my mother as a tom, kept her short of money and drugs, to make her reliant and desperate. Anyfing I earn from Lily and the Brig, she takes to feed her habit. Even if I hide it in the toes of my trainers, she finds it. Does my head in. What'll happen to her? She's not beautiful any more; Harley'll kill her.'

As Feral got up to wave away a swarm of flies settling on a plate of beefburgers, Emlyn noticed him hobbling.

'So you're no good for the trial on Monday?'

'Fanks to Mr Rupert Fancy-Black, I've gotta let

162

the Brig down.'

'Does Harley give you a hard time?'

Feral nodded bleakly. 'He went ballistic I wouldn't deal when I got access to all those rich Bagley kids. Nearly buried me when I turned down that boarding place.'

Now the howling baby was sleeping in her arms, Janna wanted to howl herself. Feral had been so proud, so brave, his constant lack of funds the only giveaway. Emlyn was being wonderful too. With one child on each muscular thigh, and the third watching, he was singing nursery rhymes to them.

'They're not going into care!' Feral became almost hysterical. 'They'll never come back.'

'Only for a bit, while we sort ourselves out,' promised Janna. 'Everyone needs a leg-up occasionally. I accepted money from Randal Stancombe to keep Larks going.'

With trepidation she called Nadine who, fired up by a new scheme to unite social services and the education and health departments, turned out to be an absolute star.

The Brigadier, who had just been cleared by the Criminal Records Bureau to teach history at Larks, had grown so fond of Feral, he asked him to stay until things got straight. Janna would be up the road with Lily next door, so Feral wouldn't be lonely, and he could do the odd job round the house. Nadine then arranged for the children and the baby to be taken into temporary care with a good, kind family in the next village, so Feral could pop in and see them whenever he wanted. Feral listlessly agreed to everything because he saw no other way out. He loved Bianca, but like Juliet she was not yet fourteen; Rupert would always show

163

him the door.

'Rupert called me a "black bastard",' he kept telling the Brigadier.

Feral moved in, but like a feral cat, he couldn't bear being trapped and begged the Brigadier not to lock the doors at night. 'I'll be your guard dog, man.'

86

Janna had worked flat out throughout the summer holidays supervising the rebuilding of Appletree, because the moment she stopped being busy, she was wiped out by guilt, sadness and despair. These feelings were reinforced by record temperatures, dire news of global warming and melting icebergs. Would there be a world at all for the children to inherit?

Despite gallant work by the remaining teachers, there had been so much disruption during the summer term that in the end only eight per cent of Larks children achieved the Magic Five. Ashton was on the telephone in seconds.

'Dear, dear, dear,' he gloated, 'how lucky for you we OK'd Appletwee first. If we'd had a sight of these wesults, you'd never have got your building. I do pray you do better with Year Ten.'

The *Times Educational Supplement* had reported that the proportion of U grades was the highest ever.

'Most of them from Larks,' observed Ashton bitchily.

Janna had also observed a faint neglect of late. Throughout July, Hengist had frequently rolled up at Appletree around dusk to admire work in progress, before making love to her in the long, pale, dry grass of Smokers' with the stars emerging as voyeurs overhead.

'Do you know it's illegal to have sex out of doors?' Janna had teased him on his last visit. 'I'm sure Miss Miserden's got a periscope.'

'It's called outreach, because I reach out for you,' said Hengist.

Above them on the right of an apricot-pink harvest moon, Mars, like an angry red-gold lion tossing his mane, dominated the evening sky.

'This year's belonged to Mars,' said Hengist, as he zipped up his trousers, 'that's why you won your battle over Year Ten, but you must watch Ashton. I don't know what he can still do to hurt you, but I don't trust him. Two thousand and four, thank God, will be Venus's year. She'll shine so brightly, I'll fall in love with you all over again.'

As he smiled down, he noticed, like scratches on a scraper board, new lines on her face.

'Darling, you must get a break. Why not come and crash out for a few days in the house we rent in Tuscany? I'll call you.'

But after that visit in late July she had heard nothing for nearly five weeks. She knew he was back because she'd read in the *Independent* about the fundraising evening and Rupert's GCSE, which he'd only finally agreed to take because all the papers claimed he'd never pass. Janna had been tempted to drop him a line and ask him if he'd like a place at Larks. That would solve any woman-teacher recruitment problem.

Throughout the summer, her thoughts had flickered too often to Emlyn. She was so grateful to him for helping sort out Feral that she called him to say the Welsh National Opera were doing *Turandot* at the Bristol Hippodrome. If she got two tickets, would he like to come?

'And I'll buy you dinner afterwards.'

'I can't, lovely; I've got a lot on.'

And Janna felt snubbed.

166

'When I suggested another night,' she told Lily, 'he said he was going to see his mother. He hasn't flown anywhere to see Oriana this summer. Do you think'—Janna loathed the thought—'he's got someone else?'

Lily shook her head.

'I'm sure he's still crazy about Oriana and thinks that somehow, if he's faithful, God will reward him.'

'How complicated,' sighed Janna. 'What's she like?'

'Bit chilly and critical. Ambitious like her father, but she lacks Hengist's warmth and *joie de vivre*.'

87

Hengist was full of joy as he changed for dinner at St Matthew's, his old Cambridge college. He and Sally had had such a magic evening last night, listening to Mahler Three at the Proms and watching a rainbow soaring out of the turning trees, which after rain were all glittering gold in the setting sunlight. They had then rushed up to bed and made such warm, passionate love that they had forgotten their mobiles, lying like lovers side by side on the terrace table, both still working perfectly in the morning, despite a further shower of rain—like our marriage, thought Hengist.

He was still battling not to be too triumphalist over Bagley's leap in the league tables; they were only a place below Fleetley. What matter if, to Alex's fury, St Jimmy's were only five places behind Bagley?

Dear Theo had, once again, got everyone through everything. He must put him forward for a Teaching Award, it would so annoy Alex.

The evening at St Matthew's was all Hengist could have wished for: exquisite food and wine and, although he loved women, as a man who had always charmed his own sex, he found there was something so wonderfully uncorseted about an all alpha-male evening. He loved keeping the table in a roar. He adored the wheeling and dealing, the superior gossip, learning of a brilliant undergraduate who, after he came down, might like to spend a year or ten teaching at Bagley, and dropping in turn hints about a brilliant Bagley boy.

'We plucked him out of the state system and a children's home. Theo's been coaching him.'

There was a lot of chuntering about admissions tutors being forced to accept lower grades from poorer students and a great deal of laughter over Rupert Campbell-Black's GCSE.

'You know him well, Hengist.'

'Love him—but he'd rather die than fail.'

'His son is a rare pianist, I never thought the Grieg could reduce me to tears.'

Over the port, people started table-hopping and the Master drew Hengist into a window seat, and in a voice as soft as the bloom on the black grapes asked him if he'd be interested in Fleetley.

'Hatchet Hawkley's retiring in two thousand and five.'

'The end of a great era,' said Hengist lightly.

'May we put your name forward, Hengist?'

Hengist looked at the wise, knowing face:

'I don't know how delighted Hatchet would be. I used to be one of his junior masters . . . Our son Mungo . . .'

Hengist didn't add that his passionate affaire with Hatchet's wife, Pippa, had only been discovered by Hatchet after her death.

'I know you have painful memories,' said the Master.

'Sally more.' Through the dusk Hengist could see the first yellow leaves falling on yellowing lawns.

'Hatchet has always been laid back about recruitment,' urged the Master, 'you could raise it to new heights.'

'I'll think about it very seriously,' said Hengist with that smile that could melt icebergs.

After a college restoration meeting the next morning, followed by a light, excellent lunch and a trip to buy a lovely oil of a greyhound for Sally, Hengist was in celebratory mood, and picked up his mobile:

'Darling, I'll be with you around eight and don't wear any knickers.'

As he left, he noticed a mower cutting to pieces any fairy rings on the college lawn.

* * *

In Hamburg, negotiating the building of a hypermarket, Randal Stancombe rang Ruth Walton between meetings. Their relationship had recently suffered a setback. Lorraine, his estranged wife, had not been amused when reports on Randal, goading Rupert into taking a GCSE, had referred to Ruth as 'the utterly gorgeous new love of his life'. Nor had Milly; outraged at being banned from seeing Graffi, she had promptly accused Randal of groping her. Ruth had staunchly dismissed this as fantasy on Milly's part, but did suggest it might be better if she and Randal cooled it until next week, when Milly was safely back at Bagley.

Randal now rang in the hope that the coast might be clear. Sadly it wasn't.

'We've got to do Milly's trunk. She's put on seven pounds in the holidays, most of it round the bust.'

Like her mother, thought Stancombe. He must keep his hands off Milly.

'And I've got a Bagley's governors' meeting early

evening. After that Milly and I are getting a takeaway; she says we never talk these days.' Ruth added more hot water to a jacuzzi as big as the Bagley lake. 'But once term starts, I'm all yours.'

'What a lovely "all",' purred Stancombe.

Ten minutes later, racked with lust, he decided to kill the meeting and fly home for the night. He bought Milly a bottle of Obsession at the hotel shop and he would sweep her and Ruth out to the La Perdrix d'Or. Somehow he must persuade Ruth to marry him. To hell with Lorraine taking him to the cleaners; he could afford it. Ruth made him feel like a god in and out of bed and after all the surgery he'd paid for, he felt he owned most of her anyway.

As he let himself into the Cavendish Plaza flat he allowed her to live in for nothing, he was touched at first to find candles on a table. Ruth, like the good mother she was, was taking her bonding session with Milly very seriously. Two bottles of his Krug, lobster and strawberries in the fridge were pushing it a bit, as was the Château d'Yquem. There was even a rocket and asparagus salad and, most caring of all, home-made mayonnaise.

On the triple bed, on the other hand, was a Janet Reger carrier bag with a suspender belt, tutu and negligee spilling out, too good even for Milly's trunk, and sweet-scented roses and lilies everywhere.

Stancombe flicked on the machine. The deep, lazy, patrician tones were unmistakable.

'Darling, I'll be with you around eight and don't wear any knickers.'

Clearly this governors' meeting was only for two people. Quivering with clumsy rage, Stancombe

171

removed flowers, food, bottles, underwear—all Ruth's seduction kit—from the flat. He wanted to kill them both so badly, he nearly ran his Ferrari into the Casey Andrews sculpture adorning the exit to Cavendish Plaza. The bastard, the bitch, the bitch, the bastard. His brain was a red fuzz. He'd cancel the Stancombe block at Bagley, but it was already a quarter up, which was more than he was. Desperate for a pretty shoulder to cry on, he drove straight round to Janna's.

*   *   *

Janna had been anticipating a quiet evening. She was delighted to see Lily off on a date with the Brigadier, which would include watching a recording of *Buffers*. Emlyn had swept Feral off to see a Welsh rugby sports doctor about his ankle and spend the night with Emlyn's mother in Wales.

The birds in Janna's garden had stopped singing, too exhausted by caring for their young at the end of the summer holidays. She had just opened a tin of Pedigree Chum for Partner when she heard a car outside.

At first, when she saw the bottles of Krug in Randal's hand, she thought he'd come to exact payment in kind for financing the rebuilding of Appletree. When he plonked them on the kitchen table, along with a bottle of Château d'Yquem and a carrier bag spilling over with pink underwear, she asked him if he'd won the lottery.

She was just hastily washing Pedigree Chum off her hands, when he returned with armfuls of flowers and a carrier bag containing two lobsters, strawberries and a bowl of mayonnaise and told

172

her to put them and the Krug in the fridge.

'How lovely,' squeaked Janna. 'Would you like some of your own drink, or shall I put these in water first?'

Then she noticed Stancombe was wearing a suit and tie, as though he'd just come from the office, that he was shuddering and there was a green tinge to his permatan.

'Whatever's the matter?'

Stancombe slumped down at the kitchen table and started to cry.

'Oh, my poor love.' Running round, Janna put her arms round him. 'Is it Jade? What's happened?'

'Ruth,' sobbed Stancombe.

'Oh my God, is she OK?'

'She's OK, the fucking bitch. She's seeing someone else.'

'Are you sure? She always seems mad about you!'

Ashamed of breaking down, Stancombe blew his nose on a piece of kitchen roll and proceeded to pace up and down the tiny kitchen like a tiger penned in a travelling crate.

Janna took down a vase and as the roses were beginning to droop, found a rolling pin to bash the stems.

'God I loved her, the bitch,' said Stancombe despairingly.

'She was just probably being friendly with whoever.'

'Like hell. I decided to surprise her and she had dinner prepared and my flat decked out for your friend Hengist.'

'Ouch!' The rolling pin crushing her fingers and the rose thorn plunging into her thumb were

173

nothing to the pain. 'Hengist? It can't be. He and Sally . . .'

'Fucking hypocrite. "My darling Sally", indeed.'

'How long's it been going on?' asked Janna numbly.

'Dunno. A bit—he left a message on her machine telling her not to wear any panties.'

Ouch, thought Janna. Why can't men get a new script?

'He's always treated me like shit,' went on Stancombe, getting the Krug out of the fridge. 'No wonder he wouldn't make me a governor—interrupt their little footsy footsy under the boardroom table. It's the lies I hate, pretending Milly needed some quality time with her mother, when she only wants to be shagged by Mr B-T.'

They went outside and Stancombe and (mostly) Janna drank the first bottle of Krug. Janna had the sprinkler on, defying the hosepipe ban, and kept drenching herself as she moved it round the parched lawn, or leapt up to liberate a Japanese anemone or late delphinium bent double by bindweed. Occasionally an apple thudded to the ground.

Partner, sensing her desolation, stayed very close as Stancombe ranted on and on about expensive trips, surgery, designer clothes for both Ruth and Milly and Milly's school fees.

'Ruth'll be begging for a place at Larks. She won't be able to afford Bagley any more.'

In the middle, Janna rushed next door to Lily's to feed the General and found, instead of cat food, she had emptied a tin of pineapple chunks into his bowl. On her return with the second bottle of Krug, Stancombe was still cataloguing grievances.

'And I'm getting those emeralds back. I really loved Ruth.'

And I really, really loved Hengist, thought Janna. In the dark Stancombe couldn't see the tears pouring down her cheeks.

'I'm so sorry,' she muttered. 'Shall we open this?'

'I've got a better idea.' Seizing her hand, Stancombe dragged her upstairs. 'Nice little property, this.'

' "What gat ye to your dinner, Lord Randal, my son?" ' cried Janna wildly. ' "Make my bed soon, For I'm weary wi' hunting and fain wald lie down." '

'Say again?' asked Stancombe.

'Only an old lay—rather like me,' muttered Janna. Was she going mad? Aware what a pathetic figure she must cut, compared with radiant, bosomy Ruth, she dawdled over undressing, tripping as she tried to escape from her knickers. Stancombe, by comparison, was resplendent, far sleeker than Hengist.

'Why should she cheat on me?' He flexed his muscles in the mirror, then added curtly: 'Put on her underwear.'

'It won't fit.'

Janna's much smaller breasts went straight through the cut-outs for nipples of Ruth's pink lace bra. To stay up, the suspender belt had to be tied behind. The black fishnet hold-ups had to be folded over like long socks.

'God. She knew how to please men,' groaned Stancombe. As he lay back on ivory satin sheets bought to please Hengist, his cock was almost a kingpost supporting the beam. Without any foreplay, Janna was dry as the fields outside and

175

screamed as he tried to force his way in.

'Get that fucking dog out,' yelled Stancombe as Partner rushed yapping to the rescue.

Terrified he might mistake Stancombe's cock for a particularly splendid stick, Janna shoved Partner outside and cautiously rejoined Stancombe on the bed, wondering what to do next. Stancombe had no doubts. Waving his penis like a torch, he said:

'Suck it, you bitch, it won't suck itself.'

So Janna went down on him, hands going like pistons, licking, sucking, flickering, to an accompaniment of whining and scratching from an incensed and banished Partner. Thinking of Mrs Walton's leisurely expertise as she despatched Hengist to heaven, Janna gave a despairing sob.

'Keep going, darling.' Stancombe's hand clutched the back of her head. 'Keep going. Aaah.' And he shot into her mouth.

Stancombe was showered and dressed in five minutes. On the way out he said:

'Sorry. I dumped on you in every way.'

Seeing the misery on his face, she said:

'I'm sure she'll come back.'

'No one cheats on Randal Stancombe.' And he was gone.

Janna felt dirty and utterly desolate. Unable to stop crying, she gulped down the second bottle of Krug to take away the taste of Stancombe.

'Forgo your dream, poor fool of love.'

The pain was so excruciating, she couldn't go on.

Ripping some October pages out of her diary, much aided by Chateau d'Yquem, she settled down to write a suicide note. Lily was away; no one would find her until it was too late.

'My heart has been utterly broken by Hengist

176

Brett-Taylor,' she began. 'My life is no longer worth living.'

When she'd finished, she couldn't find the bottle of paracetamol. As she tried to climb upstairs to look for it, she fell in a crumpled heap on the bottom step and passed out.

*   *   *

Driving back from Wales early next morning, marvelling at the white biblical rays of sunlight falling through the thinning tree ceiling, Emlyn fretted that he'd snubbed Janna over the Welsh National Opera and *Turandot*. He was so fond of her and in such a muddle about Oriana. He'd almost sensed Oriana's relief when he'd announced he wouldn't be flying out to see her this summer, but it had in no way diminished his longing. Lily, the Brigadier and Sally kept encouraging him to take Janna out. But although he wanted her friendship and her body, he knew if Oriana walked through the door, he'd be as hopelessly hooked as ever, so his muddle was unsorted.

The trip to Wales had at least been a success; the Welsh expert on rugby injuries said Feral's ankle needed only rest. Emlyn's mother had spoilt them both rotten. As he'd just dropped Feral off to visit his brothers and sisters in the next village, Emlyn decided to call on Janna.

Partner was ecstatic to see him and promptly led him to his mistress, who had somehow got herself on to the sitting-room sofa. As she was still asleep (and, he noticed, wearing some very saucy underwear beneath her dressing gown), Emlyn

177

wandered off to the kitchen, taking in the empty bottles, the flowers, the fridge door open, the lobsters inside and blood from Janna's rose-pricked fingers everywhere.

'I wish you could talk, boyo,' he told Partner as he fed him and filled up his water bowl.

Then he picked up an envelope on which was scrawled: 'To whom it may concern—no one probably'.

Inside was Janna's suicide note, scrawled on pages from Yom Kippur to Halloween. Whistling as he read it, Emlyn felt amazement, sadness and fury. Bastard Hengist, bastard Stancombe.

Having fixed himself a cup of very sweet black coffee and a plate of lobster and home-made mayonnaise, he proceeded to mark the suicide note: F for grammar—'two split infinitives and tenses all to pieces'; G for spelling; U for handwriting—'almost indecipherable towards the end'; C for imagination; E for narrative skill—'confused and repetitive'; D for vocabulary—'somewhat repetitive'. Only for melodrama did he award her A star.

Janna came round at midday to find Emlyn polishing off the strawberries.

'How long has Hengist been shagging you?'

'Don't be ridiculous.' Then, slowly registering the suicide note in his hand: 'About a year and a bit.'

'And Stancombe?'

'Oh, not at all, at all.'

Again Emlyn waved the note.

'Well, maybe last night.' Janna frowned, trying to remember. 'Only to stop the pain.'

'Which must be even worse now judging by the booze you've shipped.'

When she reread the suicide note, complete with Emlyn's marking, Janna started to giggle helplessly.

'You shouldn't make horrible jokes when my heart is broken. Why do I get so hurt?'

'Shouldn't sleep with married men.' Emlyn handed her a glass of Alka-Seltzer. 'If they cheat on their wives, they'll cheat on you.'

'According to this, I didn't sleep with Stancombe.' Janna shuddered.

Emlyn had caught the sun yesterday, his face was tawny brown rather than ruddy, but the expression on it was unreadable. Janna longed to collapse sobbing into his arms. She put a cushion over her face. 'I can't go on. I love Hengist so much.'

'Don't be wet,' said Emlyn briskly, 'you've got forty kids to get through GCSEs. Mrs Walton's the one in trouble. Who's going to bankroll her now? Hengist certainly won't leave Sally.'

'You won't tell anyone about Hengist and me?' pleaded Janna. 'Stancombe hasn't a clue'—she shivered—'but he's out to bury Hengist.'

'Ruthless in both senses of the word,' sighed Emlyn.

*　　　*　　　*

Hengist was in fact extremely twitchy. Not since David Hawkley went through the effects of his late wife Pippa had he been caught out. At first he and Ruth thought the flat had been burgled, then they saw a copy of the Hamburg evening paper. Hengist had made himself scarce. Only later, after Randal had come round and had it out with her, did Ruth ring him at home in hysterics. Sally, thankfully, was

179

staying with her mother.

'Randal heard the message about me not wearing knickers'—Hengist went cold—'and he's keeping the tape as evidence. He didn't beat me up, but he's chucking me out in the morning and he's stopped all my credit cards and taken back the Merc.'

'God, I'm sorry.'

'It's all your fault,' screamed Ruth. 'Where am I going to live and what about the school fees? You'll have to give Milly a bursary.'

As Milly was definitely C/D borderline, Alex wouldn't be at all amused. Oh dear, how rash he'd been.

'Where did Stancombe go when he found out?'

'Straight round to Janna Curtis.' Then, bitchily: 'You're always saying how good she is with difficult children.'

'Christ.' Hengist had gone even colder. 'What did she say?'

'Evidently they talked for hours, and probably ended up in bed. What the hell am I going to do—sue him for palimony?'

Hengist even in extremis couldn't resist a joke.

'You could get a flat in the catchment area of St Jimmy's. Everybody's doing it for A levels, then the universities couldn't discriminate against Milly for being at a public school.'

'Oh, for Christ's sake, be serious. There's no way Milly's going to a state school. My life is ruined.'

So will mine be if the news reaches Sally, thought Hengist.

In the middle of Friday afternoon, more flowers arrived at Jubilee Cottage. For a moment Janna's heart leapt, hoping that they might be Hengist

180

apologizing, but the card said, 'Thank you for listening, Randal Stancombe'.

Stancombe had already decided to make a play for Anthea Belvedon. It would infuriate Ruth, who disliked her intensely, and it would mean access at last to Little Dora.

88

Hengist did not officially announce that he would be leaving Bagley at the end of summer 2005, because neither the job as Jupiter's Minister of Education nor as head of Fleetley had been firmed up. But from the start of the autumn term 2003 he began dropping hints, setting in train a hunt to find his successor, who must be both a giant and a genius at recruitment. The procedure was to appoint someone at the end of the penultimate year of the departing head, which in Hengist's case would be summer 2004. A small sub-committee of governors would be elected to look for a new head.

Alex Bruce, already hell-bent on getting the job, was consequently even more determined to improve his own house's results by chucking out potential failures like Xavier Campbell-Black. Poppet was already meddling in the leadership struggle by trying to get herself elected to the sub-committee and urging it to monitor applicants to maintain a gender balance. She then encouraged Joan Johnson to put herself forward as a suitable candidate, to which Hengist exploded that after his predecessor, Sabine Bottomley, he wasn't having 'another bloody dyke at the helm'.

A shocked Poppet reproached Hengist for homophobia.

She's probably right, reflected Hengist ruefully.

He had never stopped regretting that he had passed up Artie Deverell as deputy head in favour of the robotic Alex. He had done this not just because he'd wanted Alex to take over all the tasks he detested, but because he'd felt that having a self-confessed homosexual in the job might deter parents. He had been quite wrong. The parents adored Artie, who in his sweetness had never once reproached Hengist for such a betrayal.

Now Hengist was paying for it. Alex, the tortoise to his hare, was slowly imposing his stranglehold. Last term Alex had tried to sack Rufus because missing coursework had been discovered by a cleaner under his bed. Now, on the first Friday of term, the school photograph was being taken and Alex in a frenzy of bossiness was making sure everyone was wearing correct uniform, their hair was brushed and their heights similar. A diversion had been created by Dicky Belvedon, one of the smallest boys in the school; in a desperate attempt to make himself look taller, he had coaxed his hair upwards with pineapple gel, which on a warm, windless September afternoon had attracted a swarm of wasps.

It was only after a blushing, mortified Dicky had returned from washing out the gel, and Alex had finally got everyone settled, that Dicky's sister Dora pointed out that all the Upper Fifths taking GCSEs with Mr Graham were missing, including two star pupils: Cosmo and Paris.

The glorious thing about Theo Graham's classes was that he was not only inspiring on his own subject—the ancient world being populated with people he seemed to know intimately—but also easily diverted onto others.

On Wednesday, the Upper Fifth had discussed in what kind of ship Ulysses would have returned to Ithaca. Today, Theo had produced a cutting about Sutton Hoo, where a lot of Anglo-Saxon remains had been unearthed. They'd even dug up an entire eighty-nine-foot-long ship with its warrior captain buried inside it. Another warrior had been found buried with his horse.

'Imagine your father being buried beside Penscombe Peterkin,' mocked Jade.

Not a road Xav wanted to go down. Peterkin had been scratched from the St Leger. He doubted if his father would ever speak to him again.

'Siegfried was carried down the Rhine on a funeral ship,' murmured Cosmo with an evil smile, 'but he was already dead. Black shit no-hopers like Xavier Campbell-Black ought to be buried alive.'

Theo was about to rebuke Cosmo savagely when Alex Bruce burst in, purple with rage:

'You have forgotten the school photograph, Theo, how dare you keep everyone waiting. You were reminded of this yesterday—very black mark indeed.' Then, as the class poured out of the room: 'And why aren't you using the whiteboard?'

Arriving at the last moment as usual, Hengist ran his eyes over the rows. Xavier looked dreadful, covered in spots, narrowed, dark eyes sliding in his squashed flat face. Hengist was off to London this evening, but tomorrow he'd have the poor boy in for a drink.

He also noticed how grey Theo was looking and hoped Alex wasn't bullying him. And there was Dora's twin, Dicky, cringing behind a couple of bruisers from the first fifteen. Pulling Dicky to the front, because his awful mother would raise hell if he weren't in the picture, Hengist took his place in the middle of the front row beside Sally. God, he hoped Stancombe hadn't shopped him to Alex, who would tell Poppet, who would certainly feel it her duty to tell Sally all about Ruth. Hengist felt extremely exposed.

*   *   *

After the utter humiliation of the school photograph, Dicky Belvedon was still curling up with embarrassment on Friday evening. Dicky was so pretty he had even received a Valentine from Tarquin Courtney. At thirteen, his voice was only just beginning to break, he had little pubic hair and it was a nightmare being called Dick and only having a tiny one, particularly with Cosmo Rannaldini poncing around in the showers brandishing a cock a kilometre long.

Dicky had a passion for Bianca Campbell-Black, but appreciated the competition was too stiff. He was confused because he'd had a wet dream about Paris the other night. He also idolized David Beckham and back in February had written a letter to Beckham commiserating with him for being hit by Alex Ferguson's boot. Beckham hadn't replied.

Dicky had been even more devastated than Dora by the death of his father but, unlike Dora, loved his mother. He tried to overlook her deficiencies and prayed for her in chapel:

'Make my mother marry again, but someone very kind and very rich, who likes me and Dora.'

Like Dora, however, Dicky was a pragmatist, and lionhearted. Running his own shop at Bagley, he did a roaring trade in drink and fags. Wearing one of his mother's wigs, he would make sorties into Bagley village, returning in a buckling taxi, which the more louche and lustful house prefects helped him unload.

185

Anthea, noting so many pupils hailing Dicky on Speech Days, was always boasting that her son got on with all ages. Little did she realize most of them were customers. One of Bagley's punishments for bad behaviour was having to run ten or twenty times the two hundred yards down to the boathouse and back. Dicky hid a stash of booze in the boathouse. It kept both vodka and white wine cool.

Because his housemaster Alex Bruce was devoted to Anthea, he tended to leave Dicky alone. Not so Xavier, whom Alex had asked Boffin to spy on and who, that Friday evening, was in an explosive mood, fuelled by fast-diminishing supplies of drink and drugs. How dare Cosmo call him a no-hoper and black shit in front of the class?

It was only a week into term and Xav had run out of money. He couldn't help himself to Rupert's cellar or his cocaine stash any more. He was heavily overdrawn at the bank and had gone back to school in such a rage that he'd forgotten to ask for a top-up. He already owed Dicky Belvedon a hundred pounds from last term. Dicky was too frightened of Xav to press for it, but when Xav came storming into his dormitory after supper that Friday night and demanded a bottle of vodka, Dicky stalled.

'You owe me a hundred.'

'So fucking what? D'you want to make an issue of it?'

Dicky didn't. There was something so mad, Neanderthal and truculent about Xav. Dicky extracted a half-bottle of gin from under his mattress. 'You can have this, but it's the last you're having till you've paid up.'

'We'll see about that.' Xavier lurched off.

Dicky sighed. He'd promised the gin to Amber

186

for a midnight feast. He'd better sneak down to the boathouse and get some more. Unfortunately Mr Fussy and Poppet were in the garden celebrating yet another ghastly brat on the way with a supper party, to which Boffin, as Charisma's boyfriend, had been invited, so Dicky didn't manage to escape until after eleven.

It was very dark; only a sliver of moon was mirrored in the depths of the lake as Dicky ran past. The boathouse formed a covered link between the lake and the river. Boats, which could be pushed out into either, floated in rows: long ones known as eights in which the school eights competed at Henley; Biffo's dinghy; and little rowing boats in which juniors occasionally paddled round the lake and where, under a tarpaulin, Dicky hid his booze.

It was spooky inside, just the slap of the water against the boats' sides and a snatch of distant song from the Junior Common Room.

As Dicky emerged with a bottle of gin under his pyjama top and tweed jacket, three figures emerged from out of the curtains of a willow tree and grabbed him. 'Come here, you little bastard.'

Dicky's blood froze. It was Cosmo.

Earlier in the evening, as part of a fiendish plan, Cosmo had pretended to make friends with Xavier.

'I've got some crack,' he lied. 'It'll take your mind apart. And some Charlie—we'll have a party to make up for calling you "black shit" earlier. I was only joking.'

Xav, who had already demolished the half-bottle of gin or he might have been more suspicious, was absurdly flattered.

'Why don't you get some booze from Dicky

187

Belvedon?' suggested Cosmo.

'He refused me any more earlier,' grumbled Xav, 'but we'll see about that.'

'We certainly will. High time Master Belvedon was done over. He's in your house, Xav, you'll have to lure him out.'

Dicky wasn't in his dormitory and Poppet, Alex, Charisma and Boffin were still squawking away singing madrigals, so Xav had crept out of the house again and he, Cosmo and Lubemir, after a line, had walked in the direction of the boathouse. Meeting Dicky creeping back along the edge of the lake, they had relieved him of his bottle.

'We've other plans for you,' said Cosmo softly. 'We're going to stage your funeral and send you down the river, Dicky.'

'No, please,' begged Dicky, frightened witless, gibbering with horror as they tugged off his clothes and tied his hands behind his back. 'You can have all my booze, it's stored in the last boat under the tarpaulin.'

'We'll have it anyway,' said Lubemir, roping together Dicky's frantically kicking feet, before tying two scarves tightly over his mouth and his eyes. 'This is to punish you for cheeking Xav earlier and refusing to give him any more credit.'

Xav was confused. None of this was quite right, but he was so flattered to be in league with Lubemir and Cosmo.

'Come on, Dicky, into the boat,' said Cosmo. 'Great warriors were buried in eighty-nine-foot ships. Wimps like you don't need anything that long.'

As he identified seats, slides and shoe fastenings beneath his naked back and felt the boat rocking in the water, Dicky realized he was in one of the eights and wriggled and bucked in terror.

'Look at his tiny little dick,' mocked Cosmo, giving it a vicious tweak. 'You don't deserve to live with a cock that tiny, Little Dick. You're in the river now; off you go.'

Panic-stricken, totally disorientated, drenched in icy sweat, Dicky felt the eight give and sway as it slid into open water and moved away.

'Bon voyage,' murmured Cosmo, 'or rather, farewell.'

Then there was silence.

Dicky tried to scream through the scarf as the cold wet fingers of a weeping willow stroked his bare body. In a few minutes the boat would reach the whirlpools and the weir. With his hands and feet bound, he couldn't swim. He couldn't breathe. I'm going to die, thought Dicky, I mustn't shit myself.

89

Charisma Bruce had fallen in love with Boffin after he caringly held her long mousy hair out of the way whilst she threw up into a flower bed during a teenage party.

Now, humming madrigals, she and Boffin walked hand in hand round the lake.

' "A maid and her wight Come whispering by",' quoted Boffin sententiously. ' "War's annals will cloud into night Ere their story die." '

Charisma was wearing a new floaty dress. Her long face looked rather lovely in the moonlight. She and Boffin could hear the croak of frogs and compared notes on the dissecting of other frogs and on future A levels.

'I enjoy *Cracker*,' confessed Charisma. 'It's popular television, of course, but, like Mother, I'm a people person, so I'm going to take psychiatry as one subject.'

When Boffin kissed her, she tasted of cider and her mother's prune and fig sorbet. As a black cloud, indistinguishable from the ebony trees, edged over the moon, Boffin turned on his torch and in its beam, caught sight of one of the eights in the middle of the lake. On closer inspection, he found it contained a wriggling, moaning, naked body.

Charisma, who'd obtained all her life-saving medals, flung aside her shawl and plunged into the water in her floaty dress, which Boffin, diving after her, found floated up most excitingly. Together they towed the boat to the shore.

'Why, it's Dick Belvedon,' said Boffin as Charisma untied the black scarves and wrapped her own shawl round Dicky's frozen, shuddering body.

'Poor little boy, who could have done this wicked thing?'

Cosmo and Lubemir, lurking inside the weeping willow, made a successful run for it, but Xav, off his face with drink and drugs, tripped over a log and went flying.

'Stop,' cried Charisma. As Xavier, trying to struggle to his feet, was caught in the light of Boffin's torch, she picked up her mobile. 'Dad, Dad, come down to the lake and alert the sick bay, Xavier Campbell-Black's tried to murder Dicky Belvedon.'

*   *   *

Rupert and Taggie were in Provence. As neither of their children were speaking to them, they had decided to get away for the weekend and had just enjoyed a most delicious dinner, for once not cooked by Taggie, and reeled upstairs drunk and happy.

Only when Rupert undressed his wife did he realize quite how much weight she'd lost over the summer, particularly on her breasts, which had not dropped because she'd never fed the babies she'd so desperately longed for. Instead she and Rupert had derived incredible happiness from adopting Xavier and Bianca, aware that both had lost parents, vowing to do everything in the world to make them feel happy and safe.

'We will again,' Rupert had promised Taggie over

dinner. He found it much easier to forgive Xav now because Peterkin was nearly sound.

Rupert had ordered that on no account should they be disturbed, so the manager had to come upstairs and bang on the door.

'Monsieur Campbell-Black, telephone, it's urgent.'

'Fuck off.'

'It might be one of the children,' said Taggie, wriggling out from under him. Rupert reached for the telephone.

'It's Alex Bruce here, I'm afraid I've had to exclude Xavier. He's not only drunk and stoned but, desperate for a fix, he raided Dick Belvedon's store of booze, then tried to murder him.'

'How?'

'Tied him up, stripped him naked and blindfolded him.'

'All by himself?'

'So it would appear, then put him in one of the eights' boats and, telling him it was the river, sent him out on the lake.'

Rupert went cold.

'Probably just a prank. Is Dicky OK?'

'Far from it. He was in the middle of the lake hyperventilating. Luckily Bernard Brooks and our daughter Charisma were out for a midnight stroll and managed to rescue the lad. Trying to escape the scene of his crime, Xavier fell over a log, so drunk he couldn't get up.'

'If he was that drunk, he couldn't have done all that on his own.'

'Our daughter and Bernard saw no one else. Xav's too inebriated to testify; we've locked him in the sick bay and will have to wait for him to sober up.'

'Fifteen-year-olds don't talk. Where the fuck's Hengist?'

'Our Senior Team Leader's away.' Alex nearly added, As usual.

*   *   *

Hengist was incandescent with rage when he got back next morning. Why the hell hadn't Alex tried to sort it out internally? But by this time, Dora, equally furious with Xav for trying to kill her brother, had leaked the entire story to the *Mail on Sunday*.

Alex, who'd longed to kick Xav out for years, was in heaven, particularly over the publicity. At last, he was man of the hour who'd made the tough decision to rout out bullying. His photograph appeared in all the papers alongside G and T Charisma, Dicky's courageous saviour.

The press, who loved any story about Rupert, proceeded to dig up all his past misdemeanours: drinking and drugging and particularly bullying fellow showjumper Jake Lovell on the circuit.

'Chip off the old Campbell-Black', said the headlines, accompanying a particularly evil photograph of Xavier, with monotonous regularity.

Almost the worst part was being in emotional debt to Anthea Belvedon, who was really milking it.

'Thank God Sir Raymond is no longer alaive. My Dicky is such a plucky little fellow, he'll bounce back. Of course I won't hold it against you, Rupert, but I do feel, at the very least, we should take a holistic approach and get round the table for family counselling. I and Dicky wouldn't want Xavier excluded. If we discover what happened and why, Dicky and Xav can achieve closure.'

Xavier, who was utterly mortified when he realized what he'd done, had written a letter of apology to Dicky, but he never shopped Cosmo or Lubemir.

Dicky was allowed a few days at home. On the Monday after his terrible boat trip, his mother, having tucked him up in bed, indulged in a little daydream. If Dicky had passed away, heaven forbid, she would have set up 'Dicky's Fund' and campaigned to stop bullying in schools. She would have fundraised tirelessly and lectured in schools and to Government ministers.

'Lady Belvedon talks such good sense and always looks so lovely.'

She could just imagine herself getting an OBE from the Queen, or, with a huge blow-up of Dicky at his most blue-eyed, blond and adorable behind her, talking to Dermot and Natasha on breakfast television.

Heaven forbid, she wouldn't want darling Dicky to die. Dora was a different matter. Anthea had opened an envelope addressed to Dora from the *Scorpion* containing a cheque for three thousand pounds the other day. Dora could jolly well pay her own school fees in future. Perhaps Rupert could pay them for a bit—to make up to her for not suing. Rupert was so attractive—pity about Taggie.

Anthea's musings were interrupted by the telephone and by such an exciting, intimate voice.

'Lady Belvedon, sorry about little Dick, is he OK? Nasty piece of work that Xav Campbell-Black, takes after his dad more than you would

194

think.'

It was Stancombe. Anthea thought of his handsome, sensual face, his dark devouring eyes and his billions.

'Wondered if we could go out for a meal this week.'

'I must be there for my Dicky, but he should be back at Bagley by Wednesday. What about Wednesday evening?'

'Perfect. To avoid the tabloids, as you're such a high profile lady, why not come to my place?'

Life was full of surprises. Lady Belvedon gave Stancombe the best blow job he'd ever had.

*   *   *

Things were also looking up for Dicky. He received a signed football shirt and a get-well card from David Beckham, who was a friend of Rupert, and if Dicky and a friend would like to watch a Real Madrid match one Saturday, Rupert's helicopter was also at their disposal. Dicky definitely thought he'd live.

Xav, who'd gone into rehab, wasn't sure.

'Perhaps he'll meet Feral's mother in there,' said Bianca wistfully.

Such bad publicity for Rupert and Bagley was not good for Jupiter's New Reform Party and he had the temerity to tell Rupert so.

'You're chairman of his governors, why don't you tell Hengist to spend more time there?' Rupert had howled back and wandered off to Venturer to watch a recording of *Buffers*.

Here he had found his father, as one of this week's panel, downing large whiskies in the green

195

room.

General Broadstairs, the Lord Lieutenant and a governor of Bagley, was also on the programme, which resulted in lots of apoplexy and cries of: 'I couldn't agree less.'

Fortunately the contestants were too old to storm very fast off the set and the Brigadier kept the whole thing under excellent control.

Afterwards Rupert had a drink in the bar with the Brigadier, who said he was thinking of asking Ian Cartwright on the programme, what did Rupert think?

'Bit young, isn't he?'

'Sound tank man, read a few books.' Then, after a pause: 'Might get him to bring young Paris with him. I might bring young Feral too. Fun for them to see the inside of a studio, still fascinated by it myself. Think the two boys miss each other.'

The Brigadier longed to tackle Rupert about calling Feral a 'black bastard'. Feral was still so miserable about Bianca, but Rupert was after all the Brigadier's boss, paying him a splendid salary, so he turned to the more neutral subject of Ian Cartwright and then realized Rupert hadn't taken in a word.

'Sorry about Xavier. Couldn't have been the only one. Dicky's small but he's a wiry little chap. Strong mentally too, refusing to shop anyone, like your Xav won't. Where's Xav now?'

'In rehab. Terrible that one doesn't see what's going on under one's nose. Christ knows what we do with him once he's dried out.'

Rupert's despondency was as unusual as it was touching.

'Why not send him to Larks?' suggested the

Brigadier. 'Janna Curtis is a genius with disturbed children. The classes are going to be tiny, might get some GCSEs.'

'God in heaven,' cried Rupert in horror, 'it'd make him ten times worse.'

'Christian Woodford suggested we send Xav to Larks,' he told Taggie when he got home. 'Of all the bloody silly ideas. "Do you want to finish him off completely?" I said.'

90

Meanwhile, over at Larks, Janna was heroically forcing herself not to betray her heartbreak over Hengist and having a mad scramble to get Appletree ready in time. She was still searching for a maths master when Mike Pitts called and, having asked for a meeting, rolled up clear-skinned, bright-eyed, with no wine and food stains all over his clothes and asked if he could have his old job back.

'I haven't touched a drop for two months. I so much admire what you've done and I'd like to see my students through to the end.'

Janna leapt up and hugged him, realizing how much paunch and flab he'd lost and how his shakes were from nerves rather than booze—and what courage had been needed to approach her.

'Come back immediately. That is the best news in months,' she cried and, glancing at her watch, added, 'It's nearly six, let's have a vast drink to celebrate.' Then, realizing what she'd said, she screamed with horrified laughter. 'Oh God, sorry, at least we can have a cup of tea and a piece of lardy-cake my auntie sent me from Yorkshire.

'I'm desperate for a maths teacher, and I so need your experience,' she went on, pointing to a rough timetable on the wall as she switched on the kettle. 'I hope it'll work. With only forty-odd children, no one need do more than two and a half days a week. So many of your friends are still here: Skunk, Mr Mates, Basket, Cambola, Mags, darling Sophy Belvedon and Gloria. Lily Hamilton, who speaks masses of languages, is helping out Mags. Brigadier Woodford, who's madly in love with Lily and taught at the Staff College, is tackling history. Wally's going to lend a hand in D and T.'

'What about IT?' asked Mike, mouth watering as Janna cut off two big slices of lardy-cake and drenched them in ruby-red plum jam.

'Rowan's very sweetly staying on to teach it and look after me; she also confided that anything was better than staying at home full time looking after Meagan and Scarlet.'

Mike knew the feeling. For a second, like a butterfly on his upper lip, his ebony moustache quivered. What he didn't tell Janna was the utter nightmare of the last months. No one had wanted to employ him, except Poppet for maths coaching which had come to nothing. His wife had never stopped complaining about having him under her feet, as though he were lying permanently on the kitchen floor singing and waving a whisky bottle, which had not been far from the truth until he forced himself on to the wagon. He felt giddy with relief.

'The place looks superb,' he said, looking round. 'I like all these fawns and sand colours—very soothing.'

'We thought we'd give primary colours a miss, make the children feel it was more like a college.' Janna poured out Mike's tea, remembering the two sugars. 'The only exception is the hall which doubles up as a theatre. Graffi's painted the ceiling sky blue, and covered it in stars, suns and angels, who all have faces like Milly Walton.'

Janna winced, thinking of Milly's mother.

'I'm right glad to see you, Mike.'

199

'You've cut your hair,' said Mike looking at her for the first time. 'It—er—suits you.'

'Chally would say it's much neater,' said Janna acidly. 'It takes minutes rather than hours to wash in the morning.'

In a gesture of defiance and despair after she'd found out about Hengist and Ruth, she'd rushed into Larkminster and had her shaggy red mane cut off. Now it fell from the crown in a straight hard fringe to an inch above her eyebrows and to an inch above the collar at the back—typical middle-aged head teacher hair: hideous, or rather headious. But Hengist had gone. It was her farewell to love.

Sally Brett-Taylor had popped in several times, replacing many of the dead saplings with new ones from the Bagley plantation, creating a herb garden with Wally and planting plenty of bulbs, so 'we'll have lots to cheer us up in the Hilary Term.'

Each time she arrived, Janna felt glad she and Hengist were over but it didn't lessen her helpless longing.

With Mike on board, everything seemed to be falling into place. Wally hated the sand colours: too much like Iraq where his son was still serving, but he'd applied them with his usual expertise. Only the blue board outside the school had been left empty so the children could think up their own name. Thank God, now Janna was her own mistress, she could call the shots and start term when she chose—several days after bloody Bagley.

Thank God too for Debbie, who would love working in such a shiny new modern kitchen and who had already been freezing curries and pies.

But just a few days before term began, Debbie

had sidled into Janna's office with a piece of shortbread for Partner, who immediately leapt on to her knee. Then, eyes cast down, she muttered, 'I'm so sorry, but I won't be staying on at Larks after all.'

'Why ever not?'

'I'm going to work for S and C—or more precisely for Ashton Douglas.'

'You can't. He's a monster!'

Debbie's face went dead.

'I take as I find. He's always been very courteous and pleasant. It'll be nice cooking for one gentleman, dinner parties and things.' Her face softened. 'I've loved working for you, Janna, and little Partner.' She stroked his ginger forehead. 'But there's been a lot of sadness and I'm tired. Forty kids and their teachers is a lot with just me, Moll and Marge. Mr Douglas has got such a lovely quiet house in the Close with a nice top floor for me, Wayne and Brad. And he's promised to get them into the choir school, just two minutes away.'

Wow, thought Janna, Ashton has pulled out the stops.

She felt like the final runner in the relay race, who reaches out for the baton and finds it bashing her over the head.

'I can't bear it,' she wailed. 'I don't mean to rubbish Ashton, but he's been no friend to Larks. I'll try and put up your wages.'

'Thanks all the same, but my mind's made up.'

Where do I find Larks's answer to Nigella Lawson in twenty-four hours, thought Janna.

Bloody Debbie to walk out without notice. Even bloodier Ashton. Then she flipped and sent him an email.

'How dare you poach my cook, you conniving shit. Poaching means dropping into boiling water, so don't you dare hurt or bully Debbie, or I'll cut off your goolies. Janna Curtis'.

The bastard, it was the dirtiest trick he could have played. No army could march on unfilled stomachs.

'Who's going to keep back the best bits of chicken for you?' she asked Partner.

It was dark outside; the wind had risen. The trees were doing aerobics, swaying and tossing their branches from side to side. It was too late to start ringing catering agencies. Then she saw lights. Was it Ashton come to fire her? But Partner, having jumped on the sofa to check the window, first wagged his tail then snuffled madly under the door. Definitely not Ashton. Next moment, Emlyn barged in. He was sweating and wearing a dark blue tracksuit.

'Ashton's poached Debbie,' cried Janna.

'I know.' Emlyn waved an email at her. 'You pressed the wrong button.'

'Ashton deserved it, the bastard. He bribed her with a massive salary and places in the choir school for Brad and Wayne, who both sing like crows with laryngitis. Lemme get at that computer.' Plonking herself down, Janna was about to fire off her rocket to the intended target.

'Pack it in,' snapped Emlyn, 'or you'll get sued for libel and suspended before term begins. Debbie'll come back when she realizes what a shit he is. I'm sorry, lovely.' Then he stopped in his tracks. 'Kerist, what have you done to your lovely hair?'

'I know, it's horrible,' said Janna despairingly. 'But as I'm clearly not a sex object any more, I'm

202

putting all my energies into looking like a head.'

Emlyn smiled ruefully. 'You haven't got the big ass and dinner-lady arms to go with it, angel.'

In the past, Janna had been able to soften and hide the effects of her exhaustion behind long hair and a floppy fringe, but the hard new style exposed the dark circles and the added lines, leaving her with the face of a novice monk unsure of his vocation.

Crossing the room, Emlyn took her in his arms, his big hands ruffling the short crop, then coming to rest on an expanse of bare neck, which reminded him agonizingly of Oriana. But the cut that enhanced Oriana's flawless features did nothing for Janna.

'It'll be easier to keep,' she mumbled into his warm, comforting chest. 'Keep men away, I mean. My love life is over.'

'Bollocks. Ask Sally for some Gro-more. It'll be rippling over your shoulders in a month or two. Mind you'—he squinted down at her—'you'll appeal to a completely different market now, and have Artie, Theo, Biffo and Joan after you—even Ashton might start pressing his pale grey suit.'

'Yuk,' shuddered Janna, but she started laughing.

It was nice holding her in his arms, reflected Emlyn. Reluctantly, he released her.

'I must go, I'm supposed to be in a staff meeting. It all looks great.' He admired the big collage Janna had made from photographs of every member of the new year Eleven and their teachers.

'I'll have to remove Debbie's photo,' sighed Janna. 'Where the hell am I going to find another cook, and how do I know if any of the children will turn up on the first day?'

'Turn it into a party,' said Emlyn.

*   *   *

And so Janna did—dispatching every child an invitation to 'A launching party at Appletree House to welcome Larks Year Eleven. Buffet 12.30 onwards, no uniform to be worn.'

On the following Monday, the staff settled in, rejoicing over the labs, the IT suite, the light airy classrooms, the big windows that didn't rattle, and the roof which didn't leak despite a downpour outside. They particularly liked the new staffroom, with its circle of comfortable chairs, coffee percolator, fridge, bar, dishwasher and a television with Sky. Randal had done them proud.

On the Tuesday from midday onwards, the children began to drift in. Making the most of the warm September sunshine, many of the girls showed off bare shoulders and midriffs, their flares sweeping the floor. Both sexes, however, looked edgy. Were they going to be the centre of too much teacher attention, drawn into an exam factory and sweatshop?

'It's weird,' grumbled Johnnie Fowler, 'there's no one above us and no one beneaf us.'

But gradually their fears vanished as they were welcomed by a hug from Janna and a glass of Buck's Fizz from Mags, and Bob Marley over the loudspeaker. Everything was certainly going to be all right as they raced round Appletree, admiring the whiteboards and the big windowed dining room, designed with a bar like a Wild West saloon. They were soon swinging on ropes in the gym and screaming with excitement over the boys' lavatory, where as you peed into a shiny steel trough, turquoise and indigo water gushed out and swept it away.

They also loved the hall, with the sky-blue ceiling full of angels looking like Milly Walton. Most of all, they loved the sand colours and beiges.

'Wicked, wicked, wicked, miss, it don't look like a school any more,' shouted Pearl. 'Oh look, TV's arrived. Anyone want mike-up?'

Partner was in heaven to see all his friends again. Janna was particularly pleased to see Aysha. The Brigadier's great coup had been to make a special journey to see Mr Khan, who only dealt with men and whose own father had been in a Punjab regiment. Invited on the set of *Buffers*, flattered to have his brains picked on the Punjabs' courage when the Japs invaded Burma, Mr Khan had finally agreed to let Aysha return to Larks. She looked so pretty in her apricot-pink headscarf and was knocked out by the new labs.

'Kylie Rose has put on a lot of weight,' whispered Cambola. 'Hope it's not what I'm thinking.'

'This drink is yummy,' said Kitten Meadows, 'can I have another one?'

'If you mop it up with some food,' said Mags, running in with a huge shepherd's pie from the Ghost and Castle. Lily, who'd offered to help out in the kitchen, had made several plum tarts and blackberry and apple crumbles.

'We'll start hellfy eating tomorrow,' said Rocky, who'd already had two showers in the changing rooms.

'Like your hair, miss, it's cool,' said kind Kylie.

'It's gross,' said Pearl. 'You'd better let me cut it next time.'

Outside, where the ground had been levelled for a small pitch with goalposts, Feral was playing football with Graffi, Johnnie, Monster and a frantically yapping Partner.

After everyone had had lunch, Janna called them into the hall for a group photograph and Pearl went round taking the shine off everyone's noses.

'I saw Chally in Tesco's this morning,' moaned Basket. 'She was so unkind.'

Janna put her hands over her ears. 'I don't want to hear it.'

'She said, "None of those no-hopers could ever get a job, that's why they're hanging on at Larks for another year." '

'Bitch. We'll show her,' said Janna, clapping her hands for silence. 'I'd like to thank Brigadier Woodford so much for providing the champagne. Is everyone's glass filled up?'

As Sophy and Gloria rushed round with bottles, Cambola played the theme tune from 'Band of Brothers' on the piano, then, as the music faded away, Janna smiled round.

' "We few, we happy few, we band of brothers",' she said softly. 'Today is for welcome and celebration. The purpose of the year ahead is to get some grades and have a ball. You're students now. This is a college. You may have noticed that Wally hasn't painted anything on the board outside because we thought you could kick off by naming your school yourselves.'

'What about Curtis College?' shouted Pearl.

'What about Cool School?'

'What about Shakespeare School?'

The suggestions came from all sides.

'What about Larkminster High School?' Aysha

206

said.

'Because larks fly high, and we're aiming for the stars.' Graffi pointed up at the sky-blue ceiling. 'Bloody good.'

Everyone cheered.

'Larks High it shall be,' went on Janna. 'We've also decided to dispense with a few rules. What causes most rows in schools?'

'Uniform and short skirts,' shouted Pearl, 'and jewellery.'

'Smoking,' said Johnnie, throwing his cigarette into a fire bucket, 'and chewing gum.'

'Mobiles,' said Kylie, as hers rang. 'Hi, Jack, ay can't talk to you right now.'

Everyone roared with laughter.

'Right,' said Janna, 'in future you can smoke, but not in the classrooms, and as long as you don't stub your fags out on our lovely new floors. Ditto chewing gum. You can use your mobiles as long as you ask permission and go out of the classroom to take calls. You can also wear what clothes you like and any jewellery, but be sensible: no hoop earrings and tie back your hair in the labs.

'You've all seen how beautiful your new building is. So please cover the walls with examples of good work, not graffiti. And as we're a band of brothers, please don't bring in any guns or knives. PC Cuthbert'—loud cheers from the girls—'will be popping in and out. You can also call us by our Christian names if you like.'

'We do, Janna,' yelled Johnnie to more cheers.

'The only sad news,' went on Janna, consulting her notes, 'is that Debbie has left us, so I'm putting up a rota of people who'll help clear away after lunch and load the new dishwasher.'

'Terrific,' interrupted Rocky, 'as long as it's only the women,' which caused a howl of protest from the girls.

'We'd also like two of you to take it in turns to sit in reception doing homework and welcoming guests to the school and offering them tea, coffee or hot chocolate from our wonderful new machine. And please remember to fill up Partner's water bowl.'

'She's very good,' murmured Lily to the Brigadier.

'That's all.' Again Janna smiled round at them. 'Don't hurry home, look around and enjoy yourselves. We may have been called "no-hopers" in the past, but we're going to prove everyone wrong.'

Rocky, who'd been gazing into space, suddenly shouted hoarsely, 'God bless Larks High and all who sail in her. Three cheers for Miss Curtis, I mean Janna.'

'Janna,' shouted everyone, draining empty glasses.

'We few, we crappy few,' sang Graffi happily.

*   *   *

'That went really well,' said Mags as she and Basket loaded up the dishwasher. 'Johnnie must be drunk, I've just seen him doing a high five with Monster.'

'I don't mind doing this today,' Janna said as she shared the last bottle of the champagne between their three glasses, 'but I've got to find a cook. The one I interviewed yesterday was a battleaxe who wanted six hundred pounds a week. Taggie

Campbell-Black's coming to see me at three-thirty, I wonder what she wants.'

91

Pupils were still hanging around gossiping when Taggie arrived. Kylie Rose, recognizing her from *Hello!* and most of the papers and determined to be the hostess with the mostess, rushed forward to welcome her, offering her hot chocolate.

'I'm sure there are some biscuits in the kitchen, Mrs Campbell-Black, I'll bring them in.' She ushered Taggie along the corridor, passing Monster and Johnnie, who, having suspended peace talks, were having a fight, then Pearl, in a micro skirt, smoking and shouting, 'You can fuck off,' into her mobile.

As Taggie entered Janna's office, she was shaking worse than Mike Pitts. She was also so tall, long-legged, huge-eyed and vulnerable, Janna felt they were taking part in some Aesop fable about a red squirrel and a giraffe. Partner immediately curled up on Taggie's knee to make her feel at home.

'What a sweet dog.' Taggie had a surprisingly deep, gruff voice. 'Reminds me of my little mongrel, Gertrude. I've got a lurcher now, who's adorable, but you can't cuddle them on your knee. They fall off. All dogs are best dogs, but Gertrude was my best, best dog. What a lovely office.'

Taggie was rattling now and when Kylie Rose arrived with hot chocolate and some Bourbon biscuits, the cup Taggie took from her rattled in accompaniment like a woodpecker.

'Can I get you a tea, miss, I mean, Janna?' asked Kylie, dying to find out why such a star had descended to earth.

'I'm fine thanks. Shut the door behind you, Kylie. How can I help you?' Janna smiled at Taggie.

'I'm looking for a school for Xav when he comes out of rehab next month.'

Janna nearly fell off her chair.

'He was just going into Year Eleven, like your children,' stammered Taggie, 'and Christian Woodford says you're a genius with d-d-d-difficult, unhappy children.'

Janna brightened. 'He did?'

'You can hardly have failed to notice how Xav was expelled from Bagley. Such a public humiliation for both him and Rupert, who's hardly bullied anyone since he left school. Poor Xav's been so difficult since he went to Bagley, I feel terrible not realizing he was drinking and drugging.'

'Tell me about this summer.'

Feeling horribly disloyal, Taggie did so.

'Marcus and Tabitha have done so well,' she said finally, 'and Bianca just floats through life. Xav feels so hopeless. I was the same, the really thick one, between a brilliant brother and sister. Alex Bruce always thought Xav was stupid and was waiting for an excuse to sack him.'

'We have to prove him wrong then.'

Taggie glanced up, not daring to hope. 'D'you mean . . . ?'

'I certainly do. We'd love to have Xav. He was so kind to Paris on the geography field trip and he worked terribly hard during *Romeo and Juliet*. Aysha, who got on very well with him, is staying on at Larks, so he'll have a buddy to look after him.'

Taggie's stammering ecstatic gratitude was cut

211

short by the telephone. The call was equally short.

'Bugger, bugger, bugger.' Janna switched off the handset. 'A cook I interviewed yesterday has decided not to take the job after all. Our wonderful Debbie has been poached by Ashton Douglas.'

Taggie's silver eyes widened like rain rings in a pond.

'Not that horrible smoothie at the public meeting?'

'That's the one.'

'What does the job involve?' asked Taggie.

'Well, basically, dinner every day for about forty. The staff and lots of the children will only be working a two- or three-day week and many of them just have baguettes or salads and rush off and play in the grounds. I've got a very good temp for September starting tomorrow, but after that . . .' Janna splayed out her fingers in despair.

'I know someone who might be able to help you,' said Taggie, colour suffusing her pale face. 'Before I married Rupert I used to cook for dinner parties. I could give it a try until you found someone.'

Taggie had been so desperately low about herself both as a wife and mother that the sun really came out when Janna jumped to her feet in delight and pumped Taggie's hand.

'I can't think of anything more wonderful for Larks's street cred. The children will be so chuffed to have two Campbell-Blacks here.'

'You don't think it'll embarrass Xav?'

'Some mothers, yes, but not you. And I think, as he'll have just come out of rehab, we'll have to keep an eye on him.'

Taggie loved the new kitchens, 'much more modern than ours at Penscombe'.

'I'd like to start a breakfast club,' said Janna as she walked Taggie to the front door, 'even if it's only orange juice and a bacon sandwich. So many of our children face a wall of indifference and hostility beyond the school gates. Xav will find himself one of the very lucky ones. Some of them lead such deprived lives. This is one of the worst cases,' she whispered as, on cue, bouncing his violet and yellow football along the corridor, came Feral. He had lost his sheen like a conker forgotten in a coat pocket. Poised for flight, he looked at Taggie warily as if awaiting blows.

'Hello, Feral, I'm so sorry about the other evening,' she stammered.

'Xavier's coming to Larks,' said Janna.

'Wicked,' said Feral and skittered past them into the dusk.

*   *   *

Back at Penscombe, Rupert was in a foul temper. Where in hell was Taggie? There was no sign of dinner. He'd taken advantage of her absence to have a look at one of his GCSE set books, which he'd found in the library next door: a first edition of *Pride and Prejudice* with the pages uncut, which he'd scribbled notes all over. He hadn't been able to make head nor tail of *Macbeth* and even less of the Ted Hughes poem he'd tackled yesterday. Why had he ever let himself be bullied into taking this bloody exam? If by some miracle he passed, he wouldn't give a penny to Alex Bruce's science block after the way he'd treated Xav.

Hearing a car and joyous barking as dogs bounded down the stairs and along from the

213

kitchen, and old Bogotá looked up hopefully through his sightless eyes praying it might be Xavier, Rupert shoved *Pride and Prejudice* under a cushion. As Taggie ran in, eyes shining, colour back in her cheeks for the first time in days, he thought she'd never looked prettier. How enticingly that white T-shirt clung to her. Dinner could wait; he took her hand: 'Let's go to bed.'

'Something wonderful happened,' gasped Taggie, 'I must just tell you.'

*   *   *

'Are you out of your mind?' asked Rupert two minutes later, in the soft bitchy voice that always made Taggie want to bolt like a hunted hare. 'Xav is totally unstable, and you're throwing him to the wolves: the flower of the Shakespeare Estate who'll force-feed him glue, steroids and crack cocaine; brutes like Feral Jackson who whip out guns at public meetings, nick cars and beat up old ladies.'

Rupert's icy rage could halt global warming, but Taggie stood her ground.

'Christian Woodford's teaching there, and Lily. They love Feral. You liked Janna. You went out of your way to try and save Larks.'

'For other people's children. You're committing Xav to a crap bunch of teachers and geriatrics, only clinging on because they can't find work anywhere else.'

'Most of them are your age.' Taggie was appalled at her own bitchiness. 'They've just led more stressful lives. Xav's going; I've signed a form.'

'Which you couldn't even read,' said Rupert

214

brutally.

'Janna read it to me. I'm going to give it a try.'

'Shouldn't you have involved Xav "in the decision-making process" as Mrs Bruce would say?'

Taggie lost her temper. 'You haven't tried to find him anywhere. Why are you being so bloody negative?'

'I'm going out.' Rupert snatched up his car keys and stormed off, slamming the door.

Returning at two in the morning, he couldn't have insomnia in the spare room, because he'd given it over to Bianca, so he had to go and freeze in a musty deserted bedroom and let in all the dogs to keep him warm.

'I miss him as much as you,' he mumbled as he hoisted poor blind Bogotá up beside him.

*   *   *

Bianca, next day, was angrier than Rupert.

'I can't tell people you're going to be a cook like Mrs Axford. Who's going to take me to school? You'll have to drop me off at eight in the morning if you're going to get Xav to Larks by eight-thirty. I might as well board, I'm not going to be a latchkey kid.'

Running upstairs, Bianca threw herself down on the pink and lilac quilt and sobbed her heart out. She'd never believed anything could hurt so much. Only this afternoon, as one of the grooms was driving her home, she'd mistaken a rain-soaked trunk halfway down the chestnut avenue for Feral and, leaping out of the car, raced towards him.

If her mother went to Larks, Feral would fall in

215

love with her like everyone else did, she thought despairingly.

*   *   *

What enraged Rupert was the ribbing from Jupiter and Hengist.

'Why don't you take your GCSE at Larks, and make it a full house?' suggested Jupiter. 'Estelle Morris is always ticking off ministers for not sending their children to maintained schools. Think of the brownie points if you sent yourself.'

'Did Taggie say how Janna was?' asked Hengist.

'From that picture in the *Gazette*, she's acquired an Eton crop and completely lost her looks,' said Jupiter.

Hengist missed Janna terribly. He felt so sad and so guilty about her, as if he'd plucked a bunch of wild flowers on a walk and found them dead in the porch three days later because he'd forgotten to put them in water.

216

92

It was arguable who was more terrified, Xav or Taggie, when they arrived at Larks in late September. Xav had just emerged from rehab, utterly mortified he had nearly killed Dicky and written off Rupert's best horse.

Learning his destination, he panicked: 'I can't go to Larks, they'd skin me alive. They'll have read what I did to Dicky. They'll think I'm some pervy Hooray. Have you seen the hulking brutes like Monster Norman and Johnnie Fowler?'

'Give it a try,' pleaded Taggie, 'I so need your help to read recipes and tell me everyone's names.'

'You do?' Xav looked dubious. 'What'll you do if the other guys slag me off?'

'I'll thump them,' said Taggie.

Xav smiled slightly.

'And there's a sweet girl called Aysha looking forward to seeing you.'

Xav's face brightened. 'I thought she'd gone to Searston Abbey.'

'Brigadier Woodford talked her father round.'

Inside, Taggie was quailing. What if Xav hadn't stopped drinking? She had been comforted by her father, Declan, who was passionately opposed to private education, particularly boarding schools. 'Xav'll get to know all the local children,' he told Rupert.

'Hardly, at thirty miles away,' said Rupert sourly.

'We're to roll up after assembly around ten o'clock so it won't be too public,' Taggie reassured Xav. 'And you don't have to bother with uniform, although you've lost so much weight, we'd better go and buy you some jeans.'

'They'll look too new,' grumbled Xav.

*   *   *

There was a row as they were leaving. How could they possibly abandon Bogotá? He'd get so confused.

'He'll have all the other dogs and the stable lads,' begged Taggie.

'But he's used to having you or me.' Xav was nearly hysterical, particularly when Bogotá tried to jump into the car, missed, fell and, tail drooping, unseeing eyes bewildered, was lifted back into the house.

'Poor old boy,' said Rupert, who'd been deliberately keeping his distance, 'abandoned like everyone else.'

More frightened of his father's icy disapproval, Xav shot into the car. God he could use a drink, or a line. How could he possibly slide unobtrusively into Larks with Taggie in tow, looking utterly gorgeous in a pale pink polo shirt and black jeans?

Dora, who had not forgiven Xav, had also been at work and they arrived to find the school gates swarming with press and television cameras.

Xav grabbed the door handle. 'I'm going home.'

'We can't let Janna down.'

A blond woman thrust her tape recorder through the window. 'Why are you sending Xav to Larks?'

'I've heard wonderful things about it,' stammered Taggie.

'Oh, come on,' said a repulsively familiar toad face with olive-green teeth: Col Peters had turned up in person. 'Larks has just been closed down.'

'Janna Curtis has very kindly offered Xav a place. He's into his second year's GSE'—mumbled Taggie, who could never master initials. 'GECS course. Xav knows a lot of the children and the staff.'

'After the way Xav nearly totalled Dicky Belvedon, he won't have any difficulty holding his own,' sneered Col.

'Is Rupert going to take his GCSE at Larks?' asked a man from the BBC.

'Find his own intellectual level if he did,' quipped Col.

'And Rupert knows all about bullying, doesn't he, Taggie?' The crowd of press were making it impossible for Taggie to push through. Out of the corner of her eye, she could see Wally and PC Cuthbert belting down the drive, but Xav was too quick for them. Leaping out of the car, he grabbed Col's lapels.

'You're one to talk when it comes to bullying,' he yelled. 'Leave my mother alone, you great asshole.'

To his amazement, he was then given a round of applause by the rest of the press.

Next moment, PC Cuthbert had moved in:

'That's enough. Morning, Mrs Campbell-Black, morning, Xav.' He directed them to the car park, then on to reception, where a huge banner said: 'Welcome to Larks High, Taggie and Xavier'.

Cambola played 'The Campbell-Blacks are coming, hurrah, hurrah' on her trumpet, and Kylie stepped forward and presented a bunch of orange freesias to Taggie to a chorus of wolf whistles. No one seemed to be at lessons. Janna came out and hugged them both.

'That your sister, Xav?' shouted Johnnie.

'We're doing media studies, Xav,' giggled Kitten, 'and we just sit round reading the tabloids and about you and your farver all day.'

'Thank goodness you're here, Taggie, we're starving,' shouted Graffi. 'And who's going to win the big race this afternoon, Xavier?'

'Probably Hellespont,' muttered Xav, and a score of mobiles were switched on.

The warmth of his and Taggie's reception was due first to their novelty factor in arriving a fortnight after the beginning of term on a beautiful day, and secondly because Janna's no-hopers were having the time of their lives. In small classes of half a dozen, they were really blossoming, and the teachers who'd stayed on, her 'Golden Oldies' (except for Sophy, Gloria and Rowan) as Janna called them, were regaining their skills, their confidence, and at last having time to teach and prepare their lessons.

After initial doubts about the Brigadier—'He looks old enough to have been in the First World War,' grumbled Johnnie Fowler—both sexes had been utterly captivated by his lessons, playing war games all over the park, moving pepper pots round polished tables.

An additional advantage was an excellent press, except from the *Gazette*, on Xavier's first day, with several references to his challenging Col Peters for cheeking his mother. His street cred rose even higher when Hellespont won by five lengths.

Xav arrived a scarred, angry, screwed-up ex-junkie, terrified he was going to be beaten up for being posh, thick and black. Instead, he found he was brighter and further ahead in most subjects, particularly in Spanish.

Gradually, as the acceptance of the other children won him over, he began, as Janna had predicted, to appreciate the horror of so many of their lives.

It was Taggie who, because people talked to her, learnt that Johnnie Fowler supported the BNP because his mother had been nearly beaten to death by a black lover and that Monster's dad had arrived last weekend after an absence of five years and left again after a blazing drunken row. Feral's mother had also vanished like smoke, but any moment she and Uncle Harley might roll up and ruin everything. Feral was getting on all right with the Brigadier. His brother and sisters were thriving with the foster parents, but kept escaping to the amusement arcades in Larkminster. Feral had bought the two eldest mobiles, so he could keep track of them, but they kept running up bills. All this Taggie explained to Xav.

Rocky, who was madly in love with Taggie, was building a dog kennel for Bogotá in D and T.

Fearful fights still broke out, particularly between the boys who were so in need of a father figure. Christian Woodford was much admired but a bit old, as were Skunk, Pittsy and Mr Mates. Janna thought longingly of Emlyn, who instantly diffused rows whenever he appeared.

For the first time, Xav found himself looking forward to PE with the glamorous Gloria. He could now get into size 32 trousers; his spots had gone; his hawk-like South American-Indian features were emerging, and suddenly he discovered he was attractive to girls. Pearl and Kitten were both giving him the eye, but Xav still only had eyes for Aysha. Sad, beautiful and timid as the deer that sometimes invaded his father's woods, she was working on her first science module, which had to be finished by Christmas.

'Ask her out,' urged Feral.

'Her dad wouldn't let me near her,' sighed Xav.

Feral knew the feeling. Bianca was boarding at Bagley now and it crucified him to think of her at the mercy of Cosmo, Anatole and the predators of the lower and upper sixths.

During Ramadan, on top of all her school work and helping out at home, Aysha was expected to fast from sunrise to sunset. One afternoon she fainted in the corridor. Xav, who found her, was demented. As he loosened her headscarf and her top button, he couldn't resist kissing her pale lips. Aysha had fluttered open her lashes, smiled as if she'd gone to Mecca, then realized this was earth, cried out in terror, staggered to her feet and fled.

Another of Xav's momentous encounters was with Mike Pitts. Returning to Mike's classroom to collect some forgotten maths homework, Xav found Mike about to take a slug of whisky from a bottle. He had had a gruelling afternoon, with Monster and Johnnie refusing to understand quadratic equations. Xav took a deep breath.

'If you're anything like me, sir, you don't really want to drink that.'

Mike had nearly jumped through the roof, but he lowered the bottle.

'Shall I take it, sir?' Xav felt an awful prig as he emptied it out of the window. 'I'm desperate for a drink whenever I get stressed,' he confessed, 'but if I can somehow get over the moment . . .'

'Thank you.' Mike wanted to beg Xav not to tell

anyone. 'Shall we make a pact? If you feel like having a drink, you call me.'

'And if you feel like it,' said Xav, 'you call me—any hour of the night,' he added gravely.

He could feel the dampness of Mike's hand as they shook on it. Xav told no one, but was gratified that he and Mike exchanged three or four calls a week.

Xav was almost proudest that Taggie's cooking had encouraged all the children to switch to school dinners and of how Taggie enslaved them with her gentleness and sweetness when she started helping them with their food technology GCSE. Part of the coursework was to provide a menu and food for Larkminster Rovers Football Club. Taggie was determined to put in a good word for Feral.

As the weather grew colder, more and more children started rolling up to her breakfast club to eat bacon and eggs or croissants with apple jelly from the Penscombe orchard. In addition they joined an after-school club where they could do their homework, undisturbed by yelling families.

The children also saw Xav with his arm round Taggie's shoulders as he deciphered memos and recipes for her, and told him how lucky he was.

'Christ, I wish I was adopted,' sighed Graffi. 'Paris's foster muvver looks like a horse. Yours is like a gazelle, she's beautiful.' Graffi had done some lovely drawings of Taggie, which Xav would have shown to his father if Rupert had been in a better mood.

Sally Brett-Taylor, who often popped in to tend the garden, always sought Xav out to see how he was and give him the gossip, to which Janna was unable to stop herself listening.

223

Oriana was due home at Christmas for a long stint. Hengist was utterly obsessed with the rugby World Cup.

'If there's any possibility of England reaching the final, he's been asked by Venturer to fly out and cover it. So exciting,' confided Sally. 'He's also been terribly busy writing speeches for Jupiter for the Tory Party conference.'

* * *

Once Larks was up and running, Janna was distracted by a constant stream of visitors. Wendy Wallace wrote a lovely piece for the *Times Educational Supplement*. The BBC in Bristol came over to interview the children and told the viewers how well the experiment was working.

Ashton Douglas was not happy with this publicity, particularly if it established a precedent and failing schools all over the country started clamouring for buildings and funding to enable them to keep going for another year for the sake of a few Year Tens.

* * *

Meanwhile Rupert was keeping his distance. He'd enjoyed *The Mayor of Casterbridge*, and in his present mood, was very tempted to auction Taggie at Sotheby's. He'd struggled to the end of act one of *Macbeth*. He only thawed fractionally when Taggie brought him a bottle of Jack Daniel's and a foot of Toblerone with her first pay packet. He yawned like Jonah's whale when Xav and Taggie gossiped about Larks.

'Is Janna interviewing cooks? I thought this was a temporary job?'

'She's trying, but she's got so much to do,' mumbled Taggie, who also had so much to do and was as distressed by Rupert's rage as by Bianca's refusal to come home at weekends.

Bianca, who was too proud to tell her parents how much she loathed boarding, was also furious Xav was having such a good time.

'He gets away at four and often doesn't have homework even in the subjects he's taking. I have to work until six o'clock and have two hours' homework after that.' And she stormed into Miss Painswick's office to ring Childline.

In the second week of October, when the gutters were filling up with leaves and conkers crashing down, Cosmo, Anatole and Lubemir, armed with a huge bottle of vodka for Janna, rolled up at Larks, uninvited, to see what sort of cock-up Xavier was making of his life.

In the corridor they bumped into Xav himself, who started to shake. Fortunately, he was flanked by Johnnie, Monster, Feral and Graffi.

Any skirmish was averted by Janna coming out of her office and offering the Cosmonaughties a cup of tea and lardy-cake and expressing profound gratitude for the vodka.

The trio returned to Bagley absolutely furious.

Why couldn't they smoke, use their mobiles in class, not wear uniform, call the teachers by their Christian names and have cosy lessons on sofas?

'It's great at Larks,' Anatole admitted to the rest of a madly curious Upper Fifth. 'Xav is doing really vell and getting A stars.'

'Boffin Black,' mocked Cosmo, 'born in a Bogotá

gutter, he's found his own level. How could Mr Fussy have let such a genius slip through his fingers?'

'Oh, cool it, Cosmo,' snapped Lubemir, who was profoundly grateful to Xav for not shopping him over Dicky Belvedon's boat trip. 'Xav looked really good, he's lost so much weight, and Pearl, Feral, Graffi, Kylie and Johnnie—all of them—sent their best to you,' he added.

'That's nice,' said Amber.

'To me?' asked Paris, looking up.

'No, how funny,' drawled Cosmo, 'no one mentioned you at all, not even Janna, who's had the most awful haircut. They've all forgotten you.'

93

Paris was faring patchily at Bagley. Work, particularly in English, Latin and Greek, was miraculous. He had caught up with and overtaken the class. Playing regularly for the third fifteen had given him a rugger bugger swagger and the friendship of Lando, Junior and Jack Waterlane, who all found his help with both homework and coursework invaluable. In turn they protected him from Cosmo and Boffin, who were furious he had so often supplanted them as teacher's pet.

Things were going less happily at home, where Paris kept on drinking Ian's drink, staying out late, and being sullen and uncommunicative when Ian and Patience's friends dropped in.

Ian was already uptight because of a fee-fixing scandal, which had just broken. As a comparatively new bursar, he had received emails and telephone calls from other independent school bursars round the country, and assumed it was standard practice to compare notes on fees. Now two major public schools had turned supergrass and the independents were being accused of forming a cartel and denying parents the chance to seek cheaper options.

Alex Bruce, predictably, had gone into a frenzy of disapproval, demanding total access to Ian's files and accusing him of sharp practice.

As Alizarin Belvedon, Sophy's husband, was working flat out for a major exhibition in New York and London, and Sophy was working at least three days a week at Larks, Patience frequently looked after their three-year-old daughter Dulcie, which, as well as the yard, meant a lot of work. Dulcie, with blonde curls and huge dark blue eyes, was utterly adorable and very self-willed. She adored Paris and, accompanied by Northcliffe, trailed constantly round the house after him, interrupting his homework.

The afternoon Cosmo returned from Larks and taunted Paris that no one had asked after him, Paris had stormed out of the classroom and Lando had run after him, trying to comfort him.

'Don't rise, man, Cosmo's just winding you up because he's jealous. I'll walk back to the Coach House with you, I need to check Barbary. He was lame yesterday, and on the way you can tell me the plot of *The Mayor of Casterbridge*.'

But as they shuffled through a burning fiery furnace of leaves, Paris snapped, 'Look it up in the *Oxford Companion to English Literature*, you idle sod. I'm pissed off doing your donkey work,' and ran ahead into the gloom.

Reaching the yard, he found Patience giving the horses haynets and Dulcie, in pale blue denim dungarees and a blue and white shirt, trying to sweep up straw with a fork. Both called out to Paris, but he belted upstairs and slammed his bedroom door.

How could Janna not ask after him? How could Graffi, Pearl and Feral forget him?

' "I am—yet what I am, none cares or knows",' he quoted bitterly. ' "My friends forsake me like a memory lost." ' Glancing round the room, he flipped.

Whoosh went the fixtures, cards and photographs on the mantelpiece. Whoosh off the shelf by the window went the china Labrador head bookends containing his poetry books; crash went pots of felt tips, marker pens and biros, and piles of files and videos, as he tipped over his work table and upended chairs.

'Fuck, fuck, fucking Cosmo.'

'Pawis, Pawis,' said a voice, accompanied by banging on the door. 'Pawis, let me in.' It was Dulcie.

'Fuck off,' screamed Paris, hurling a stapler on the floor so its innards spilled out.

Dulcie looked round in delight. 'Whatyerdoin', Pawis?'

'Trashing this room, now sod off.'

The radio hit the wall with a sickening crunch. A vase of winter jasmine, picked and arranged by Patience, crashed to the floor.

'Let's play twashing,' screamed an enchanted Dulcie, picking up a video of *Macbeth*.

'No,' yelled Paris as she chucked it against a skirting board, following it with a bust of Homer, which lost its nose.

'All fall down.'

'Not that either,' howled Paris as she grabbed a leather-bound copy of the Greek *Epigrams* given him by Theo, and dropped it in the winter jasmine water, before smashing Paris's alarm clock on the floor.

'Twashing, twashing,' crowed Dulcie, pulling books out of shelves.

Only when she grabbed the snow fountain containing the Eiffel Tower, given him by his mother, did Paris finally come to his senses. Catching it just in time and returning it to the window sill, he burst out laughing, and gathering up Dulcie, tossed her in the air until she screamed with even more delight. It was thus how Patience found them.

'We'd better tidy things up before Grandpa gets home.'

Ian was less amused and rang Theo to ask him over for a drink and to seek advice about Paris.

*   *   *

Putting down the telephone, before taking up his translation of Sophocles, Theo looked out of his study window on to the playing fields and woods of the school he loved so dearly. Maybe he'd last another year? He was in terrible pain, but he must cling on to finish Sophocles and to set Paris on course. One felt the ecstasy of teaching and opening up such a receptive mind half a dozen times only in a career.

Hearing a thud, Theo noticed Hindsight, his vast ginger tom cat, had landed on a table by the window, endangering a bust of Socrates, and in greedy pursuit of a peacock butterfly clinging to one of the brown curtains. Groaning, Theo crossed the room and cupped the butterfly in his hands, pulling down the window handle with his little finger. He hated chucking butterflies out in winter but today was perhaps mild enough for it to survive. He laid it on a wisteria stem. Next moment it had taken off into the dusk. Perhaps he could do the same for Paris.

Ignoring Hindsight's filthy thwarted look, he pressed three emerald-green Anadin Ultra out of their silver wrapping and washed them down with neat whisky from the bottle.

Later, he limped over to the Old Coach House, admiring a huge fox-fur ring round the moon—a presage of storms to come.

He liked Cartwright, who poured a good mahogany whisky. He was a little inflexible for Paris perhaps, but kinder and more down to earth than some silly, sandalled, muesli-munching liberal. Noticing a yellow brick road of Wisdens along the bookshelf, Theo was touched when Ian shyly produced Theo's own translation of *The Bacchae* and asked him to sign it. They then got on to their favourite topic, bitching about Alex Bruce.

'The archives are definitely for the chop,' grumbled Ian. 'What does it matter to Alex if Bagley old boys won six VCs or that one got the Templar Prize for a biography of Auchinleck?'

'He's got an even more sinister plan for reports,' growled Theo. 'A computer program limited to a choice of a hundred and forty different phrases to describe a pupil and his work. Christ, when one considers the infinite riches of the English language. "Think of the time you'll save," said Alex. "You've only got a handful of pupils anyway, Theo Graham, and they'll drift away as the classics lose their relevance." '

' "He loves no plays, As thou dost, Antony," ' sighed Ian, ' "he hears no music." '

'I hear the scratching of new brooms,' shivered Theo, 'scratch, scratch, scratch along floorboard and carpet, sinister as the dry snake scales crawling up the roof in Rikki Tikki Tavi. I'm sure Hengist is going to Fleetley.'

'God, I hope not,' said Ian in horror as he topped up both their glasses. 'We'll all be for the high jump. Hengist is spending too much time away, not

231

even doing anything worthy like fundraising. He must watch his back. D'you think a word with Sally?'

But the door had burst open and in ran Dulcie, wearing a blue dressing gown and mouse slippers.

Ian's angry face softened. 'Come to say goodnight, darling?'

'Let's play twashing,' cried Dulcie, picking up a photograph of her Aunt Emerald and smashing it on the floor, followed by a cranberry red glass bowl, which Ian, once a fine slip, leapt forward and caught.

'That's enough, Dulcie,' he said sharply, as *The Bacchae* flew across the room.

'Twashing,' cried Dulcie, beaming at her grandfather and briskly upending Theo's overflowing ashtray on the carpet, followed by a Staffordshire milkmaid. 'Pawis and I played twashing this afternoon.'

She took a swig of Theo's whisky and spat it out.

'Ugh, poison.'

'Very possibly,' agreed Theo.

After Patience had bustled in and whisked Dulcie off to bed, Ian said, 'Paris's influence, I'm afraid. He's being tricky at the moment.'

'Testing you,' said Theo. 'He's terrified of losing you and the comfort and security you've given him. I'm photostatting a very good poem called "Yearning Difficulties" he wrote this week. Don't let him know I've shown it to you.'

Upstairs, as Patience read *Jemima Puddleduck* to Dulcie, she was aware of Paris stealing down the landing. He loved listening in, particularly when Patience was teaching Dulcie nursery rhymes. He also loved playing with Ian's old train set, showing

Dulcie how to work it with infinite patience because he was enjoying himself so much. It broke Patience's heart that he'd missed out on a childhood.

Pretending they were presents from Dulcie, she'd brought him a teddy bear, a duck for his bath and a CD of nursery rhymes. She'd also rooted out Emerald and Sophy's old copies of *The Just So Stories*, *The Jungle Book* and Hans Andersen.

Dora insisted Paris was like Little Kay in *The Snow Queen*. 'His heart must be melted before it freezes over completely.'

Paris had filled out from rugby, was nearly six foot and so beautiful, Patience couldn't take her eyes off him. She felt so sorry for poor besotted Dora, who put sweets in his locker, and who was having a horrid time at home.

Randal Stancombe was in hot pursuit of her mother, piling on the presents, inviting Anthea on thrilling trips. He was clearly very taken. Anthea was pretty, clear-sighted, excellent at running a home—Ruth had been a slut and very lazy—and wonderful in bed.

Anthea, in her turn, was captivated by Randal's money, but found him difficult to control; and she'd rather wait until he got his K, so she could move seamlessly from Lady Belvedon to Lady Stancombe. She was touched by the way he wanted to win over her children, but she wished he wouldn't try quite so hard with Dora. So did Dora who, when she was at Foxglove Cottage, slept with Dicky's camel-hair dressing gown buttoned up to her neck and Cadbury, who loathed Stancombe, across her legs.

'I'm going to make myself a chastity belt in D and

T,' she told Bianca.

Anthea had made a huge fuss about Stancombe's birthday one Sunday in late November, giving him a beautiful glass engraved with his initials and buying a card to which she insisted Dicky and Dora added their names.

'I don't ever wish him to return happily,' stormed Dora.

Randal was charmed by his present. Then, having said the only thing he'd rather drink from the glass was Anthea herself, spoilt it all by murmuring that:

'Of course, the most precious gift a woman can give a man is her daughter.'

Anthea had gone bright red.

'Don't make disgusting jokes. Dora hasn't had her first period yet and she's not remotely interested in boys except for that gormless Paris Alvaston.'

While Anthea was cooking his birthday lunch next door, an unrepentant Randal had stroked Dora's cheek.

'I'll have to put you down for a few years, then you'll mature like the finest wine.'

Revolted, Dora had stormed off to tell Paris and Dicky as they queued in the drizzle to go into chapel that evening.

'Randal Stancombe is desiccating our father's bed.'

'And we've got to spend Christmas with that poisonous Jade,' sighed Dicky.

'Jade had the gall to complain to Joan she was a victim of peer abuse because Amber chose to go to the cinema with Milly rather than her,' said Dora scornfully. 'Joan took Jade's side. That woman's getting such a hold on Bagley. She's finally got permission for her all-female window in the chapel. She's chosen Elizabeth Fry, Florence Nightingale and Marie Curie, I ask you!'

'Who's Elizabeth Fry?' asked Dicky.

'She was a penis reformer,' said Dora.

'I wish she would do something about mine,' said Dicky gloomily.

Worst of all for Dora, Cadbury was in jeopardy again. He'd been banished from the kennels for gobbling up all the beagles' food, and was back in the air-freshened, floral-print femininity of Foxglove Cottage with Anthea. 'Mummy forgot to get him any Butcher's Tripe, so she fed him on cat food. No wonder he farted throughout their romantic candlelit dinner, just like the bombardment in Iraq. Any minute you'd expect Oriana Brett-Taylor to pop up announcing Breaking Wind.'

Paris laughed. He loved Dora in this mood.

'Now Mummy's threatening to have him castrated because he growls at Stancombe. She's longing to give him away,' exploded Dora, 'so I must go home again next weekend and sort it. I feel so guilty deserting Bianca. She's too proud to go home and I won't be around to protect her from Cosmo.'

I'd protect her, thought Dicky wistfully.

'Poor Bianca's jealous because Taggie and that murderous brute Xavier are getting on so well with Feral.' Grabbing hymn and prayer books, Dora handed them to Paris and Dicky. 'Bianca loves Feral so much and he never rings or texts her.'

Not by a flicker of expression did Paris betray how interested he was.

235

94

Bianca was indeed miserable. Joan continually hassled her to work harder and she desperately missed Rupert and Taggie and the cosseting at Penscombe. In the past, she had flirted with everyone but escaped in the evenings; now there was nobody to shield her from Jade's bitchiness or Cosmo's lust. So many parents were splitting up. If Taggie and Rupert weren't getting on they might be next. Cruellest of all, Feral had never got in touch.

The following Friday, smelling baked cod which she detested, Bianca decided to skip lunch and wander down the pitches. She had been slightly cheered by an excellent dancing lesson and intimations that she might land the part of Cinderella in the Christmas ballet. Most of the trees were bare now, but the beeches still hung on to a few orange leaves, reminding her of the towering wood behind the house at Penscombe. Feeling the familiar crunch of beech husks beneath her feet, overwhelmed by homesickness, Bianca decided to bury her pride and go home tomorrow. Turning two cartwheels, she started practising dance steps.

Paris, who'd been stalking her like a deer-hunter for days, never revealing his presence, had watched her setting out with that dancer's strut, feet in flat pumps turned out. She was the one everyone wanted: how satisfying to snatch the prize— particularly from Cosmo.

As she reached Badger's Retreat, where smaller

trees were protected by larger ones, leaves were still falling. Laughing, shrieking, dark hair escaping, Bianca bounded about trying to catch them like some rite of autumn. Swinging round to catch a red, wild cherry leaf, Bianca caught sight of Paris.

Smiling, she showed no fear.

'What are you doing?' he asked.

'Every time you catch a leaf, it gives you a happy day.' Reaching out, grabbing a dark brown ash frond, she thrust it into his breast pocket. 'Seven leaves. That'll give you a happy week.'

Paris just stared with those light, utterly focused eyes, exciting and unnerving her, lean jaw moving as he chewed gum.

'My father fell in love with my mother when he saw her racing around catching happy days for him.' Bianca snatched a falling yellow hazel leaf and shoved it in his side pocket. 'Daddy kept all the leaves, but felt he was too old and wicked for Mummy. He'd had billions of women before her, like you've had'—she peeped up at Paris from under a thicket of black lashes—'but Mummy persisted and they've been happy for almost eighteen years—at least they would be if she hadn't taken this stupid job and Daddy wasn't taking this stupid GCSE. So stupid of Feral to say I was out of his league.'

She kicked a red spotted toadstool, did a pas de chat and fell into Paris's arms. Glancing down he saw the despair in her eyes.

'I'm not out of your league, am I?'

'Totally'—Paris spat out his chewing gum—'but I don't care.'

Once he'd kissed her, she was lost. Scrabbling to

remove his school tie, tugging at the short end, she nearly throttled him.

'Lemme do it.' Paris yanked off his own, then hers, then unbuttoned her shirt, pulling her down on a dry, crackling bed of yellow sycamore leaves, black-spotted like leopard skin.

Like both Feral and her father, he had laid so many girls—in the open air, in parks at dusk or on banks in the gardens of care homes—but none as delicately desirable as Bianca as she beamed up at him in ecstasy, her face the same soft shiny umber as the ash frond she had given him.

As he peeled off her tights and knickers, he could smell her body, already hot and excited from dancing and even more so from him.

'D'you really want it?'

'Oh yes, definitely yes.'

Her tiny clitoris was hard as a ball bearing; below lay a buttery sticky cavern, measureless to man and terrifyingly narrow.

'I don't want to hurt you.'

'You won't, you won't.' Then as Paris produced a condom, 'We don't need that, my period's due tomorrow.'

'Better be safe.'

'Well, I'm not going to be sorry.' Unzipping his trousers, she released a cock hard and white as ivory.

'Why isn't it green like one of Mrs Sweetie's courgettes?'

Paris gave a gasp of laughter. 'Shut up.'

'Please, please go on,' begged Bianca, writhing against his lovingly stroking hand as it travelled down her belly, up the insides of her thighs, sliding into her pubes, fingering, stoking, slowly bringing her to ecstasy. 'Oh pleeeeese.'

For a second his cock buckled at the entrance, then straightened.

'Ouch, ouch,' cried Bianca, 'oh bloody ouch.'

Blokes were supposed to recite something boring to stop themselves coming. Paris had been learning the Latin verb *vastare*, to lay waste, but he only reached the future perfect third person singular when Bianca's sleekness and tightness overcame him; three more stabs and it was over.

'I am so sorry,' he muttered.

'Thought you didn't do "sorry".'

Paris slowly opened his eyes to find her laughing up at him.

'I was dying to lose it. Goodbye, virginity.'

Paris wriggled free, falling back on the leaves, ashamed of having come so quickly.

'I'll do it properly next time.' A year ago he'd have said 'proper'.

'When did you get that tattoo?' said Bianca, fingering the Eiffel Tower on his shoulder.

'When I was ten. Saved up my pocket money for a year, sneaked out of the home. Once it was done, nothing they could do.'

Bianca leant up on her elbow, pushing the straight blond hair out of those pale unblinking eyes. 'Do I look like a mature woman of experience?'

'You look beautiful.'

But as the light filtering through the remaining leaves fell on her warm brown skin, her thick dark lashes (such a lovely contrast to her white teeth and the whites of her eyes), Paris was suddenly and agonizingly reminded of Feral, whose great love he had just stolen.

Sitting up, Bianca examined herself.

'I don't seem to be bleeding much. Dora reckons she's ridden such a lot she hasn't got a hymen any more.' Bianca giggled, then squeaked, 'Oh my God, Dora!'

'What about her?' Paris dried Bianca with a handful of leaves.

'She loves you so much.'

'Well, I don't love her. I like her when she's outrageous and funny, but when she hangs around like a kicked spaniel, she does my head in. I don't need a dog, I've got Northcliffe . . .'

He could see the athletics team pounding towards the all-weather track.

'Will your dad horsewhip me?'

'He mustn't know.' Bianca looked aghast. 'I don't want anyone to know—not Feral. Although he probably wouldn't give a stuff. I've just slept with the best-looking guy in the school, and I don't want Jade or Amber scratching my eyes out, or Dora ringing the *News of the World*.'

'Or Cosmo challenging me to a duel,' agreed Paris, tugging on his trousers and buckling the leather belt Dora had given him. ' "Twere profanation of our joys To tell the laity our love." '

'What's that?'

'Some poem.'

'You'll have to help me with my homework, now Dora won't—well, may not want to any more.'

Dora, Bianca reflected, had listened and listened when she'd been miserable about Feral and her mother and boarding. Dora had helped her endlessly with homework, acting out poems so Bianca would remember them. Last week it was one called 'Death the Leveller', and Dora had

240

thrown her riding hat and Bianca's baseball cap down the Boudicca's stairs to illustrate:

Sceptre and crown
Must tumble down,
And in the dust be equal made.

'I feel a pig. What an extraordinary tree'—Bianca patted the trunk—'all writhing together like dancers.'

'Hengist calls it the Family Tree,' said Paris. 'Look, he, Sally and Oriana have carved their initials on the bark, symbolizing a family clinging together against winter and tempest,' he added bitterly. 'Oriana's supposed to be coming home for Christmas, so Emlyn will be happy again.'

'Talking of families,' said Bianca, testing the water, 'I was going to ring Mummy and ask if I could go back to being a day girl.'

'Don't!' snarled Paris, taking her face between his hands, for a second betraying his need for her. 'Just don't.'

'I'm not going to.' Bianca flung her arms round his neck, kissing him, until her heart was beating louder than the pounding footsteps of the athletics team.

'You're my boyfriend now, aren't you, but above all, we mustn't hurt Dora.'

95

Christmas approached. The erection of Stancombe's Science Emporium seemed to be taking for ever. General Bagley and Denmark, their view of the Long Walk impeded, rose out of a sea of mud. Dulcie spent a lot of time with the builders, who brought her a little wheelbarrow so she could help them. Progress, however, was repeatedly held up by the Lower Fourth doing moonies at the builders from the fire escape.

'Rubble, rubble, toil and trouble,' sighed Hengist.

Poppet Bruce, who was pregnant again, said there was no way she would curtsey to the Queen if she opened the emporium.

'I wish Rupert wasn't taking this GCSE,' grumbled Jupiter. 'He's always working and he's getting even more left wing than Mrs Bruce.'

'He's so seriously stuck into *Macbeth*,' warned Hengist, 'he'll knife you in your bed and take over the Tory Party.'

Nothing could dim Hengist's high spirits. The end of term was nigh and so was his darling Oriana, who was due to arrive at Bagley in time for Christmas and stay at least a week.

Janna's end of term had been a great success, with trips to the pantomime and a carol service at the cathedral, where Kylie Rose had sung 'Mary's Boy Child'. On the last day, the food technology candidates helped cook a glorious Christmas lunch, ending up with more carols, mulled wine, mince pies and every boy in the school trying to manoeuvre Taggie under the mistletoe hanging in reception.

Driving home through the twilight, seeing a fuzzy newish moon like a little pilot light, Janna turned on the car radio to find a voice of exceptional beauty singing 'See Amid the Winter Snow' and burst into tears. She'd thrown herself so wholeheartedly into Larks High, she hadn't given herself time to mourn the loss of Larks Comp or of Hengist, or even her sweet mother, whom she always missed most at Christmas. It was probably exhaustion and still not having a man in her life and wild jealousy of Oriana, because Hengist and Emlyn were so excited about her return.

Among her post on the doormat, however, was a letter from Sally. 'Darling Janna, If you're not busy we'd simply love you to join us for Christmas dinner. Oriana's home and we need some bright attractive young to amuse her. Black tie for the chaps so do dress up. So hope you can make it. Love, Sally'.

Hardly pausing to open a tin for Partner, Janna shot next door to find Lily making fudge and salted almonds.

'Sally B-T's asked me to Christmas dinner.'

'Well, that's very nice, you must go.'

'But I was coming to you.'

'Never mind, you can come on Boxing Day. It'll be fascinating for you to meet Oriana.'

Relieved to see Janna, who'd been very near the edge recently, looking ecstatic, no doubt at the prospect of seeing Hengist again, Lily was too kind to say she and Christian had already refused Sally's invitation to Christmas dinner because they didn't want to desert Janna and Feral.

'Sally said dress up.' Janna glanced at herself in

243

Lily's kitchen mirror, hardly able to see her reflection for photographs of General slotted into the frame. At least her fringe covered her eyebrows now, and Rowan had had a whip-round and the staff had bought her a day of pampering at the local health spa. What could she wear to win Hengist back? But she mustn't think like that, it was so kind of Sally to ask her.

'Naughty Dora's given me a Christmas hamper full of pâté, plum cake and some lovely red,' announced Lily. 'Shall we have a glass now? The end-of-term party was fun, wasn't it?'

'Lovely. Amazing how the Golden Oldies have mellowed; Skunk's so loyal to Larks High he even snogged Basket in the store cupboard.'

'The nicest sight was Xav dancing with Aysha,' said Lily, who was rootling around for a corkscrew, 'so happy, both of them. You'll never guess what Christian has got Feral for Christmas: two tickets for an Arsenal match.'

'Lovely,' said Janna, who wasn't listening. 'Do you really think I should go?'

'You will anyway,' said Lily.

Sally had in fact invited Janna because, a week before Christmas, Oriana had rung and dropped the bombshell that she'd be bringing her producer Charlie Delgado with her for Christmas.

Sally couldn't help being thrilled as she asked Alison Cox, their housekeeper, to make up the bed in the spare room. She'd always known that Emlyn wasn't the answer for Oriana—too chippy and the wrong class; things like that grated in the end. Emlyn also seemed to have been seeing a bit of Janna recently, so with any luck he wouldn't be too upset about Charlie Delgado.

What a shame Christian and Lily couldn't join them. Christian, she knew, was anxious to have Oriana as a guest on *Buffers* and was longing to hear about the war in Iraq. It was a tragedy too that Artie Deverell couldn't make it. Artie and Oriana loved each other, and he had such a wonderfully emollient effect on both her and Emlyn and could discourse on any subject. But Artie and Theo had decided they needed some sun and taken off to Greece together. Nor could Ian and Patience, who had both daughters staying, make it, so in the end it would be a cosy family party: Janna and Emlyn, Charlie and Oriana, herself and Hengist.

Sally went to the present drawer and found Charlie some cufflinks, English Fern aftershave (which was liked even by men who regarded scent as sissy), David Hawkley's lovely translation of Catullus in paperback, and a jokey yellow silk tie decorated with pink elephants from Elaine.

Sally had been feeling tired, what with all the presents and parties to organize and over a thousand cards now slotted into the drawing-room books in a huge patchwork of glitter and colour, but the prospect of Charlie Delgado had given her a second wind. Not that she was a snob, but Oriana Delgado had a nice ring to it. Although, knowing Oriana, she'd keep her maiden name.

Emlyn, who'd been told in a very casual way that Oriana was bringing some workmate, was getting increasingly twitchy and poured his heart out to Artie on the eve of his and Theo's trip.

'I don't know what she feels any more. She's always been a workaholic, but in the old days she always found time for me and we had fun together.

Now I see her on TV growing harder and more glittering. She never answers my emails and puts herself out of communication—as though she and her mobile are both switched off. I'm sure she's got someone else.'

'Only Mungo and the desire to compensate for his death. If he'd lived, she could have shown how much in everything she excelled him. What's she like in bed?'

'Like playing Rachmaninov Three on a soundless piano. Pouring out love and emotion to no effect somehow. I teach lovesick schoolboys; I don't want to act like one.'

'Sorry to desert you, dear boy, but Theo needs to get away—he wants to see Attica.'

'For a last time?'

'Probably. Poor Paris. He loves Theo and Theo's so desperate not to abandon him. When are you going to Wales?'

'Tomorrow and driving back on Christmas Day.'

*   *   *

On Christmas morning it started to snow, just a few flakes drifting down; by five o'clock it had settled, but Hengist couldn't. He was playing Charpentier's *Oratorio de Noël*, which had reached the jolly jiggy tune of the shepherds on their way to the stable. The house looked ravishing, filled with crimson roses, flame-red amaryllis and white candles everywhere. Holly and pine branches were banked in corners. The whole house smelled divinely of jasmine, pine, orange zest, beeswax and the heady sweet scent of Sally's indoor hyacinths, waxy white and pink flowers rising out of their

246

mossy earth. In the hall, the blond head of the fairy on the top of the Christmas tree touched the vaulted ceiling.

Hengist and Sally had opened their presents earlier. They had so many, and they didn't want to embarrass Charlie Delgado who would have so few. So many of the cards had congratulated Hengist on his wonderful reporting of the World Cup. He still had a dark tan and had not come down to earth. He had managed to get a signed photograph of Jonny Wilkinson for Dora.

He had already received ten copies of Martin Johnson's autobiography and five copies of Lynne Truss's book on punctuation and a digital camera, on which he had just photographed Elaine in an emerald-green paper hat watching a squirrel raiding the bird table, whose roof was already covered with snow three inches thick.

Newspapers kept ringing up for his reaction to Saddam's arrest—pity, strangely—and for his New Year's resolution. To get stuck into his biography of Thomas and Matthew Arnold, vowed Hengist.

Sally had given him an 1867 first edition of Matthew's poems, which included 'Dover Beach', 'Rugby Chapel' and 'Thyrsis'. 'Ah, love, let us be true To one another!' read Hengist. 'And we are here as on a darkling plain ... where ignorant armies clash by night.'

Sally should have been washing her hair but, ever conscientious, was scrabbling round in old address books to reply to a card from a cook who had left ten years ago. Hengist was therefore delighted to welcome Dora, who'd turned up to waitress, and gave her a glass of champagne.

Dora then told him about lunch at Randal's.

'Dicky got drunk, kept mistaking Randal's furry cushions for cats and apologizing to them. Mummy and Randal are now at home, offering most surprisingly to dogsit. Probably because they want a good bonk.'

After taking a frantically over-excited, capering Elaine for a run in the snow and failing to teach her to catch snowballs, Dora retreated to the kitchen to help Mrs Cox. She had great hopes of tonight. Oriana was a huge star since Iraq. Several newspapers were interested in any titbit about her. Dora couldn't believe her luck when Mrs Cox, who had never really warmed to Oriana and who was utterly devoted to Emlyn, let slip in her indignation that Oriana was rolling up with a new man.

Concentrating on washing up saucepans, Dora didn't reveal how fascinated she was, particularly when Sally breezed in, wet hair in a towel, to check the goose was browning and to remind Coxie that the roast potatoes in their goose dripping should go in at seven-thirty.

'That smoked salmon pâté is delicious, Mrs B-T.'

'I'm glad, Dora. There's plenty of food in the fridge if you're hungry,' suggested Sally, noticing that the parsnip purée and the bread sauce, as well as the salmon pâté, were pitted with Dora's finger marks.

To distract her, Dora said she'd dropped in on Patience and Ian on the way. 'Dulcie's so sweet, she asked me if I was going cattle singing.'

'I'd like a grandchild just like Dulcie,' said Sally.

'I'd like a mother just like you or Mrs Cartwright.'

Sally had written people's names on little cards decorated with holly and mistletoe.

'Shall I put them round the table?' offered Dora. 'You'll catch cold if you don't dry your hair.'

'That's kind. Janna on Mr B-T's right, Emlyn on my right,' said Sally.

'Hengist, Sally, Janna, Oriana, Emlyn, Charlie,' read Dora.

In the shadows of Hengist's study, she switched on her mobile. 'Oriana's got a new boyfriend coming called Charlie,' she murmured. 'I'll keep you posted. So pants for Mr Davies.'

*　　　*　　　*

Out of the window, the snow was still falling, transforming the laurels into an army of lop-eared white rabbits.

'She's here, she's here!'

The crunch on the gravel was softened by the snow. Oriana wriggled out of the dark green Peugeot, gathering up parcels and pashminas, a bunch of red freesias between her teeth like Carmen.

'Hi, Mum.'

Oriana had never been a cuddly child, arching her back to wriggle out of every embrace. Now she rested first in Sally's, then in Hengist's arms, pressing her smiling red lips to their cheeks. Softened and glowing as never before, she took Hengist's breath away.

'Hi there, Coxie.' She hugged a startled Mrs Cox before handing her a squashy, scarlet-wrapped present.

'Here's yours, Mum and Dad, Charlie'll be here around eight-thirty. The house looks glorious—I'm so used to New York minimalism and neutral colours . . . and that's new, and that too!' She paused in front of a John Nash of weeping ashes, then a William Nicholson of a child and a dog asleep in a haycock. 'Lovely, both of them.' Then, peering into the dining room: 'That green wallpaper's great.'

'Show's how long you've been away,' said Sally.

From a dark corner of the hall, Dora took pictures on her mobile.

'Who's coming tonight?' asked Oriana.

'Just a very small party. You are staying for a bit, aren't you, darling?'

'Well, at least till the New Year, if that's OK. I want to show Charlie the West Country,' said Oriana, running upstairs to her old bedroom.

'Oh, how lovely you haven't changed anything, except for that sweet little blue chair.' Fingering the Christmas roses and snowdrops in a vase on the dressing table, she said, 'You do know how to make things pretty, Mum.'

She must be in love to be so complimentary, thought Sally.

Hengist gasped when Oriana came down a good hour later. Her slenderness was enhanced by a sleeveless dark brown velvet dress, split to the thigh to show off long greyhound legs and very high heels. Her short spiky hair was softened by pearl drop earrings and, for Oriana, a lot of eye make-up, blusher and scarlet lipstick. She reeked of familiar scent.

'You look absolutely gorgeous, darling.'

She must be bats about this Charlie. Where the hell did that put poor Emlyn?

'Can I take a photograph of you and Mr Brett-Taylor?' asked Dora, sliding in with a champagne cocktail on a silver tray.

Before long, Oriana reverted to being as spiky as her hair.

'You've obviously been fundraising,' she told Hengist. 'Place looks more like a country club than ever, I nearly got lost on the way in. What are you teaching at the moment?'

'First year,' said Hengist, unstoppering the whisky decanter. He intended to get gloriously drunk this evening.

'Hardly extending yourself.'

'It's a very good way of acquainting oneself with a new intake, and, quite frankly, teaching is something I do in my spare time these days.'

Then he tried to tell Oriana about Paris and the brilliant poem he'd written about England winning the World Cup, because for once David (Jonny Wilkinson) and Goliath (Martin Johnson) were on the same side. But he soon realized Oriana was interested neither in Paris nor the World Cup: 'It wasn't reported in the States; it was irrelevant on a global scale!' nor in him fulminating about the dumbing down of the GCSE history syllabus, which now included the restoration of historic houses and the producing of television documentaries.

'The aim is to make it more vocational, Jesus! They're even talking of combining history and geography as one subject. It's madness.'

Noting Oriana yawning, probably jet-lagged, Hengist put another log on the fire and switched to Iraq.

'Seeing Saddam's statue pulled down reminded me of Ozymandias, "round the decay Of that colossal wreck". But I felt unaccountably sorry for the poor sod when he was arrested. Looked as

251

though he'd been sleeping rough outside the Savoy. What's going to happen about Iran?'

'Oh, please don't interrogate me, Dad. We've got all next week, I just need to unwind.'

'Sorry.' Hengist patted her rigid shoulder. 'I'm just so proud of you. Wonderful if you could talk to the school about Iraq, you've got such a fan club here.'

But Oriana was rearranging her spikes in the mirror, a muscle rippling her flawless jawline. She's hellishly nervous, thought Hengist, as he put on a CD of carols sung by his old college choir.

96

Sally knew Oriana was home because her bedroom had been ransacked for tights, shampoo, dental floss; Beautiful had been left unstoppered, Hengist's aftershave ditto. Toothpaste lay like patches of snow in the basin, towels all over the floor. The hairdrier, still plugged in, was on the carpet. Favourite pearl drop earrings were missing from her jewel case.

Sally smiled and put on sapphire earrings instead.

'It came upon a midnight clear . . .' floated up the stairs as she pulled on a midnight-blue skirt and a turquoise frilled silk shirt. A dash of lipstick, a touch of mascara. Thank God for a good skin. Sally hoped Charlie Delgado would think her pretty. She imagined him dark-eyed and slightly Latin; perhaps he'd kiss her hand.

*   *   *

A second champagne cocktail hadn't cured Oriana's nerves; she glanced yet again at the clock and tried to ring someone on the remote control, then, cursing, punched out the number on her mobile.

Emlyn was the first to arrive as the grandfather clock in the hall chimed eight. He'd had a gruelling time with his mother, who was missing his father dreadfully and hinting that the only thing that would cheer her up was grandchildren. Nervous about the evening ahead, he'd done little justice to the Christmas lunch she'd spent so much time preparing. She had cried when he left. He longed to sweep her up and bring her to Bagley, but the contrast between their tiny overcrowded terrace house and the Brett-Taylors' splendour, with all the candles, crimson roses, great glittering tree and the fire leaping in the lounge, would have been hideous.

Aware his dinner suit was crumpled and his face red from lurking outside in the cold, he felt horribly bucolic compared with Hengist, whose cream shirt open at the neck showed off his tan and whose dark green smoking jacket, another present from Sally, emphasized his merry dark green eyes.

'Come in, dear boy. Happy Christmas.'

Emlyn's spirits drooped even further as Oriana ducked her head when he tried to kiss her.

'You look fantastic,' he said, addressing her lowered grey and brown streaked eyelids, then handed her a small square parcel. 'Happy Christmas.'

'Thanks, I'll open it later.'

Was she scared it was a ring?

Dora had no such inhibitions as she swept in with more champagne cocktails.

'Hello Mr Davies. Merry Christmas. What's that, a ring? Randal Stancombe gave my mother a lovely brooch, green enamel mistletoe with pearls as the berries. "Either wear it or put it in a safe," he told Mummy. Then, so she'd find out how much it cost, told her to insure it at once. So pants! Do open it.' She edged forward.

'Come on, Dora.' A grinning Hengist dragged her out of the room. 'Give Oriana and Emlyn a moment together.'

After a long pause, during which Emlyn longed to enfold and kiss the life out of her, he asked, 'How was the flight?'

'OK, except I can't get used to being recognized and pestered for autographs everywhere. It's impossible to be an observer when you're constantly observed.'

'Hasn't hurt John Simpson or Kate Adie,' said Emlyn, more sharply than he meant. 'You're a superstar now, and you look like one. Lovely dress.'

*   *   *

The snow had stopped and the clouds parted to reveal Orion in his glittering glory. Janna wished she could pluck him down from the skies as her escort this evening. She hadn't seen Hengist since before Stancombe caught out him and Mrs Walton. How would she feel about her great lost love? She was so nervous, she couldn't understand why her car wouldn't start until she realized she was trying to jam her seatbelt buckle into the ignition keyhole.

Her lovely day at the health spa yesterday had only made her realize, as hands massaged her face and body, how desperately she needed love in her life.

The snow was falling quietly and steadily again, blotting out caution. Hearing a scrunch on the gravel, Oriana raced to the window. It was not Charlie, but a surprisingly pretty redhead running up the steps as an icy wind blew aside a pashmina the colour of faded bracken to reveal a clinging

255

dress in leopardskin print.

'Darling, darling, "a pardlike Spirit, beautiful and swift".' Opening the front door, Hengist drew Janna into a muscular, lemon-scented embrace. Then, when she glanced up, he kissed her on the mouth, holding her steady as she swayed in amazement and wonder. 'So nice to see you again,' he murmured. 'Have you forgiven me?'

Janna's heart leapt in hope. Did he still care for her? Then he swept her into the lounge, grabbed her a drink and introduced her to Oriana, who had Sally's delicate features but Hengist's colouring, and who, because of her courage and left-wing views, had long been a heroine of Janna's, but who was now looking at her with hostility. Particularly when Elaine, who'd hardly budged when Oriana arrived, now jumped down sleepy-eyed from the sofa to nudge and chatter her teeth in welcome.

'So pleased to meet you. I'm such a fan,' said Janna, taking Oriana's damp hand; then, turning to Emlyn: 'How are you, how was Christmas and your mum?' which made Oriana even frostier. Perhaps she'd heard Emlyn and Janna were friends.

'How's Larks?' Hengist laced her champagne with a slug of brandy. 'You've got to fill me in on everything—and how's Xavier getting on?

'Good,' he said when Janna finished telling him. 'I felt we let him down really badly. And how's the divine Taggie? Is Rupert unfreezing at all?'

It was clear Hengist was on automatic pilot, firing questions, not listening to a word, because he was trying to overhear what Emlyn was saying to Oriana. Not a lot, it seemed. Oriana, equally clearly, was trying to find out what Janna was saying to Hengist.

256

'How's Xav getting on?' repeated Hengist, and Janna was overwhelmed with sadness.

'Since nothing all my love avails, Since all, my life seemed meant for, fails . . .'

Emlyn looked as though he'd been turned to stone, or rather red brick.

Hengist was deploring universal ignorance again.

'Ninety per cent of secondary-school children interviewed couldn't name a single composer, and seventy per cent of them thought Churchill was the dog in those insurance ads, which is quite funny if it weren't so dreadful. Mind you, teachers aren't much better. Forty-seven per cent, according to the *TES*, couldn't name Charles Clarke as the Education Secretary.'

'They're too busy to read newspapers,' protested Janna.

'Or too out of touch to teach children,' mocked Oriana.

'Janna's head of Larks,' said Hengist.

'I thought it was about to close.'

'It did,' said Janna.

'Not entirely,' said Emlyn evenly, 'it's called Larks High now. I'm going to switch to Scotch, if that's OK, Hengist?'

The restless Oriana had just put on *L'Enfance du Christ* when Sally rushed in.

'Sorry, everyone. Mini crisis with the goose. Janna darling, how lovely you look, such a saucy dress. Emlyn dear, how nice. Hengist, look what Dora's given us, it's an American greyhound calendar, with different photographs of greyhounds for every month.'

Armed with her camera and following Sally into the room, Dora said, 'February's has such a look of

257

Elaine, and April's the spitting image of my father's dog, Grenville, who lives with my sister now, and November's just like Maud who— Smile please, Janna and Mr Davies, and er, Miss Brett-Taylor.'

Headlights shone into the room. There was another crunch on gravel.

'Can you answer the door, Dora?' said Hengist to shut her up, but Oriana had already flown from the room, past the banks of holly and pine, past the white candles and the crimson roses, letting in a blast of icy air before falling into Charlie Delgado's arms.

'Oh, thank God you're here.'

'How's it going?'

'Hairy, but I'm safe now.'

'You are. Now I'm here.'

'So good you've already changed. Let's get your stuff out of the car.'

Two minutes later, with shouts of laughter and excitement, they came back into the house. Charlie's arms were now full of presents and, carrying coals of fire to Newcastle, a huge bunch of crimson roses. Oriana dropped Charlie's very smart suitcase in the hall.

'Come and meet everyone.'

Dora emerged from the shadows and shot back in again in a state of profound shock. For Charlie Delgado was around five foot eleven, lean, raven-haired, lynx-eyed, handsome, wearing an exquisitely cut dinner jacket and very, very female.

'My God.' Hengist's hand flew to straighten his tie and smooth his hair.

Next, thought Janna wearily.

'Oh dear,' said Sally gaily, 'I've screwed up the

258

numbers. Give Charlie a drink, darling, and take her up to the spare room.'

'Oh no, Charlie'll be sleeping with me,' announced Oriana.

97

It was as though a suicide bomber had blown the conviviality of the party to smithereens. An evening of excruciating embarrassment followed.

Dora put her head back round the door, eyes on stalks, and belted off to tell Coxie.

Oriana filled up a glass for Charlie, and was just about to take her upstairs when Hengist said, 'Mummy'll take her,' and dragged Oriana into his study, where neither of them noticed Dora's charging mobile.

Like some outer Mongolian warlord, Ghengist Khan no less, Hengist's eyes had narrowed to slits in his furious brown face.

'What the fuck are you playing at?'

All the radiance had drained out of Oriana. Unfazed by snipers or Scud missiles, she now looked white and utterly terrified.

'I didn't know how to tell you.'

'You could have bloody well tried.'

'I'm gay, Dad. I'm sorry I can't marry Emlyn and provide you with the son who'll play for England.'

'Don't be fatuous. Have you told Emlyn?'

'Not yet. I've never really fancied men.' She was trembling violently. 'I've been so unhappy about it.'

'For Christ's sake, it's just a phase. Scores of people are bisexual.'

'Not me. You and Mum wanted me to be a boy so I guess I tried to please you.' When Hengist opened his mouth to protest: 'No, let me finish. I walked into the Palestine Hotel in Baghdad in

260

April; Charlie was at the bar. Another journalist introduced us. Charlie just stared at me, then said in that glorious deep voice of hers, "Why are you so late?" "What d'you mean?" I stammered. "I've been waiting all my life for you," she said. "I knew the moment you walked into the room." '

Oriana collapsed on the red leather fender seat.

'It was the *coup de foudre* for both of us; we've been living together ever since. I wanted to tell you, Dad.'

'You could have found a better time to do it. Poor Emlyn.'

'I know. But don't think it's been fun.' Having reeled on the ropes, Oriana was beginning the fight back. 'Usually when people announce they've met Mr Right, the champagne comes out and everyone starts ringing round the family. We don't get any of that. No engagement in *The Times*, only being brushed under the carpet and an awareness of murdering one's parents' happiness. I can't help my sexual orientation.'

Through the open curtains, the snow was covering the past, stifling feelings.

Hearing voices, Hengist said, 'We better go back and cause as little hurt as possible.'

Oriana scuttled upstairs.

Next door, Emlyn had turned grey, megalithic, anguish carved on his face. Janna tried to comfort him, but it was like offering junior aspirin to an elephant with a spear through its heart.

Sally, having returned from upstairs, looked equally stunned.

'I'm so sorry.' Janna found herself hugging her. 'I'd better go.'

'No, please don't, we need you,' begged Sally,

then lowering her voice: 'It isn't so big a thing.'

Next moment Hengist walked in, also pale, but totally in control, and he put an arm round Sally's shoulders.

'More drinks all round, I guess,' and he poured champagne for Sally and Janna and much darker whiskies for himself and Emlyn.

'I'm afraid our daughter's "come out".'

'Poor Emlyn,' gasped Janna.

'Poor Sally,' snapped Hengist.

They were then joined by Charlie and Oriana, with all her lipstick kissed off.

'Mrs Brett-Taylor, you are so kind,' cried Charlie. 'I've just opened my gifts. These cufflinks are so neat, look'—she shot out her silken ivory cuffs—'and I'm wearing the perfume, it's delightful.' She held out a wrist for Sally to smell. 'And this is so appropriate.' She waved the pink elephant tie. 'From what Oriana tells me about Brett-Taylor hospitality, I'll be seeing pink elephants of my own in a day or two, and finally Catullus is one of my favourite poets, and translated by Lord Hawkley. He came and lectured us at Smith.'

' "Let's live and love, my Lesbia," ' muttered Janna, who was starting to get drunk and lippy. ' "Heed not the disapproval of censorious old men," ' and received a filthy look from Oriana.

'I've brought you some bottles of fine wine,' went on Charlie.

Dora, snapping away on her telephone camera, was livid when Hengist gave her twenty pounds and told her to buzz off.

'How are you going to manage? Coxie can't wait on her own, she was hoping to put her feet up with a plate of goose and *The Wizard of Oz*.'

262

'Go on, hop it.'

Dora rushed off across the snow to the Old Coach House.

'Guess what, Oriana's a lesbian; she's turned up with a tall woman called Charlie. They're sharing a bed, imagine them licking each other, it's so pants.'

Ian and Patience, who'd had several drinks after a gruelling day with Paris, had great difficulty not laughing.

'Shall I go and cheer him up?' asked Dora wistfully. 'Oh well, I'd better toboggan home.'

*   *   *

Charlie proceeded to dominate the conversation. She had spent six years teaching English at Smith before going into television on the news side. She had been everywhere and knew everyone. She was also a know-all, decided Janna, although it might have been to impress the Brett-Taylors.

She immediately recognized *L'Enfance du Christ* on the record player but, on picking up the CD cover, said she preferred Sir Colin Davis's version with Janet Baker singing Mary.

The mistletoe hanging in the hall on the way into dinner was an excuse for a little lecture on druids gathering it by moonlight.

'Mistletoe was alleged to cure infertility,' continued Charlie, 'ill humour and offer protection from lightning.' Then, tucking her arm through Oriana's: 'There should have been some hanging in the Palestine Hotel the night we met.

'Omigod.' She clapped her hands as she entered the dining room. 'How glorious.' Yet the scarlet napkins, crimson roses and army of white candles

263

lighting the room and casting a sheen on the frozen snow outside seemed less suited to the mood of the evening than the dark jungle wallpaper.

Glancing at the place cards, Sally wondered if Charlie ought now to be on Hengist's right rather than hers, particularly as Emlyn was on her left, glowering like some huge cliff face across at Charlie, who was unfolding her red napkin like a matador and banging on about the New York apartment.

'Oriana and I have kept things neutral. Then we can vary the look by adding cushions and throws.'

'We've done the same at my school,' piped up Janna. 'Alas the boys do most of the throwing.'

But Charlie had been sidetracked by a lovely Nevinson of Battersea Power Station, opal smoke drifting in the morning sun, which had been recently hung on the wall opposite.

'Although I prefer the gritty realism of Nevinson's war oeuvre. Oriana, like him, is a war artist. The tautness and poetry of your daughter's reportage, Hengist and Sally, will become TV classics.'

'Oh Charlie.' Oriana blew her a kiss.

They're bitches. Poor Emlyn, thought Janna furiously. How could they chatter away as though everything was normal?

Hengist, who never squandered an opportunity to work a room, was quizzing Charlie about the American political scene, which he and Jupiter were busy cracking. Who were the movers and shakers? Charlie dismissed most of the ones he knew as right-wing bigots.

The first course of smoked salmon mousse and poached scallops was delicious but the latter were

264

definitely undercooked, like eating chunks of female flesh.

Emlyn gagged and put his knife and fork together, suddenly overwhelmed with longing for his wise kindly father, who'd so disapproved of any link with the Brett-Taylors. What was he to do? He could hardly challenge Charlie to a duel. And how did you compete for a woman with another woman, who was so self-assured, so smart and who looked so much better in a dinner suit and her own skin than you did yourself? Emlyn drained his glass of Pouilly-Fumé and poured another one.

Charlie was a slow eater, because she talked so much, which was a good thing, because Coxie was so incensed to be abandoned that she refused to do much waiting.

Oriana and Sally helped her in with the goose, parsnip purée, roast potatoes, sprouts and bread sauce. As Hengist began carving, Elaine sidled round the table, dark eyes bright and loving in anticipation of goodies. On learning her name, Charlie launched into Tennyson:

' "Elaine the fair, Elaine the loveable, Elaine, the lily maid of Astolat." '

'Oh, fuck off,' muttered Emlyn.

'Pardon me?' asked Charlie, then demanded what aspect of American history Emlyn was teaching. Learning it was the Wild West, she hoped Emlyn was stressing the victimization of the Native Americans.

'No one more than Emlyn,' snapped Janna.

'Here you are, Emlyn.' A sympathetic Coxie shoved a huge plate of goose in front of him. 'I've given you the breast.'

And so it went on. Glasses were filled several

times as candlelight etched the deepening crisis on each face. On the surface, people contradicted each other, some with passion, some with dogged authority, while everyone watched. Was Charlie revving up to ask Hengist for Oriana's nailbitten hand? wondered Janna. She had been worried about which fork to use. This lot would hardly have noticed if she'd rammed one into Charlie's arm.

The crimson roses were shedding petals on the polished table like drops of blood. Janna shivered, remembering Cara Sharpe and the scarlet anemones.

Oriana, in truth, was irritated Emlyn was behaving so angrily and gauchely. She could see Charlie was wondering how Oriana could have attached herself for so long to such a boor. Emlyn could be so funny and sharp, but every time Charlie threw him a question, he ignored it like a great vegan sea lion rejecting fish. She also wished her father were less right wing, and her mother less like a crystal lustre, tinkle, tinkle, filling in silences with inane chat.

Janna she couldn't read. She'd been convinced she was her father's latest, but from the way Janna was sticking up for Emlyn, Oriana wasn't sure.

The food was sublime. Never were sprouts more crunchy, potatoes more golden crisp and creamily soft inside, or goose more tender without being fatty. Charlie, who hadn't had any lunch, was particularly taken with the parsnip purée and had a second helping.

'It's Taggie Campbell-Black's recipe,' said Sally, who was now gazing into space.

As Charlie proceeded to annihilate the Bush administration, and make disapproving comments

266

on 'not forgetting the starving worldwide' as more food seemed to go back on everyone else's plates than was put on them in the first place, Elaine was having a field day.

Sally, who'd been fingering the cut-glass ridges of her water glass, suddenly filled it up from the gravy boat without realizing it.

'It's my turn to clear away.' Janna leapt to her feet, stacking up the plates and grabbing Sally's glass.

In the kitchen, she found Coxie in tears and attacking the brandy.

'My dinner's ruined and poor Mr Davies.'

'It was a wonderful dinner. Everyone's upset, that's all.' Janna put an arm round Coxie's heaving shoulders as Emlyn walked in with the goose.

When she and Emlyn came back to the kitchen with vegetables and sauce boats, Janna murmured that Charlie and Oriana were fearfully anti-Bush.

'Except each other's,' snarled Emlyn.

Janna screamed with laughter, then stifled it, stammering how desperately sorry she was about everything.

Returning to the dining room with hot plates, Christmas pudding and brandy butter, they caught Oriana and Charlie in a clinch in the hall.

'Christ!' exploded Emlyn. 'Shall we unjoin the ladies?'

Ignoring him, as a further act of solidarity, Charlie and Oriana moved their chairs together, pulling crackers, putting on paper hats and giggling over riddles. Inside Charlie's cracker was a yellow whistle which she kept blowing.

Janna put the Christmas pudding on the sideboard; Hengist defiantly emptied half a bottle of brandy over it. As he set fire to it, blue flame nearly scorched the ceiling. Emlyn felt similar anger flaring up inside him: Oriana should have levelled with him. Even if there was a certain relief that it wasn't him specifically she didn't fancy, just blokes in general, her lack of response had constantly humiliated him, eroding his masculinity. He'd felt so heavy and ham-fisted, like a rhino trying to shag a gazelle.

'D'you remember how you used to put silver 5ps in the Christmas pudding, Mum?' asked Oriana.

'It was bachelor's buttons in my day,' said Hengist, scooping Christmas pudding into silver bowls, which Janna handed round.

'I wonder who'd qualify for that,' said Sally in a high voice.

Seeing she was shivering, Janna took Emlyn's seat next to her, praising the brandy butter, saying what joy her indoor bulbs had brought the children.

'How nice.' Sally attacked her Christmas pudding, then, putting her spoon down, said:

'D'you remember the time you got Elaine a doggy bag from La Perdrix d'Or, pork chops wrapped in silver foil, and forgot and put it under the tree? By the time you opened it on Christmas night, it had gone orf and stank like hell.' Sally started to laugh shrilly on and on. Janna put a hand on her arm.

'It's OK,' she murmured, 'you're doing fine.'

'I haven't had much practice.'

Hengist, who'd been trying to get some sense out of Emlyn about rugger, glanced across at his wife with such concern.

She's the one he loves, thought Janna. Me, Ruth

Walton, even Oriana aren't in the frame compared with her.

'Don't know why everyone goes on about Taggie's cooking,' said Hengist, 'my wife's is just as good. Let's all drink to her.'

After they'd drained their glasses, Hengist filled them up again and proposed a toast to absent friends.

'Mum,' said Janna.

'Mungo,' said Oriana bitterly.

'Dad,' muttered Emlyn with a break in his voice.

He was looking so sad, Janna poked him in the ribs with a cracker. Inside was a key ring attached to a perky little black dog with pricked ears.

'How darling,' said Charlie covetously, 'an Aberdeen terrier. My mother has one.'

'We call them Scotties in England,' said Janna tartly, 'and Emlyn's going to have it.' She dropped it into his dinner jacket pocket.

'Where are Artie and Theo?' said Oriana fretfully.

'Gone to Athens,' said Hengist, 'staying in the Grande Bretagne, lucky things. Artie's hiring a car and they're going on day trips to Corinth and Sparta.'

'Such a shame, I so wanted Charlie to meet them.'

'They're both such dear persons,' said Sally.

'Why are male couples "dear persons" and not women?' said Oriana, who was getting punchy. 'Dad's always slagging off Joan Johnson and Sabine Bottomley, but if they're men, it's fine.'

Hengist and Janna escaped with the pudding bowls.

'Save it for the birds,' he cried as Janna started to

269

tip rejected pudding into the bin. 'Christ, what a bloody awful evening. Is that appalling Charlie going to stay behind and drink port with me and Emlyn?'

But as they returned to the dining room, the grandfather clock struck ten-thirty and Charlie, looking at Oriana with sleepy suggestive eyes, announced she was exhausted.

'Thank you so much, Sally and Hengist, for letting me invade your evening and for your wonderful gifts. If it's OK, I'll give you mine tomorrow after I've unpacked. A very merry Christmas.'

Then she kissed Sally, shook hands with Hengist and Janna and told Emlyn it was good to meet him, and turned towards the door.

'I'm coming with you,' Oriana leapt to her feet.

'No, you're not.' Emlyn grabbed her arm. 'We've got to talk.'

'Tomorrow.' Oriana winced at the exerted pressure, then, thinking her arm would snap like a wishbone: 'Oh, OK then.'

They went back into the drawing room, where neither could be bothered to bank up the dying embers.

Out of nerves, Oriana put a Christmas compilation on the CD player, hastily turning down the sound when the first track was 'O Come, All Ye Faithful'.

Emlyn watched as she idly flipped through the white invitation cards on the chimney piece, then wandered to the window, gazing out at the snow, which, growing too heavy, was sliding off branches and had bowed down her mother's beloved ceanothus to breaking point.

Snow might have fallen on the stretch of white neck between Oriana's dark hair and her brown velvet neckline. This can't be happening, thought Emlyn.

'I'm so desperately sorry.' Her voice was so low he had to move closer. 'I hadn't the guts to tell you. I thought you might have guessed. I'll always love you in my head, but not between my legs.'

'Thanks.' Emlyn helped himself to several fingers of Hengist's whisky. 'How long's it been going on?'

'About eight months. War forces people to take chances, but I just knew it was right.'

She ought to be more contrite, thought Emlyn. She has all the self-righteousness of the infatuated.

'Couldn't we be friends?' she begged.

'I doubt it, not when one's shot down by friendly fire.' As a log fell into the grate in a shower of sparks he went on, 'Hengist won't get his rugby Blue grandson now.' Emlyn removed Hengist's pale blue tasselled Cambridge cap from a bust of Brahms.

'He could.' Oriana swung round. 'Can I ask you a favour? It's a compliment really. Charlie and I want a baby.'

Emlyn caught his breath. Fuck, he'd pulled the tassel off the cap.

'Unto us a boy is born,' sang the CD player.

'Not unto us, it ain't,' said Emlyn flatly.

'It could be. I can't think of anyone in the world I'd rather have as father of my child. You're brave, loyal, funny and such a wonderful athlete.'

'And thick,' said Emlyn. 'You'd provide the brains presumably.'

'Oh, Emlyn.' If he could joke, the worst was over. She reached out and took his hand, irresistible in

271

her hopeful beauty. 'Daddy'd be so pleased too, he's so fond of you. Will you sleep with me while I'm here, Charlie truly won't mind, but if you can't face that, at least be the donor?' Then when he didn't answer: 'You could have access,' she added.

'You fucking bitch,' said Emlyn softly. 'I joined this school because of you, and sold my principles down the River Fleet. You ruthless bloody bitch. Using your rough trade to provide hybrid vigour. No fucking thank you.'

'No need to be obnoxious,' said Oriana huffily, as though he'd refused to give her a lift to the station. 'I could easily have married you and had women on the side, taken the easy route. But Charlie and I thought about this long and hard.'

'Hardly the operative adjectives.' Emlyn's voice grew in fury. 'There is absolutely no way a child of mine is going to be brought up by a couple of lesbians.'

'Pity,' sighed Oriana, 'our gay male friends have been very supportive and are very happy to oblige. They see the bigger picture.'

'Or bugger picture—we are talking about a child.'

'Charlie would actually prefer IVF to make sure of a girl, but she knows I so want to give Dad a grandson.'

'You've had it all planned,' said Emlyn softly. 'I never, never want to see you again,' and, fumbling with the French windows, tripping over the door ledge, he stumbled off into the blizzard.

Hearing doors slamming and shouting, Hengist, who'd just seen Janna, who should not have been driving, into her car, marched into the drawing room.

Towering over Oriana, terrible as an army with banners, he roared, 'Your mother's devastated. I can't think of a crasser way of hurting her. I'm amazed you didn't announce it on television. Heartbreaking News. And what the hell have you said to poor Emlyn?'

When Oriana told him, adding that she hoped it would be some compensation to Emlyn to feel he was involved, Hengist flipped.

'How can you be so fucking insensitive?'

'You wanted a son, a grandson; I'm doing my best.'

'Not one brought up by two dykes.'

Oriana winced. 'Why are you and Emlyn so homophobic?'

'Children need a father.'

'Charlie and I love each other,' said Oriana. 'You've always surrounded yourself with children who you love more than me. You loved Mungo more than me. I'm just trying to give you another Mungo,' she sobbed.

'Don't drag Mungo into it. Get out, GET OUT, I never want to see you or Charlie again.'

*　　　*　　　*

Charging upstairs to her bedroom, Oriana discovered the long, lean, olive-skinned nakedness of Charlie, stretched out across the four-poster. Her high breasts and sleek flat belly would never have need of surgery. Arms on the pillow behind her head showed off armpit hair as glossy as her dark brown Brazilian. On the bedside table awaited oil for fingers that went everywhere, releasing Oriana utterly, driving her to heaven.

'Come to bed, my darling,' called out Charlie softly, then, seeing the anguish on Oriana's face, asked anxiously, 'Whatever's the matter?'

'It's a good thing you haven't unpacked yet,' sobbed Oriana, 'there's no room at this inn.'

*   *   *

Out on the pitches, it was as light as day. In contrast to her master's anguish, Elaine skipped and cavorted, white on white, snorting excitedly, tunnelling her nose along the snow. Hengist, who had no treads on his black evening shoes, fell over twice and heaved himself up. Reaching Badger's Retreat, he found a tall big ash had been blown over in yesterday's gale, knocking most of the branches off the east side of the Family Tree, smashing every sapling springing up around it.

Like Charlie, invading our Christmas, destroying us, he thought. A few remaining branches swung loose like broken limbs. Others were bandaged in snow. Hengist gave a howl and flung his arms round the trunk trying to hold the family together.

From now on, his sights would be set on Paris.

*   *   *

By the time he got home, Oriana and Charlie had departed and he was greeted by a tearful Sally, furious with him for chucking Oriana out.

'It was the way she was born, poor child.'

'Bloody wasn't. How could she treat poor Emlyn like that?'

'She loves Charlie, who was sweet when they left. She apologized and hoped she hadn't come on too strong at dinner, but she didn't know how to handle Emlyn and she was so nervous about meeting us.'

'Bollocks,' raged Hengist, 'she's as nervous as a basking shark.'

98

Dora, of course, leaked the entire story to the press, who came roaring down to Bagley, wildly interested in the coming out of Oriana.

'Of course we support Oriana,' Sally told the *Telegraph*, 'Hengist and I are naturally disappointed as we've always longed for grandchildren and feel life is easier if you have a conventional marriage.'

'If your daughter does something reprehensible,' Hengist was quoted as saying, 'you take it on the chin.'

Rupert put down *Lord of the Flies*, which he was rather enjoying, to ring Hengist to commiserate.

'Same thing happened to us with Marcus. Hell of a shock at the time. But he's very happy with his boyfriend and it didn't do his career any harm.'

Bianca was absolutely fed up with Rupert staying at home to read his set books during the holidays, which meant she couldn't slope off and see Paris. Why the hell couldn't he take up blood sports again?

Although most of the staff at Bagley were very sympathetic towards Hengist, Sally and Emlyn, there was a faction, headed by Poppet Bruce, who felt the Brett-Taylors had been a little too smug about Oriana's achievements.

Janna tried to comfort a monosyllabic, devastated Emlyn, who was outwardly stoical, thinking more of Hengist and Sally. Inwardly he identified with the Brett-Taylors' Christmas tree, which had held up the lights, the tinsel, the fairy and the coloured balls, with everyone oohing and aahing. Now the decorations had gone back into their box until next year, but the tree had been chucked out on the terrace on Twelfth Night, destined for the bonfire. That's how he felt Oriana had treated him.

Somehow he had survived the beginning of term, welcoming back boys, taking lessons and rugby practice, drinking only a little more than usual, refusing to talk to the press, who nevertheless quoted him as saying: 'I feel a proper Charlie, although that's probably Oriana's role now.'

On the other hand, history mocks were never marked down more savagely. Even Boffin Brooks only got a D, while one boy ordered to run ten times down to the boathouse on frozen ground was carted off to the sick bay with a broken ankle. Emlyn was again taking no prisoners. He coped until the second week of term when he and Sally were wandering towards the lake discussing the situation.

The snow had nearly thawed. The brightest thing in the landscape was the warm brown keys of the ashes and Elaine in her red tartan coat, bounding ahead. A soft grey mist was coming down. The press, thank God, had retreated.

'I'm so worried about Oriana's career and her relationship with Hengist,' Sally was saying as she tightened her dark blue silk scarf under her chin. 'He so adores her. When you and she were together, you always made room for him, but Charlie seems to be all-consuming. I doubt, even if he came round, she'd let him back in again.

'I like lesbians,' she added firmly, 'Joan's a dear. But I just feel their chances of happiness are limited and it's more difficult to gain social acceptance because the world is so ignorant and the press is so cruel.'

Emlyn gathered up a remaining patch of snow and hurled it into the lake. 'Guys get excited by the idea, but only if it's two lush blondes on a bed and they can watch or join in. They're threatened by the reality.'

He and Sally were so engrossed they didn't notice Poppet Bruce waiting like Horatius as they stepped on to the Japanese bridge which crossed a narrow stretch of the lake. Poppet looked very cheery in a woolly hat, muffler and gumboots all in orange and, because she was pregnant, she had added a blue and orange wool cloak. She was full of her own Christmas.

'We enjoyed goat's cheese quiche for the festive meal and instead of exchanging Christmas gifts, we donated a goat to a family in Africa. I'm very excited by my latest project: swimming for Asian women.' Then, eyes sparkling with malevolent enthusiasm, she went on, 'I'm so pleased to bump into you, Sally, because I so rejoice for you.'

'Whatever for?' Searching for carp in the grey water, Sally braced herself.

'That Oriana's gay. What a thrill for you and Hengist. What a new and fascinating take it will give you on life, with particular resonance for Hengist who's so homophobic. I would urge him to have immediate counselling. As a professional, I'd be happy to oblige.'

Reading their silence as approval, Poppet turned and walked back across the bridge with them. 'What is more, I much look forward to meeting Charlie Delgado. I so admire her oeuvre. Might

Oriana be prevailed on to address the Talks Society, not just about the war, but about coming out? She and Charlie could do a fascinating double act.'

They had reached the other side.

Sally, quite unable to speak, was gazing in horror at Poppet. Not so Emlyn, who was so angry, he gathered up his deputy headmaster's wife and threw her into the lake.

'It's not just Asian women who go swimming. If you were a bloke,' he roared, 'I'd smack you round the face, you insensitive bitch. And you're *not* going to rescue her.' He seized Sally's arm.

As he hurried her away, Sally reflected on life's ironies. She had been so delighted when she thought Oriana had a new man, but now, how lovingly and gratefully she'd have accepted Emlyn as a son-in-law. Furiously spitting out pond weed, Poppet swam to the bank.

Emlyn had hardly got back to his flat and poured himself a vast whisky when Alex Bruce, glasses steaming up in righteous indignation, barged in.

'How dare you chuck Poppet in the lake? You could have killed her and our babe.'

'Witches deserve drowning,' yelled Emlyn. 'My only mistake was not to do it sooner. If you come down to the lake, I'll be happy to hold you under.'

Such was Emlyn's fury, Alex backed hastily away, knocking over a chair overloaded with unopened Christmas presents.

'You're only resorting to vulgar abuse, taking it out on your colleagues, because you can't handle rejection. Oriana is clearly seeking closure.'

'Shut up about Oriana!' Emlyn drained his glass of whisky and got to his feet, his massive frame

279

blotting out any light from the window. Next moment, he had grabbed Alex's lapels, dislodging his spectacles. 'You little weasel.'

'You'll get fired for this.'

'Good,' said Emlyn, 'I couldn't work under the same roof as you and that vindictive cow a moment longer,' and his fist propelled Alex through the air on to a rickety sofa, sending flying piles of rugby shirts and unmarked mocks papers and face-down photographs of Oriana.

Despite a possibly cracked cheekbone and his terror of this vast, fire-breathing Welsh dragon, Alex felt a surge of satisfaction. Emlyn, with his working-class, state-school background, was an ace in the Hengist-Artie-Theo pack, because he saw good in their traditions, whereas Alex only saw evil. Emlyn was also young, left wing and progressive and so loved by parents and pupils alike that Alex feared him as an outside candidate for headmaster. His loss to the old guard would be immeasurable.

'Can I accept this as your resignation?' he spluttered.

'You certainly can, now get out.'

*   *   *

That day Emlyn walked straight to Janna, who took care of him. For twenty-four hours he was delirious, ranting and raving in the pits of drunken despair. It was hard to tell if the bitch he was inveighing against was Poppet, Charlie or Oriana.

Janna, therefore, hid a letter she had been amazed to receive from Oriana, which apologized for being rude.

'I'm protective towards my mother and I mistakenly thought you were after Dad. Will you keep an eye on her and on Emlyn? I really do care for him and I bungled the whole thing. Charlie sends her best. We hope to see you when we're next in England.'

Janna felt oddly comforted.

'What are you going to do?' she asked Emlyn when he finally sobered up.

'I've been screwed by the Brett-Taylors.' Emlyn gazed moodily into a cup of black coffee. 'Until Charlie rolled up, they had no real desire for me to marry Oriana. To that lot, being working class is worse than being lesbian. Fucking upper classes, fucking independent schools.'

He rubbed his stubble reflectively. 'I might go back to the maintained system; I might go and work for the Welsh Rugby Union. I dropped in on them when I was home at Christmas. They said there was always a job going. I'd like to be part of building up a team to bury England at Twickenham. But for the next two terms, I'd like to help you out at Larks, if you'll have me?'

Janna gazed at him, eyes and mouth opening wider and wider. '*Have* you?' She frantically wiped her eyes. 'It's the best news ever. Are you sure? God, we need you. They love the Brig and Pittsy and tolerate Skunk and Mates, but they worship you. The Brigadier's awesome on Nazi Germany, but he's rusty on the Russian Revolution and it'd be wonderful to have someone to referee fights and see off Ashton Douglas and just have you around.'

*   *   *

281

Hengist, by contrast, was devastated. He'd lost a marvellous master, a soulmate and a favoured heir apparent. He tried to persuade Emlyn to reconsider.

'We could always claim Poppet provoked you. None of your class has completed its coursework. Their parents are going to be livid. You can't let them down. Look at the way Janna stood by her no-hopers. What the hell are you going to do?'

'Go to Larks to help out Janna,' which didn't please Hengist one bit.

'Well, don't break her heart then. And what about our rugger teams?'

'Denzil will have to get up in the afternoon for a change.'

'Where are you going to live?'

'I've got temporary digs in Wilmington High Street, opposite Brigadier Woodford,' which pleased Hengist even less.

The pupils were equally enraged at Emlyn's departure. Posters and graffiti everywhere demanded his return. Alex was shouted down and booed in chapel and he wrongly blamed Theo when someone painted 'Ite domum' on the roof of his house.

Nor did having Boffin caringly applying rump steak to one's black eye compensate for being called 'Alex Bruise'. Alex festered as he corrected the proofs of his *Guide to Red Tape*, which was due out in June.

Poppet, on the other hand, was nauseatingly forgiving. 'Emlyn was hurting,' she told everyone, 'it came out as anger.'

Artie and Theo walked to chapel past the lake, on whose banks, as a result of the gales, twigs, branches and even ivy-mantled trees were strewn like an antler factory. The wind of change blowing out dead wood, thought Theo, with a shiver.

'How's Emlyn?' he asked.

'Resigned,' replied Artie sadly.

'Is that a verb or an adjective?'

'Both.'

'We have lost our Hector,' said Theo mournfully.

Dora leaked the story to the papers, who all came roaring back to Bagley: 'Top rugby school loses star coach'.

99

The despair of Bagley at losing their star coach was only equalled by Larks's joy at inheriting him. By blacking one of the detested Mr Fussy's eyes, Emlyn had achieved cult status and it rocketed morale to have such an attractive man round the place. Even though it was winter, the gap suddenly increased between jeans and crop tops, skirts climbed, Rowan's dark bob was highlighted for the first time, even Miss Basket, sparked up by snogging Skunk at the Christmas party, drenched herself in lavender water.

'Lovely for the boys to have a role model,' said Mags.

'I'm a roly-poly model,' sighed Sophy, who'd put on seven pounds over Christmas and now joined the netball team in the lunch hour.

Weatherwise, Emlyn's first morning was unpromising, with lowering skies and a bitter east wind sending leaves scuttling like mice across the playground. Inside, all was warmth. Graffi had designed a banner for reception showing a red dragon being greeted by a lot of larks. Pupils wandered in and out of a staffroom thick with cigarette smoke when they wanted to talk to a teacher. The purple and cyclamen-pink ball dresses worn by Pittsy and Skunk as Ugly Sisters in the staff pantomime still hung on a rail with everyone's coats. The noticeboard was thick with cuttings about Larks and a mocks timetable with a red line through it. Thought for the week was: 'Chewing gum: we're gumming down.'

Sophy had brought in her daughter, Dulcie, who was playing with Kylie Rose's Cameron and being monitored by several pupils taking GCSE child care.

Miss Cambola rushed up and kissed Emlyn on both cheeks.

'At last, we have a baritone. We aim to sing the German Requiem in the cathedral.'

At break, Taggie Campbell-Black brought in a rainbow cake she was trying out for coursework and gave Emlyn the biggest slice.

After break he gave his first lesson on the Russian Revolution: a great success, particularly when Rocky retreated once more to the cupboard at the back of the room and kept the class in fits of laughter.

Emlyn told them about the first general strike in Moscow when there was no electricity and Tsar Nicholas, in his amber room, had to read and write his letters by candlelight.

'What was he experiencing for a first time?' asked Emlyn.

'People power,' boomed the voice from the cupboard.

'Excellent, Rocky. Well done.'

Knowing their attention span was short, Emlyn moved on to the Monk with the burning eyes who had such a hold on Queen Alexandra.

'Can anyone tell me his name?'

'Omar Sharif,' intoned the cupboard.

Rocky, who liked talking to adults, wandered into the staffroom during the lunch hour.

'Get out before I kill you,' bellowed the Brigadier in mock fury as Rocky helped himself to Lily's last cheroot.

Both Brigadier and Lily, Emlyn noticed, were in fine fettle, the Brigadier arranging his teaching days to coincide with Lily's so he could give her a lift in and out.

In the afternoon, Janna went through the children's mocks papers with the Brigadier and Emlyn, expressing doubts whether any of them would manage a decent grade in history.

'If they'd been marked down as ruthlessly as they're supposed to be, they'd have been in minus figures,' she added dolefully.

'If it's any comfort'—the Brigadier patted her hand—'Rupert Campbell-Black asked me to mark his English lit. mocks papers for him. I'm afraid I had to fail him too. In an exam, one really cannot say: "Sylvia Plath's the most fucking awful woman I've ever come across," or, "Mrs Bennet's exactly like Anthea Belvedon."'

Emlyn grinned.'He got that bit right.'

*   *   *

Emlyn was keen to improve Larks's history marks but, filled with underlying rage against the whole arrogant, elitist public-school system, his ambition was to thrash them at the game at which they considered themselves invincible: rugby football. The boys at Larks were already fired up by the World Cup, so Emlyn had no difficulty in forming a rugby team, who grew markedly less enthusiastic when they had to run through the frozen water meadows before sunrise and train after school in the dark evenings. Admittedly, Emlyn jogged with them and shed twenty pounds and his gut. With his soft Welsh lilt becoming a sergeant major's roar, he had no difficulty keeping the roughest, toughest boys in order, particularly when he dropped them from the team if they didn't shape up.

Johnnie Fowler was kicked out for two weeks because he rolled up in a dirty shirt.

'You're meant to be covered in mud at the end of a game, not the beginning.'

'The washing machine's broke.'

'Go to the launderette.'

'Haven't got no money.'

'Wash it by bloody hand then.'

Emlyn's genius was to draw the most out of players, so they achieved way beyond their own and everyone else's dreams. He knew which boys, like Johnnie and Monster, to slap down and which, like Xav and Rocky, to build up. He was an expert at pinpointing a player's weakness and finding a solution, adapting teaching to the individual. Rugby, above all, taught boys teamwork and to keep their temper. As a result, flare-ups and loutish behaviour within the school dramatically decreased.

Emlyn increasingly appreciated the difficulties in getting these children through GCSE. Not that they were thick, but they were flowers planted in stony, dry, infertile soil, buffeted by winds.

'Try and speak French with your family at home,' he heard Lily urging, *c'est très bon.*'

'Our family don't even speak in English,' said Johnnie. 'They just throw fings at each other.'

But as the weeks went by, the children gradually mastered the basics of volcanoes, earthquakes, heredity, the rise of Hitler, the Cuban missile crisis, the effect of tourism on world debt, the splitting of the atom, the circulation of the blood, the reflexes of the eye, electricity, dissecting sheep's hearts and learnt how to book a ticket in French or to go shopping in Spanish.

They had fun with geography coursework, deciding where to locate a factory.

'In Miss Miserden's front garden,' said Pearl.

'That won't mean a lot to the examiner,' said Basket.

'Well, Baldie Hyde's back garden then.'

In his coursework, Graffi wrote eloquently about how roadworks in Shakespeare Lane, which ran into the Shakespeare Estate, inconvenienced people. 'Makes me late for school. Mum can't get to Tesco's. Dad can't get to the pub. Cavendish Plaza can't get to their hairdressers. Randal Stancombe takes a helicopter, so the rich get inconvenienced less than the poor.'

Emlyn found the teaching much tougher than Bagley; it was like having to crank up an old Ford for the shortest journey when one had been driving a Lamborghini, but the rewards were greater, seeing understanding dawning on children's faces. Increasingly too he admired Janna, how she exhausted herself worrying about Wally's son in Iraq, Mags's premature grandchild, Mr Mates's arthritis.

She was outwardly cheerful, but he realized how near cracking up she was when, one late February morning, she wandered wailing into his history class.

'Look, look, Sally Brett-Taylor gave me these hyacinth bulbs back in October, I put them in a black dustbin bag at the back of the stockroom and forgot about them.'

Thus imprisoned in darkness, the white leaves

and stems, from which sprouted tiny, colourless, misshapen flowers, had struggled to a hopelessly etiolated twenty-four inches, hanging pathetically down over the edge of their blue china bowl. Their whiskery roots had completely clogged the bulb fibre.

'They were so desperate to reach the light and flower like the children in the Shakespeare Estate,' she sobbed. 'I left them in the dark; I failed to give them water and light.'

Jerking his head towards the door to tell Feral and Co to scarper, Emlyn put the bowl on his desk and took Janna in his arms.

'It's all right, lovely, it's all right.'

'I killed them.'

'You didn't—it's only this year's hyacinths. The bulbs themselves are fine, they'll flower again next year. Look, already the leaves are turning green in the light, like your kids'll blossom because you've given them love and hope.'

To cheer her up, he took her to the new James Bond film that evening and she slept right through it.

The children at Larks had been so furious when horrible Rod Hyde won a Teaching Award in October that when a small ad appeared in the *Gazette* asking for nominations for next autumn's awards, they decided to enter Janna.

'Miss is such a good filler-in of forms, but we can't expect her to fill in her own,' said Kylie. 'Let's ask Emlyn.'

Gradually Janna became calmer and happier. It was so great to have someone to kick ass so she could concentrate on cherishing.

Emlyn was still gutted about Oriana; he missed

289

Artie and Theo and the pupils at Bagley, but he loved the Brigadier and Wally and even grew fond of Skunk, Pittsy and Mr Mates—and they of him, because he treated them as equals, even regarding them as young enough to be roped into refereeing.

Gradually, as the almond scattered its pink blossom, crocuses purpled the emerald-green spring grass and the days grew longer, Xav's remaining fat turned to hard muscle, Monster, Johnnie and Rocky formed an impenetrable back row, Graffi, talking Welsh to Emlyn to annoy the others, and Danny, a Belfast boy, known as 'Danny the Irish', grew fleet as forwards. Feral, to crown it, was a natural, with the wisdom, the speed, the ability to pass, kick and dodge of a potential international. Like a feral cat, his eyes swivelled the whole time, assessing danger, checking where everyone else was on the field and where they were going to be in five seconds' time.

Emlyn longed to keep him for rugby, but he had made a Faustian bargain. If Feral gave him one term and a sporting chance of beating Bagley, he would put Feral on to the football map. At heart, he hoped Feral might become sufficiently enamoured of rugby to convert.

With Stormin' Norman on the sidelines yelling the heroes on, Larks was gradually transformed into a 'lean, mean, killing machine'.

100

Hengist meanwhile, aware that Bagley needed to do more to bond with the community, challenged Larks to a fun charity rugby match on the last Sunday of term.

Randal Stancombe, as Larks's increasingly self-confessed backer, immediately donated a rugby ball in gold plate, on which the name of the winning team would be engraved.

'And when you move on to your next school,' he told Janna, 'you must carry on the fixture,' murmuring that he had great plans for a new school on the water meadows below the Cathedral, 'a city academy, which you would run.'

Janna couldn't fail to be flattered and although Randal gave her the creeps since their hideous sexual encounter back in September, she had to recognize that with the £120,000, the rebuilding of Appletree and the minibus, which could now take half the school to matches or outings, he had provided fantastic support. So she smiled over gritted teeth when he popped in to show off her brave experiment to high-powered friends, hinting she'd never have pulled it off without his six figure leg-up.

Emlyn detested Randal sauntering in as though he owned the place. As if he could possibly build a school on the water meadows, when they were well below the flood plain. Randal was far more likely to flatten the Shakespeare Estate.

Nor did Randal miss an opportunity to drop in on Taggie's classes. Lady Belvedon might be the blow-job queen, but Mrs Campbell-Black was the stuff of dreams and far too sweet to patronize or put him down as Anthea often did.

'How's your hubby's GCSE going?'

'He's working very hard,' sighed Taggie.

Taggie had another admirer, Pete Wainwright, the new Larks Rovers under-manager, a bluff, tough Lancastrian, with whom she'd been liaising over her class's coursework. As well as lunch in the director's boxes, this included a pre-match meal for the players and snacks for the crowd.

Pete Wainwright was so impressed, he was thinking of adopting Taggie's menus for the club. Taggie, in turn, was determined 'to screw her courage' (a phrase that came from one of Rupert's set books) to ask Pete to give Feral a trial.

*   *   *

Despite Taggie's success at work, things were not easy at home. Rupert, displaying the same competitive streak that took him to the top as a showjumper and an owner-trainer, was hell bent on winning his bet. Having ploughed his mocks, he had given up drink for Lent and incessantly mugged up his set books as hounds checked between coverts or his helicopter flew him to race meetings round Europe.

Xav seemed much happier, although in despair that Aysha, having completed her coursework in record time, had reluctantly gone back to Pakistan to meet her future husband. Xav was also panicking about the proposed match against Bagley. Would they flay him alive?

Taggie was more worried about Bianca who, on

the occasions she came home, was moody and detached: the dancing sunbeam permanently hidden behind dark clouds. Over half-term she'd shut herself away in her room. On the Sunday afternoon, Taggie was wearily clearing away lunch and planning her lesson for tomorrow: 'a cake for a celebration: christening, birthday or wedding', when Bianca rushed in in tears.

'Darling! Whatever's the matter?'

'I don't want to go back to Bagley tomorrow.'

'Oh, angel.' Taggie's heart leapt guiltily: how blissful if Bianca had decided to go back to being a day girl. 'Whyever not?'

'Because I want to go back tonight,' sobbed Bianca, 'but bloody Daddy's so busy writing an essay on *Pride and Prejudice* he'll only take me first thing tomorrow morning. He says I'm obsessed with boys, like Lydia Bennet.'

With the lighter evenings, Bianca had made plans on her return to drug Jade Stancombe's cocoa, climb out of her dormitory window and run to Middle Field, straight into Paris's arms. The effort required for the two of them to be alone added frisson to their affaire. They had made love in Plover's loose box, behind the bicycle shed, in the science lab and the boathouse and had somehow escaped discovery.

Bianca adored Paris; she was reduced to jelly when their eyes met in chapel, or their hands clasped in the corridor. But she found him very difficult to talk to. He was wonderful at making love, his touch so sure and tender, but he was undemonstrative; he told her that she was beautiful, but never that he loved her. There was a detachment and cool about him that fascinated while intimidating her. He was so clever: he sent her witty text messages, wrote her poems she didn't understand and he was always reading. Bianca, who never read, liked chatting, dancing and shopping. It was also impossible to escape Dora who, like a dog suspecting its owners are about to go out, clung ever closer.

Paris had been devastated by Emlyn's departure. Rugby, such a release of aggression, had lost much of its charm. He could always talk to Emlyn, who understood the demons and anger lurking beneath the surface.

Hengist, stung by Oriana's accusations that he'd given up teaching, was now taking the Upper Fifth's history set abandoned by Emlyn. This was a revelation to the pupils because he made the subject so vivid and amusing. On one occasion, they acted out the Munich Conference. Boffin, with his supercilious, toothy face, made the perfect Chamberlain, Lubemir was Mussolini, and the nasty German diplomat demanding more and more of Czechoslovakia was naturally Cosmo.

Lessons went in a flash. Paris wanted to tape every word. You could hear the tramp of jackboots, smell the gas of the concentration camps as Hengist built up the nightmare menace of Nazi Germany.

Hengist, desperately missing Oriana, found great solace in teaching Paris. So did Theo, whose back grew increasingly painful as he laboured to finish Sophocles, but was somehow soothed as he and Paris talked long into the night, devouring the great classical writers.

Obsessed with work, Paris had less time for either Bianca or Dora, but he still went back to the

Old Coach House on Sundays, shutting himself in his room to read and work and never too busy to admit Dulcie and Northcliffe, who both loved nothing better than to curl up on his bed.

Paris's over-active imagination was invariably triggered off by things he read. When a Sunday tabloid, early in March, claimed that badly abused children often torture animals and abuse smaller children, he grew utterly distraught, banishing a tearful Dulcie, pushing away a bewildered Northcliffe, terrified of harming them, before trashing his room.

Ian, under continuing pressure from Alex Bruce, was fed up with Paris and increasingly muttering about returning him to care. Only last week, when he had merely removed a leaf from the boy's hair, Paris had clenched his fists and nearly thumped him.

This terrified Patience. As Paris was doing *Macbeth* for GCSE coursework, in a desperate attempt to cheer him up and provide him with inspiration, she drove him, on the third Saturday in March, to see a Royal Shakespeare performance. Paris, who'd wanted to slope off and see Bianca, hardly spoke and listened to a tape of *Lord of the Flies* all the way there.

Poor Patience, no intellectual, was desperately tired and, despite the thunderclaps and battle din, fought sleep throughout the play. She was worried Paris minded being seen in public with such an old scarecrow and tried to keep her raucous voice down. When they went to the bar in the interval, lots of people gazed at the white beauty of Paris in his severe dark grey school suit and then at her, pondering the connection. She had ordered half a bottle of white and some smoked salmon sandwiches, cobwebbed in cellophane, and thought what a ghastly middle-class, middle-aged thing to do.

' "Screw your courage", "Is this a dagger"? We always intoned, "Out, damned spot!" when we had spots at school. *Macbeth*'s so full of quotations,' she gabbled, desperate to keep the conversation going.

Paris answered in monosyllables. Patience longed to get tanked up, but she had to drive home. Conscious of Paris's set, white face beside her on the return journey, she was filled with despair. Ian was right. It wasn't working. He clearly loathed living with them. A small voice inside her also said: He might be more grateful.

It was after midnight when they reached home, greeted by a grinning, sleepy-eyed, singing Northcliffe.

'I do hope the play didn't upset you too much,' said Patience. 'It is very harrowing and so sad at the end.'

As Paris went towards the door, she asked if there was anything about it he'd particularly liked.

'The bogs in the theatre were nice,' muttered Paris and shot upstairs.

Patience went out to check the horses, who at least whickered and were pleased to see her, even when she sobbed into Plover's dappled grey shoulder. When she finally came to bed, she found Ian in a martyred heap. 'Of course I haven't slept, I've been worried stiff about you on those roads.'

*   *   *

296

Next day was Mothering Sunday—a traditional day for children in care to go berserk because they were made so aware of not having a mother around. Remembering last year's hysterical scenes, when Paris had broken up his room yet again, screaming how he missed his mother and that Ian hated him and anyway, Ian and Patience were so old, they'd die soon and he'd be sent to another foster home, Patience steeled herself.

She'd fed the horses and, as it was a mild day, turned them out in their rugs. She was simultaneously frying bacon, grilling sausages and mushrooms and emptying the bins when Paris walked in. Grabbing the black bin bag and taking it to the dustbins outside, he dropped an envelope on the kitchen table.

He's leaving, thought Patience in panic, oh please God no, but, opening the letter with trembling hands, she found a Mother's Day card of shocking pink roses, with the words 'To a Wonderful Mother' on the front.

'Dear Patience,' Paris had written inside. 'Thank you for *Macbeth*. It was so awesome I couldn't speak afterwards. Love, Paris'.

She had to read it three times before the words swam before her eyes, then she broke into noisy sobs.

'I'm sorry.' An appalled Paris, returning, snatched the card from her. 'I didn't mean to—'

'No, no.' With one large, red hand, Patience reached for the kitchen roll, with the other she snatched back her card.

'It's the most wonderful thing that ever happened. It's just unexpected, that's all. I was worried we were old and boring and you didn't like

297

living here.'

Paris shrugged. 'Well, I do.'

'We want you to stay with us more than anything,' muttered Patience. 'We've tried to act cool because we didn't want to frighten you or make you feel claustrophobic.'

Paris said nothing, but his normally ashen face was flooded with colour.

They were brought back to earth by the smell of burning sausages. Next moment Dulcie marched in with the little wheelbarrow given her by the builders working on the Randal Stancombe science block. Today it was full of sand.

'Those men better get their arses into gear,' announced Dulcie, 'or the building won't be fucking ready in time.'

Patience turned to retrieve the sausages and Paris rescued the bacon on the Aga, both trying to hide their laughter, which diffused the situation.

101

The match between Larks and Bagley's third
fifteen took place a week later, on an unexpectedly
mild evening. Unbeaten all term, Bagley regarded
victory as so certain that the entire team had
raging hangovers from a tarts and vicars party the
night before. For those in need of succour, Cosmo,
still in his dog collar, was circulating with a big
brown jug frothing with Alka-Seltzer.

'Attila the Hunk can't work miracles,' he said
bitchily, 'even if he does have scores to settle.'

'It'll be more than fifty–nil,' said Lando, who
hadn't bothered to wash off his tart's eyeliner and
scarlet lipstick. 'I've had a bet.'

Over at Larks, Xav was refusing to get on the
bus.

'Please don't make me go back to Bagley,' he
begged Emlyn. 'They'll lynch me for bullying
Dicky.'

'Not if I'm around. You're the only player with
big match experience, who knows the capabilities
of the Bagley team.'

As a V-sign to Alex Bruce, who'd sacked them
both, Emlyn had made Xav captain. It had been
worth it to see the terror and delight on Xav's
broad, normally impassive face.

Now terror predominated.

'Cosmo and Lubemir are in the team, they'll bury
me.'

'Feral's the one they'll try and bury. You've got to
be there for him, to stop him losing his rag. He
didn't sleep last night.'

'Nor did I,' grumbled Xav.

*   *   *

Feral ricocheted between longing and panic. Pete Wainwright from Larkminster Rovers was coming to the match and, if impressed, might offer Feral a trial. He might also see Bianca again. Agonizing rumours had filtered through that she and Paris were an item. How could he not murder Paris?

Under his cheerful air of imperturbability, Emlyn was churning worse than his team at the prospect of returning to Bagley, 'the land of lost content', where he'd been so happy and hopeful and so hurt and humiliated by Oriana's coming out. Hengist wouldn't miss an opportunity to emphasize the good he was doing for the community, so the press would be out in force—raking things up.

Hengist, who'd combined a governors' meeting over lunch, had laid on a bar and buffet in the pavilion and buses to transport Larks supporters to the game. He had also invited local bigwigs: the Mayor and the Bishop. Ashton and Cindy who, like Randal, loved to pretend they'd been responsible for saving Larks, had also rolled up.

Ashton, eyeing up the Bagley boys, who were certainly pretty, was in fact feeling bleak. The business pages that morning had launched blistering attacks on S and C and other private companies that had specialized in education. Not only were LEAs they'd taken over not meeting their targets, but the buildings they'd imposed on schools had turned out to be shoddy, poky, taking too long to build and not able to withstand the wear and tear of children. S and C badly needed a hit.

Still, it was hard to be bleak on such a lovely evening. Crowds already thronged the touchline and, although the daffodils were nearly over, primroses starred the banks and a pale haze of green leaf softened many trees, while others were pinky roan from buds about to burst. Heavy rain earlier enhanced the jade green of the pitch.

It was even mild enough for Randal Stancombe to descend from his chopper in a new, exquisitely cut off-white suit. Still smarting from being cuckolded by Hengist, he had rolled up with Anthea Belvedon, radiant in Parma violet, with a calf-length mink flung round her shoulders and a huge sapphire ring on her right hand.

'What a ravishing fur,' sighed Vicky Fairchild.

'A gift from Randal,' said Anthea, loudly enough to be heard by Ruth Walton, who'd just arrived, flushed from lunch, in last year's Lindka Cierach. 'I didn't realize it was going to be so warm—hello, Ruth—Randal and I feel for Dicky, Dora and Jade's sake it's so important to show one's face at such functions.'

'And I'm reporting you to animal rights,' hissed Dora, feeding roast beef sandwiches to Cadbury. 'That coat is so pants.'

Alex Bruce was fuming. How dare Hengist schedule a rugby match on the same day as a GCSE science revision workshop, which no one would now attend. Even Boffin had defected and, already miked up with a silver whistle round his scrawny neck, was poised to referee the game. And how dare Hengist invite back Emlyn, who had nearly drowned Poppet?

'Ten Downing Street is deceptively large once

you get inside,' Poppet, several months pregnant, was now boasting to Anthea.

Noticing Mrs Walton looking a shade disconsolate, Cosmo thrust a large vodka and tonic into her hand.

'Ever considered a toyboy?' he murmured.

Hengist, not confident of shaven-headed Denzil, who preferred any game to rugger, was himself revving up the rest of the Bagley third fifteen. 'Never take any team coached by Emlyn for granted. He'll have told them to attack and attack and that nothing matters except getting points on the board.'

'It's still going to be three hundred to nil,' grumbled Lando. 'Christ, my head hurts.'

'Here they are, here they are,' went up the shout as Randal's crimson minibus rumbled up the drive.

'Larks wouldn't still exist without Daddy,' boasted Jade. 'He's given them so much financial support.'

'Oh shut up,' muttered Dora.

Bagley, incensed by the loss of Emlyn, watched Larks emerge with mixed feelings.

'There's Graffi, still lush,' sighed Milly.

Graffi, still grinning although black under the eyes, was reeling with relief because he'd completed his ten-hour art exam earlier in the week and was happy with what he had produced.

'My God,' said Amber, cutting off her conversation with the Master of Beagles at Radley, 'is that really Xavier? He must have lost a couple of stone and grown a foot. Looks quite attractive.'

'Very attractive if one remembers his trust fund,' agreed Milly.

'Hi, Xav.'

'Hello there, Xav,' purred Jade.

'Welcome back, Xav,' shouted Amber.

'Booo!' shouted Dora, who'd been at Dicky's hipflask. 'Have you forgotten he tried to kill my brother?'

'Shut up,' hissed a discomfited Dicky, as an equally discomfited Xav belted across the grass to the visitors' changing room.

'And here comes the Larks Lothario,' shouted Amber.

A pair of black-jeaned legs, as long and pliable as liquorice, were finally followed down the bus steps by a Nike scarlet jacket and a haughty black face.

'God he's awesome,' sighed Milly.

Glancing coldly round, reluctant to take a first step on enemy territory, Feral caught sight of Bianca standing on top of a car, in a bright orange poncho, her dark hair lifting in the breeze; he started violently as they gazed and gazed and gazed at each other.

'Move it, for fuck's sake.'

From behind, Johnnie, Monster and Rocky ejected Feral on to the gravel.

Oh God, thought Bianca in panic, I still love him.

Thank God, thought Feral in ecstasy, she still loves me.

In a daze he glanced up to see if she was real, then, smiling, shaking his head, waving his hands, he reeled after Xav.

Paris, who'd witnessed this eye-meet from the home changing room, felt punched in the gut. Then he saw Janna jumping out of Emlyn's muddy Renault. At first he was shocked how tired, pale and old she looked, but when both Larks and Bagley pupils ran forward to welcome her, and her

303

face was illuminated by that tender, joyful smile, he realized how her new, short, curly hair became her, and how protectively Emlyn was towering over her, sheltering her from the mob as it surged around them.

'Mr Davies, Mr Davies, look, it's Mr Davies back.'

Paris wanted to join the throng and beg Janna's forgiveness and friendship. He wanted to bolt back to the Old Coach House and hide. He couldn't play rugby with so many cross-currents.

'Janna, darling.' It was Hengist, hugging her and then shaking hands with Emlyn. 'Marvellous to see you both. Sally sent her apologies, she's had to go and see her mother.'

Like hell, thought Janna. Normally such a trooper, Sally had taken Oriana's coming out very badly, particularly the press delving around and raising the ghost of Mungo. Today, with Emlyn's return, they would be out in force, and she hadn't been able to face it.

'Tell her her bulbs are being miraculous,' said Janna. 'Sheets of daffodils and hyacinths, even fritillaries; they've cheered everyone up so much.'

'I will; she'll be so pleased. Come and have a drink.'

'Janna can,' said Emlyn. 'I'm going to crank up my team.'

Emlyn found his Larks players strangely silent as with clumsily shaking hands they tried to find the necks of their crimson and yellow striped shirts and zip up shorts less white than most of their faces.

'Ouch,' yelled Johnnie Fowler, as he bit the inside of his cheek instead of his chewing gum.

Emlyn smiled round, steadying them, then placed

a rugby ball on the floor in front of them.

'This is your best friend, so don't give him away. He has one destiny, over the line or between the posts. Don't let them bait you, don't swear at the ref, don't spit, or bite, kill the ball, or collapse in the scrum. However much you want to, it'll only put points on the board for the other side, not for us. Watch, watch the whole time.'

Larks parents were out in force. Cigarettes slotted into their lower lips, fathers with tattoos, earrings and T-shirts, they looked so young compared with the tiny sprinkling of Bagley parents.

'S'pose you have to grow old before you're rich enough to afford fees here,' observed Graffi's father, Dafydd, who was getting tanked up with Stormin' Norman.

Pearl's boxer dad had a whole quiche in one hand and a pint of red in the other.

Pearl and Kitten, in crop tops showing off grabbable waists, their purple flares sweeping the damp grass, tossed their shining, straightened manes as they paraded up and down, giggling and being eyed up by the Bagley boys.

Randal moved around pressing the flesh, getting himself and his beautiful suit photographed as much as possible, distributing largesse to the inhabitants of the Shakespeare Estate.

'So pleased Larks is doing well; what subject is your youngster taking in GCSE?'

'Sex and violence,' quipped Dafydd cheekily and regretted it when Stancombe's face blackened and he made a note on his pocket computer.

Through the cobweb-festooned window, Xav could see everyone nudging and staring as his

305

parents arrived. Bianca, full of chat, dragged Taggie off to the bar. Rupert, who had no desire to socialize, stayed in the car with a bottle of brandy and *Opening Lines*, the OCR poetry set book, which, after repeated slugs, he was finding increasingly difficult to understand. He'd never met such a bunch of whingers moaning on about their dreadful childhoods. He could relate to Philip Larkin or Simon Armitage stealing from his mother's handbag and punching an irritating wife, but what the fuck was this guy Stevie Smith going on about?

> To carry a child into adult life,
> Is good, I say it is not.
> To carry the child into adult life
> Is to be handicapped.

In his wild youth, Rupert had had a Rolls-Royce with black windows. He could have done with it now, to stop so many ghastly mothers waving and gazing in. Nor could he avoid seeing Taggie being welcomed by all her dreadful new friends: Pittsy and fearful stinking, whiskery Skunk and that ghastly football manager, Pete Wainwright, who'd clearly got the raging hots for her, not to mention that fat Welshman who seemed to have bewitched Xav.

Rupert knew he was in the wrong. Since he'd decided to take this wretched exam and Taggie had proved such a hit at Larks, he'd been vile to her and ratty with the children.

Christ, she was even allowing the caretaker Wally to peck her on the cheek. Rupert was finding it as hard to climb out of his mega sulk as to break out

306

of Broadmoor. Bloody hell, Stancombe, looking an absolute prat in his white suit, was now kissing Taggie—pity a snow plough couldn't run him over. Rupert was going to win this bet if it killed him. He took another slug.

*   *   *

Knowing they would expect great things, Paris observed that Ian and Patience had formed a merry party with Artie, Theo, the Brigadier and Lily.

'Larks look alarmingly fit,' grumbled Jack Waterlane as Monster, Johnnie and Danny the Irish thundered past chucking a ball to each other.

'Only because they stayed in last night,' said Anatole.

Bagley's shirts, sea blue with white collars, gave them a look of deceptive innocence. The sun, darting in and out of big white clouds, spotlit the Mansion one moment, an acid-green lime in Badger's Retreat another, Mrs Walton's laughing face as a passing Cosmo waved to her the next.

It was Larks's first glimpse of Paris for eighteen months. He had shot up and filled out, his jewellery had gone, his white blond hair, no longer gelled upwards, was longer with a side parting and, like Rupert Brooke's, poetically brushed back from his forehead. He was as dead pan as ever, but he had a new confidence. Nodding to his old classmates, but not stopping to say hello, he turned to Junior Lloyd-Foxe, yelling at him to pass the ball.

'Parse, parse,' mocked Monster.

'Lord, la-di-da,' shouted Johnnie, 'listen to the

Prince of Posh "parsing" the "bawl". He's too grand for his old friends now.'

Paris ignored them, but a flush crept up his cheek.

Bagley won the toss, and chose the Mansion end, with the soft west wind behind them.

'Bagley to kick off.'

'OK, boys,' quietly Xav echoed Martin Johnson, 'let's take this game.'

'Very plucky of your lads to take on Bagley,' Poppet was saying patronizingly to Janna.

'Have you ever seen anything so gross as Boffin's bum in those shorts?' hissed Dora as Boffin blew a shrill plaintive note on his whistle.

Lando booted the ball over the heads of the Larks forwards. Next moment Feral moved into its path, caught it and set off for goal, dodging round Anatole and Lubemir, flashing his teeth at them, charging straight for the Hon. Jack, aiming for his right side, luring him on to his right foot, then bolting past on his left.

'Tackle him,' bellowed Lando, but Lubemir, hurling himself at Feral, only caught air as Feral skipped out of the way, streaking over the line, burying the ball under the posts to ecstatic, flabbergasted cheers.

'That gorilla won't kick it ten yards,' drawled Cosmo, as Rocky, having laboriously readjusted the plastic stand, finally managed to balance the ball on top of it.

'Our Farver,' mumbled Rocky and belted it over the bar to even more flabbergasted cheers.

'Very plucky of you to take on Larks,' Janna told Poppet.

'I ain't no gorilla.' Rocky marched up to Cosmo,

308

shoving a huge fist in his terrified face.

'Rocky, no!' howled Xav.

Reluctantly Rocky lowered his fist.

'If you do that again, Rocky,' Boffin's miked voice echoed round the field, 'I shall send you to the sin bin.'

Three minutes later, Rocky leapt miles in the air in the line-out and catching the ball, passed to Xav, who passed to Graffi, who trundled down the field like a little Welsh pony, black hair tossing, slap into the Bagley defence, powering his way through them and crashing face down in the mud over the line, but with the ball staying firm between his palm and the pitch. Again Rocky converted.

'Rocky by name, Rocky by nature,' yelled the increasingly intoxicated crowd of Larks supporters.

'Steady, steady,' pleaded Emlyn, a great golden bear prowling the touchline. 'Oh Christ, well done,' as Xav kicked eighty yards up the field into touch.

Bagley rallied. Lubemir, winning the scrum, passed to Anatole, who passed to Jack, who found himself running into a solid Berlin wall of defence: Monster, Rocky and Johnnie Fowler, who brought him crashing down. Xav took the ball off him and kicked it up field, where it was gathered up by Feral, who with Ferrari acceleration charged up to the Bagley defence, their gumshields glaring, waiting to flatten him, and popped over a glorious left-footed drop goal.

As he sauntered back, festooned with cheering, thumping, ecstatic Larks players, Miss Cambola, who'd been practising with Kylie Rose and the choir, started to sing 'Swing Low, Sweet Chariot', as, from all sides, crimson Larks banners were

309

waving.

'That's our tune,' snorted Biffo Rudge.

Bagley were now displaying all the symptoms of nerves, losing in the line-out, high tackling, killing the ball, sledging, biting, resorting to every dirty trick. What was also plain to everyone was that Paris was out of it, passing to the wrong people or the other side, kicking in empty spaces, and when Boffin blew the whistle, first on Monster for high tackling, and then on Johnnie for swearing and spitting at Cosmo, Paris missed two easy penalties.

'Lord Posh, Lord Posh,' barracked the Larks crowd.

'Lord, la-di-da, nose in the air,' bellowed Stormin' Norman to the edification of the entire field, 'you're as useless as tits on a bull.'

Pete Wainwright laughed happily because he was gaining intense pleasure watching Feral. You could see the boy thinking, glancing around each time he had the ball, using his brain. The others mostly kicked and hoped. Xavier was playing beautifully too. It was gratifying to see two black boys working so well together, cleaning up in the white heartland of an English public school. Pete was so pleased to see the delighted pride on Xav's sweet mother's face.

'The directors loved your lunch—it was a great success,' he told Taggie.

Johnnie Fowler's mother, Shelley, swayed up to Rupert's car. 'Your Xav's playing like a little king, Lord Black.' Then, when Rupert lowered the window a millimetre: 'My Johnnie's the good-looking one, didn't go into Larks much in the old days, had a lot of days off, but since Emlyn, Taggie and the Brig's taken over, he's hardly missed a

310

day.' Noticing how handsome Rupert was, she added, 'Would you like me to get you a drink?'

'If you're going that way.'

Seeing Rupert looking more friendly, Poppet Bruce rushed over. 'Rupert, Rupert, how's your GCSE Eng. lit. going?'

'Fine,' snapped Rupert.

'Oh! You're reading *Opening Lines*. Charisma's finding it so enriching. Each poem yielding its meaning.'

'Not to me, they don't. I can't make head nor tail of this chap Stevie Smith.'

'Oh, how priceless.' Poppet went off into peals of laughter. 'Smith's a woman, Rupert.'

'Explains why the poem's such crap.'

'Don't be so sexist. You'll never pass your GCSE that way. Why not join our workshop in the Easter holidays?'

Fortunately relief arrived in the form of Shelley Fowler and a large brandy and ginger.

'Get in,' hissed Rupert, winding up the window.

'Johnnie's got that book too,' said Shelley, picking up *Opening Lines*. 'Didn't understand a word till Janna explained it.'

*   *   *

Half-time. The sides gathered in two groups, towelling away sweat, swigging bottled water, pouring it over their heads. Hengist strode on to the pitch.

'What the hell are you playing at?'

'They're as tough as shit,' protested Jack Waterlane. 'I think I've cracked a rib.'

'They really vant to vin,' grumbled Anatole.

311

'I've fucked my ankle, sir,' lied Cosmo.
'Well, you better go off for the second half.'

*   *   *

Larks were down to fourteen men: Danny the Irish had cramp. Wally was working on his instep.

Emlyn was talking in a low voice to his team, praising them to the now pink and blue flecked sky, isolating individual triumphs.

'But the second half's going to be tougher; you'll be getting tired. If I sub any of you, it's a compliment, means you've played your hearts out. Rocky, you've been awesome, and Monster and Johnnie.' Emlyn's square face glowed. 'I can't tell you how great it's been, good as scoring for Wales.'

Janna, watching Emlyn's joy, felt conflicting emotions. How glorious to see Larks ascending, but she felt so sorry for Paris.

Dora's despair, on the other hand, was total. She could see Hengist giving the team hell. Poor Paris, head hanging, face concealed by a damp curtain of blond hair, must be feeling suicidal, not just about his dud performance, but about Feral and Bianca as well.

'Stop bullying him,' she shouted. 'It's so unfair.'

Cadbury, who'd been stuffing his face all afternoon, wandered off to drink from Middle Field Pond. Following him, Dora decided she must save Paris.

102

As the pep talk ended and the teams changed ends and took up their positions, they were distracted by howls of laughter and wolf whistles as a streaker came running out of Middle Field and raced across the pitch skipping and dancing, arms outstretched. Her high breasts and bottom were too small to wobble. The waist, in between, as yet lacked definition, the racing legs were still a little plump. A pale blonde triangle was just discernible between her thighs. Her face was hidden by a pulled-down baseball cap.

'Who is it? Who is it?' yelled the delighted and cheering crowd. Then, as the streaker did a cartwheel and two handstands, her baseball cap fell off, her blonde plaits tumbled out and a chocolate Labrador bounded on to the pitch after her.

'My God, it's Dora,' said Lando. 'Look, sir, a streaker.'

Hengist swung round and laughed.

'Good heavens, so there is.'

'Gone away,' brayed Jack Waterlane as Siegfried's horn call rang out joyfully on Miss Cambola's trumpet.

Binoculars and little oblong silver cameras were being raised all round the pitch as the cheers escalated. The press raced along the touchline.

'Go for it, Dora,' yelled both teams, momentarily distracted from despair and elation.

' "Like an unbodied joy whose race has just begun",' murmured Theo.

'Lovely little bottom,' sighed Artie.

Northcliffe growled at the sight of a passing Cadbury. Boffin clamped his hands over his eyes in horror. Anthea, who had been upstaging Poppet, turned back to the pitch.

'Oh look, a streaker, how common. We should never have allowed this bonding with Larks!' Then she gave an almighty squawk: 'My God, it's Dora. Dicky! Randal! Do something!'

Randal, only too happy to show how fit he was, set off in pursuit.

' "The Assyrian came down like the wolf on the fold," ' murmured Ian Cartwright.

Hot on Randal's heels came Joan. 'Dora Belvedon,' she bellowed, 'come here at once.'

'Sit!' howled Cosmo to roars of laughter. 'Stay!'

Evading capture, circling, Dora galloped up to Paris.

'Get your stupid finger out,' she panted, breasts quivering, face red from running, eyes flashing, hair escaping from her plaits. 'You've got to loosen up and win this game. You can't let Feral beat you.'

As she slid to her knees in the mud, pretending to shake an imaginary football shirt at the crowd, Paris started to laugh. Then he heard footsteps and caught a whiff of aftershave; Randal was thundering in from the left, Joan, like the Paddington-Larkminster Intercity, from the right.

'Come here,' yelled Randal.

'Come here,' bellowed Joan.

The crowd were in uproar. Both Hengist and Emlyn tried to contain their laughter as Dora gave her pursuers the slip again.

Scenting danger, detesting Randal, Paris tugged off his sea-blue shirt to more wolf whistles and belted after Dora, grabbing her and forcing the shirt over her head, but having to loosen his grip as he tried to shove both her arms in. Next moment Dora had scuttled off giggling—slap into Randal.

Alas, in the slippery patch near the goalposts, Randal's Guccis had no grip, and he slid past her flat on his back, covering his lovely new suit in mud. The press went berserk.

'This is the way the gentlemen ride,' shouted Amber, 'gallopy, gallopy, gallopy and *down* in the mud.'

'That ain't no gentleman,' said Cosmo, topping up Mrs Walton's glass.

Dora, running away, turned to laugh, and promptly hit the buffers of Primrose Duddon's vast bosom.

'I've got her, JJ.'

Thundering up, Joan flung her duffel coat round a frantically wriggling Dora.

'How dare you bring Boudicca into disrepute?'

'I had to jolt Paris out of his despair.'

'This way, Dora, to me, Dora,' yelled the photographers, as, clapping and punching the air, Dora allowed herself to be frogmarched up to Anthea.

'Take your daughter home, Lady Belvedon.'

'You little slut,' hissed Anthea, and the next minute had slapped Dora viciously across the face, then again with the back of her hand, catching Dora's pink cheek with Randal's huge sapphire, so blood spurted down Joan's duffel coat and Paris's blue rugby shirt underneath.

'Stop that.' Outraged, Janna shot forward. But Cadbury was quicker. Leaping to the defence of his mistress, he threatened Anthea's tiny ankle

315

with his big white teeth, making her scream her head off.

'Get away, you brute.' Randal, racing up, aimed a vicious kick at Cadbury.

'Don't you hurt my dog,' squealed Dora, kicking Randal in the ankle, spurting blood all over the part of his white suit that wasn't coated in mud, before grabbing Cadbury by the collar.

On cue, Partner, who'd been chatting up his old friend Elaine, rushed up to Cadbury, jumping up and down, licking his ears in congratulation.

'My leg,' shrieked Anthea, pretending to faint into Alex Bruce's skinny arms, as a tiny drop of blood seeped through her flesh-coloured hold-ups. 'I must have a tetanus jab.'

'And a tourniquet,' murmured Amber.

Randal was howling abuse at Cadbury and Dora. It took Hengist to restore order.

'Neither you nor Dora are allowed back on to the field with blood injuries,' he told Anthea. 'You all right, Dora, darling?' Whipping out a blue spotted handkerchief, he mopped Dora's cheek. 'Looks nasty. We better get on with the game. I'm sure First Aid'll sort you out, Anthea. The ambulance is over there. Meanwhile we'd better find Paris another shirt and you take Dora to the sick bay, Joan.' Then, when Joan looked mutinous: '*Now.*'

There was no way he was going to abandon Dora to the untender mercies of Randal and Anthea.

'She can't bring that dog,' announced Joan. 'Hand him over to your mother, Dora.'

'I can't.' Tears, near the surface, spilled over, mingling with the blood on Dora's cheeks. 'Randal will put him down. He and Mummy hate Cadbury.'

'I'll take him.' Ian Cartwright took off his tie for a

lead but Northcliffe's golden hackles were up, his teeth bared.

'I'll take him,' said Dicky, borrowing Ian's tie.

*   *   *

As the second half began, Paris, in a no. 16 shirt, could hardly bear to see Dora being dragged off, defiantly yelling: 'Come on Bagley,' to deafening applause from both sides. Joan looked absolutely furious.

Amber shook her head. 'How can that woman, who has no heart, teach us about the heart in biology?'

The heat of the day had subsided; the horizon was ringed with rose; through still bare trees a moon to match the yellow stripe in Larks's shirts was rising to aid the floodlighting switched on for the second half.

'What a dreadful waste of electricity,' chuntered Poppet. 'Why couldn't Hengist schedule this match earlier in the day?'

Johnnie and Graffi, who'd played their hearts out, had been subbed, which gave Graffi the chance to chat up Milly, and Johnnie a chance to chat to the media.

'Emlyn's cool,' he was telling the BBC. 'I always got sent off at football because I had scraps. Emlyn's helped me wiv my anger management.'

'He could give Lady Belvedon a few lessons,' said the interviewer.

Primrose and Pearl were discussing their respective revision of the Russian Revolution.

'We've been watching a video of *Doctor Zhivago*,' volunteered Pearl proudly.

317

'Hengist is taking us to St Petersburg for a long weekend after Easter,' said Primrose.

The roaring and cheering were continuous now. Bagley had come back with a vengeance and two tries from Paris who, feeling he owed it to Dora, was playing like a man possessed. Rupert had abandoned his sulks and Stevie Smith, and was yelling his handsome head off. 'Come on Xav, come on Larks.'

' "You'll Never Walk Alone",' sang Kylie, her sweet voice ringing out to the accompaniment of Cambola's trumpet, and all the Larks parents, children and teachers joined in.

Janna wiped her eyes. It was wonderful seeing Skunk and Pittsy really cheering, and she was so proud of Emlyn.

Probably the only people not concentrating were Cosmo and Mrs Walton.

'I've always wanted you,' murmured Cosmo. 'Will you come back to my cell?'

'I thought you were injured,' teased a once more radiant Ruth.

'I've sprained my ankle, not my cock. You must give me lessons. One cannot be too good in bed.'

*   *   *

Five minutes to go. Bagley was playing catch-up. They were six points behind Larks. A try and a conversion would do it. Somehow Larks hung on with heroic tackling and covering work, but gradually their defence was driven back.

Only a minute to go. Janna couldn't bear to look. Please dear God, for Emlyn's and the children's sake.

318

Paris had the ball and was scorching down the pitch.

'Come on,' yelled Theo, Artie and the Cartwrights. He was through, but with Aston Martin acceleration, Feral stormed in from the right, tackling him five yards from the line, his arms clamping round Paris's hips, bringing him crashing to the ground. The line was a foot away— beyond it, the heavenly city. Wriggling forward, Paris lost control of the ball, which fell forward over the line.

'Let go of me, you fucker,' he howled, trying to struggle forwards in the mud to touch it down. But Feral clung on. A second later, Rocky had pounded up and kicked the ball into the crowd as the whistle went.

Feral and Paris lay on the ground, hearts thumping, both winded, checking they weren't hurt. Then they turned to look at each other, both faces caked in mud, Paris's as brown as Feral's. For a second, panting and exhausted, they scowled.

Then, as if in a dream, their hands stretched out and, as they grinned, their hands met in a grounded high five.

'You was wicked, man,' gasped Paris.

'We've won, we've beaten Bagley.' All restraint gone, screaming her head off, Janna raced on to the pitch, running from exhausted Larks player to player, kissing their dirty faces before falling into an equally ecstatic Emlyn's arms:

'We did it, we did it.'

Tipping her head right back, Janna smiled up into his rugged, ruddy, overjoyed face, feeling his hot sweating body and his heart pounding against hers. They were brought back to earth by the jeering of Johnnie Fowler.

'Cheer up, you fat commie. At least you came second.'

'Take zat back, you smug little vanker,' howled Anatole.

It was only Emlyn's lightning reaction, dropping Janna, swinging round and catching Anatole's arm before his fist smashed into Johnnie's face, that prevented a riot.

'Break it up, you two,' he roared, in addition grabbing Johnnie's shirt collar, 'or I'll bang your thick skulls together. It's only a game.'

'That's not what you told us in the dressing room beforehand,' panted Johnnie, aiming a kick at Anatole. Then seeing Emlyn's face blacken: 'Sir!'

'That's enough, Anatole,' said Hengist, taking him from Emlyn. 'Be more gracious, you were outplayed.'

103

Ashton, Cindy and Randal, having had a good stretch of their legs to take in Badger's Retreat, were now claiming credit for Larks's victory to *The Times*.

'We felt it crucial to give these disadvantaged youngsters a second chance,' Cindy was saying. 'Yes, "Payne" with a "Y".'

'We're keeping a close watch, of course,' purred Ashton. Catching sight of Hengist, he added, 'Bad luck, you must be very disappointed and surprised.'

'Not when you consider Emlyn's been coaching them,' said Hengist lightly. 'After those rather worrying reports in your Sunday paper today'—he smiled at *The Times*'s reporter—'about S and C's catastrophic involvement in the educational field, they must regard Larks High, particularly after today's triumph, as the jewel in their crown.' Then, nodding at a scowling Ashton and Cindy: 'Do grab a drink before the presentation.'

Captain Xavier went up to shake hands with Randal in his muddy suit and to collect the gold-plated rugby ball to deafening applause from his parents and those from the Shakespeare Estate, who were already legless.

Xav was followed by his players who, in the floodlighting, cast giant shadows in two directions. But Randal, on the podium (provided by himself), cast the biggest, blackest shadow of all.

Feral was Man of the Match.

'Well played,' said Pete Wainwright, handing him his card. 'For once your supporters didn't exaggerate. Football isn't that different to rugby. Give me a bell and I'll fix a date for a trial.'

'That's wicked, man,' muttered Feral.

Maybe, maybe Bianca soon wouldn't be so out of reach after all. 'Give me time, baby.'

Inside, Hengist was seething, but he'd learnt to be magnanimous in defeat.

'Fantastic victory, Emlyn, terrific entertainment for the spectators.'

Emlyn grinned. 'I think Dora should have won Man of the Match rather than Feral.'

'That bitch of a mother,' exploded Janna.

'Hush, darling,' Hengist took Janna's arm. 'Come and have a drink. You'll want to be with your boys, Emlyn.' It was an order. 'Join Janna and me later. You must be so proud,' he told her as they set off towards the pavilion.

The first pale stars were coming out, as if the deepening blue sky wanted to boast it had primroses too.

'So pleased about Feral's trial,' said Hengist. 'If he needs any advice about converting to soccer . . . ?'

How generous and sweet you are, thought Janna.

'Paris played really well in the end,' she said. Then, as they were out of earshot: 'Do you think he's still hung up about us?'

'Not at all, he's working incredibly hard. Well played!' Hengist ruffled a passing Xav's black hair. 'Really good to see you back. Your parents must be ecstatic.'

As they moved on through a copse of young wild cherry trees, he murmured, 'Are *you* still hung up about us, darling?'

Janna started. Hengist turned her to face him,

322

gazing down at her, laughing eyes for once serious. 'I truly didn't mean to hurt you.'

'But you love Sally,' finished Janna. 'I know—and it doesn't hurt any more,' she added, realizing in amazement it was true. 'It's just lovely we can be friends. I do love you.'

'And I, you,' and he dropped a long kiss on her forehead.

*   *   *

Emlyn, still euphoric, accepting congratulations from Artie and Theo, about to round up his team for the plunge bath, reflected that he hadn't thought about Oriana since he arrived. Irked by being dismissed by Hengist, he glanced idly towards the pavilion, then saw Hengist and Janna had not even reached it but were lurking in the wild cherry copse, talking intimately, smiling at each other; now Hengist was stealing a kiss. Emlyn felt his great blaze of euphoria turn to ashes.

Then soft dark hair brushed against his cheek, and a childish little voice said:

'Well done, Emlyn, I couldn't help cheering like mad for my old school.'

It was Vicky, pretty as ever in a turquoise blazer, with a schoolboy's turquoise and olive-green scarf round her neck, looking as young as any of her pupils.

'I'm having a party at my flat here tonight. Why don't you come? Lots of Bagley people will be there. You can always stop over in the spare room, if you don't want to drive.'

'I've got to take the team home,' said Emlyn, noticing Hengist and Janna were still gazing into each other's eyes. 'But thanks, I might well look in later.'

*   *   *

Paris wandered towards Badger's Retreat in total confusion. He cringed at the memory of the missed penalties. He'd played atrociously, only redeemed by those tries in the second half, when Dora's streak had shaken him out of his despondency. As if he were coming round after an operation, not knowing how much it would hurt, he hadn't worked out how he felt about Feral and Bianca. Like Philip Larkin in their poetry set book, he'd probably been 'too selfish, withdrawn And easily bored' to love Bianca.

Now he was haunted by the thought of Anthea cutting up Dora's round, sweet face. Randal had ruined his suit; Lady Belvedon had ruined her image as a 'lady'—the vicious bitch. Neither would forgive Dora.

After half an hour, when Emlyn hadn't joined the uproarious party spilling out of the pavilion, happily remembering how lovely his arms had felt round her earlier, Janna went in search of him. She found him among the crowd waving off the still stunned Larks fifteen.

'Are you coming back to the Dog and Duck to celebrate?' Janna tucked her arm through his. 'Lily and Christian and Cambola are just leaving.'

'I'll give it a miss tonight,' said Emlyn brusquely. 'Some of the Bagley teachers are having a party; I said I'd join them.' Not meeting Janna's eyes, he didn't see the hurt and disappointment. 'Can you get a lift with the Brig?'

'Of course,' said Janna in a small voice. 'Thank you for all you did for Larks today.'

But Emlyn had stalked off towards the car park.

*   *   *

As Graffi's father and Stormin' Norman were decanted on to the last bus and went home singing ' 'Ark, 'Ark! the Lark', Hengist reflected that being a host without Sally was very hard work.

How sweet Janna had looked; he'd have loved to whisk her upstairs to bed. All the same, he felt unusually tired—must be the end of term.

Back in his study in the Mansion, he poured himself a large whisky, put on a CD of Fischer-Dieskau singing *Winterreise* and, picking up his note-laden copy of Matthew Arnold's poems, settled down on the sofa with a weary Elaine's head on his lap. Headmasters' dogs get tired too, trailing after them, her gusty sigh seemed to say.

These holidays, vowed Hengist, he was going to write his book rather than politicking. Jupiter was too bloody demanding.

There was a knock on the door. Elaine, a good judge of character, didn't wag. It was Alex.

'A word, headmaster.'

The bloody man would only accept Perrier and sat bolt upright, as though it would be an act of decadence to collapse into the bear hug of one of Hengist's armchairs.

'That was a catastrophe.'

'Losing to Larks, I agree.'

'No, Dora Belvedon's disgusting display. How should we address the problem?'

'Having that bitch of a mother, not to mention

325

the odious Stancombe as a possible stepfather, should be punishment enough.'

Alex looked pained and cracked his knuckles, his Adam's apple wobbling as he swallowed. 'Anthea and Randal are supportive friends.'

'Not to poor Dora, they aren't.'

'She must be excluded for the rest of the term if not permanently.'

'Don't be fatuous, there are only a few days left. It was just high spirits.' Hengist drained his drink. 'At least she shook Paris out of his doldrums and brightened a dire afternoon.'

'Tomorrow's press will be disastrous.'

Hengist's anger boiled over.

'If you hadn't engineered the departure of the best bloody rugger coach Bagley has ever had, we'd have walked it today.'

'Too much emphasis is placed on competitive sports.'

'Bollocks,' roared Hengist. 'It's crucial for strengthening character, fostering qualities of leadership and channelling aggression. Look how Xavier Campbell-Black blossomed. He looks great and played a terrific match. But you had to kick him out without any kind of investigation. We failed him—and we've made an enemy of Rupert. How d'you think it feels having Campbell-Blacks yelling for Larks? Well, you're not getting rid of Dora. Now get out and wreck someone else's evening.'

*　　　*　　　*

Janna gave herself a talking-to as she made herself a cup of tea the following morning.

'You prayed and prayed that Larks wouldn't be humiliated by Bagley, so for heaven's sake be grateful for very large mercies, and don't go slipping in any prayers about Emlyn. I'm lucky to have you,' she told Partner, who wagged his tail in agreement. Emlyn was amiable enough, but had big feet for treading on paws.

Janna left early to buy a big celebratory cake from the baker's and to drape banners across the gate and reception. She felt the fifteen should tour Larkminster in an open-top bus like the World Cup players.

It was an exquisite morning, with only her and the sun in the quiet street, and celandines opening like more little suns on the banks.

She slowed down as the postman approached.

'Saw you on TV last night, Janna. Great result. That Feral played a blinder. *Scorpion*'s got a cartoon of a Red Dragon carrying lots of larks on his back.'

Janna was enchanted. She must get it framed for Emlyn. Why shouldn't he whoop it up with his Bagley mates. His car wasn't outside his digs. He probably never came home.

As she drove down Wilmington High Street, however, she was flagged down by a scarlet windmill—it was Vicky in a red rugger shirt nearly reaching to her knees, about to get into her pale blue Golf. She wore no make-up; her hair was drawn back and falling in a Jane Austen cascade, pretty as always.

'Jannie, how are you? So sorry to miss you yesterday.'

'What are you doing here?' Janna made no attempt to look friendly.

'Emlyn celebrated victory so full-bloodedly last night,' simpered Vicky, 'I had to bring him home. I'm coaching Jack and Lando at eight o'clock—not that they'll be in any fit state, after drowning their sorrows—so I borrowed one of Emlyn's rugby shirts. Rather fetching.'

I'm not hearing this, thought Janna.

'Emlyn is so gorgeous.' Vicky stretched voluptuously. 'Oriana needs her head—or rather the lower parts of her anatomy'—Vicky giggled coarsely—'examined. You must come to kitchen sups in my little flat in the hols. Shall I ask Ashton to make up a four, or don't you two still get on? Anyway, must fly.'

'Fuck, fuck, fuck,' said Emlyn looking down from his first-floor window. That had not been the way to get over Oriana.

Dora's streak ensured that Larks's victory over Bagley was headlined in most of the papers.

'Welsh dragon turns heat on old school', said *The Times*.

'Full back', was the *Scorpion*'s caption on a charming, naked rear view of Dora, which she agreed was one way of reminding all her press contacts what she looked like.

104

Larks High's pupils were on such a high on the morning after the match, they failed to notice that both Janna and Emlyn were very subdued. Over at Bagley, an equally ecstatic Cosmo was spending a free period stretched out on the fur-covered triple bed in his study. As token coursework, he was making notes on Andrew Marvell's 'To His Coy Mistress', and thinking about Ruth Walton, who wasn't at all coy and might very soon become his mistress. What a coup. Cosmo was so elated, he had no need of his elevenses spliff.

As it was nearly Easter, he was also playing a CD of his father's recording of the Good Friday music from *Parsifal*. Hearing distraught sobbing and finding Dora and a worried Cadbury outside, he pulled them into the room and slammed the door.

'Whatever's the matter?'

'The music,' wailed Dora. 'It was Daddy's favourite. They played it at his funeral. I miss him so much.'

Cosmo let her cry, tempted to comfort her in the only way he knew. She'd looked extremely fetching streaking round the pitch yesterday.

'Daddy would have saved Cadbury. He liked dogs almost more than people. Hengist's Elaine is the great-niece of Daddy's greyhound Maud. Mummy's so furious about me streaking and Cadbury threatening her, she's insisting he's got to be put down, or castrated, or go to the nearest rescue kennels. I can't let him go. He's my only friend except for Mrs Cartwright,' she added, as

Cadbury put a large paw on her knee in agreement.

'Bianca was a best friend, but after she took up with Paris, she got too embarrassed to talk to me. And having sworn she couldn't help herself because he was the great love of her life, she's now bats about Feral again and I so don't want to hear how dreadful she feels about breaking Paris's heart.'

'No, I can see that.' Cosmo handed her a handkerchief and a glass of orange juice.

'Thanks,' sniffed Dora. 'I daren't keep Cadbury at Boudicca, because if Joan finds him she'll shunt him straight back to Mummy and the gas chamber. Mummy's terrified I'll be expelled and she and Randal won't be able to have revolting sex all the time. I think Randal's a paedofeel. He groped my non-existent boobs last time I fell off my skateboard.'

'Hum,' said Cosmo.

'I've got a double period of English. Can Cadbury stay here for a couple of hours?' pleaded Dora.

'Sure.' Cosmo looked at his watch. 'I've got maths, but he'll be OK on his own.'

'Can I use this for water?' said Dora, emptying some alabaster eggs out of a Lalique bowl.

'Yeah,' said Cosmo, 'it's insured.'

*   *   *

Left to his own devices, Cadbury whined for a bit, scratched at Cosmo's door, jumped on to the bed, peered out of the window, growled at Theo's cat Hindsight, then started to sniff round the room.

330

Finding an open packet of biscuits, he devoured them, then smelt something much more exciting under the mattress. Pink nostrils flaring, snorting wildly, tail frantically waving, Cadbury began burrowing.

*   *   *

Double English with Miss Wormley droning on about *The Tempest* seemed to go on for hours. Wheedling a Pyrex bowl of shepherd's pie out of Coxie, Dora rushed over to Cosmo's study to find Cadbury sitting on Cosmo's bed, swaying from side to side, yellow eyes glazed, an inane grin on his panting cocoa-brown face.

'Whatever's the matter with you?' wailed Dora.

Concern turned to panic when Cadbury refused the shepherd's pie. Labradors have to be dying not to eat. Hearing a step in the corridor, Dora leapt to close the door and leant against it. Cosmo, however, shoved his way in.

'Cadbury,' gasped Dora. 'He's been poisoned.'

'Don't be silly, there's nothing poisonous in here; he's probably stuffed his face with too many biscuits.' Cosmo picked up the remains of the packet.

'He's never been ill before—look at him,' sobbed Dora as Cadbury, pink tongue lolling, swaying like a windscreen wiper, beamed up at Cosmo.

'Looks more like the village idiot than ever.'

'He does not. The vet's too far away'—Dora's voice was rising hysterically—'You must help me get him to the sick bay.'

'I must not,' snapped Cosmo, who was expecting a call from Ruth Walton. 'I'll get thrown out for harbouring an illegal immigrant.'

Dora didn't care. Rushing outside, she found one of the builder's trolleys which had been nicked last night to wheel home a drunken Anatole.

'Help me,' she begged Cosmo.

'I'm bloody well carrying the front end then. Christ, he's heavy. I'll rupture myself,' grumbled Cosmo as they heaved Cadbury on to the trolley. 'You're on your own now.'

Stumbling, swearing, diving into alleyways and behind trees to avoid Poppet Bruce, who as eco-chief was furiously fingerprinting dropped empties, Dora trundled him round the back of the school.

'Please don't die,' she pleaded. 'Don't give up on me. Please God, save Cadbury, don't make Matron shunt him back to Mummy.'

Luck, however, was on Dora's side. Only two pupils were in the waiting room: a boy with athlete's foot and a girl from Boudicca wanting the morning-after pill.

'It's an emergency,' panted Dora. 'Can I go in first?'

Even better, as she dragged Cadbury through the door, a deep, expensive voice exclaimed, 'Why, Dora, darling, how lovely to see you.'

'Dr Benson. It's even nicer to see you.'

James Benson was the raffishly handsome, ultra-charming private GP who for the last thirty years had looked after her family, the Campbell-Blacks and the France-Lynches.

'Whatever are you doing here?'

'A locum. Rather like working in a sweet shop with so many gorgeous girls around, and talking of gorgeous, you've grown really pretty, Dora.' James Benson smoothed his black and silver hair. 'And so like your father, such a sweet man.'

'Thanks so much.' Dora had no time for pleasantries. 'It's Cadbury I'm worried about, I think he's been poisoned or having some kind of fit. I haven't got time to get him to the vet. Please help.'

Cadbury, dopier than ever, collapsed on the rug, pupils vast, beaming inanely and swaying rather more slowly from left to right.

'He's going to die.' Dora burst into noisy sobs. 'I bet it's Mr Fussy or Poppet who's poisoned him.'

James Benson shot his very white cuffs and looked at Cadbury's eyes, his tongue, listened to his heart, then proceeded to laugh a great deal.

'It's not funny,' exploded Dora.

'I think he'll live.' Dr Benson wiped his eyes. 'If I were you, Dora, darling, I'd take him home, turn down the lights and put on a Bob Marley record.'

'I don't know what you mean,' said Dora huffily.

'I don't know where your dog's been, but he's completely stoned.'

Even Cosmo found this amusing. In fact he was in such a good mood after hearing from Mrs Walton, he forgave Cadbury for tunnelling between two mattresses and locating and swallowing a whole eighth of skunk wrapped in cellophane, and agreed that Cadbury could sleep off his excesses on the fur-covered bed.

'He could have a brilliant career as a sniffer dog,' said Dora in excitement. 'According to the *Daily Mail*, dogs get paid five hundred pounds a morning searching for drugs in state schools.'

'He can start by sniffing out all the drugs at Bagley,' said Cosmo evilly, 'and then we can confiscate them.'

Returning for the summer term, Bagley discovered that Poppet Bruce as eco-chief was becoming more and more of a bully, waddling very pregnant round the corridors, charging vast fines for lights left on or doors not closed to preserve heat.

On a late-night patrol on the first Friday of term, Poppet discerned noises coming from the art department. Hammering on the door, she found it locked and, hearing a crash, fumbled for her master key. 'Let me in, let me in.'

Switching on the light, she was confronted by the excesses of the Upper Fifth's coursework, which included a six-foot straw donkey, a robot Christ on a steel cross, and Lando's sin bin: a flame-red tent painted with demons. Hearing a cough, her gaze was drawn to a naked member of the Upper Fifth, who was clutching a palette in an abortive attempt to hide a very large penis.

'Cosmo Rannaldini,' squawked Poppet, 'what are you doing?'

'You're not going to believe this,' mumbled Cosmo, 'but I come here to be near you.'

'How d'you mean?' asked Poppet, thinking how beautifully the lad was constructed.

'Your p-p-p-picture,' stammered Cosmo, pointing a trembling finger at Boffin's half-finished but already absurdly flattering portrait of Poppet breastfeeding little thirteen-month-old Gandhi.

'What a caring interpretation,' cried a delighted Poppet.

'Indeed. This is seriously embarrassing,' went on Cosmo, 'but I'm so obsessed with you, Mrs Bruce. I

334

come here sometimes to, er, jerk off in front of your portrait. I have such strong sexual urges, which I don't want to impose on my fellow students. It helps me to destress. Please don't be angry with me.' Cosmo hung his dark, curly head, a tear glittering like a diamond on his cheekbone.

Poppet was deeply moved and very understanding. She appreciated the pain of young love. Cosmo mustn't feel guilty about masturbation. He would get over her and find some lovely young woman of his own.

'Never,' swore Cosmo, 'I think of you constantly. At least let me have hope.'

'Alex and I have a very strong partnership.' Poppet perched on a fibreglass wildebeest. 'Not that I haven't had my admirers.'

'I bet you have.'

Cosmo's penis was pushing most excitingly through the hole in the palette. Alex was rather meanly endowed, although Poppet knew size had nothing to do with pleasure. A snort from the direction of the sin bin made them both jump.

'What was that?'

'Probably a rat. Lando keeps leaving half-eaten Cornish pasties around.'

Poppet noticed Cosmo was shivering. 'You mustn't catch cold.'

'Could you bear to leave me to get dressed?' begged Cosmo adoringly. 'And have a moment of quiet reflection on your words of wisdom?'

'Of course, I'll lock up in a quarter of an hour,' said Poppet. 'Good night, Cosmo.'

'Good night, sweet princess,' said Cosmo soulfully, then, ten seconds later, 'All clear,' and a naked Ruth Walton, who'd been stuffing Cosmo's

335

shirt into her mouth to stop her laughter, emerged from the sin bin into his arms.

'Thank you for saving me.'

'We've got ten minutes.'

'No, we haven't, it's not safe—well, perhaps it is,' gasped Ruth as Cosmo pushed her down on Primrose Duddon's ethnic quilt and plunged his cock into her. 'Oh God, what heaven!'

They escaped down the corridor just in time.

'You are the biggest thing in my life,' confessed Cosmo, kissing her in the shadows of the car park.

'And your thing is the biggest I've ever had in my life,' teased Mrs Walton to hide how enamoured she was.

Cosmo was chuffed to bits. He and Ruth couldn't get enough of each other and the pillow talk was as exciting as the sex. He was learning so much about the governing body and the sexual and social habits of Randal Stancombe. The only blot was that Poppet Bruce, unable to keep a secret, revealed Cosmo's passion to Alex, who was casting even blacker looks in Cosmo's direction.

A fortnight later, Poppet had her baby, another girl, Cranberry Germaine, a little Taurus, whom Poppet breastfed in public at every opportunity, particularly in front of Cosmo: 'To domesticate his passion and help him see my breasts in a different light.' She also bombarded him with leaflets from SHAG: the Sexual Health Action Group.

105

Over at Larks, Feral's football trial, a midweek friendly at Larkminster Rovers, approached. Good as his word, Emlyn spent hours helping Feral transfer back to football, increasingly conscious that he was dealing with genius.

When the trial day arrived, Feral in turn felt more positive than ever before. Emlyn had given him such confidence. If he could get a place with the Rovers, who looked like they'd be going up to the first division next season, he'd soon be on serious money, then he'd be in a position to look after his mother, his brothers and sisters and even ask Bianca out. Suddenly he had hope.

It was a perfect day for football, warm but slightly overcast. The Brigadier, Lily, Janna, Emlyn and, to Rupert's intense irritation, Taggie were all going to the ground to cheer him on. As it was midweek, Bianca couldn't get out of school. Feral was relieved. He needed nothing to distract him.

*   *   *

Feral and Xav, who'd come along to give moral support, made their way to the football ground through the Wednesday market. Xav had already handed Feral a good-luck card of a sleek black velvet cat. Inside it said, 'Stay cool, thinking of you, all love, Bianca'.

Feral was nervous but terribly excited. He was wearing the same socks which brought him luck against Bagley and, doing scout steps, running twenty paces, then walking twenty, dreamt of becoming the next Thierry Henry. No footballer's wife would be lovelier than Bianca; she would light up any stand.

Oh please, God of footballers, this is my one chance to break in.

They were early and as they passed the cheese stall, then breathed in the smell of beefburgers and rotating golden brown chickens, Xav asked Feral if he were hungry. Feral shook his head. He couldn't have kept down a potato crisp as he skipped to left and right practising moves. They stopped to admire some leather jackets. Xav tried on a black one.

'How does it look?'

'Cool,' said Feral absent-mindedly.

'My father, stupid twat, thinks leather coats are common, so I'm going to buy one. My mother always sides with my father. "Why can't you wear that nice denim jacket?" Parents get on my tits.'

Xav, who was very antsy about the GCSEs ahead, tried on a brown jacket, then decided the black one was nicer.

'Blacks look good in black,' agreed Feral.

'I'll have it.' Xav produced a Coutts cheque book, a sheaf of identification and wrote a cheque for £160.

'Parents are never off your back,' he went on irritably as he pocketed the receipt. 'My father never gave a stuff about my working hard until he started this stupid GCSE. My mother's over the moon because Larkminster Rovers are so excited by her coursework ideas. If you land this job, you'll probably live on Steak Taggie for the rest of your life.'

'Shut up, you spoilt bastard,' snapped Feral. 'You don't deserve no respect, man. Every kid in the school wants to be you, living in a palace wiv horses, buying coats wiv what would keep most families for a monf. You've a beautiful sister, your mother's a lovely woman—your dad's a shit, admittedly, but he's always been there for you. You're fucking smuvvered wiv love, and you can't stop dissing them. For Chrissake, stop whingeing.'

A gust of wind blowing blossom out of the trees scattered pink petals over them, as they scowled at each other, fists clenched. Then Feral said:

'Sorry, man. I'm uptight about the trial, didn't sleep last night.'

They did a high five. Feral glanced at Xav's Rolex; there was still time to buy Janna some flowers.

'She's always been there for me.'

Just as he was paying for a bunch of red carnations, he felt a faint scratch on his back. Swinging round, he saw a corpse—almost a skeleton—with a white scabby face, thinning hair, unseeing bloodshot eyes: a nightmare life in death against the technicoloured riot of the flower stall.

She had bruises and cuts all over her arms, was wrapped in stinking rags and trembled uncontrollably in what Feral instantly recognized as an advanced state of heroin withdrawal.

'Have you got a pound for a cup of tea?' she mumbled.

'Mum,' whispered Feral in horror.

Xav took Feral firmly by the arm.

'You've got a trial, it's your big chance. You've got to walk away from her.'

'Fifty pence for a cup of tea,' whined Feral's

339

swaying mother.

Xav gave her a fiver and frogmarched Feral towards the football ground. They could see the flags and the stands ahead, but as they reached the High Street, Feral turned and bolted back, disappearing into the crowd. Janna's red carnations fell from his hand and were trampled underfoot.

*   *   *

Xav searched for Feral everywhere, but fruitlessly. By the time he turned up at the match, play had been going on for half an hour and everyone had washed their hands of him.

Pete Wainwright, who'd set the whole thing up, was apoplectic with rage. 'Made me look a complete prat. It's obvious the lad's got no commitment.'

Lily, Janna and Taggie in the stands were devastated; the Brigadier and Emlyn hopping mad with fury. How could Feral have bottled out of the thing he wanted most in the world?

'It isn't as though any of the trial players are a quarter as good as him. He'd have walked it,' exploded the Brigadier.

Rupert who, not trusting Taggie with flash football managers, had at the last moment rolled up as well, said the whole thing was 'absolutely typical'.

Seeing Xav, they all charged down the stands.

'What the hell's happened?'

As Xav finished explaining, Rupert launched into blistering invective. 'It's not worth investing a bloody penny in him.'

'It was his mother, for Christ's sake,' shouted back Xav. 'You wouldn't leave someone like that.'

'I'll come and help you look for him,' said Janna.

'So will I,' said Emlyn.

Having combed the market and the main streets, they tried the Shakespeare Estate. Janna ran up the path past the burnt-out car and the stinking dustbins. A pretty black girl, reeking of sex and booze, her great body shown off by tight orange vest and rucked-up yellow mini, answered the door.

'We're looking for Feral,' begged Janna, then flinched as the girl was joined by a leering Uncle Harley, clearly off his face and zipping up his trousers.

'Nice to see you, Miss Curtis.'

'Have you seen Feral?'

'He's not here. He in trouble again?'

'Feral obviously daren't go home,' Janna told Emlyn as she jumped back into his car.

A distraught Xav didn't get back till late evening. There had been no sign of Feral or his mother, so Emlyn had called the police.

'I'm sorry,' Xav told Rupert defiantly, 'but I admire Feral more than anyone I've ever met.'

*   *   *

Next day the police found Feral hiding out under the railway bridge. His mother beside him, drifting in and out of consciousness, was rushed to hospital. The police had been searching for her anyway on three drug-related offences. The following day, she just avoided a prison sentence by promising to go into rehab and was admitted to a local drying-out clinic.

'I'm jolly well going to pay for six weeks of it,' said Taggie.

'Don't be bloody stupid,' snapped Rupert, particularly when Taggie threatened to sell her diamonds.

Feral, suicidally aware he'd let everyone down, ashamed that he'd been too frightened of her getting arrested to take his mother to hospital, was amazed that the Brigadier allowed him back. Lily was there when, head drooping, a picture of dejection, he walked through the door.

'Come and sit down.' Lily patted the sofa.

Collapsing beside her, Feral broke into the most piteous sobs.

'So sorry, Lily, so sorry, man.'

It broke the Brigadier's heart.

'Poor fellow, poor fellow,' he said, patting Feral's heaving shoulders. 'So pleased you're home. Missed you around the place very much. Tried my hand at cooking corn beef hash for tonight, but have a dry Martini first.'

106

All round Larks, as the summer term began, Wally had nailed up signs saying: 'Get your finger out and your coursework in. All your hard work will be worthless unless you write tidily.'

The teachers stood over the children, reading, redrafting, adding, criticizing handwriting, improving spelling and grammar and finally marking each piece of coursework.

Staff teaching the same subject, like Skunk and Mates, or Janna and Sophy, would then read coursework by each other's pupils, to see if they felt the grades given were fair.

'I do feel this mark's a little too generous for Feral,' sighed Janna.

'A little,' agreed Sophy, 'but marking him up seemed the only way of helping him get a grade.'

There was a drama over the food technology coursework, which included lunch for the hospitality boxes at Larkminster Rovers. The chicken and vegetable jalousie, which consisted of chicken legs wrapped in ham with pepper and tomato sauce, smelt so delicious that Rocky wandered in and scoffed four of the entries. As the external examiner was due in an hour, Taggie felt justified in remaking them herself, just in time.

Other members of staff felt it was like Christmas all over again, as they packed up coursework and despatched it to the examining board. They needed a pantechnicon to accommodate the contribution from design and technology, which included Danijela the Bosnian girl's beautiful blue and green embroidered wedding dress and Rocky's six-foot dog kennel. On the side he had written in pokerwork: 'Dog house I will live in if you do not pass me'.

Other packages included geography projects on traffic-calming and the shaping of industrial development and RE dissertations on death and dying, which seemed a welcome option to the exams ahead, which began on 14 May with Urdu listening.

*   *   *

In Xav's view, Aysha had been listening to a great deal too much Urdu claptrap from her bullying father.

He and Aysha had revised together in the Larks garden, she helping him with science, he her with Spanish and French, occasionally getting electric shocks when their hands touched.

'You must get an A star in Urdu to beat my vile ex-housemaster's wife,' said Xav. 'She and her awful daughter Charisma are taking the subject to show off.'

'How's your dad getting on with English lit.?' asked Aysha. Her little diamond nose stud glinted in the sunlight. Her face and hands were the soft brown of Penscombe Peterkin's glossy coat. As she raised big, brown, almond-shaped eyes to him, Xav's heart shook his body like an overloaded washing machine.

'My dad is very short-fused and not concentrating enough on the yard,' he replied gloomily. 'Hasn't had as many winners as last year. I tried to give him a few tips I'd learnt in business studies, but he

344

told me to get stuffed. Got a good horse called Fast running on the twenty-eighth.'

*   *   *

' "Do not adultery commit; Advantage rarely came of it",' intoned Rupert.

What a ridiculous syllabus! Of all the sins teenagers committed, adultery must be bottom of the list. Half the poems on the other hand seem to be cooing over new babies, the last thing one wanted to encourage in the young. A poem by some woman called Pilkington (who'd only lived thirty-eight years, so God had struck her down) claimed the only way to get on in politics was to tell lies, which didn't dispose Rupert to join Jupiter and Hengist in their proposed coup.

The whole anthology was deeply silly.

Fed up with poetry, Rupert slotted *Pride and Prejudice* into his Walkman. Not a bad book, quite funny, and he completely identified with Darcy: sound fellow, looked after his friends and his tenants, ran his estate well, couldn't be bothered with riff-raff like Mrs Bennet.

Rupert was still spitting because he'd received a letter from Aysha's father, Raschid Khan, who owned a curry house in Larkminster, asking him to stop Xav pestering Aysha. Damned cheek. Both children were black. Xav was clearly desperately in love. Rupert's daughter, Tabitha, had been besotted by a tractor driver called Ashley and got over him, thank God, but he hated to see Xav so unhappy about Aysha's arranged marriage.

*   *   *

As soon as the summer term began, the press, nudged by Dora, had started ringing Bagley for reports on Larks's Golden Boy, only to be told by Hengist that he was confident that not only Paris, but all the school's candidates, would excel in their forthcoming exams. They were all working extremely hard.

This was not strictly true. Boffin and Primrose Duddon had been working steadily all their school careers. Paris had worked hard since he'd been at Bagley. The rest of the year had been cramming knowledge into their heads, aided by caffeine and speed, but only for three weeks. Even the promise of an oil well and his own six-bedroom dacha hadn't motivated Anatole. Even the promise of a Ferrari if he achieved straight As had not halted Cosmo's nightly visits to Mrs Walton, whom he had installed in a cottage on the far side of Bagley village.

Disapproving of all work and no play, Poppet urged her RE students to keep up their voluntary work and 'enrichment activities', which enraged Lubemir, Anatole and Cosmo. How could they enrich themselves by flogging exam papers, when Alex Bruce had once more changed the combination on the school safe? Why should generations of Bagley pupils profit from their enterprise and not they?

Primrose Duddon was overwhelmed how popular she'd suddenly become, enjoying heady weekends staying with the Lloyd-Foxes, helping Amber and Junior with English revision, and at Robinsgrove where, with his dark, sleek head resting on her splendid breasts, she had initiated Lando France-

346

Lynch into the mysteries of the double helix and the circulation of the blood.

*   *   *

Paris's first exam was Latin on the afternoon of 18 May. The night before, Hengist, just off a plane after a big speech in Washington, summoned Paris to his study in the Mansion to check things were all right.

Still in crumpled off-white trousers and a purple shirt, Hengist had hung his jacket and tie over Darwin, the ancient stuffed gorilla, which Alex and Joan had recently sacked from the biology lab on the grounds that he would be too scruffy for Randal's Science Emporium. In an excess of Bruce-baiting, Hengist had rescued Darwin from the skip, placing him beside the stuffed bear and topping him with his own mortar board. Elaine, enchanted to have her master home, was following Hengist round, nudging him in friendship, sweeping off with her long tail the pile of faxes, emails and letters Hengist couldn't be bothered to look at.

Switching off his telephone, Hengist hung a 'Do Not Disturb' notice on the door, tore the gold paper off a bottle of Moët and prepared to give Paris his full attention.

It was a perfect evening. Cricket games were in their last overs. Cow parsley foamed along the rough meadow between pitches and golf course; buttercups streaked the fields beyond. An overpoweringly sweet scent of lilac drifted in through the big open windows.

'Don't be silly,' Hengist murmured fondly as

347

Elaine jumped then trembled as the champagne cork flew out. 'You've heard enough of those in your time.'

Perched on the dark red Paisley window seat, Paris could just see the lake. Here Artie Deverell lounged in a panama hat and a deckchair, with several bottles of Sancerre cooling in the water among the forget-me-nots, reading his favourite poems in his gentle bell-like voice to his favourite GCSE candidates.

'I bet he's chosen Lamartine's "Lake" or Baudelaire's "Voyage to Cythera".' Hengist handed Paris an excitingly large glass. 'Poetry that no longer appears on any exam syllabus. Great literature, as William Rees-Mogg was saying recently in *The Times*, teaches us to understand human nature. People still sulk like Achilles, get mad with jealousy like Othello, loathe their stepfather like Hamlet, have happy marriages like Hector and Andromache.' For a second Hengist's finger caressed Sally's sweet face in the photograph on his desk. 'Literature, Rees-Mogg rightly claims, is the road to the general understanding of the heart and the head. History's the same. If you study William's conquest of England in ten sixty-six, you can appreciate how the Iraqis feel today.'

'Mr Bruce doesn't feel like that.' Paris rose to his feet, gazing at Hengist's books with a longing most boys would reserve for Sienna Miller. 'He's hell-bent on chucking out the classical library and Theo's archives.'

'Not while I'm running this joint. This bloody Government is already destroying public libraries. Wants them to replenish their entire stock in five years, in the name of multiculturism and vibrancy. Jesus! I can accommodate Darwin'—he patted the gorilla on the shoulder—'not sure there's room in here for the archives.'

'You will protect Theo. He's such a cool teacher,' Paris stammered and blushed. 'He read us Plato's description of the death of Socrates the other evening, tears pouring down his cheeks the whole time. It was awesome, but I think he's very near the edge.'

'I'll make a note of it,' said Hengist gravely, noting how exhausted Paris looked. His bloodshot eyes glowed like rubies in the intense white face.

'I know how hard you've been working, but this time in a month, you won't remember a single equation or date you've forced into your tired brain.'

'I have to say, sir'—Paris took a gulp of champagne, and moved to sit down on what was left of the sofa by a stretched-out Elaine—'I was gutted when Mr Davies left, but your classes are wicked, just as interesting as Mr Graham's. I can relate now to Lenin, Khrushchev, the Tsar, even to Hitler and Stalin. You don't make us take sides. Emlyn was always pushing for the underdog, the peasants, the Jews or the communists, but you show us tyrants don't start off wrong, they're often convinced they were doing right. Like in Euripides. I suddenly find I'm right behind Medea. You're like Euripides, sir.'

'Why, thank you, Paris. I've been called a lot of things. Which English set book did you like best?'

'*Macbeth*. Wish I'd been able to take it in the exam, rather than just as coursework.'

'Rupert Campbell-Black has very strong views on

349

Macbeth.' Hengist shook his head. 'I so hope he's going to pass. I toned down some of his ideas in which he described Malcolm as a "heartless shit" for being so bracing with Macduff just after his wife and children had been butchered. The Prince of Wales would have handled it far more sympathetically, according to Rupert.'

'That's right,' said Paris.

Down below, he could see Dora scouring the ground with her eyes one moment, looking round for him the next, with Cadbury bounding after her. He'd had a disturbing dream last night: Dora had rescued him from a particularly horrible children's home, and held him safe and kissed him. It had been lovely, but Dora was only a child, sexually light years behind Bianca. He must stamp on any feelings.

'Dora's been great,' he added to Hengist. 'She's helped me to revise, testing me on everything. Pity she's not taking her GCSEs. She knows the textbooks backwards.'

'I'm devoted to Dora,' said Hengist. 'I'll never forget inviting her in for a glass of champagne on her birthday her first term and asking her with what adjective would she best like her friends to describe her. She said, "There." I said, "That's not an adjective." And Dora said, "I'd like my friends to say I was there for them." '

'And she is,' said Paris.

'How are you getting on with Ian and Patience?' he asked.

'OK. Patience took me to *Macbeth*. Brilliant production, except the weird sisters were sleek, young and glamorous, which is garbage: Shakespeare categorically states they had beards

350

and were ugly. And they can't have been in Macbeth's imagination, because Banquo saw them too.'

'Rupert explained it as Macbeth and Banquo being off their faces with drugs,' volunteered Hengist, 'like the entire US Army in Iraq.'

'Magic mushrooms, perhaps,' suggested Paris.

' "The instruments of darkness tell us truths",' murmured Hengist, then, regretfully: 'I must go and change. We're dining with the Lord Lieutenant—such a sweet, boring man, I'll never stay awake. Look, you'll walk these exams. Try and write legibly and read through if you've got time. Examiners are awfully keen on inessentials like punctuation and spelling. Easy to ignore if you're writing at the gallop.'

Paris finished his glass of champagne. If he hadn't been a bit drunk, he would never have tried on Hengist's mortar board. With it tipped over his long nose, and shielding his red eyes, his blond hair floating, he looked so ravishing, Hengist caught his breath.

'Certainly suits you better than Darwin. You must go to my old college, and get the first Matthew Arnold and I, upsetting our fathers so dreadfully, didn't get.'

*   *   *

As Hengist showered, watching the black hairs flowing down in deltas over his strong muscular chest and thighs, he was gripped with excitement. What a transformation in two years! Paris was able to relax, joke, put forward opinions, even exchange compliments. Hengist imagined his first book of

351

poems, dedicated to 'Hengist Brett-Taylor, without whom . . .'

Ian, Patience and Theo, too, must be doing a good job. All the same, the boy would have fared even better with him and Sally. If he took the job at Fleetley, could he take Paris with him? If he went into politics, a beautiful adopted son would be great for his image. Christ, he mustn't think like that. He missed Oriana so much. Even in Washington he hadn't rung her. Not a word had been exchanged. Was Sally speaking to her secretly?

Wrapped in a big red towel, wandering to the window, Hengist saw Paris sprinting down to the lake to join Artie and his friends.

In the Bruces' back garden he could see Boffin, his nose in his revision folder, and Alex smugly rereading a proof of his *Guide to Red Tape*. He must get on with Tom and Matt. Please God, prayed Hengist, make Paris do better than Boffin.

107

'Before the GCSEs, you can expect panic attacks, moodiness, tears and temper tantrums,' Janna sighed to Taggie, 'and that's just the parents.'

The staff weren't behaving much better. Despite the outwardly convivial atmosphere, Pittsy was desperate his maths candidates should do much better than Skunk's scientists. Basket wanted better grades than Sophy and Cambola. Even sweet, calm Mags and jaunty Lily got snappy with Emlyn and the Brigadier over hijacked marker pens. There was so much at stake.

Discounting art and Urdu, which Graffi and Aysha had already taken, exams started in earnest with business studies on the morning of 21 May. The evening before, Janna took refuge among the cow parsley on Smokers', breathing in a heady mingling of wild garlic and balsam, watching the last scarlet streaks of the sunset jazzing up the black silhouette of the cathedral and listening to the exquisite singing of the nightingales in the laurels. Partner, who'd been rabbiting, was drinking out of the pond, avoiding the tadpoles the children had been too busy revising to collect in jam jars.

Like Orpheus visiting the underworld, Janna was still shaking from dropping off good-luck cards to houses in the Shakespeare Estate. If her children scraped just a few GCSEs, they could escape from that hell-hole. Johnnie, Rocky, Monster, Danny the Irish, whose father had just been arrested for punching a particularly irritating female social worker, were all light-fingered and, with no job prospects, would revert to crime and the streets.

Aysha would be beaten within an inch of her life if she didn't get the Magic Five. Kylie was expecting a second child any minute and her voice would need to take off like Charlotte Church's to support them both. Feral had the back-up of the Brigadier and Lily, but although he'd tried hard, she doubted if he'd get any grades except PE. At least Rocky was ensured a good D and T grade with his massive dog kennel.

Graffi worried her the most. Ever since his da Dafydd had been sacked for cheeking Stancombe at the rugby match, he'd been blacked by other firms and drunkenly out of work. Dafydd's mood had not been improved by his dotty mother, known as Cardiff Nan, moving in with them. Graffi, stacking shelves all night in Tesco to make ends meet, was constantly hijacked during the day to mind both his little handicapped sister Caitlin and Cardiff Nan in their enclosed worlds.

Graffi was clever. He'd already got a starred A for art and could easily notch up the Magic Five if he could get some sleep and somewhere quiet to revise. Earlier, she had found him fallen asleep in reception, brush in his hand dripping black gloss on to the floor, in the middle of painting a lucky black cat ringed with gold horseshoes.

The sun and the nightingales had disappeared into the darkness. Going indoors, Janna checked the gym, where in the half-light, like a chessboard, each white square table a metre apart, awaited exam papers. Partner's claws clattered on the floorboards as he sniffed around.

Going into her office, Janna jumped as her

354

mobile rang. Emlyn? she thought ever hopefully, but the number was unfamiliar. The sinister, lisping stammering voice was not.

'Pwepared for tomorrow, Janna? After all our effort, support and financial commitment, I hope you're not going to let us down. Wemember how you hassled us to give your kids a chance to get some gwades? Now it's your turn to deliver; the world is watching, you owe us spectacular wesults.'

'You've got the wrong number, this is not Sadists Anonymous and I'm taping this conversation, so bugger off.'

Janna slammed down the receiver. How dare Ashton wind her up when she needed to be at her most calm and cheerful? She longed to unlock the safe and photocopy every paper. Not that it would help the children unless she wrote the answers for them. By the time Rocky, Feral and Danijela had struggled to the end of the business studies case histories and worked out what questions needed answering, time would be up. Oh God, had she pushed them beyond their capabilities?

If only she could call Emlyn, but since the rugby match their stand-off had continued. But whatever his sadness over Oriana, Emlyn had gallantly thrown himself into the Larks GCSEs, even to the unprecedented step of getting himself to the breakfast club most mornings and conducting question-and-answer sessions until the history candidates were date perfect. Often the Brigadier had joined him, performing a splendid double act.

*   *   *

Over at Bagley, Alex Bruce tiptoed along the

355

landing after lights out. Hearing murmuring coming from the junior dormitory, he drew closer, then smiled as he heard Boffin's voice: 'Please remember in your prayers that over the next four weeks I'll be taking my GCSEs.'

*   *   *

It was nearly midnight at Penscombe, but still stiflingly hot. The shrill neigh of a horse trembled on the night. Earlier, Xav had bravely delivered a good-luck card to Aysha's house and been sent packing.

Now he looked out on a tossing silver sea of cow parsley and ebony woods menacing as an approaching tidal wave on the horizon. Bogotá panted at his feet. *Understanding Business*, black with notes, lay open on his bed.

Xav had never more wanted a drink to take the edge off his nerves and his sadness. He had shouted at his poor mother for asking for the hundredth time if he were all right, and threatened to punch Bianca for pestering him for the millionth time not to forget to pass on Feral's good-luck card, which she'd put in his school bag. There was a knock on the door.

'Bugger off,' hissed Xav.

It was Rupert, bearing a cup of cocoa.

'Thought this might help you sleep. Know what you're going through. I'm shit scared already and I'm doing only one subject; you're doing loads.'

'Thanks.' Xav took the cup. 'Not so much money on me. You've got to wipe that smug smirk off Stancombe's face.'

The cup of cocoa, the first and last Rupert would

ever make, was absolutely disgusting. The cocoa was still in powdery lumps, sugar hadn't been added and, by not sieving the milk, Rupert had left a thickening layer of skin on the top. Xav was so touched by his father's concern, he drank the lot, managing not to gag.

'Those marketing ideas aren't bad,' admitted Rupert, 'although I doubt if direct mailing the Shakespeare Estate would find us any new owners.'

To Xav's amazement, the cocoa sent him to sleep.

* * *

' "Nessun dorma!" ' sang Miss Cambola, but pianissimo so that it wouldn't wake her fellow lodgers.

When she'd taken O levels, far too many years ago, her English had been so poor, she'd failed everything except music. Her set pieces had been Brandenburg Four, the Egmont Overture and the 'Waldstein'; she could still remember every note. The last year had been such a joy; Cambola absolutely dreaded the future. Kylie had such an exquisite voice, but would she ever be able to use it?

* * *

Over at Wilmington, the Brigadier couldn't sleep. All his unrelaxed bones were aching. Had he simplified the Great War enough? Would they ever remember the essentials? Feral had received a lot of good-luck cards—even one from his mother in

357

rehab, whom he'd promised to ring after every exam. Business studies this morning, however, had been considered beyond him, so, getting up at five, the Brigadier left him to sleep.

Out in the deserted street, every car had a cat stretched out on the bonnet or underneath, like a union meeting. Lily's cat, General, obviously the shop steward, lay in the middle of the road, and strolled off huffily as the Brigadier started up his car. Noticing ominous pewter-grey clouds over Larkminster, he prayed the forecast rain would hold off. As had been proved in elections, the working classes tended not to come out in bad weather. He and Emlyn would have to jump into Stancombe's minibus and round up the defectors.

The cuckoo was singing in a nearby wood as he reached the next village. In the churchyard, the graves, like swimmers in a marathon, nearly disappeared in a white sea of cow parsley and wild garlic flowers. The yellow roses he'd put on his wife's grave on Ascension Day were shedding their petals. He wondered if she'd rest in peace if she knew he was plucking up courage to propose to Lily.

The church door creaked as he went in, followed by another creak as Lily, kneeling in a front pew, struggled to her feet.

'Don't believe prayers work unless one kneels down,' she confessed. 'Couldn't sleep, just popped down here to wish them luck.'

Without rouge and lipstick, Lily looked pale; pink moisturizer ringed her nostrils; her face was as rumpled as the bed in which she'd tossed and turned. There was a white hair on her upper lip and a big bunch of dark and light purple lilac, with stems bashed, on the pew beside her.

'I so want them and Janna not to be humiliated.'

The Brigadier's heart expanded with love.

108

Over at Larks, from eight o'clock onwards, Partner, sporting a smart crimson bow tie, welcomed everyone with joyful barks. Across one whole wall of reception, defiantly defacing Ashton's property, Graffi's grinning black cat juggled gold horseshoes and lashed a tail at a lark ascending into gold clouds. In black letters, Graffi had also named each candidate and wished them all luck.

The heady smell of Sally and Lily's flowers, however, couldn't disguise a reek of cheap scent, sweat and terror. No one could face Taggie's cornflakes and croissants; they could hardly keep down a cup of tea.

With their hair drawn back and twisted up into knots, their smocks with shoelace straps showing off bare shoulders, and their jeans flopping round their ankles, the girls looked like extras in a BBC Jane Austen ball scene above the waist, and the technicians making the film below it.

But their pale faces, seamed with strain and weariness, came straight out of a Dickens slum scene. Every so often, one of the girls would break into terrified sobs and trigger off the others.

'Got the runs, miss.' 'Toilet's blocked, miss.' 'Stink makes you frow up.' 'Fink I've come on.' 'Miss, I'm goin' 'ome.'

'No, you're not,' said Janna firmly.

After quick prayers in assembly—'May an angel ride on your shoulders'—Cambola played them out with 'Hark, Hark! the Lark' on the trumpet.

Now at the far end of the gym, Mags Gablecross sat calmly smiling, ticking off candidates as she called out their names in alphabetical order.

Xav being Campbell-Black was one of the first in. Taggie gave him a huge hug.

'Can I have a hug too?' asked Rocky.

Danijela's little teeth were chattering frantically.

'Even my buttyflies have buttyflies.'

Danny the Irish, who'd only come in because she had, held her hand.

'I'm so exhausted I can't remember my candidate number,' moaned Pearl.

'Can I have a hug?' Monster begged Taggie, his lower lip trembling like a little boy's.

Inside the gym, the windows were too high to reveal anything except ever-darkening purple sky.

'At least we can hang ourself on the ropes,' sighed Kylie, whose bulge was so big she could hardly get at her desk.

'That's not a metre between your desks, Danny and Danijela,' called out Mags as she checked everyone had written their names and numbers properly. 'If you want to hold hands, do it after the exam.'

Aysha, a bruise darkening her cheek, cast down her eyes, terrified of looking at an anguished Xav.

As Janna watched the tail-enders forlornly filing to their doom, she wanted to ask if they'd packed their pencil boxes themselves.

'Perhaps we should strip search you for mobiles,' she joked.

'Yes, please,' giggled Kitten, 'but only if Emlyn does it.'

'Kitten Meadows, you've never worn a long skirt in your life, what have you got hidden?' shouted

361

Pearl.

'Shut up, all of you,' yelled Cambola.

Turning, Janna noticed Emlyn leaning against the wall watching her. He had just rounded up and brought in Johnnie Fowler. 'Worse than getting a mustang into a lorry.'

'I feel like Gérard Houllier,' confessed Janna, watching through the door as Mags handed out the papers. 'Once they're on the field you can only pray, we can't even substitute Boffin or Cosmo.'

'Don't expect too much, they've crammed a two-year course into one year, but it's been such a fantastic year. It'll stand them in good stead for ever,' said Emlyn. As his big, warm hand gathered up hers and squeezed it, she let it lie there.

'Everyone here?' demanded Mags, consulting her list. 'No Feral?'

'He's not taking business studies, miss.'

Mags looked round the room. 'Graffi's not here either.'

At that moment, a schoolmaster bringing back the birch, the rain lashed the window panes.

'I'll go and find him,' said Emlyn, letting go of Janna's hand.

Torrential rain scrabbled and clawed at his windscreen; rotting fruit, veg, fag ends and needles flowed into the cul-de-sacs of the Shakespeare Estate. Emlyn found Graffi wandering down Hamlet Street. It was hard to tell if his face was soaked by tears or rain; his black curls hung in rat's tails.

'Cardiff Nan's fucked off.'

'Hop in and leave her.'

'Can't, she's left all her clothes at home.'

'A Welsh undresser.'

'She'll catch her death.'

'I'll find her after I've dropped you at Larks.'

'Can't do the exam now, it's too late. My hands are frozen.' Graffi was shaking uncontrollably. 'I can't write.'

'You can have a go.'

Five minutes later, having swapped his drenched T-shirt for Emlyn's jersey, which reached his knees, Graffi slid into the gym to giggles and cheers from his supporters.

'I've got the shakes, I can't do this.' He picked up the paper and read: 'Greenstreet PLC are planning to build their fifth supermarket on the edge of an ancient and much-loved country town. Question one: How should they set about winning local acceptance and planning permission?'

Familiar territory, Mr Randal Greenstreet, thought Graffi.

'Well, maybe I can.' He picked up his pen.

The silence of the exams was interrupted only by occasional expletives, rain grapeshotting the windows, sweet papers rustling, tummies rumbling, the click of Mags's knitting needles and the pacing of Cambola, the invigilator, up and down the rows, to be replaced after thirty minutes by the clattering of Gloria's high heels.

Gloria, dreaming of PC Cuthbert, didn't notice Kitten's denim skirt falling open to reveal useful business terms and formulas written on her succulent thighs. Distracted by the sight, Monster lost his train of thought. Pearl opened her KitKat, turning it over thoughtfully. On the back, with a compass, she had also scratched terms and formulas.

Sweating when they came in, the bare-shouldered girls were now shivering.

I'm three-quarters through. I can do it, thought Xav joyfully. Looking across, he met Aysha's eyes. He wanted to kiss her purple bruise better.

Even Rocky, vast in his tiny desk, like Bultitude Senior in *Vice Versa*, was writing slowly but steadily.

'Got my period,' announced Pearl. 'Got to go to the toilet.'

Out she went, returning in a spitting rage.

'Who removed *Understanding Business* out of the toilet cistern?'

*   *   *

Over at Bagley, Stancombe's Science Emporium was being built for the Queen's visit in the first week in November and the builders continued to make an unconscionable din: bang, bang, drill, drill, setting the children's teeth on edge, so the GCSE exams were being taken in the newish sports hall.

Well into business studies, Primrose was writing steadily. Paris was thinking, then scribbling frantically, wishing he could instead write a short story about the idealistic young couple in Question Three, who were trying to make their garden centre break even by taking in another director.

Amber was writing to her boyfriend at Harrow. Boffin was filling pages and pages, between smirking and cracking his knuckles. Cosmo had polished off his paper in half an hour and was writing to Mrs Walton. He did hope Milly wouldn't want to come home and veg for a week at half-term.

Plugged into Jade Stancombe's ear, and hidden by a curtain of tortoiseshell hair, was a little mobile, the latest technical device from the Philippines, which as she tapped in the number, gave her the answers to each question as slowly or as fast as she chose. For this relief, she had almost forgiven Daddy for shacking up with Anthea Belvedon, particularly as he'd promised her a thousand pounds for every A grade.

*   *   *

Gloria had been replaced as invigilator by Basket, whose spangled flip-flops, daringly acquired in Skunk's honour, flapped as she padded up and down, doing everyone's heads in.

'Turn down the fucking volume,' snarled Monster.

The rain was easing, the windows framing grey clouds topped with white rather than purple.

Mags put down the shawl she was knitting for Kylie's baby.

'You've got five minutes left.'

Danijela burst into tears, gazing helplessly at her hardly touched pages. Others scribbled final answers or tried to reach into the depths of their memories, as one might rootle in a bag for a taxi fare, and find nothing.

'Put down your pens, please.'

Dazed, like miners coming up into the light, they spilt out into the drizzle. They had an hour and three-quarters to eat and drink something before PE theory that afternoon. Feral, bouncing his football, had just arrived; Partner, barking round his feet, hoped for a game.

'Howdya do?' Feral asked Xav.

'Not bad, once I got going. I've got a card for you.'

Pearl the drama queen was making her usual fuss.

'I've failed, I've failed. Couldn't do any of it. We wasn't taught the syllabus.'

'Yes we was,' said Kitten. 'I thought it were easy.'

Janna rushed round encouraging and consoling.

'First one's always difficult. Sure this afternoon'll be much easier. Just make certain you have a proper dinner.'

It had been hard to settle to anything this morning, all she could think was that Emlyn had held her hand.

*　　　*　　　*

PE theory lasted two hours. Feral had got top marks in the practical exam, but he couldn't make head nor tail of this paper. So he slowly deciphered Bianca's card.

It was her parents' last-year's Christmas card, with a picture of Penscombe Peterkin gambolling in the snow with Rupert's Jack Russells.

Inside were printed the words 'Merry Christmas and a Happy New Year' and at the bottom 'Rupert and Taggie Campbell-Black'. There was no way Rupert would ever wish him any happiness, thought Feral wearily.

'Dearest Feral,' Bianca had written. 'This card is the right one because I want to know you next Christmas and the next and the next, for ever. Good luck, I miss you, please ring me. All love.'

With a groan of despair Feral shoved the card in

his pocket and gazed at the blank pages of the booklet in which he was supposed to write down his answers. The princess and pauper: how could he ever give Bianca the life she deserved?

*   *   *

When Graffi got home from his night shift at Tesco, the dawn was already breaking and his father roaring drunk and raging mad.

'How dare you let out Cardiff Nan? Day centre brought her back and fucking charged me for the loan of a dressing gown,' and he hit Graffi across the lounge.

109

PE theory was followed by information technology, German listening and religious studies, leading up to the big one, English lit., on the Friday morning before half-term. For Rupert, the Thursday had been punctuated by telephone calls from skittish Bagley mothers, including the fearful Dame Hermione, saying that as they'd pledged large sums of money, they did hope to be rewarded with a party if he got a good grade. The final call at midnight had been from ghastly Stancombe, saying he hoped Rupert was going to honour his promise and roll up at Cotchester College tomorrow.

'There's a lot at stake.'

'The stake should be through your fucking heart,' howled Rupert and hung up.

Randal turned gleefully to Anthea, stretched out naked on his bed beside him. 'Pressure getting to his Highness.'

'Good,' said Anthea. 'Ay hope he gets a U. He's always been far too big for his raiding boots.'

Rupert was so livid, he'd never sleep now. In the old days of showjumping, or when he was Minister for Sport, he could always ease the tension by pulling a groom or a groupie. Now he was mocked by an entire library of books, which he'd never read, and by *Lord of the Flies* reminding him how horribly he was bullying darling Taggie at the moment, by being so sulky and resentful. Thank God term would be over in a few weeks and she'd be back home with him again. But would she be bored? Had Larks whetted her appetite for more company and excitement: for bloody Pete Wainwright or that fat Welshman?

Rupert wished he could have taken the exam at Larks instead of Cotchester College, which would be swarming with press. But when he'd dropped into Jubilee Cottage to ask Janna, she had very sweetly said his presence in the exam room would be far too distracting.

'The girls would all gaze at you, and the invigilators too, enabling all the lads to cheat like mad and no one would notice. You're still the most attractive man in the world,' she added, blushing furiously.

'Huh—doesn't get me anywhere.' Rupert had stalked off into the sitting room and been blown away by Graffi's mural.

'That's so bloody good. Christ! There's Rod Hyde and ghastly Ashton in one of his poncy mauve shirts and that asshole Bishop. What's he called, Graffi? He must come and do one of the hunt before bloody Blair closes it down.'

Rupert's mood didn't improve on the morning of the exam. Taggie and Xav had left for Larks and weren't even there to wave him off. The forecourt of Cotchester College was swarming with press, including a grinning Venturer camera crew.

'To me, Rupert', 'Look this way, Rupe', 'Over here', they shouted, as Rupert deliberately parked his dark blue BMW in the space reserved for the Dean of the College, and, gathering up *Lord of the Flies*, *Death of a Salesman*, and *Opening Lines*, leapt out like a snarling tiger.

'God, he's lush,' sighed a presenter from Sky.

'What have you learnt from your studies of English lit. ?' asked the *Guardian*.

'That the term "mature student" is an oxymoron.'

'Randal Stancombe says you haven't got a hope in hell,' taunted the *Scorpion*.

'Stancombe's an expert on hell,' snarled Rupert. 'Now, get out of my way.'

He was about to pick the *Scorpion* reporter up by his lapels when he was distracted by a vast fluffy black pantomime cat padding up to him, purring loudly and rubbing itself against his thighs.

'What the fuck?' Rupert was about to punch or kick the cat away, when a deep gasping familiar voice spoke.

'I've just come to bring you luck.'

Rupert's scowl widened into a huge smile, his voice cracked: 'Oh Tag, darling, oh Tag,' as he pulled the cat to its feet and into his arms.

'Purrrr, purrrr,' giggled the cat, tickling his face with its whiskers.

Rupert was still laughing as he sat down. Oblivious of his fellow candidates, he got out a blue fountain pen and wrote his name and number. Then, opening the paper, he read the first question on *Lord of the Flies*: 'Describe the importance of Jack in this novel.'

' "This is a good island",' wrote Rupert, with a sigh of relief. ' "We'll have fun." '

Finishing his answer on *Death of a Salesman*, he had half an hour left for poetry and to explain the ways Seamus Heaney and Dannie Abse wrote about the father/son relationship in two poems, which he'd enjoyed and identified with. Heaney was sound on ploughing and he liked the Abse line about his son playing pop music and 'dreaming of some school Juliet I don't know'. He'd never get a chance to meet Aysha if Raschid Khan had his way.

Thank God there wasn't a question on that whining bitch Sylvia Plath.

Having finished the paper, Rupert felt very flat. Cursing himself for things he should have put in, he shook off the press, and drove straight to Larks to collect Xav. Taggie would already have left to collect Bianca from Bagley.

As he hurtled down the back roads, he noticed the cow parsley turning green and going over and the chestnut candles scattering their creamy petals. He'd been too busy to appreciate them and now he'd have to wait until next year. The baton had been taken over by hawthorn, exploding everywhere in white-hot fountains, its soapy bath-day smell competing with the reek of wild garlic, much stronger now the leaves were yellowing and decaying.

Thank God he'd be able to concentrate full time on racing once more. A new dark brown filly called Fast was running in the first race at York. Pulling into the Larks car park, where, judging by the 'Please Be Quiet' sign, Eng. lit. was still going on, he switched on the little television on his dashboard.

Next second, a white van with Star of Lahore Curry House printed on its side drew up, driven presumably by Raschid Khan. Rupert had been about to take a large swig of brandy out of his hipflask, but Khan looked the sort of evil bugger who'd report him to the police.

Fast was dancing round the paddock looking almost too well. The bookies had her at twelve to one. Rupert was about to ring Ladbrokes, when he

371

noticed Mr Khan, despite his air of extreme disapproval, sneaking a look at the television.

'Hi,' said Rupert.

'Good afternoon,' replied Mr Khan stiffly.

'I know who you are,' drawled Rupert. 'You have an exceptionally clever daughter. In my experience, the more you tell teenagers not to see each other, the more they want to.'

Mr Khan was about to close his window, when Rupert added:

'The attachment is as abhorrent to me as it obviously is to you.' Then, when Mr Khan looked astounded: 'Do you honestly think I want Xavier, with all he is likely to inherit, to chuck himself away on a total nobody?'

'A nobody?' Quivering with fury, Mr Khan inflated like a turkey cock.

'By comparison,' said Rupert coldly.

'That's a racist remark.'

'You're the racist,' snapped back Rupert, 'being foul about my son, who's much blacker than your daughter, who I gather is utterly enchanting. My wife Taggie is almost more devoted to her than Xav is.'

'There is nothing more to be said. Aysha is engaged to be married.'

'Right. If you'll forgive me,' said Rupert, punching out Ladbrokes' number, 'I've got a potentially very good horse in this race. If you want to take a chance and have a bet, the odds are excellent.'

There was a long pause. In the dust of the car park, two robins were quarrelling over a feather. Mr Khan, unable to resist a flutter, extracted a tenner from a paperclip full of notes in his breast pocket and handed it over. 'I will have a bet.'

Matters dipped when Fast, no doubt excited to be carrying Rupert's dark blue and emerald green colours for the first time, took off at the start and ran halfway round the course, before her jockey could pull her up. She then lined up with the starters, set off at a cracking pace, and with Mr Khan and Rupert both yelling their heads off, lived up to her name by flying down the straight to win by six lengths.

'You've made a hundred and twenty pounds,' said Rupert jubilantly, 'and I've just bought one fantastic horse.'

When Xav and Aysha wandered wearily out of English lit., deliberately keeping their distance, utterly dejected at the prospect of not seeing each other for ten days, they were flabbergasted to see Rupert and Raschid Khan leaning against Rupert's car, deep in conversation.

'Xav tried to introduce marketing to my yard.'

'Aysha tried to introduce food technology to my restaurant, which I would be honoured if you would visit one evening.'

'How did you get on, Dad?' asked Xav nervously.

'Not bad, might have scraped a G. How about you?'

'Not great, I've never understood that Heaney poem. Is his father senile, or is he haunted by his memory?'

'Senile, if he's anything like me. Have you met Mr Khan? Fast just won by six lengths.' Rupert turned back to Raschid: 'Why don't you, your wife and Aysha come to Epsom one day next week?'

'How could you schmooze up to that terrible guy?' exploded Xav as Rupert drove over the

373

bridge towards Penscombe. 'He blacked Aysha's eye last week.'

'No, he didn't, Aysha's younger sister did that. Aysha wanted to revise and turned off *EastEnders*. Raschid told me,' said Rupert smugly.

Winding down his window, narrowly missing a jogger, Rupert chucked Sylvia Plath into the River Fleet.

110

Half-term wasn't helpful. The candidates felt they deserved a break, but guilty if they eased off and lost momentum, particularly on the Monday after, when faced with two heavyweights: geography and double science. As a result of being in a confined space, everyone had colds or tummy bugs and the heat wave had kicked in. At nine-thirty it was already like an oven in the gym. Sophy was invigilating and unless she walked in the straight line required of sobriety tests, her splendid bulk sent papers flying and candidates into fits of nervous giggles.

They were just about to start geography when Johnnie Fowler was found to be missing. Then Janna ran in saying Johnnie's sister had rung to say at the prospect of two such gruelling exams, Johnnie had gone 'on the booze, then on the rob' and been arrested.

'Go and bail him,' Skunk Littlewood begged Emlyn, 'he's got double science this afternoon. He could get a B.'

Emlyn found Johnnie in a cell, cross-eyed with hangover.

'What happened?'

'I got hammered, mugged an old lady for anuvver round, but I was so drunk I didn't realize it was Graffi's Cardiff Nan, what had escaped. It's not funny,' he grumbled. 'Anyway, I don't want bailing. Can't I stay here and miss science, maffs, French, D and T, English, anuvver bleeding geography and German and history and more science?'

'Come on,' said Emlyn.

Outside, he fed Johnnie black coffee and later chicken soup and dry toast and got him back in time for science.

'Don't,' groaned Johnnie, clutching his head as the other candidates gave him a round of applause.

Monster had had baked beans for lunch; consequently, his farts were worse than Skunk's heat-wave armpits.

'I'm going to faint,' said Johnnie, even more so a minute later when he opened the paper, which was a brute. 'And to fink I could be kipping in some nice cell.'

'Holy shit.' Feral screwed up his paper and walked out, bouncing his football.

'Don't give up,' the Brigadier, who was hovering in the corridor, begged him, 'you've got plenty of time and an extra half-hour for being dyslexic.'

'If I stared at that paper for a hundred years, I couldn't do a word of it, so don't get yer hopes up, Brig, I'm going to play football.'

Pearl unfurled another KitKat weighed down with equations. Within twenty minutes the room was almost empty; only Graffi, Aysha, Xav (because it gave him the chance to gaze at Aysha), Kitten and Pearl were left.

'Bloody hell,' said Graffi, 'I need a fag and a piss.'

'Hush,' said Basket in horror.

'And for you to take off those fucking, squeaking shoes.'

'Nuffink on circulation, nuffink on the heart, nuffink on the solar system, or electricity or radiation,' raged Pearl as they came blinking and utterly dispirited into the sunlight.

'I thought it were easy,' said Kitten and got punched in the face by Pearl.

*   *   *

Over at Bagley earlier, Mr Fussy hung round the sports hall, hurrying in his students, 'Don't be late, don't be late,' hell-bent on smashing Theo's record of getting everyone through.

Milly, practising a yoga relaxation technique Poppet had urged on her, was nearly asleep. Jade made another mental note not to thrust her fingers through her hair and reveal the tiny transmitter in her ear.

Lando was at the back, murmuring, 'Define a quark, define a quark. It's the sound that an upper-class duck makes,' and laughing at his own joke so much, he was furiously hushed by Boffin. From where Lando was sitting, he could admire the splendid swell of Primrose's left breast. Cosmo, having finished his paper, was reading *The Secret History*.

*   *   *

When it came to the two-hour maths exam the following day, Xav was determined not to let Pittsy down. Ex-alkies should stick together.

'If Mrs Rock borrowed £2,000 at ten per cent compound interest and paid it back together with total interest after two years, what would be her total repayment?' read Xav.

'£2,420', he wrote a minute later.

*   *   *

Over at Bagley, the Philippine gremlin whispered £2,420 in Jade's ear, in answer to the same question. Jack Waterlane, utterly defeated by the same paper, was relieved to receive a text message on his smuggled-in mobile, saying Kylie Rose had gone into labour.

When in doubt, take the easier option. As Jack ran out of the exam hall, Biffo, who was invigilating, leapt down from his chair and chased after him. The best way of stopping Biffo following him, decided Jack, was to take Biffo's car. Although he was only sixteen, Jack had been driving tractors round his father's estate since he was ten and, leaving a furiously windmilling Biffo, set off at ninety miles an hour for the hospital.

Kylie Rose's face when he walked into the maternity ward made everything worthwhile.

'I thought you'—groan—'was in the middle of a maffs paper,' progressed to, 'Oh'—groan—'of course I'll marry you.'

Chantal spent the rest of the labour crying with joy.

Lord Waterlane, when he rolled up some hours later, was in a towering rage. On the other hand, Jack's mother, Sharon, who insisted on referring to herself as Lady Shar, had once been a nightclub hostess and a hell of a goer. David had always suffered from *nostalgie de la boue* and found Chantal, who was only thirty, extremely pretty and, after all, Kylie had given birth to a boy.

'We're going to call him Ganymede David,' she told her future father-in-law proudly.

*　　　*　　　*

378

The first English paper, which also contained literature questions, was on 10 June. Dora, knowing this was a crucially important subject to Paris, had finally tracked down five four-leafed clovers and, with Patience's help, had glued them on a card. 'Dear Paris,' she had written inside, 'Good luck in English and all your other exams, you'll do brilliantly. Love, Dora'.

Her timing, admittedly, was lousy. A thoroughly strung-up Paris, flanked by Junior, Lando and Jack, was just going into the exam when Dora had rushed up, thrusting the card into his hand. Paris glanced down.

'What the fuck?'

'Please open it.'

Paris gazed at her in disbelief.

'Just fuck off, can't you see I'm busy? Get out of my life and leave me alone.'

Dora cried great rasping sobs all round the pitches, missing French. Artie Deverell, who'd picked up on the exchange, dispatched Bianca, not the ideal person, who found Dora sitting on a log sobbing into Cadbury's shoulder.

'Good thing Labradors like water,' observed Bianca.

Dora went on crying.

'Paris is heartless, Dor. Even when he was crazy about me, he couldn't show it. It's his upbringing; he doesn't know how to express love, he hasn't had any practice. He's got a slice of ice in his heart.'

'Put not your trust in Arctic Princes,' sobbed Dora.

Jade Stancombe, in the evening, was more brutal. 'You were like an autograph-hunter interrupting

Tiger Woods as he teed up at the eighteenth hole. Paris just tore up your card and chucked it in the bin. Stop making a fool of yourself; he's out of your league.'

*   *   *

In the sports hall earlier, Paris dispatched Housman and Hood's rosy view of childhood: 'Lands of Lost Content'. Poets all seemed to have had wondrous childhoods and gloomy, insecure old ages.

I've had a gloomy, insecure childhood, thought Paris; God help me if the rest of my life is even worse. I remember, I remember the children's homes where I wasn't born.

He turned to the next question: 'Describe a place you hate.'

I hate my own heart [wrote Paris] because it is cruel and hard. My best friend, Dora, is honourable and good like Piggy in *Lord of the Flies*. She has helped me revise all my exams: where the world moves and sits in space, Martial's recipe for happiness, drumlins, the Battle of Arginusae and the trials of the Generals. She gave me a beautiful good-luck card decorated with four-leaf clovers, but I tore it up and told her to piss off, because I was uptight. I would like to apologize to Dora on behalf of all my sex. Where women are concerned, we always get things wrong and I most of all. Dora is well named because she is adorable.

I hate my heart because it lets me down; its

380

beat quickens when I hear beautiful music or poetry, but when a friend tries to get close, it freezes over. To twist Catullus: whenever I love, I seem to hate or resent as well. We dissected a pig's heart in biology, but if you dissected my heart, it would pump not blood but poison.

'A place I hate,' wrote Boffin Brooks, 'is the headquarters of the Tory Party.'

The place I hate is my deputy headmaster's drawing room. He calls it a lounge, which is a complete misnomer because no one could lounge in such an uncomfortable place [wrote Lando]. The chairs are ramrod hard; the sofas murder your coccyx. No parents stay more than five minutes because he offers such tiny glasses of indifferent sherry and doesn't want anyone to linger. There are no pictures, no books except the very odd scientific manual. When you enter, you always get a lecture on bad behaviour.

'The place I hate is a vivisectionist's laboratory where the animals' vocal cords are cut on arrival so their screams cannot upset the staff or visitors,' wrote Amber and made herself cry even more cataloguing other iniquities.

Glancing round, Primrose Duddon smiled sympathetically and shoved a box of Kleenex in her direction.

I like Primrose, decided Amber, I like her much better than Milly or Jade. Primrose had helped her with revision beyond the call of duty. Amber

381

resolved to buy her a cashmere jersey as a thank-you present. On the other hand, it would take a lot of cashmere to accommodate Primrose's splendid bosom and might be rather expensive. Better to give her scent instead.

111

The sun had long since set, but it was still so hot that, despite wearing only shorts, a cotton shirt and loafers, Theo had left his study windows wide open. In the past month, he had been soothed by the 'liquid siftings' of the nightingales in the laurels. Tonight they had all departed—like pupils at the end of term. Would he still be alive next year to hear them?

He had been wrestling with a difficult letter in answer to a telephone call telling him one of his favourite old boys, Jamie Pardow, had been killed in Iraq.

'We knew you were fond of each other,' Jamie's father had said, 'in fact in his very last letter home, he said: "If you see Theo, tell him I'm still not tucking my shirt in." ' The father's voice had cracked then and he'd had to ring off.

Such a lovely boy. Theo shook his head. He should be writing reports. He should be working on Sophocles. Instead, he poured another large Scotch to wash down a couple more painkillers. A bottle of morphine, illegally prescribed by James Benson, was hidden behind the books, for when things became unendurable.

Would he could take something to ease the ache in his heart that after the end of term he wouldn't see Paris for eight weeks. In a way it would be a relief. He needed to be alone to calm his fever, to think about the boy. He knew Ian Cartwright, Cosmo and even Dora were jealous of their friendship. He must try not to favour him next term.

On a positive side, he was delighted Paris was on course for A stars in Greek and Latin. Hengist, who had a key to the school safe and, against all the rules, often looked at finished papers, had reported exquisite translations of Homer and Virgil, wise, witty, lyrical comments on Ovid and Horace and Iphigenia's pleading for Orestes and flawless unseens in the language papers. How Socrates would have loved him.

Paris, according to Hengist, had also submitted brilliant papers in other subjects, including a matchless first history paper. 'He writes so entertainingly.'

Paris had science tomorrow morning and a second history paper in the afternoon, covering the Russian Revolution and Nazi Germany, which had both fascinated and haunted him. Then it was all over.

Although it was after eleven, golden Jupiter was the only star visible in a palely luminous blue sky. The trees on the edge of the golf course, olive green in the half light, seemed to have faces, hollow-eyed, too, after a month of exams. The mingled stench of rank elderflower and decaying wild garlic was overwhelming.

As Hindsight padded in, leaping on to the table, Theo grabbed his glass—there was enough whisky spilt over the reports and his translation of Sophocles already—and guided the cat's fluffy orange tail away from the halogen lamp. A mosquito was whining around his bald head looking for a late supper; Theo lit yet another cigarette to deter it.

He smiled briefly as he caught sight of a poster

on the wall Paris had had framed for him for his birthday, which showed a woman with a balloon coming out of her mouth saying: 'I'm voting for Martial, he's not clever, he's not honest, but he's handsome.' Alex had banished it from Theo's classroom as being too sexist.

Theo had seen a lot of Paris in the last ten days. Not entirely, he was realistic enough to recognize, because Paris relished his company. The boy, it appeared, had been so gratuitously cruel to poor little Dora that that dear, kind, soul Patience Cartwright had ticked him off roundly. This had so shocked Paris, he had since shunned the Cartwrights' and spent his evenings working in the library or talking to Theo. Theo suspected and genuinely hoped Paris was much fonder of Dora than he let on. He could do worse. Dora was brave, resourceful and good-hearted.

The evenings together had been an exquisite pleasure. They had listened to music and discussed books and Paris's choice of AS levels: Greek, Latin, theatre studies and English. Paris also brought Theo the latest gossip. How Lando had been caught listening to the Empire test match on his walkman during science, how Anatole had mistaken downers for uppers and slept peacefully through French, and how Boffin, 'stupid twat', was already immersed in one of next year's set books: *The Handmaid's Tale*.

*　　　　*　　　　*

Hengist was in Washington, due back this evening, but grounded by a strike. He had nevertheless rung in to wish Paris luck in his final history paper

385

tomorrow.

Theo emptied the bottle into his glass. On his desk lay an advance copy of Alex's *Guide to Red Tape* (or *Tape* as it was now known), which the self-regarding idiot had presented to Theo to illustrate that he, Alex, despite being busier than anyone, was capable, unlike Theo and Hengist, of meeting deadlines.

Theo, instead, turned to Aeschylus, whose *Philoctetes*, covered in drink and coffee rings, he'd been reading earlier. Philoctetes, driven crazy by a snake bite, as he was by his ransacked spine. How admirable was Maurice Bowra's translation:

> Oh Healer death, spurn not to come to me.
> For you alone, of woes incurable, are doctor,
> And a dead man feels no pain.

Theo hoped this were true. Awful to reach the other side and immediately find oneself bound on a wheel of fire, like Ixion.

*   *   *

Back in his cell, Cosmo peeled off his mother's blond wig, which she'd worn for *Norma* and in which he had disguised himself in his walk down to Bagley village to pleasure Ruth Walton.

He had finished *The Secret History*, the best book he had ever read, in which young people had totally waived morality and taken justice into their own hands. He had put on Matthias Goerne, a voice of unearthly beauty, singing Bach cantatas and was flipping through scores for the end-of-term concert. But he was not happy.

He had spent half an hour earlier mending Theo's DVD machine, but Theo's eyes still didn't rest on him with as much tenderness as they rested on Paris. No matter that he was going to get straight A stars and one for shagging from Ruth Walton, Cosmo wanted to be loved best by all the people by whom he wanted to be loved best. Even Hengist had rung from Washington to wish Paris luck.

He never rang me, thought Cosmo bitterly.

Cannoning off the walls on his way to bed around midnight, Theo saw a light on in Paris's room and went in. On the Thomas the Tank Engine duvet lay the boy's dark green history revision folder. In his sleeping hand was clutched the Greek *Epigrams* which Theo had given him for his sixteenth birthday. Theo was touched.

Paris looked so adorable with the lamplight falling on his long blond lashes and silky, flaxen hair. Playing cricket without a cap had brought a sprinkling of freckles and a touch of colour to his pale face. In sleep, the wolf cub relaxed and one could appreciate the beauty and casual grace of his body. Theo removed the Greek *Epigrams*.

Cosmo, skulking on the landing on the lookout for trouble, froze at the sight of Theo's battered copy of Philoctetes and his late-night whisky outside Paris's bedroom.

Suddenly terrible screams ripped the night apart, followed by anguished sobbing, which slowly subsided. Five minutes later, Cosmo, lurking in the shadows, saw Theo, a faint smile on his cadaverous features, coming out of Paris's room and going through the green baize door into his own apartment.

Cosmo retired to his cell and, setting aside the end-of-term concert scores, lit a fag, poured himself a large brandy and reflected. Alex Bruce wasn't his greatest fan, particularly since the Poppet art department incident. Poppet had even asked Cosmo to address the Talks Society on the morality of onanism. It wouldn't hurt to win some brownie points.

After a preliminary rootle round Theo's study, Cosmo let himself out of the front door, dropped his empty brandy bottle in Poppet's bottle bank and knocked on the Bruces' door. Alex, awake, much enjoying a third read of *Tape*, was soon reassuring Cosmo that he had done exactly the right thing.

Telling each other it was for Paris's sake, they let themselves into the house and to Theo's study, which thankfully looked out over an entirely deserted golf course. Judging by the bottles in the waste-paper basket, Theo was unlikely to wake up.

Alex's lips pursed at the overflowing ashtrays and the pile of reports unmarked, except by whisky stains. From Theo's desk drawer, Cosmo unearthed some love poems to Paris in Greek.

'Who was it said Greek letters on a blank page look like bird's footprints in the snow?' asked Cosmo, then when Alex clearly didn't know the answer, added, 'These are pretty explicit, sir, and those letters here, here, here and here, spell Paris, although it could be the Paris who triggered off the Trojan War.'

'I doubt it.' The gleam of triumph in Alex's eyes was obscene, particularly when, from under Theo's desk drawer lining paper, Cosmo pulled ravishing nude photographs of Paris, with the Eiffel Tower

388

tattoo on his right shoulder, as well as a DVD in a plain brown wrapper.

Hearing a crash, they both jumped out of their skins, but it was only Hindsight arriving through the window.

'I'm amazed that cat hasn't died from passive smoking,' said Alex, shoving him out again. Breathing more heavily than a French bulldog on the job, Alex then fastidiously parked his bottom on Theo's rickety chair and put the DVD into the machine, which came up with a film of ravishing naked youths re-enacting classical myths with men sporting curly hair and ringleted beards.

'That's Narcissus and that must be Ganymede,' volunteered Cosmo.

'Don't look.' Alex clapped a sweating hand over Cosmo's eyes.

'All part of my development,' said Cosmo, tugging the hand away.

The mosquito, earlier deterred by Theo's cigarettes, whined, circled and plunged her teeth into Alex's arm.

*   *   *

'I thought Mr Fussy was going to pounce,' Cosmo told Anatole next morning. 'I couldn't tell if he was more turned on by the porn or the chance to nail Theo. The Martial voting poster on the wall and *Red Tape* chucked in the bin were the *dernière paille.*'

112

Arriving at the police station in the early hours of the morning, Theo was locked in a windowless cell measuring five foot by eight foot and strip-searched. This included a policeman getting out a latex glove and telling him to bend over. He was then moved to another cell, by which time, deprived of whisky, cigarettes and morphine, he was crawling up the walls. Every so often, officers lifted the flap in the door to look at him.

He realized he had entered the twisted world of the morally repulsive when he saw the stony contempt on the faces of the two interrogating officers, one man, one woman, who obviously wanted to find out if he were part of a wider paedophile ring.

'I'm innocent.'

'Those photographs and that DVD weren't innocent, sir.'

'They were planted. Look, I need to make a telephone call, I'm worried about my cat.'

'Cat's least of your worries, sir.'

The policewoman clearly found him distasteful. He'd grabbed a maroon polo neck knitted for him by an aunt, but was still in his shorts, knees continually knocking together. Stinking of booze, fags and sweat, grey stubble thickening, he must cut a repugnant figure. They had removed his shoelaces and his belt, so his shorts kept falling down.

As the night wore on, they kept trying to make him confess.

'I'm innocent, I never laid a finger on the boy.'

'What about those nude photographs?'

'Never saw them before in my life; you won't find any of my fingerprints; must have been taken years ago—Paris has got a completely different haircut.'

'And the images of an obscene nature on the DVD machine?'

'The sixth form gave it to me as a Christmas present. I can't work the damn thing.'

'And the poems?'

'Certainly, I wrote those.' Theo groaned; his back was excruciating. 'Nothing obscene about them. I've been framed.'

'They all say that. You're in denial, Theo. Admit your guilt, you'll feel so much better. Then you can be put on a course for sex offenders.'

'And never teach again.'

'You were carried away, you'd had a bit too much to drink. Do you always entertain young boys alone? D'you sit close to them? D'you always make a habit of going into their rooms at night?'

Sadness overwhelmed Theo. Paris must have shopped him.

'If you confess,' the policewoman was now saying cosily, 'you might easily get off. Crown won't want a lengthy trial; happens a lot.'

The only reason he might confess, thought Theo, as the sky turned from electric blue to the rose pink of sunrise, was to get some more morphine.

In the morning, he came up before the magistrates and was given police bail, on condition that he didn't get in touch with anyone from the school.

'You must not speak to any members of staff,' he was told, 'or discuss the incident with anyone.

391

You're to have no contact with the boy or any of the pupils. You must give an address well away from the school.'

Theo gave them the name of a dilapidated cottage on Windermere, left him by the aunt who'd knitted the maroon polo neck.

The case would now be adjourned for a pre-judicial review, which might take three weeks. Theo would come up in court three weeks after that. If the magistrates decided there was a case, it would be tried in a Crown court, probably not before Christmas.

Outside the court, Theo found Biffo, who had been selected by Alex as a safe bet to pack up his belongings. Biffo had also driven over in Theo's ancient Golf, which was loaded up with books, clothes, bottles of pills. He had also packed Theo's credit cards and cheque books, the seven plays of Sophocles, the manuscript in progress and Theo's notebooks.

'Where's my cat?' demanded Theo.

'I couldn't find him.' Biffo couldn't meet his eyes. 'All the police cars and disturbance must have scared him.'

'You must find him!' Theo was nearly in tears. 'I've had him since he was a kitten.'

'You often left him in the summer holidays.'

Biffo, Theo felt, at last had a legitimate excuse for detesting him.

'You've got to help me, Biffo, I must talk to Paris and Hengist.'

'You can't talk to anyone. Hengist is still away, anyway. You can ring me, here's my number, but only about things unconnected with the case.'

'I'm not resigning, I'm innocent.'

'I can't discuss it.'

Theo gave Biffo the address and telephone number of his cottage in Windermere. 'At least give it to Artie.'

'I can't promise anything. I've filled your car up with petrol.'

'Please try and find Hindsight, I'll pay for someone to come and collect him.'

*　　　*　　　*

Theo was still missing when Paris returned from his history exam. Barging into his housemaster's sealed-off study, he found whole shelves of books and Theo's manuscript gone, and Biffo nosing around.

'Is Theo back?'

'Gone away.'

'Where?'

'I'm not at liberty to say.'

'Don't be fucking stupid. I need to phone him. He never said goodbye; what's he supposed to have done?' Paris was nearly hysterical, particularly when Hindsight jumped in through the window and, mewing piteously, started weaving round his legs. 'Theo must have been pushed; he'd never leave without Hindsight. Tell me.'

Biffo backed away as, from a miniature Greek urn on Theo's desk, Paris grabbed a pair of scissors.

'I'll have those,' said Dora, grabbing the scissors as she marched in with a plate of cod from the kitchens and the *Larkminster Gazette*, which she handed to Paris.

'Page three,' she added as she started to cut up

the cod for Hindsight.

'Bagley master arrested over sex abuse claim', Paris read the headline, then, with dawning disbelief, the copy: 'Theo Graham, aged 59, a housemaster who frequently took groups of boys on trips to Ancient Greece, was arrested last night for harbouring images of an obscene nature, but was released on police bail this morning.'

Paris turned on Dora. 'You didn't flog this story?'

'Certainly not. Poor Mr Graham's been victimcised.'

'Who's he supposed to have jumped on?'

'Why, you, of course.'

*   *   *

The temperature had dropped; a mean east wind was systematically stripping the petals off Sally's shrub roses. The A Level candidates were still wrestling with law and French papers and police cars were parked outside the Mansion when Hengist finally got back to Bagley.

Marching into Alex's office, he found his deputy head in a high state of almost sexual excitement, forehead white, eyes gleaming more than the gold rims of his spectacles, whole body shivering with self-righteous disapproval, damp patches under the arms of his shirt, whose sleeves were held up by frightful garters.

'What the hell's going on?'

'Very grave news, S.T.L. Theo Graham's been arrested.'

'Whatever for?'

'Sexually abusing Paris Alvaston.'

'Don't be ridiculous, Theo'd never jeopardize a

394

boy's exams like that.'

'His baser nature overcame him,' said Alex heavily.

'Is Paris OK?' demanded Hengist. 'Did he take his history paper?' Then realizing how self-interested that sounded: 'What's he got to say?'

'He became hysterical and leapt at both Biffo and the policeman when asked the simplest question, which pre-supposes . . .'

'Bloody nothing,' roared Hengist.

'Theo entered Paris's room last night. Bloodcurdling screams were followed by desperate sobbing.'

'Probably a nightmare. Too much *Macbeth*, or mugging up Stalin's purges and the death camps, for Christ's sake. The boy's always been highly strung. Who reported this?'

'One of his peers, Cosmo Rannaldini.'

'Whoever believed a word Cosmo says?' said Hengist contemptuously. 'He'll have rung up the *Scorpion* by now.'

'I think not.' Alex put steepled fingers to pursed lips. 'Concerned for a fellow student, Cosmo behaved caringly and approached me late last night. I phoned the police instantly. They arrested Theo in the early hours.'

'For Christ's sake, Alex, why didn't you talk to Theo or ring me?'

'Your mobile was switched off. I consulted with Biffo, Joan and the bursar who, as the foster father, was very concerned.'

'You always wanted Theo out because he resisted your bloody modernizing.'

'We are accountable for our students' safety. In Theo's drawers were found naked photographs of

Paris'—let Hengist think the police discovered them—'poems dedicated to Paris of a homo-erotic nature and an obscene DVD of child pornography.'

Hengist looked out of the window at a blackbird splashing in the bird bath: such an innocent joyful pleasure. He felt a great sadness and said with less certainty, 'Theo's been framed.'

'I'm sorry, S.T.L.' Alex pinched the bridge of his nose. 'I know you were fond of the old boy. I was fond of him too. The whole thing has been most distressing.'

And you want me to feel sorry for you, thought Hengist.

'When did Paris find out?'

'We didn't apprize him this morning. I didn't want to stress him before a science paper.'

'Your subject, natch,' snarled Hengist. He wanted to hurl Alex to his death through the window.

'By lunchtime, Paris was searching for Theo. Rumours were circulating. The story had broken on Radio Larkminster. So Poppet broke the news to Paris, saying Mr Graham was helping the police with their enquiries.'

'Poppet? How did Paris take that?'

'Hard to tell, he never says much.'

'Jesus, if he's screwed up history, deputy heads will roll. I'm telling you, Alex, it's a set-up. Cosmo was clearly jealous of Theo's closeness to Paris.'

'Even if Paris does deny everything,' said Alex smugly, 'the photos and the pornography are enough to suspend him. I emailed the parents first thing. Better they knew before it hit the press. I've already received several back, and many supportive phone calls.' Alex handed Hengist a sheaf of paper.

396

On top was a fax from Randal Stancombe: 'Hope that bloody nonce goes down and gets the thrashing he deserves. He's always sidelined my Jade.'

The second came from Boffin's mother: 'I don't want my Bernard at risk.'

'With an arse that size, he'd hardly be in jeopardy,' said Hengist contemptuously.

'That was uncalled for. I've arranged for Jason Fenton, who knows a little Latin, to take Theo's classes. Fortunately, the classics don't attract many students. Goodness knows who's going to write Theo's reports.'

Alex paused as Miss Painswick, who'd never been berserk about Theo either, rushed in in a state of high excitement.

'Oh, you're back, headmaster. Thank God, there are so many messages.' Then, turning to Alex: 'The police want to talk to you, Mr Bruce, and afterwards, the press would like a word.'

Quivering with self-importance, Alex bustled off.

'The *TES* want that piece on the advantages of the baccalaureate by tomorrow,' Painswick added to Hengist.

*   *   *

Finding the general office empty, Hengist unlocked the safe and took the GCSE history papers, which had just been handed in, upstairs to his office and groaned when he saw Paris's booklet. The boy had scrawled his name: Alvaston, Paris; his candidate number; and signed his name at the bottom. The rest was gibberish, the work of a fast unravelling mind. What did they expect with yet another father figure snatched from him?

Hengist was demented; his great scheme fucked. He turned to Boffin's booklet. In his greed to get at the paper, the little beast had forgotten to put his name at the top, only his candidate number which ended with a three which could easily be curved and billowed out into an eight.

Hengist glanced through the questions.

'The main reason for the collapse of the provisional Government in 1917 was the work of Lenin and the Bolsheviks. Discuss.'

That was a doddle.

'Do you agree that the increased Nazi support in the period 1930–32 was due to the personal appeal of Hitler?'

Hengist suddenly had a better plan. Picking up the telephone, he rang Painswick.

'I better get shot of that *TES* piece before anything else blows up, Miss P. Won't take more than an hour. I don't want to be disturbed.'

*   *   *

Alex was relishing his interview.

'Mr Graham was a scholar of the old school, officer. He had that rather Greek thing of cultivating friendships with boys, never girls, and insisted on working one to one with vulnerable youngsters like Paris Alvaston. He liked to flout convention.

'Believing in transparency, officer, I installed glass panels in classroom doors so one could monitor practice. Theo Graham deliberately hung his coat over the panel. He could be very subversive.'

An hour later, Hengist was just deciding how best to handle the Theo debacle when his office door was pushed open and Elaine flew in, throwing herself on him, chattering her teeth in delight, circling and sending all the urgent messages flying. She was followed by Sally, who'd clearly been crying.

'Darling, why didn't you tell me you were back? This is so terrible.' Quickly she kissed Hengist. 'Thank God you're here. Poor Theo could never have done this. We've got to rescue him.'

'I'm just off to nail Alex, come with me.'

In Alex's office, they found Poppet dropping some herbal painkiller made from drops of valerian into a glass of water, which Alex gulped down noisily, his Adam's apple heaving. Hengist couldn't bear to look at him and went to the window, from which he could see pupils, aware of some great crisis, milling about, talking, glancing worriedly up, then looking away.

'What did the police say?'

'They're taking it very seriously.'

'So am I. They've hijacked my best teacher,' snapped Hengist.

'And granted him bail,' said Poppet, who was now massaging her husband's shoulders. Alex closed his eyes.

On a side table, copies of *A Guide to Red Tape* rose to the ceiling.

'I've signed you a copy, S.T.L.'

Then, when Hengist didn't answer, Poppet said accusingly, 'Alex didn't get any sleep last night.'

'Didn't bloody deserve to.'

'Alex has a duty of care for young people,' reproached Poppet.

'Theo's name should never have been released to the media before there was any proof of guilt,' said Sally furiously. 'Why couldn't it have been dealt with internally, Alex?'

'Things are so much better handled in the maintained system,' piped up Poppet. 'Theo could have sought help from the union. We could have called an emergency meeting of the governors. The union rep would have then rolled up with the offending member.'

'If they can persuade the offending member to withdraw,' added Alex—for a second Hengist's eyes met Sally's—'i.e. resign at once, things can be hushed up.'

'Why should Theo resign?' shouted Sally. 'He's innocent.'

*   *   *

Theo drove north until he found a church that was open, such was his need of sanctuary. How would he cope without James Benson's morphine? But the pain in his heart was far crueller.

Gasping for breath, he collapsed in a front pew, resting for a long time . . . When he looked down, he saw a pool of tears on the stone floor of the church.

*   *   *

Over at Larks, insulated against the outside world, the Brigadier and Emlyn heaved sighs of relief to find the history paper had included a question about the number of people killed on the Somme.

'On the other hand,' said Emlyn, 'Rocky's just informed me he was so pleased he remembered to tell the examiner we'd never have won World War I if Hitler hadn't attacked the Russians. How d'you get on?' he asked Feral.

'Bad as usual.' Feral shot outside to join his friends, who, euphoric the last exam was over, were playing football. Partner raced about yapping encouragement, particularly to Feral, who seemed to have wings on his heels. No one could stop him as he found goal again and again.

But what was the use? I'm thick, thick, thick, he told himself as he psyched himself up to ring his mother to let her know he'd screwed up yet again.

*   *   *

Pete Wainwright had just rolled up with a crate of wine to say thank you for the suggestions Taggie and her class had put forward for the Rovers' next season's menus. Bottles were therefore being opened in the staffroom to celebrate the end of the GCSEs when Emlyn walked in looking wintry.

'Afraid I can't stay.'

'Whyever not?' asked the Brigadier, who was mixing a pink gin for Lily.

'I've got to go over to Bagley. Artie's just phoned. Theo was arrested last night for possession of child porn and sexual abuse.'

'Paris?' whispered Janna.

'So it seems.'

'I don't believe it.'

Oh God, she thought, we should never have let him go to Bagley.

113

The last exam at Larks was followed two nights later by the end-of-term prom. Janna and her staff had such a frantic scramble getting everything ready that they had scant time to agonize about Paris and Theo—particularly as they were full of their own regrets that the year of grace was almost over.

Lily spent the day of the prom at home making sausage rolls and mushroom vol-au-vents for the buffet supper and trying not to cry. She was going to miss her Larks friends horribly, particularly seeing so much of the Brigadier. They'd planned a dance routine of Fred Astaire songs as a cabaret. Christian, rather smug he could still fit into them, was going to wear tails, and Lily had been forced to sell a last piece of Georgian silver to pay for a blue silk ball dress and pretty silver shoes in which to perform. Her cottage was achieving fashionable minimalism faster than she would have liked.

Lily was nervous of making an idiot of herself. If she drank enough to give herself courage she'd probably fall over. One of the numbers was 'Stepping Out with My Baby', and how could she pass as a 'baby' when she was over eighty with hair drawn into a dreary bun? If only she could afford to go back to Sadie, her darling Larkminster hairdresser, who'd cut her hair so beautifully.

As she packed bottles of elderberry wine into a cardboard box, she wondered who would feed the birds at Larks or the silver carp gliding, like Concorde, through the pond. She mustn't cry.

Weeping at her age so devastated one's face. Sometimes she thought Christian loved her, but she was terrified her bridge might dislodge if he kissed her, leaving a great red toothless gap, and her body undressed was not a pretty sight, and with her too-long grey hair down, she looked like a witch.

Despite being poor, Lily had never stinted on General, who, too fat for the cat door, was mewing to go out. Wiping her eyes with a drying-up cloth, she opened the front door to find Pearl on the doorstep, weighed down by make-up kit.

'You've been so kind to me Lily, I fort I'd give you a make-over.' Then, at Lily's look of alarm: 'You've got such pretty hair, I'd love to cut it, and there's a new blue rinse called Sapphire Siren to bring out your blue eyes.'

'It's very kind. I'm not sure.'

'You'll look great.' Pearl marched into the house, dumping her cases in the kitchen. 'You've got such lovely skin. Christian says you're wearing blue tonight for the cabaret.'

'It's a secret,' squeaked Lily. 'We may not do it, depends how the evening pans out.'

'Everyone's looking forward to it,' said Pearl. As she unpacked her bottles, six tenners from the Brigadier crackled comfortingly in her breast pocket.

'I think I'll cut your hair before I wash it. Have you heard about Paris? Do you think Mr Graham's really been giving him it up the bum?'

'I'm sure not,' said Lily faintly.

'I often wondered whether Paris wasn't a woofter. Never made a pass at me,' said Pearl.

*   *   *

The rest of the staff kept trying to send Janna home early to make herself beautiful. Twenty years wouldn't be enough, she thought wearily; she'd need her jaw wired up in a permanent smile to get her through the evening.

She had been trying to complete the children's year books and certificates of achievement, when Sally had popped in with 'a bit of blotting paper': namely a mountain of smoked salmon wrapped in cling film and 'some nice white wine for you and Emlyn to drink behind the bus shelter'.

Janna thanked her profusely and, thinking for the first time Sally looked her age, begged her to stop for a cup of tea.

'My dear, I'd have loved to—look how well those oriental poppies are doing—but we're all in a bit of a state over Theo and Paris. Paris hurled a brick through Alex's window last night, because no one will give him Theo's address. Emlyn's been wonderful with him, but the poor boy's hysterical, says he'll only talk to the police if he's allowed to talk to Theo first, which the police say is impossible. Nadine and Cindy Payne are putting their oars in; press everywhere.'

The sympathy in Janna's eyes prompted Sally to further revelations. 'Emlyn's also had a bit of a shock, poor boy. Oriana's expecting a baby—I'm not sure who the father is—due in November.' For a second Sally's face crumpled. 'I'm sure I'll love it once it's born, but Hengist doesn't want anything to do with it or Oriana. He's terribly cut up about Theo. Oh Janna, I do hope you don't feel we've failed Paris.'

404

Janna was reassuring Sally she didn't and was kissing her goodbye when Randal Stancombe came on the line. God, how she now hated his oily, over-intimate, threatening voice.

'Hi, Jan, can I be frank? Feel rather let down; I didn't get an invite for tonight's end-of-term do. Didn't think our friendship was that shallow.'

'Oh, it isn't, it isn't.' Janna curled up in embarrassment. 'It's only small, just staff and children.'

'Don't weaken,' mouthed Rowan from the doorway.

'But do drop in,' mumbled Janna.

'I'm actually taking Jade out for a meal, but we'll look in on the way. You asked any media?'

'No. Doesn't mean the bastards won't turn up.'

*   *   *

'Gosh, you're brave,' said Bianca, 'I should so die of embarrassment if Mummy was tempted on to the dance floor.'

'Unlikely,' said Xav as he tied his black tie. 'Dad's ordered me to shoot anyone who comes near her.'

He was delighted that the waistband of his DJ trousers had had to be taken in six inches and the legs let down.

Downstairs, Rupert helped his wife, ravishing in a scarlet halterneck, load chocolate torte and bowls of strawberries into the car.

'Keep an eye on her,' he said to Xav. 'You both look marvellous.'

He wouldn't have admitted to a soul, that he couldn't wait to get back and finish *Emma*.

Mrs Elton was even more like Anthea Belvedon than Mrs Bennet.

*   *   *

'I'll be down in a minute, pour yourself a drink,' Lily shouted down the stairs as Christian Woodford put the elderberry wine, the crumbles and the sausage rolls into the car.

The Brigadier choked on his drink as Lily came down the stairs. Her short silver-blue hair softly caressed her cheekbones, brought out the intense blue of her eyes and matched a dress short enough to reveal the most charming ankles. She had pawned all her jewellery except her sapphire engagement ring and her pearls, which she asked him to do up.

' "My precious Lily! My imperial kitten!" ' sighed the Brigadier, letting his fingers linger on her neck.

With his white tie and tails setting off his golfing tan, his fine square features and his thick silver hair, the Brigadier looked infinitely handsomer than Fred Astaire and Lily told him so.

'Could you also zip up my dress, which is beyond my arthritic fingers?'

'Much rather unhook it,' said the Brigadier, who had this afternoon signed a two-year Venturer contract to make another series of *Buffers*, along with some poetry drama documentaries kicking off with 'Horatius' and 'Morte d'Arthur'.

' "Steppin' Out With My Baby",' sang the Brigadier, smiling at Lily as they reached the outskirts of Larkminster. For a moment, he thought he was back in the last war, as, like submarines gliding stealthily through the blue evening, stretch limos with black windows kept overtaking them. Then out of these limos on to the Appletree forecourt, like a conjuror's coloured handkerchief, spilled the children, the boys in hired tuxedos with red, blue, green and tartan bow ties, the girls in pink or mauve satin trouser suits or ball dresses showing off pearly shoulders and pretty legs, enhanced by jewelled high heels and sparkling ankle bracelets.

With their hair descending in ringleted waterfalls and secured with combs decorated with flowers, their faces glittering with excitement, they could have been re-enacting the Netherfield ball from their set book. Intoxicated by their new beauty, they tore around Appletree, taking photographs, shrieking how wicked each other looked. Judging by the giggling, they'd already been at the booze.

The boys were fingering the Brigadier's tailcoat.

'That retro shawl collar's dead cool, Brig, did you get it from Matalan or the internet?'

'It's my own,' confessed Christian, 'I used to wear it night after night to dances. I like your gym shoes, Graffi.'

'Fort I'd treat myself.' Graffi waved a dark blue and pale blue trainer with a two-inch heel in the air. 'They cost a hundred and ten quid. What d'you think of Beckham's new hair?'

'Not as good as mine,' said Rocky, patting four-inch-high vermilion-gelled spikes. 'And you look even gooder, Lily.'

As the others laughed and agreed, Lily told them they all looked wonderful too.

The hall had been utterly transformed. Mags had blocked out any light from the big windows with full-length black curtains, which she and the other teachers had covered in silver and gold paper stars. On the stage below a huge glittering blue sign saying 'Larkminster High School Prom 2004', a group of suntanned men in black, known as the Butchers (as in 'I'm butcher than you'), were belting out 'American Pie'.

From the ceiling, concealing Graffi's angels, who all looked like Milly Walton, hung hundreds of coloured balloons like an inverted bubble bath. The floor was carpeted with dancers, gyrating under the flickering lights, clapping their hands above their heads. Many of the boys wore luminous rings in blue, emerald or red round foreheads or necks. The air was a dense fog of cigarette smoke.

Chairs for spectators had been grouped along one wall on either side of a trestle table, offering Coca-Cola, lemonade and Fanta. Officially, because Ashton or Cindy might gatecrash, the evening was dry.

I could murder a proper drink, thought Lily.

As if reading her mind, Janna glided out of the dancers. She had at long last had a chance to wear her slinky black velvet dress, off one freckled shoulder and split to the thigh on one side. With the front of her hair coaxed upward in smaller russet spikes than Rocky's, her huge eyes ringed with raw sienna, her big trembling mouth painted scarlet, she looked as young suddenly as any of her pupils.

'You look stunning! Isn't Pearl a genius,' she and Lily shouted to each other over 'American Pie'.

'Keep this for yourself,' added Janna, filling a glass with Sally's white, then handing bottle and glass to Lily.

'What's that?' Lily noticed Janna was drinking straight from a Fanta bottle.

'Teachers' lemonade, taught me by a primary head. No one can tell it's half filled with vodka. Will you crown the Prom King and Queen for us?'

'As long as I don't have to make a speech. Who's won it?'

'Wait and see. But it's a grand result.'

Next moment Pearl had rushed up.

'I want a group photograph of my favourite teachers,' she said bossily. 'That's you, Pittsy, you, Janna, you, Taggie and the Brig and Lily.'

Flattered, the five lined up as Pearl spent ages getting them in the right position. 'You go behind Janna, Taggie, and Lily in front of Pittsy, or we can't see you. Where's Emlyn? I'd like him as well.'

'Oh, get on,' grumbled the Brigadier, 'Lily and Taggie need top-ups.'

Dutifully they all waited as Pearl peered into her viewfinder, then, suddenly saying: 'Oh, I'm bored with this,' she wandered off to photograph someone else.

'Little madam,' exploded the Brigadier as Janna and Lily got the giggles.

'It's the first time I've seen Aysha's hair in four years. She looks absolutely gorgeous,' said Pittsy as Aysha timidly followed Xav on to the floor to join the big circle of dancers.

Aysha had only been allowed to attend the prom if she was chaperoned. As a result, Mrs Khan sat in the darkness watching her daughter, knowing how sad Aysha would be tomorrow. At least tonight, as she swayed in flowing turquoise chiffon before Xav, she could forget her heartache.

'Get Mother Khan some teachers' lemonade,'

suggested Wally.

'Where's Emlyn?' asked Janna for the hundredth time.

'He was here shifting furniture until the last moment,' said Cambola, who kept dragging boys on to the floor to dance; they lasted thirty seconds before belting back to their mates.

Outside, the sky was pale grey, the lace mats of elderflower caressing the window panes. Thinking Basket looked rather fetching in her tobacco-brown crimplene, Skunk led her off for a stroll.

They were passed as they went out by Feral wandering in, late because he'd been playing football. Unable to afford a tuxedo, he still looked a million dollars in black jeans and polo neck.

' "Here's mettle more attractive",' cried Cambola, bearing him off to dance to loud cheers.

114

Janna was dancing with the children again, singing along to Katie Melua as she rotated two pink luminous flowers above her head, surrendering herself to the music.

'One forgets how young she is,' Lily murmured to the Brigadier, adding doubtfully, 'You don't think our cabaret's too old for them?'

The Brigadier squeezed her hand.

'To use a mendacious expression of Randal Stancombe's: "Trust me." '

'Talk of the devil,' complained Lily as Randal, resplendent in a dinner jacket, pink carnation in his buttonhole, appeared in the doorway.

I'd like to be his arm candy, thought Kitten, running her hand through her hair and sticking out her breasts. Oh hell, he'd brought a woman. No, it was that bitch Jade.

Graffi, drunk and furious with Stancombe for sacking his father, reeled over and handed him his glass, which Stancombe was about to drink out of, then realized it was empty.

'Get me a Bacardi and Coke,' Graffi ordered him airily, then, at Stancombe's look of fury: 'Oh, I fort you was a waiter.'

'Graffi!' Anticipating punch-ups, Janna ran off the dance floor. 'Hello, Randal, let me get you a drink.'

'Evening, Janna, looks as if you're enjoying yourself.' Stancombe then dragged her into the corridor, pointing to walls on which Graffi had caricatured every child in the school. 'Made a bit of a mess of the property.'

'Nothing a lick of paint won't cure,' answered Janna defensively. 'One day, Graffi's murals'll be worth more than this place put together.'

'Your geese are always swans,' sneered Stancombe.

Suddenly photographers seemed to be everywhere.

'Go away, this is a private party,' Janna told them furiously.

'Just a few piccies,' insisted Stancombe, 'with the kids beside the minibus,' which had suddenly appeared, parked in the forecourt.

'I can't drag them off the dance floor.'

Jade, Kitten and Pearl were insincerely congratulating each other on their dresses. Jade in Versace was miffed they were looking so good. She was used to being the belle of the ball. Feral, Graffi, Johnnie, Danny the Irish, even Xav, all looked gorgeous. Why weren't any of them asking her to dance?

'Come and dance,' Rocky asked her a minute later.

'Thanks, but I'm not stopping. Daddy's about to make a statement to the press,' answered Jade as the music died away.

'As one who has enriched these youngsters' lives,' Stancombe told the reporters, 'I've been haunted by the statistics that it's six times as difficult for kids from poor homes to go to uni.'

'You did it without a degree, Mr Stancombe,' said a blonde from the *Scorpion* admiringly.

'I was lucky,' admitted Stancombe modestly. 'I only hope my not insubstantial financial contribution to Larks High has paid off and the students get some good grades.'

'Oh, shut up,' muttered Janna.

'Can we have a photograph of you dancing with the kids?' asked the *Gazette*.

'You'd better do it,' Janna urged the children, as the band started up again, 'then he'll push off.'

Stancombe, however, had turned back to Janna.

'Terrible news about Theo Graham. I'd castrate all paedophiles.'

'Hengist is convinced he's innocent.'

Stancombe was about to argue, when he noticed Xav, euphoric after another dance with Aysha, bopping off the floor and demanded, 'How did your dad get on in his Eng. lit. exam?'

'Very well,' replied Xav coldly, then as Stancombe's eyebrows shot up. 'My dad does everything well. He's got a horse running on Saturday called Poodle. I'd have a big bet if I were you. It's the only way you'll pay the money you owe the Bagley Fund when the results come out.'

Scenting trouble, it was Xav's mother this time who rushed over.

'Ah, the lovely Taggie—a quick dance?' Randal seized her hand.

'I don't think so.' Xav stepped in front of his mother, scowling up at Stancombe. 'My father asked me to look after Mum—he wouldn't like it one bit if she danced with you.'

Stancombe, who now much regretted leaving his guards behind, said furiously:

'I can only assume you've been drinking.'

'I don't drink,' said Xav.

'I'll get even with you and your arrogant bastard of a father.' Hurrying Jade towards the door, Stancombe went slap into Emlyn.

413

'I was just saying,' he yelled over the band, 'Theo Graham ought to be castrated and not allowed near vulnerable youngsters.'

'Get out,' growled Emlyn, holding open the door.

Jade suddenly longed to stay. As she watched Xav rushing back to Aysha, she decided he'd become very attractive, not least in the way he'd stood up to her father. She'd love to join the great ring of dancers. She wished she had friends like that. It was all her parents' fault for not sending her to a comprehensive.

'Come on, princess,' shouted Randal.

*   *   *

'You OK?' Janna asked Emlyn, noticing how tired he looked, but his answer was blotted out by a roll of drums. It was time for the awards.

'At least it might mean the music is a bit less loud,' the Brigadier murmured to Lily.

Janna grabbed the mike and announced she was now going to give each pupil his or her year book and certificate of achievement.

'I'd rather have some money,' shouted Rocky to roars of applause, which continued as each child went up and Emlyn took photograph after photograph, because everyone wanted a record of themselves beside Janna.

When it was Johnnie's turn, he grabbed Janna, kissing her on and on to whoops and catcalls until Emlyn tapped him sharply on the shoulder: 'That's enough.'

'Your turn now, Mr Davies,' chorused the children, screaming with laughter as Emlyn handed a blushing Janna his handkerchief to wipe

414

off her smudged lipstick.

Who would have dreamt a year ago, I could have had a ball at a ball without a drop of booze? thought Pittsy.

Janna then thanked all the children for making the year so memorable and rewarding.

'I'd also like to say on behalf of all the weird staff who came to teach you, that we've never had it so good.'

'Hear, hear,' shouted Skunk, squeezing Basket's spare tyres.

'And I'd like to thank all the teachers, wondercooks'—Janna smiled at Taggie—'terrific dinner ladies, Rowan and, most of all, Wally, who's taken care of us all, and made this evening possible.'

'Don't forget Mistah Davies,' shouted Graffi.

'And of course, Emlyn, thank you all.'

Pittsy then seized the mike and admitted:

'In twenty-nine years of teaching, this is the best year I've ever had because of that woman over there.' He pointed to Janna, to deafening applause. 'She's the best boss I've ever had—' His voice cracked. 'She's been dead good.'

Are they talking about me, wondered Janna in bewilderment, particularly when a big screen to the right of the band lit up and there was Kylie, clutching her new baby and singing: 'To Miss . . .' instead of 'To Sir, With Love'.

'Oh hell,' grumbled Pearl. 'There goes my make-up again,' as Janna's tears swept away a flotsam of mascara and glitter, particularly when Kitten curtsied and presented her with a gold pen engraved 'To a great head'.

'Thank you ever so much and I'll write to you all

with this pen.' Janna mopped her eyes with Emlyn's handkerchief. Then, desperate to get the praise on to someone else: 'And now Lily is going to crown the Prom King and Queen, voted by their peers.'

'I first have to read the citations,' said Lily, putting on her spectacles and joining Janna in the middle of the floor.

' "We thought you was very snooty when you joined Larks," ' she read, ' "but we realized you was just shy and now you're a good friend to all of us." Very nice too.' Opening the envelope: 'And our Prom Queen is none other than Aysha Khan.'

Aysha gasped and clapped her hands over her eyes:

'I don't believe it.'

As Xav proudly led her up, Mrs Khan stood up and cheered, then shushed herself in horror. Lily placed a gold cardboard crown, inset with red, blue and green jewels, on Aysha's dark head, and the room erupted.

'She looks absolutely gorgeous,' sighed Pittsy.

'She certainly does,' agreed a grinning Xav as he slid back into the crowd, but not for long, as Lily read out the next citation.

' "We was worried when you came to us, but you mixed in really well, and you was never posh." ' Hands trembling with excitement, Lily ripped open the envelope. 'And the Prom King is Xavier Campbell-Black.'

More deafening roars of applause followed as Lily had difficulty getting the crown over Xav's Afro.

'Thank you so much,' shouted Xav, 'I can't believe this.'

'Nor can we,' yelled Graffi. 'Never had a poof on the frone since James I.'

'Give your queen a kiss,' shouted Pearl, and Xav turned and kissed Aysha on the lips for the first time since Ramadan, and Aysha, after a terrified glance at her tearful, ecstatic mother, who had nearly finished her bottle of teachers' lemonade, kissed Xav back to a thunder of stamped feet.

'Look at Taggie,' whispered Lily as Xav's mother wiped her eyes with her crimson pashmina.

Xav and Aysha reopened the ball, never taking their eyes off each other. A second later, Emlyn led a laughing, protesting Taggie on to the floor.

'It's so refreshing,' beamed Mrs Khan as Janna replaced her Fanta bottle.

Supper followed and the starving hordes fell on tuna and cucumber sandwiches, bridge rolls filled with egg mayonnaise, Lily's sausage rolls and vol-au-vents, Sally's smoked salmon sandwiches, strawberries, blackberry crumbles and chocolate torte.

*   *   *

The girls were back on the floor dancing together, flashing lights picking up glossy tossing curls and gleaming bare shoulders. Janna was among them, swaying like a maenad, waving a glittering blue butterfly in figures of eight.

Why haven't I asked her to dance? wondered Emlyn. What am I afraid of?

Out in the limos, groups were drinking Cava and smoking weed. Others were signing each other's T-shirts, certificates and year books. There was a second roll of drums. 'It's now time for your cabaret,' shouted the lead singer, 'performed by Brigadier Christian Woodford and Mrs Lily Hamilton.'

Clapping and whooping, the dancers retreated to be joined round the edge of the floor by others running in from the cars.

Lily fled to the Ladies, shaking with terror. If only she'd had a little more to drink. Pearl was waiting when she came out of the loo.

'Just let me fix your face.'

Getting out a brush, she added blusher to Lily's blanched cheeks, used another brush to repaint her trembling lips and another to fluff up her hair, before spraying on some rather bold scent.

'You look great, Lily. Let's hide that bra strap, and straighten your dress, off you go. Good luck.'

The children had begun to stamp their feet and slow handclap. Christian, waiting with a mike in his hand, was looking anxious, but his smile was beautiful, even when Lily muttered, 'You got me into this bloody thing,' as he led her on to the floor.

'Doo di doo, doo di doo di, doo di . . .' sang the Brigadier in a delightful baritone, then, brandishing both mike and a large green umbrella, launched into 'Singing in the Rain', ending up with a little tap dance round Lily, before sweeping her into 'Stepping Out With My Baby'.

For a second, Lily stumbled; the Brigadier held her tightly and they were off. It was such a beautiful tune.

After that Lily was fine. In no time, Christian was singing 'Cheek To Cheek', as with faces pressed together, they glided round the floor.

Lily would never in a thousand years have

418

accused the Brigadier of showing off, but she was not displeased when he too stumbled, and this time it was she who had to hold him up.

The pupils, utterly entranced, bellowed their approval.

'Good on yer, Brig. Wicked, Lily. Come on, Fred and Ginger, give us an encore.'

'I'm out,' said Lily firmly, so the Brigadier, gazing into her eyes, sang 'Our Love Is Here To Stay'.

Seizing Basket's hand, Skunk stole off into the moonlight.

'I love you, Xav,' whispered Aysha.

'Hic,' said Mrs Khan.

How much longer can I go on staying cheerful, wondered Feral as, in the middle of the floor, the Brigadier beamed down at Lily.

'Oh, cut to the chase, Brig,' shouted Graffi, 'you know you love her.'

'I believe I do,' said Christian, kissing Lily on the forehead.

As the band broke into 'YMCA', the hall filled up again. Monster was dancing with Mrs Khan, Rowan with Pittsy, Wally with Janna, Sophy with Graffi, and Rocky with Gloria.

Aware that his wits might be needed if fights broke out, Emlyn, unlike Mrs Khan, had stayed off the drink. Watching the high jinks on the floor, he thought: They're all so pixillated by the transformation of the school and themselves, they've forgotten the dark to come.

Tonight for him had been a cut-off point. Before, despite everything, he'd had the faint hope that Oriana might realize Charlie was a dreadful mistake. Now she was pregnant, it was over.

' "You're The One That I Want",' sang the

419

bronzed lead singer.

115

It was the last dance; Johnnie hand in hand with Kitten, Pearl with Graffi, Feral with Janna, Danny with Danijela, all formed a great circle. The dope-smokers, who'd got the munchies and been raiding the buffet, came racing on to the floor, sandwiches in their hands, as the balloons came down. Yellow, emerald, blue, pink, scarlet and orange, a technicolour snowstorm cascaded into the flickering lights until the ground was one great technicolour bubble bath.

Then the boys waded in, as if this was what their huge trainers had been awaiting all evening, symbolically stamping on the balloons, bang, bang, bang, followed by the girls leaping in with their stilettos, pop, pop, pop, as though war had broken out.

Instinctively, Janna had dropped Feral and Graffi's hands looking round for the tranquillizers for Partner, then remembered he was safe at home.

'Summer Days' sang the band, as dancing went on over an ocean of shredded rubber. Some of the balloons had been saved. Kitten had six, Danijela had one and burst into tears when Rocky popped it with a cigarette. Feral kept back an orange one, in case Bianca was in the car collecting Xav.

It was stiflingly hot in the smoke-filled hall. Everyone was glad to surge out into the cool of the night.

A glittering full moon, like a halo searching for its lost saint, clearly felt upstaged by the splendid explosion of fireworks which followed. Golden fountains overflowed, surging silver snakes belched forth great flurries of blue sparks, rose-pink Roman candles and hissing orange Chinese dragons were followed by a series of colossal bangs, producing screams from the spectators.

Bounding round, setting alight Catherine wheels, avoiding squibs, launching off rockets, Emlyn was glad he'd stayed sober, particularly when Rocky lurched forward.

'Want to light a rocket, want to light a rocket,' and fell flat on his face, lit cigarette narrowly missing the remaining fireworks in the box.

Heaving him up, Emlyn allowed him to light one, which, with a sound like Velcro being ripped apart, soared gloriously upwards, before tossing its emerald and royal blue stars over the Shakespeare Estate.

At the end, more blazing white-hot stars spelt out the words 'Goodbye Larks High', then faded, bringing everyone back to reality with a bump.

Suddenly Mags was reassuring sobbing pupils: 'This school is a launching pad not a crashing down to earth.'

As Pearl in her pretty periwinkle-blue dress wept on her shoulder, Janna could feel her desperate thinness.

'I'm going to miss you, miss.'

Janna was quickly drenched as child after tearful child came up.

'Thank you, miss, for everything.'

'You're the bravest girl I know.' Mags was comforting an inconsolable Aysha.

Cambola, clinging to her trumpet, was also in floods. She had no family, no husband, no job; her pupils were all.

'Do drop in for a cup of tea whenever you're passing,' she begged as each one came up.

'Never been kissed by so many pretty women,' said Pittsy.

Even Skunk was getting his fair share of hugs and shrieks, as cheeks were tickled by his bristly beard and moustache. The girls far more enjoyed weeping on Emlyn's chest. Kitten was clinging to him, leaving frosted-pink lipstick all over his shirt, when he glanced across at Janna, seeing her tears glittering in the moonlight. Setting Kitten gently aside, he crossed the grass, gathering up Janna's soaked body, and she let herself go.

It was such a haven, amid such desolation, to feel his arms round her; he was so big, solid and warm. She knew he was still carrying a torch for Oriana, but she wished he'd go on hugging her for ever.

Emlyn, meanwhile, thought: My heart is in smithereens over Oriana, but it feels nice with my arms round Janna; I'd like to keep them there.

'Can I give you a lift home?' he murmured into her spiked hair.

Janna's heart leapt. 'Oh yes, please.'

'At last,' said Lily, turning in satisfaction to the Brigadier.

*   *   *

Gradually the limos glided away. Most of the teachers had retreated to the staffroom, where the pink and purple ball dresses still hung from the Christmas pantomime and the cuttings from the rugby match against Bagley: 'Comp thrashes Posh', curled on the noticeboard. Mags had pinned up

423

Monster's definition of a mentor: 'Someone you can talk to, an adult what ain't your parents, but is a friend.'

'Once they realized we weren't on supply, they began to trust us,' said Pittsy.

The telephone rang.

'I've been phoning all evening,' screeched Miss Miserden. 'Never heard such a noise. A rocket landed on my patio. Scamp shot up the pear tree. I'm about to call the police.'

'When we have another party,' said Pittsy sarcastically, 'we'll give you a warning,' but as he replaced the receiver, his face crumpled. 'But there never will be. Best boss I ever had.'

*　　　*　　　*

Putting off the evil day, to cheer up her staff, Janna had organized some jaunts for later in the week. The list, also pinned up, included the Barbican and Kensington Palace to see Princess Diana's clothes collection one day, a clay and archery shoot on another, with a buffet at school to include partners on another, then a fun supper just for Larks staff the next.

None of this cheered up Cambola, sobbing in the corner: it was like the end of an opera tour. Tomorrow, we rest.

As Janna waved the band off with profuse thanks, Rupert and Bianca arrived to collect Taggie and Xav, who was clutching his crown.

'He was voted most popular boy in the school,' cried Taggie.

Rupert put a hand on Xav's shoulder. 'That's better than grades, well done.'

'Is it all right if we drop Aysha and Mrs Khan off on the way?' whispered Xav, 'I think someone's spiked her drink.'

Bianca had jumped out of the BMW, big dark eyes searching everywhere for Feral. Reading her mind, Xav said, 'I'm sorry, he's gone home, I tried to keep him.'

Bianca shrugged and huddled into the back. Feral, hidden behind the big swamp cypress, watched the BMW roll down the drive, before fleeing into the night.

Emlyn was desperate to leave, suffering the edginess of not drinking, jangling his car keys attached to a black plastic Scottie with a tartan collar. He found Janna in the IT room gazing abstractedly at a computer screen, where Larks High School, like a house in a twister, rolled hopelessly over and over into a bright blue eternity.

'I saved you this.' Emlyn handed her a red balloon, splaying his fingers over hers. 'Let's go.'

'I'll just say goodbye to the others.'

Outside the staffroom, however, they found Danijela in tears.

'This school is my home.'

Emlyn gritted his teeth as Janna, the eternal hostess, put Basket's beige cardigan round Danijela's thin shoulders. Janna was just making her a cup of tea when Monster wandered in.

'My mum's not answering.'

'Where is she?'

'Moved house if she's got any sense,' quipped Rocky.

'She's asleep. Probably can't hear the doorbell,' whined Monster.

'Pissed,' mouthed Wally from behind his back.

'My bruvvers and sisters are asleep, no one won't let me in,' he whined.

'So you walked back here, poor Martin.' Janna poured boiling water over Danijela's tea bag.

'I got nowhere to go.' Monster looked round pathetically.

There was a long pause. Pittsy looked at his feet, so did Cambola, so even did Mags and Emlyn. Janna counted to ten.

'You better come home with me, Martin. We'll put a note through your mum's door: "I'm in Miss Curtis's house." You'll have to sleep on the sofa.'

Then she caught sight of Emlyn, his face a death mask.

'I'm off. Night, everybody.' He gathered up his car keys and was gone.

Janna caught up with him in reception. Graffi's black good-luck cat grinned down at her unsympathetically.

'Come in for a drink on the way home,' she pleaded. 'We can put Monster to bed.'

'Where?' snapped Emlyn.

'In the lounge. We can talk in the kitchen.'

'Talking wasn't what I had in mind.'

Janna's heart started to thump in excitement, then faltered as Emlyn said, 'And I'm not coming to any of those jaunts next week, I've got interviews.'

'You what?' Janna fought back tears of disappointment. Every trip had been planned with him in mind. 'Who with?' she asked, following him through the front door.

'The Welsh Rugby Union, among others.'

Out in the warmth of Midsummer Night's Eve,

426

the bitter acid tang of elder and the overwhelming sweetness of the white philadelphus mingled to symbolize the bitter sweetness of the evening.

'You're lovely, Janna; all things to all children,' said Emlyn bleakly, 'but you're not going to change. I'm fed up with women who want to save the world.'

As he strode towards his car, Janna ran after him. 'I'm sorry about Oriana's baby. I know you're upset: please talk to me about it.'

'I don't need any counselling. Poppet Bruce had a go earlier.' And he was in his car, storming down the drive, not even bothering with lights or a seatbelt.

Janna couldn't bawl her heart out because of Monster.

'So much food left,' she said, returning to the staffroom. 'If we put it in the fridge, the children can have it tomorrow.'

'There isn't going to be a tomorrow,' sobbed Rowan.

Cambola, however, switched off her mobile, tears drying on her beaming face.

'Jack and Kylie have just asked me to be godmother to little Ganymede.'

*   *   *

Both the Brigadier and Lily had been drinking, so they left the car at Larks and took a taxi to Elmsley church, where the Brigadier put a balloon on his wife's grave. Then they walked hand in hand down the tree tunnel with shafts of moonlight piercing the leaf ceiling lighting on Lily's pearls and the Brigadier's diamond shirt studs.

427

Pearl had forced a fish-paste sandwich on Lily, made by her mum, to keep up her strength, so Lily had to do something to sweeten her breath. Pearl's proffered Juicy Fruit chewing gum might have pulled her bridge out. Fortunately, she always kept three boiled sweets in her bag, one for the walk there, one for the walk home and one just in case. The just in case was blackcurrant, which she was sucking furiously.

Despite his outward sangfroid, the Brigadier was more nervous than he had ever been under fire.

Just outside Wilmington, they paused to rest against a five-bar gate. The Brigadier took a deep breath. Lily looked so beautiful with her silvery hair and her face bathed in moonlight.

'Darling Lily, I fell in love with you on the second of October two thousand, the day you moved into Wilmington.'

There was a crunch of boiled sweet as he took her in his arms, kissing her gently then passionately, and both their teeth stayed put.

'Oh, Christian, my Brigadearest,' sighed Lily.

'If I go down on one knee, will you help me up afterwards?'

'Of course.'

'Sweetest Lily, will you do me the great honour of marrying me?'

'Oh yes, yes I will.'

Anxious to kiss his betrothed, Christian held out a hand, Lily gave it a tug, but he was too heavy for her, and next moment had pulled her down on the grass beside him. The only way they could clamber up, some time later, still laughing helplessly, was gate bar by gate bar.

     *   *   *

Back at Larks, Graffi and Johnnie, who'd been indulging in a hilarious spot of dogging, observing Basket's plump white bottom bobbing up and down in Skunk's heaving Vauxhall, had returned to the staffroom to mob up Janna.

'Not sure Monster wants to come home with you, miss. Finks you're going to jump on him.'

'There's a perfectly good lock to the lounge door,' snarled Janna. 'Come on, Martin, I can't abandon Partner any longer.'

Having once bound a firework to Partner's tail, Monster showed even more reluctance to spend the night under the same roof.

'He'll get me in the night, miss.'

Janna drove home very slowly, tempted to knock on Emlyn's door, but there was no car outside. She had great difficulty not strangling Monster, particularly when the hulking great beast announced he was starving, then complained the scrambled eggs Janna made him were too sloppy.

Partner growled so much at such ingratitude, Janna let Monster sleep in her bedroom, and heard the key turn in the lock.

Outside, it was getting light, the longest day dawning after the longest saddest night. Except for the jaunts, which were meaningless without Emlyn, Larks was over. She must face up to the fact that she was totally, hopelessly in love with him and had utterly blown it by not being there when he needed her. Having sobbed herself to sleep, her first lie-in for weeks was interrupted by pounding on the door at six o'clock.

'Can you run me into Larkminster, miss? It's my

paper round.'

116

'Teachers should never go on holiday for at least a
fortnight after the end of the summer term,' Pittsy
was always saying. 'One needs two weeks at home
unwinding and invariably contracting some bug,
then fourteen days abroad in the sun, before a
fortnight psyching oneself up for the rigours of the
autumn term.'

Janna had no such luxury. She had to work out
her contract with S and C until the end of August,
leaving Appletree immaculate for the new
incumbents, whoever they might be, and
supervising the removal of property by
neighbouring schools, who were so avaricious, she
was tempted to put a 'do not remove' label on
Partner's collar.

To depress her further, it rained throughout July
and August as estate agents and developers
splashed through the school grounds, skips filled
with water and rubble, windows were boarded up,
machinery dismantled and cork and whiteboards
ripped down, until only Janna's office remained
operational.

In it, apart from her personal belongings, were a
framed photograph of the staff and children of
Larks High in happier days and the computer and
printer, out of which the GCSE results would
thunder.

Still on the wall was the cupboard Emlyn had put
up by nonchalantly hammering in the screws.
Janna never dreamt she would miss him so
dreadfully. Her constant companion as a child had

431

been a vast English sheepdog, whose huge reassuring presence she kept imagining round the house for months after he died. So it was with Emlyn. He had landed his grand job with the Welsh Rugby Union, but, according to the Brigadier, he was hoping to get back to Larks for Results Day on 26 August. The children so longed to see him.

Even after term was ended, they hadn't been able to accept the dream was over and still piled in every day: 'Let's play bingo, miss,' or offering to help her clean the building and littering it with Coke cans and crisp packets.

As Results Day approached, they grew increasingly jittery about not getting enough grades to qualify for sixth-form places in colleges or other schools, or for a good job, or to satisfy their parents, or to not feel a fool in front of their friends.

None of them aspired to the miracle of the Magic Five, which would give Larks a point in the league tables.

In the evenings, Janna had visited every parent on the Shakespeare Estate, trying to explain that further education didn't just mean top-up fees and the loss of a family breadwinner.

She was most worried about Feral, who'd left the sanctuary of the Brigadier's cottage and moved with his mother into a two-bedroom flat so poky there was hardly room for his football. If his mother stayed off drugs until Christmas, her other children might be returned to her. But she was so listless and easily cast down, Feral was terrified she'd lapse, particularly if Uncle Harley rolled up again. He hated leaving her, even to stack shelves

432

with Graffi every night.

As Janna was shredding confidential papers referring to the staff at Larks, she had come across one of Feral's essays which young Lydia had kept. He must have dictated it to Paris.

My dream [he had begun] is to leave home when I'm nineteen and be married by the time I'm twenty to the girl I stay with for the rest of my life and have two children. I'm going to buy a house in a nice area for my children to grow up decently. I will buy a car for my wife. She can go to work or look after the children. I'm going to give her a big posh kitchen worth £1,000 and go on holiday three times a year, twice abroad and once to Skegness.

'Well done, Feral,' Lydia had written, 'work hard and chase your dream.'

It was dated March 2002, just after he had met Bianca. Oh, poor Feral, Janna nearly wept, the desire of the moth for the star.

At least this year the incessant rain had kept alive the saplings Wally had planted last autumn; perhaps they might symbolize the survival of her children.

Against all this, she longed constantly for Emlyn and could have done without Basket popping in, flashing Skunk's diamond and saying, 'I know you'll find a Skunk of your own when you least expect it,' until Janna nearly kicked her teeth in.

*   *   *

Janna shared Wednesday 25 August with Mags and Pittsy, closeted together in her office, sworn to secrecy until the official release time which was eight o'clock on the morning of the twenty-sixth.

The results arrived by email and, as they were downloaded, were logged on to a big wall chart with a list of candidates' names in alphabetical order down the left-hand side, and the subjects starting with history along the top. It was surprising Miss Miserden didn't ring up and complain about the shrieks and yells of excitement as the trio caught sight of and analysed each result.

'We're going to need several king-size boxes of tissues tomorrow,' confessed Mags, 'but, bearing in mind how far behind they were at the beginning of the year, haven't some of our no-hopers done well?'

Pittsy was delighted he'd got more candidates through than Skunk or Basket. Serve them right for being so smug. The Brigadier and Emlyn had done very well in history, Mags and Lily in languages, Janna and Sophy in English.

Over at Bagley, the mood was less rowdy, but just as feverish, as, in scenes resembling Wall Street, department heads reached for their calculators to check if they'd beaten other departments, or set in train computer programmes to work out the crucial percentage of children who'd got the Magic Five. Could they have overtaken Fleetley, St Paul's or Wycombe Abbey, or shaken Rod Hyde off their heels?

Miss Painswick was flapping around so that the moment the official results came in tomorrow and were checked for inconsistencies, they would be faxed or emailed immediately to candidates on yacht, grouse moor, Aegean isle or, in Paris's case, the Old Coach House.

*   *   *

At six o'clock on the morning of 26 August, Janna dressed herself in a clinging new yellow and white striped T-shirt and tight sexy white jeans, in case Emlyn showed up. She then drove to the central post office in Larkminster to pick up the envelopes with coral labels containing official result slips for each candidate.

After yesterday's downpour it was a beautiful day: very hot with a bright blue sky flecked with little cirrus clouds and larger grey cumulus clouds, behind which the sun kept disappearing, as if to illustrate the miseries or splendours of each candidate.

The press awaited Janna at Larks.

'How's Rupert Campbell-Black done?'

'No idea.'

'And his son, Xav, the thick one?'

'I'm not going to tell you.'

She then rushed into her office and spent the next hour with the other staff, shoving the results into envelopes for each child, checking them against yesterday's emails. Aysha had got an A star, not an A, for maths, Kitten an E rather than a D for English lit.

'I nearly wore *my* white jeans,' said Rowan, 'but I thought it was too casual for such an important day. Oh look, here's an email from Emlyn. Oh no! He's had to fly out on some pre-season rugby tour. He sends huge love to us all and good luck. The kids will be gutted.'

Et moi aussi, thought Janna, Oh Emlyn! But she must hide her despair; it was the children's day.

Most schools just pin up the envelopes on the wall for pupils to collect. Janna, however, sat in her office determined to go through every result with every child as they lined up in the corridor, frantically chewing gum, faces dead, pacing up and down.

'I'm going to get all Gs.'

'I'm going to get straight Us.'

Pearl, shaking and sobbing, had to be carried by Mags and Cambola into Janna's office—Pearl the former truant and disaster area. Janna jumped up and hugged her.

'Oh Pearl, this is one of the best results in the school. B in English, C in history, C in home economics, C in maths, C in science. D in business studies. Well done.'

Pearl was turned to stone like Niobe, when, like the fountain, her tears gushed out.

'I don't believe it, miss. I done brilliant.'

'You certainly have.'

'I got the Magic Five,' shrieked Pearl, racing round the playground hugging everyone. Then she rang her mother and then the factory where her boxer dad worked, asking them to broadcast the results over the tannoy, then rushed off to the toilets to redo her face before she faced the press.

Back in Janna's office, there were more yells of excitement and cries of 'Good lad, well done', 'Good girl, you've got a B in RE and a C in geography and a C in home economics', as stunned candidates reeled out of the room. Graffi, despite stacking shelves, had got four Cs and an A star for art and was calling his parents. Danny the Irish had managed a B and two Cs, Kitten was over the

436

moon to get four Cs and a D in English, until she heard Pearl's grades were even better and blamed it on a social life so much more active than Pearl's.

Johnnie, against all the odds, had notched up two Bs and four Cs.

'I worked, like, hard,' he told the press, 'but I'd have screwed up, like, if it hadn't been for Emlyn and the Brigadier getting me here.'

Janna was so good at comforting the sad ones. Danijela was inconsolable. She'd only got an A in D and T for her blue and green wedding dress and a C in food technology.

'But that's brilliant. You spoke no English when you came here, you can always retake the others.'

Janna was also euphoric about Rocky, who'd been special needs level three and on the at-risk register, but had still got a B for his D and T dog kennel, a C for history and a D for business studies.

'He must have learnt more in that cupboard than we thought,' laughed Pittsy.

Kylie had notched up three Ds, a B in child care and an A star in music, which enchanted Cambola. Chantal had arrived with Cambola's little godson, Ganymede, who looked just like Jack Waterlane, and, thoroughly carried away, was now telling the press: 'My Kylie Rose is destined for music college. She done superior to her hubby, the Honourable Jack, who may well stay home and mind Cameron and Ganymede.'

'Jack'd love that,' muttered Graffi. 'He'll be able to drink and watch racing on TV all day.'

Graffi couldn't believe those results. The Magic Five. His father had just rolled up with Cardiff Nan and was looking at him with new respect.

'Good luck,' called out everyone, as, trembling and terrified, Aysha crept into Janna's office.

'I don't want to let down my dad.'

'No fear of that.' Janna clasped her hands. 'You got an A star for science, an A star for Urdu, Bs for history and English, an A star for maths and Cs for French and Spanish. Best result in the school, Aysha. Your parents will be so thrilled.'

Aysha gazed at the results slip for a moment; a storm of relieved weeping followed.

'Do you think Dad will let me see Xav now?'

'I'm sure he will.' Janna plied her with Kleenex. 'Get out,' she screamed as a cameraman shoved a lens in through the window.

Summoned by mobile and text, excited parents were soon storming the playground, bearing flowers in cellophane, cards in coloured envelopes, and accepting paper cups of wine handed out by Wally, who was beaming from ear to ear. He'd helped out all year with D and T and his pupils had done really well.

Pearl's boxer dad, who'd been allowed the rest of the day off, was hugging Pearl's mother. Pearl, thoroughly above herself, was telling the television cameras: 'The world is my lobster. I was planning to go into hairdressing, but getting the Magic Five, I've gotta refink my options.'

A dazed Aysha had already been offered places at four schools, but would she be allowed to take up any of them?

The press were now photographing pupils jumping for joy, tossing their papers in the air, the eternal cliché only before afforded to St Jimmy's and Searston Abbey.

'Where's Emlyn? What can have happened to

438

Feral?' asked everyone. 'Where's Xav?'

117

Over at Penscombe, none of the Campbell-Blacks had slept. The plan was to go into Larks to collect Xav and Taggie's results, making a slight detour on the way to Cotchester College to discover Rupert's English lit. grade. Both Rupert and Xav would have preferred to learn their fate in solitude.

The fact that Rupert had just flown in from the Athens Olympics, where his daughter Tabitha and her horse had been in the medals, had, on the one hand, made him incredibly proud. On the other, he was now even more anxious that Xav would be utterly demoralized if, by contrast, he didn't notch up a single GCSE.

To steady his nerves, Rupert was riding around the estate, followed by his pack of dogs. He admired two yearlings, Macduff and Thane of Fife, known as Fifey, checked fences and noted the casualties of summer: rusty branches hanging like broken limbs from the sycamore, field maples eaten to bits by the squirrels. The dawn redwood, prematurely russet, looked a goner too. Despite the rain, it had been an incredibly fecund year, elders already crimson black with berries, brambles covered in gorging wasps.

The sun was coming through the clouds to highlight a triangle of jade field one moment, and touch the shoulder of a beech tree—Shall we dance?—the next. Since he had read English lit., he appreciated nature and character so much more.

It was bliss having Taggie home again, but they

had all found it difficult to settle this summer, worrying about three different sets of results.

This is a good horse, thought Rupert: dark bay, strong, confident, too slow to race, the perfect hunter, but hunting would be banned soon. Democracy was gradually being eroded, but did he really mind enough to go back into politics?

There had been so much rain, the fields had only just been topped. Buzzards screamed overhead searching for carrion; a fox had caught a pigeon, its dark grey and light feathers all over the stubble— not a good omen. Nor was the single magpie rising squawking out of the wood.

'Morning, Mr Magpie, how's your wife? How many A to C grades did your children get? You piebald smartass,' snapped Rupert.

Dear God, he prayed, if Tag gets some children through food technology and Xav just one or two decent grades, he'd gladly give up his English lit. pass. Everyone knew he was a philistine. Helen, his first wife, had told him often enough.

*   *   *

Xav huddled in his room, hugging smelly, old, comforting Bogotá, who was too old to join the pack on the ride.

What if he got no grades at all? Mr Khan and Alex Bruce would gloat and say I told you so. He couldn't bear the humiliation, but he couldn't miss a chance of seeing Aysha one last time. Bianca, equally desperate for a last chance to see Feral, banged on his door.

'We ought to go, it's nearly eleven.'

She was wearing red shorts, red boots and a

441

sleeveless crimson T-shirt.

'You look cool,' said Xav.

Taggie was in the kitchen praying and unloading the dishwasher, when the telephone rang. It was Mags.

'My dears, are you coming in? Good, but I thought you might like Xav's results in advance.'

Taggie, a potato masher in one hand and two mugs hanging on the end fingers of the hand holding the telephone, sat down on the window seat, just missing Bianca's kitten.

'Can you read them again?' she gasped a minute later.

'And again?' a minute after that, then a minute later. 'And again.'

Afterwards there was a long pause.

'Are you all right?' asked Mags anxiously. 'I thought you'd like to hear the food technology results as well.'

'Yes, no.' All Margaret could hear was sobbing. 'I'll ring you back.' Taggie slotted back the telephone.

Walking back from the yard, noticing dew-spangled spiders all over the lawn, Rupert caught sight of Taggie running out on to the terrace, the same sun lighting up the tears pouring down her face.

'It's all right, darling.' Rupert raced up the lawn, folding his wife in his arms, struggling to hide his disappointment. 'He was Prom King and he's got friends; that's much more important. He worked really hard too.'

But he so wanted to pass, said a voice inside Rupert, we should have fought harder to keep him at Bagley.

Taggie was still sobbing.

'It's all right.' Rupert gritted his jaw. 'We'll look after him. I could never take exams.'

'No, no,' Taggie gulped and gasped. 'He passed. He got four Cs and a B for Spanish. The Magic Five, and D grades in all his other subjects.'

Rupert shut his eyes. Back went his head as he breathed in deeply and incredulously.

'You did it,' he muttered. 'You had the courage to send him to Larks.'

'Shall we go?' Xav walked out, saw his mother crying and knew all was lost. 'Sorry,' he mumbled.

His parents pulled him into a sodden hug.

'You got it,' said Rupert. 'They've just rung. You got the Magic Five.'

'That is really wicked,' said Xav.

Rupert put a crate of Veuve Clicquot in the car. Taggie was so happy she couldn't stop giggling. Glancing at the back, she noticed Bianca gazing out of the window, her painted scarlet lips moving: 'Please God, give me Feral,' and put a hand back on her daughter's knee.

In Cotchester, the roads were blocked with mothers frantic to collect their children's results from various schools. The forecourt of Cotchester College was swarming with mature students comparing results and with even more press, who raised their cameras and tape recorders as Rupert approached, but warily. In his time, the Golden Beast had broken more than a few photographers' jaws. Today he didn't look in a party mood. Rupert had withdrawn his bargain with God. He'd mind like hell if he failed.

Pushing through the swing doors, he entered the exam room, waving his student card.

443

'Can I have my GCSE result?'

'Oh, it's you, Mr Campbell-Black,' said the woman at the table reverently. 'We hoped you'd come in.' She coughed loudly.

As secretaries suddenly appeared, peering excitedly through the glass panel behind her, she handed him a sealed envelope, her kind round face full of concern.

'Summer 2004,' read Rupert, 'Campbell-Black, Rupert Edward. English Literature GCSE, Grade B.' He gasped. 'There's no mistake?'

'None. Many congratulations.'

'My God.' Rupert leant over the table and kissed her on both cheeks.

Out in the sunshine he sauntered over to the assembled press.

'How d'yer do, Rupert?'

'B for bloody brilliant.' He brandished the slip of paper. 'And two fingers to Randal Stancombe, who now owes the Bagley Fund a lot of money, and my first wife, Helen, now Lady Hawkley, who always told me I was thick.'

Taggie was so excited she nearly ran over an old man wheeling a tartan bag across a zebra crossing.

*   *   *

Back at Larks, Monster was moaning he'd only got Cs for English and business studies, after working like stink.

'That's terrific, well done,' said Janna, making Monster feel so good that he decided to ring Stormin', who was on nights and asleep at home.

If you can wake her, thought Janna bitterly, you horrible gooseberry, who ruined my last chance

444

with Emlyn.

Only Feral had bombed totally. Not a single grade, nothing above a G—darkness at noon. He was now on his mobile, huddled in misery.

'Didn't do enough revision, I guess, sorry, Brig, sorry, Lily. See you both later.'

As he rang his mother, Graffi and Kylie were hovering to comfort him.

'There's good news and bad news, Mum. First the bad news, I failed all my exams. Yes, all of them. But the really good news to cheer you all up, is everyone else in the school passed somefing.'

Heroically brave, he deserved an A star for courage. Janna bit her lip as she remembered the essay of hope about the girl to whom he stayed married for the rest of his life and took on holiday to Skegness.

Kylie put an arm round his shoulders. 'How was your mum?'

'OK,' lied Feral. 'Not now, perhaps later,' he added to Partner, who was nudging him to play football. Oh God, he prayed, don't let the bad news start Mum off again.

Everyone—children, parents and press—was knocking back the bottles of white and red. Graffi's dad was getting legless with Pearl's boxer dad and mum and Stormin' Norman, who'd just arrived. Even Raschid Khan, sipping apple juice, was looking quite mellow.

'I agree, Raschid,' Dafydd Williams was saying. 'None of my family's ever been to uni, we work in factories or on the building, we don't go on to better things.'

Janna climbed on to Appletree steps and clapped her hands. 'I'd just like to thank and congratulate all the children who worked so hard and made such fantastic progress. These are a terrific set of results. The greatest thing in life is an ability to pick yourself up from the floor and you all did this, and I'd like to thank your parents for all their support.'

A second later Feral had grabbed the microphone from her, clutching his battered violet and yellow football like a hot-water bottle with the other. In his deep hoarse voice, gallant in defeat, he thanked particularly Janna and the teachers.

'For being so brilliant, and giving us the best year of our lives. They've taken a year out to look after us and no one's worked harder than they have.'

What on earth's he going to do now? thought Janna despairingly.

'Oh, look,' cried Chantal, as the press went berserk, photographing a new arrival.

For a horrible moment, Janna thought it might be Stancombe, then she realized it was Pete Wainwright, grinning on the edge of the crowd. Last week, he'd been appointed manager of Larkminster Rovers and was now a god in Larkshire.

Shaking off the press, he came over and shook Janna's hand. 'How did Taggie's class do?'

'Fantastic,' said Janna.

'She coming?'

'I hope so.'

Pete Wainwright glanced across the euphoric, teeming playground at Feral, a picture of desolation slumped against the fence, listlessly tapping his football back and forth to Partner, dark head on Graffi's shoulder as Graffi patted him on the back.

446

'Ain't the end of the world, man.'

'Certainly isn't,' said Pete Wainwright, joining them. 'Here's something to cheer you up, lad.' He handed Feral a typed envelope.

Feral stared at it stupidly.

'Well, open it and read it,' ordered Pete.

'You ought to know, man, I didn't get no English.'

'I'll read it,' said Graffi. 'Wow!' he said after a quarter of a minute. 'Fuckin' hell, fuckin' wicked!' and went into a series of Tarzan howls. 'Mr Wainwright's offering you a job, man, as a junior player at Larkminster Rovers, starting next week.'

Feral swung round in bewilderment.

'I ducked out of that trial.'

'I know, and I know why you did. I saw you playing one evening after exams. Emlyn showed me some tapes. You'll have to clean a few boots to start with, spend a bit of time observing on the bench. But you're good and so was that speech you just made. I like generosity in my players.'

Feral tried to read the letter.

'It ain't no wind-up?'

Janna by this time had rushed up, hugging Feral, telling everyone the good news. 'Oh Pete, this is really wicked.'

After that Feral, like Pearl, got thoroughly above himself.

'I'm going to be the next Thierry Henry,' he yelled, punching the air, 'and I'll be so fucking rich, I'll be able to take out that bastard Rupert Campbell-Black—in fact he'll be crawling to have me marrying his daughter.'

'He probably will,' said a dry voice behind him.

It was Rupert, who'd just arrived with Taggie and

447

Xav.

'Feral's got a job,' cried Janna as the press surged forward, 'with Larkminster Rovers. And well done, fantastic results!' She hugged Xav. 'And well done, Taggie.'

'Taggie, Taggie!' The children surged round her: 'I got a B.' 'I got a C.' 'I got an A.' 'I got a C.'

'I can't believe it.' Taggie tried to hug them all.

Meanwhile, Rupert had turned to Feral.

'I've brought you a congratulatory present,' he drawled.

And Bianca erupted out of the car and, stopping, gazed at Feral, who gazed at her in wonder.

Slowly, they moved towards each other. Seizing her hand, chucking his ball to Partner, Feral led her off into the garden.

'I thought your father didn't approve of Feral,' whispered Kylie.

'He's just got a B in English lit.,' whispered back Xav, 'I think he'd even accept Tony Blair as a son-in-law.'

Having congratulated Taggie on her food technology triumph, Janna was now hugging Rupert—such a pleasure as he was so handsome.

'Randal is going to be furious about your B.'

'Good,' said Rupert. 'I should be congratulating you and apologizing for doubting that you and Larks would be the best thing for Xav. He's found himself.'

Across the playground, Xav was surrounded by friends, thumping him on the back.

'I've bought a few bottles, they're in the car,' added Rupert. 'Which one's Graffi? I want a mural in the long gallery.'

Feral, wiping off crimson lipstick and grinning like the Cheshire cat, later talked, somewhat warily, to Rupert, who said,

'Sorry I called you a black bastard.'

'It's OK, man. If I caught my daughter in bed with some no-good nigger, I guess I'd call him the same thing.'

They looked at each other, dislike melting away.

'Thank you for looking after Xav.'

'Thank you for beating Stancombe. He's a bastard, really evil, and I know, man.'

'You do interest me. Why don't you come out to lunch with us?'

'I'd like to, man'—Feral looked longingly at Bianca, who was dancing by herself, as lightly as the thistledown drifting in from the long grass— 'but actually I'm lunching wiv Lily and the Brig. I'm going to be a witness at their wedding,' he added proudly.

'Hmmmm, that sounds a party that'll go on,' said Rupert. 'You'd better come to lunch tomorrow.'

Grinning, very tentatively they exchanged a high five.

Round the back of the building, Rupert tracked down Graffi spraying in large purple letters: 'Graffi Williams for the Tate, Feral Jackson for Wembley, Randal Stancombe for the High Jump.'

'Excellent sentiments.' Rupert handed Graffi a paper cup of champagne. 'But I want something marginally more figurative for Penscombe. Are you anti blood sports?'

'Not if you pay me well enough,' said Graffi.

'Then I'd like you to do the hunt.'

*   *   *

Feral and Bianca were dancing in the hall.

Graffi's board saying 'Larkminster High School Prom 2004' had been thrown in the bin, but the silver moon and stars still curled on the long black curtains.

'And I will take Feral and cut him out in little stars, and he will make the face of heaven so fine,' said Bianca softly.

Feral picked up a fragment of balloon.

'Since Romeo and Juliet, I haven't fort of anyone or anyfing but you. I couldn't ask you to be my girlfriend when I had nothing to offer. Now I have.'

'I'll come and watch you every week.'

'Every goal will have your name on it.'

'You will come to lunch tomorrow, won't you, or it'd break my heart.'

Feral drew her into his arms. Both of them had to hold each other up, as he kissed her.

Later Bianca was approached by a man from the *Daily Express*. 'Your family's done so well today. Your mum's candidates all got through, Rupert got a B and Xav the Magic Five.'

'I've done best.' Bianca did a joyful handstand, peering back and up from between her arms and black waterfall of hair. 'They got Bs and Cs, but I got Feral Jackson.'

118

Over at Bagley, the celebrations were no less euphoric, as faxes and emails spread over the globe to Lando France-Lynch playing polo in Deauville, Lubemir in a casino, Anatole on a yacht and Cosmo on top of Mrs Walton.

'In my case, my angel,' boasted Cosmo, 'GCSE stands for Great Cock Satisfaction Ensured.'

There was as much press interest in Bagley as there had been at Larks, particularly when a jubilant Hengist announced that not only Cosmo Rannaldini and Primrose Duddon, but Paris Alvaston had achieved straight As and A stars, and Bagley appeared to have gone above Fleetley in the league tables.

Paris who, as it was still holidays, was one of the only boys in school, was bewildered by his results and ran straight over to Hengist's study.

'I couldn't have got an A star in history, sir,' he panted, 'I trashed my second paper.'

'You're imagining things,' Hengist said firmly. 'You'd been working too hard and were understandably upset about Theo. You didn't know if it was Christmas or Easter when you took that last paper. I saw it. It was fine.'

'I wrote gibberish,' insisted Paris.

'Strange things have happened this year. A boy at Fleetley evidently got an A star in English lit. and missed an entire P3 module. Your first history paper must have been exceptional. Ian and Patience will be delighted.'

They were. Ian had opened a bank account and

put in £25 for each brilliant grade, totalling £250, but Paris wasn't happy.

'I want to ring Theo.'

'You can't, I'm afraid.' Hengist went to the fridge and got out a bottle of white. 'Let's have a drink to celebrate.'

'I want to ring Theo.'

'You can't. How many times do I have to tell you the police have expressively forbidden any contact.' Hengist ran his hand through his hair. 'Imagine how I'd like to ring him, but I don't want to prejudice his case.'

'How can it, if I just thank him and give him my grades?'

'Biffo'll tell him.' Hengist was rootling round for a corkscrew.

'Who?' asked Paris quickly.

'Someone will,' said Hengist quickly. 'Oh look, Rupert and Xav are on the box, turn the sound up.' But Paris had shot out of the room.

Hengist shook his head. He must calm Paris down.

After some lovely film of Penscombe, the lunchtime news cut to Sian Williams in the studio. What a pretty thing she was; Hengist turned up the volume.

Xavier Campbell-Black, she told the viewers, who'd been excluded from Bagley Hall for bullying last September, had just notched up five A–C grades at his new school: Larkminster High. A maintained school had thus succeeded where a prestigious independent had failed.

Xav used to be such a fat slob, thought Hengist, now he was clear-eyed, smiling, good-looking and confident.

'I made so many friends at Larks,' he was now saying, 'I didn't need to bully anyone. I found teachers who believed in me and helped me to understand. It helped that my mother joined the staff as a teaching assistant. Everyone she taught food technology to passed.'

'Did you find the teaching better at Larks?'

'Much,' said Xav, who'd been at the Veuve Clicquot, 'and Alex Bruce, my housemaster at Bagley, was a twat.'

Hengist choked on his drink as the interviewer hastily asked Xav about Rupert's B.

'He's laid back, my dad, but he worked incredibly hard and we're all really proud of him.'

Now it was Rupert's turn. Age cannot wither him, thought Hengist, particularly when he's happy, mouth and long eyes lifting.

'I'm knocked out by my wife Taggie's results,' admitted Rupert, 'and Xav's and my own.'

'Who taught you?'

'Well, Miss Jennings at Cotchester College gave me some very good coaching, but mostly I read and wrestled on my own. Couldn't understand a word of it at first. Lucky to have Xav's headmistress, Janna Curtis, and Bianca's headmaster, Hengist Brett-Taylor, to tell me when my ideas were crap.'

'And by passing you won your bet with Randal Stancombe, for an undisclosed sum.'

'Not at all undisclosed, it was a hundred thousand pounds, which is not going to worry Stancombe. He spends that in a day on aftershave and greasing palms.'

'Bastard,' howled Stancombe, who was watching the same news, 'and he got that treacherous bitch, Janna Curtis, and that shit, Hengist, to help him.

No wonder he got a B. They've obviously been cramming him. After all I've done for Hengist. Building the Science Emporium and his taking Ruth off me. My God, I'll bury all three of them.'

Alex Bruce, also watching, was even more outraged. How dare that insolent brat call him a twat, and how could he have got the Magic Five? Janna Curtis must have shown him the papers. Even more distressingly, Lando and Jack had ploughed science, so Alex still hadn't equalled Theo's record of getting everyone through.

Worst of all, his star pupil Boffin Brooks had not achieved straight As. He had just had Sir Gordon Brooks in a towering rage from his villa in Portugal.

'There's no way Bernard could only have got a B in history. It's one of his strongest subjects. That's why I donated five thousand for a history prize, which will now go to some other student.'

'Rest assured, Gordon, I shall approach our Senior Team Leader and appeal. May I have a word with Charisma?' She was staying with the Brookses.

'I can't understand, Dad, I only got a B for Urdu,' whined his G and T daughter.

*   *   *

The last parents and children had drifted away; only Mr Khan lingered.

'You have a brilliant daughter,' pleaded Janna, 'won't you just consider her going on to sixth-form college?'

'She has a husband waiting for her in Pakistan. He has been very patient. He is a good man and

454

will take care of her.'

'But she's so young— Excuse me, that's my mobile.'

It was Hengist. 'Darling, I've just seen the one o'clock news. Well done, Xav, how brilliant and what a smack in the face for stupid Alex for letting him go. How did the others do?'

After Janna had told him, and about Feral's fantastic new job, she asked after Paris.

'Wonderful.' What purring content in Hengist's voice. 'Straight As and A stars for Greek, Latin, both Englishes and history. Absolutely wonderful.'

Janna was ecstatic.

'Ian and Patience must be so thrilled.'

'Relieved, as well. Little Amber did surprisingly well, too.'

'How's Paris in himself?'

'Withdrawn. We had a bit of a set-to just now. He wanted to ring Theo and tell him about the A stars to give him some comfort. But he mustn't get in touch. All the press are hanging round. They all know it's Paris, but he can't be named because the so-called "offence" began when he was fourteen.'

'Oh God, poor Theo. Will he get off?'

'Christ, I hope so. The evidence is pretty damning. Case comes up later in the year, bound to coincide with the Queen's visit. The press'll make a meal out of two old queens. One shouldn't laugh.'

Janna had taken refuge in her office; glasses and discarded envelopes were everywhere.

'Jade only scraped five Cs, which won't please Stancombe,' Hengist was now telling her, 'and, by the way, I've just seen Rupert on the box saying how much we helped him and slagging off

455

Stancombe. It's going to be a long time before dear Randal forgives either of us.'

'I don't care.'

'I do miss you. Let's have a drunken celebration before term starts.'

Dear Hengist, Janna smiled as she switched off her mobile.

Outside the playground was empty; Mr Khan had gone. Tomorrow, she thought wearily, she'd continue the battle to stop the parents chucking it all away. Lily's wedding was at two-thirty; she'd better step on it. Hastily, she toned down her flushed cheeks and shrugged on her white jacket. What did it matter how she looked, if Emlyn wasn't going to be there?

'Next week,' she told Partner as she tied a white silk bow round his neck, 'you and I will look for a job and probably somewhere to live. Today all that matters is those fantastic results.'

But as she splashed Diorissimo on her wrists, Ashton rang.

'I can see why you haven't phoned, Janna, these wesults are dweadfully disappointing.'

'Disappointing?' cried Janna in outrage. 'They're brilliant. You should focus on where those children came from. No one expected them to get any grades at all. You forget there are four pass grades below C. They may not all have got brilliant grades but they got grades. It's a miracle.'

'Janna, Janna,' sighed Ashton, 'exonerating yourself as usual. It's going to be tewwibly difficult justifying all the extwa funding you've had from the DfES. We expected far better.'

'My kids really worked, so did my teachers,' yelled Janna. 'What d'you know about work, sitting

456

in your ivory tower surrounded by hundreds of apparatchiks doing fuck all on vast salaries? Don't talk to me about wasting money.'

'No need to be offensive. You've failed, that's all, but there's no point in talking to you in this mood.' Ashton rang off.

Like a slow puncture, Janna's pride and delight ebbed out of her.

'These are the children that God forgot,' she whispered in horror as she gazed up at the happy, optimistic group photograph on the wall. 'I'm not going to change anything for them; I just suffered from hubris, putting them through exams because I wanted to prove to the world that I was a brilliant head.'

119

To ward off her desolation over Emlyn's absence and Ashton's vile remarks, Janna got dreadfully drunk at Lily's wedding and danced most of the night away with a euphoric Feral and Lily's whacky, charming family, who included Dicky and Dora. Lily, in the same blue dress she'd worn to the prom, had no need of Pearl's make-up. Never was a bridegroom prouder than her Brigadearest.

Next morning, groaning with hangover, Janna went over to Larks. She had only three days left to leave the place shipshape. Wally had lent her a van to clear out her belongings. At first, as she drove up the drive, she thought a television crew had rolled up, then she realized the place was swarming with workmen; one of them, in a bulldozer, had just smashed down half a dozen of Wally's saplings. Drawing closer, she recognized Teddy Murray, Stancombe's foreman, who'd supervised the rebuilding of Appletree.

'What the hell are you doing?'

'Taking over,' said Teddy curtly.

'On whose authority?'

'Stancombe's, of course.'

'Stancombe?' said Janna in horror as another bulldozer crushed Sally's oriental poppies. 'What's he got to do with it?'

'Owns the property. Just paid twenty-five million.'

'Don't be ridiculous.'

'See for yourself.' Teddy waved a heavily tattooed hand towards the bottom of the drive and the hayfield of a lawn outside the ruins of the main buildings, where two big crimson signs announced 'Randal Stancombe Properties'.

'What's he planning to do?'

'Search me. Slap luxury houses all over it. Flog it to some supermarket giant. Flatten the Shakespeare Estate and move in some decent customers. All part of his caring "clean up Larkminster" campaign.' Just for a second sarcasm predominated over indifference in Teddy's voice. 'Now, if you'll excuse me, Janna . . .' Revving up he smashed down two willows.

'Stop it,' screamed Janna, but he had wound up his window, so she ran into Appletree, to find all her stuff had been dumped outside her office.

She was on to Stancombe in a flash.

'Have you bought Larks?'

'I have indeed.'

'You never said anything.'

'You never let on you were coaching Rupert Campbell-Black, you treacherous bitch.'

'I didn't help him,' protested Janna. 'Rupert showed me one essay, from which I deleted a few swear words.'

'After all the support I gave you,' howled Randal, 'I don't feel predisposed to help you ever again.'

Janna gave a gasp of horror as, outside the window, she noticed a JCB gouging out the pond. What would be the fate of Concorde, the carp and the natterjack toads?

'Anyway,' went on Stancombe, 'I put up the money for Appletree, so I own it anyway,' and he hung up.

120

Boffin Brooks's sense of grievance was aggravated on his return to Bagley to find both Cosmo and Paris had better grades.

'I couldn't have got a B in history,' he spluttered to Alex. 'I remember every word I wrote, I could only have got an A star.'

Urged by Charisma, Boffin had started wearing blue tinted contact lenses, which gave him a glazed, almost defenceless look—definitely Alex's blue-eyed boy.

'I have already contacted the exam board,' Alex reassured him, 'to request a clerical check that your history marks were added up correctly. If need be, there are good friends I can phone in the exam world, but I don't want to be accused of pulling strings.'

Together they tackled Hengist, who was bogged down writing beginning-of-term speeches and welcoming new pupils and masters. He was not in a co-operative mood, telling Boffin not to be a bad loser and employing a lot of uncharacteristically hearty clichés like 'biting the bullet' and 'taking it on the chin'.

'We were also warned,' he added sourly, 'that only a limited number of candidates in each subject, irrespective of how well they did, were going to be allowed A stars. You were just one of the unlucky ones. The goalposts have been changed by this bloody Government.'

Boffin and Alex winced collectively.

'It's tough,' concluded Hengist, then begged to

be excused because the Queen's Private Secretary and the Lord Lieutenant, General Broadstairs, who was also a Bagley governor, were coming to see him about the royal visit. 'You cannot imagine the red tape. You should give them a copy of your book, Alex.'

Alex's smile creaked.

Getting up, Hengist opened the door. 'We've got just under eight weeks. I hope everything's going to be ready in time.'

Retreating down the stairs, Alex swelled with rage; after all the spadework he'd put in on the royal visit, as usual, Hengist swanned in when it suited him.

'I'm going to appeal,' whined Boffin. 'There's no way I got a B. Mr Brett-Taylor never encourages me.'

Alex was equally determined not to let his star pupil down.

'I shall request the return of your answer paper and have the marks checked, then we'll ask for a total remark. It costs around sixty pounds; Bagley can foot the bill.'

*   *   *

'What a beautiful school,' said the Private Secretary as Elaine left white hairs all over his dark suit, 'and what a beautiful dog.'

'Isn't she?' said Hengist happily. 'People think she's snarling, but she's really smiling.'

'We have Labradors, they smile too,' said the Lord Lieutenant, producing a file already as big as the Larkshire telephone book.

'I want Her Majesty to have a really nice time,'

461

said Hengist, pouring Pouilly-Fumé into three glasses. 'I know she's got to open the Science Emporium, but I thought she might like to watch some polo if the weather's fine and meet the school beagles? One of our star pupils, Paris Alvaston, might read out one of his beautiful poems and, of course, Cosmo Rannaldini, another star pupil, will be conducting the school orchestra and his mother, Dame Hermione Harefield, in a welcoming fanfare.'

'That sounds a good start,' said the Lord Lieutenant.

'Recently, we bonded with a comprehensive,' Hengist told the Private Secretary, 'who did very well in their GCSEs. It would be a miracle for them if Her Majesty could hand out the certificates.'

Later, with an entourage of press officers and detectives, they walked a possible course. Approaching the Science Emporium, still a pile of rubble, they passed General Bagley's statue.

'That's a fine beast.' The Private Secretary patted Denmark's gleaming black shoulder.

'Isn't he?' agreed Hengist. 'And his rider, our founder, General Bagley, is, I think, a distant relation of Her Majesty's mother.'

'How interesting.' The Private Secretary made a note. 'Her Majesty might like to refer to that in her speech. We'll need potted biogs, in advance, of all the people she's going to meet.'

*   *   *

No one was more excited about Paris's results than Dora.

'Ha, ha, ha, hee, hee, hee,' she sang to her friend Peter on the *Mail on Sunday* a few days later. 'Boffin Brooks has got a B.'

'Any more news of Theo Graham?'

'None, poor thing, he can't get in touch with us or we with him, until after his court case. Paris has been transferred to Artie Deverell's house. Artie's really nice, but Paris can't forgive him for not being Theo and Paris nearly strangled Cosmo yesterday for suggesting Hengist was stupid to put Paris into the house of yet another shirt-lifter.'

'How's the Queen's visit?'

'Chaos. Mrs Fussy's refusing to curtsey and wants a dust sheet put over General Bagley. No one can decide on the right shade of red carpet. But guess what, I've bought a man's wig and a white coat which I've splattered with paint so I can pose as a workman and listen in on meetings, so expect some good copy.'

'Good girl.'

'Randal Stancombe, my mum's grotesque boyfriend, is flooding the place with workmen to get his Science Emporium up in time. It's even got a space centre, so hopefully once it's finished we can land Poppet and Alex on Mars for good.'

'And your handsome headmaster?'

'Utterly euphoric we've gone above Fleetley in the league tables and off next month to Bournemouth to the Tory Party conference with my brother Jupiter.'

Awaiting Rupert's helicopter to fly him to Bournemouth, Hengist took Elaine for a quick walk down to Badger's Retreat. In one hand, he had a piece of toast and marmalade, in the other, a private and confidential letter from David 'Hatchet' Hawkley, now Lord Hawkley, the head of Fleetley.

Dear Hengist [he read],
This is a difficult letter to write. This week you will be offered the job of headmaster of Fleetley, a school I have loved and cherished for twenty-five years. I have long deliberated over whether you are the right person to succeed me. You are a genius at recruitment and getting the best out of both masters and pupils, you are hugely entertaining, charismatic, with a foot in the old world and the new, and generally filled with the milk of human kindness.
In the past we have fallen out . . .

This was a massive understatement. Hengist righted himself after nearly falling down a rabbit hole. He had feared David Hawkley would block his candidacy, but in his fairness, he had not. The letter ended: 'Look after my school, I trust you.'

Hengist was touched. It was a huge olive branch. Looking down, he saw Elaine had nicked his toast and marmalade. But would Fleetley remind Sally too much of Mungo and Pippa, David's then wife, and would it turn out to be a grander, more rigid version of Bagley?

Here he could offer Paris the odd glass of champagne and the run of his books; here he could refuse to disband the school beagles and allow Dora to keep her chocolate Labrador. Could he cope with the lack of freedom? Hengist sighed. Jupiter had just offered him Shadow Education, which would be a complete change of career and an adventure.

Sally would make the perfect minister's wife and Hengist had written Jupiter such a cracking conference speech that by next year he might have seized power. Hengist was flying down to make a fringe speech on education, before flying up to St Andrews in time for dinner at the Headmasters' Conference.

He glanced back at David's letter. He couldn't take on both Fleetley and Education. David, who was a great friend of Theo's, had added a PS: 'To sadder matters, how can we rescue Theo? I am convinced of his innocence. We must battle to clear his name and enable him to finish Sophocles. You have the greater clout.'

Hengist had reached Badger's Retreat. A robin sang in a hawthorn bush, its orange breast clashing with the crimson haws. Like a unicorn, Elaine bounded through the trees he had planted and nurtured. The ground was littered with conkers, which always gave Hengist a stab, remembering how he'd collected them for Mungo.

The Family Tree, its keys turning coral, had lost much of its charm since he'd thrown Oriana out, but, still clinging together, the three trunks and many branches had survived the onslaught of the fallen ash. Perhaps he and Oriana might be friends one day.

Bagley was a far more beautiful school than Fleetley, which, although fed by the same River Fleet, was a squat, grey, Georgian pile surrounded by very flat country. Hengist believed he would miss Badger's Retreat most of all.

Heavens! He must hurry. There was Rupert's

465

dark blue helicopter, in which it would be so cool to arrive at the Headmasters' Conference this evening.

He would earn far more money in politics than at Fleetley. The paths of glory lead but to the gravy train, reflected Hengist.

121

Jupiter's speech was a wow, constructive and marvellously bitchy about the Opposition. Then word got around about Hengist's fringe speech and the main hall had emptied, particularly of young MPs, who had crowded in to hear his good tub-thumping stuff about the real England and freedom from the stranglehold of the curriculum and Brussels.

'Let them be our allies but not dictate our way of life.'

So many interviews and congratulations followed, he only just reached St Andrews in time for dinner. The conference was being held in a lovely hotel, the St Andrews Bay, overlooking the golf course, which was being buffeted by an angry, grey North Sea.

Fiddling to get Radio 3 and the television working, emptying a miniature Bell's into a glass, Hengist called Sally.

'I'm in the most enormous suite, I wish you were here to share it. The guest speaker, some lady novelist, will address us in the Robert Burns Room.'

Sally loved Burns and had, when they first met, compared Hengist with John Anderson, my jo of the bonnie brow and the raven locks. Hengist, in turn, had recited 'My love is like a red, red rose', to her at their wedding.

'Jupiter's speech was marvellous,' cried Sally, 'terrific jokes and he seemed so warm and sort of sincere.'

'That must be a first. I'm moving towards accepting his offer, if you can cope with the incessant ripping apart by the press.'

'As long as we're together.'

'That's the only certainty. Can I fuck you the moment I get home?'

'The Bishop's coming to lunch . . .'

'I'll get there early then. I love you so much and a pat for Elaine.'

Hengist always enjoyed the Headmasters' Conference and never more so than tonight, when Bagley had finally gone above Fleetley. Whilst changing for dinner, many of the heads had seen clips of his and Jupiter's speeches, or his helicopter landing, and he was subjected to a lot of rather envious joshing.

'You going into politics, Hengist?'

'As a head, is one ever out of them?'

'Did you write all Rupert's coursework?'

Then, in lowered voices: 'Sorry about poor old Theo Graham.'

Listening to the cheerful roar of 250 like minds, anticipating a very good dinner, Hengist thought what a good bunch of chaps they were. Personable was the word. There were intellectuals, like David Hawkley or Anthony Seldon at Brighton College, who'd written a biography of Blair, or Martin Stephen, who'd just taken over St Paul's, who wrote excellent historical novels. These men had read hugely and could pick up any literary allusion. A new breed, more interested in management and marketing, had hardly read a book.

Except for a sprinkling of headmistresses, the membership was all men. Milling around they could be mistaken for army officers out of uniform, showing half an inch of clean, pink neck between hair and collar, wearing trousers that when they sat down rose to sock level above highly polished shoes.

'The *Guardian* described us as "grey men in grey suits",' grumbled old Freddie Wills of St Barnabas. 'Not true: we're in navy blue, mostly pinstripe.' With cheerfulness breaking in with flamboyant ties, thought Hengist: technicolour checks or swarming with elephants or dolphins.

They had listened all day to seminars.

'Jenni Murray was excellent on gender,' Freddie Wills told Hengist, 'but Andrew Adonis predictably told us "the Labour Party loves us", because they want to bleed us white propping up city academies. Don't seem to realize most of us have a hell of a struggle making ends meet.'

Then, a few feet away, standing in front of a mural of a 1930s' golf match, with players in pancake caps and plus fours showing off well-turned ankles, was David 'Hatchet' Hawkley, appropriately hawklike, immensely distinguished, his shyness so often coming across as brusqueness.

Hengist waved in greeting. 'Thank you for your letter.'

'You got it? Good. Better get into dinner. You're at my table.'

Hengist, already high on a successful Bournemouth and three large whiskies, found himself seated between the jolly lady novelist guest speaker and David's second wife, Helen.

As her previous husbands had included such unashamed Lotharios as Rupert Campbell-Black and Cosmo's late father, Roberto Rannaldini, it was hardly surprising Lady Hawkley insisted on

469

accompanying handsome David everywhere. A redhead with big, yellow eyes and the nervous breediness of a fallow deer, she was easily the most beautiful woman in the room.

Hengist would far rather have been seated with his chums, fellow junior masters in earlier schools, particularly as, through a vase of yellow carnations, Hatchet Hawkley was watching his every move. Would Helen follow Pippa and fall under Hengist's spell?

In fact, Hengist found Helen earnest and a dreadful intellectual snob. Having clocked him landing in Rupert's helicopter, she immediately tackled him on Rupert's B grade.

'Do we need any more proof that GCSEs are getting easier?'

'Rupert worked very hard,' protested Hengist, who hadn't eaten all day and was buttering his roll, 'and he's discovered he rather likes English lit. There's a copy of *Henry Esmond* in the helicopter and he's mellowed since the old days, when he was Lord of the Unzipped Flies. He's so delighted Taggie did so well and Xav got the Magic Five, he's thinking of turning Penscombe into a second Bloomsbury.'

Oh God. Hengist realized he'd goofed. Helen was clearly so scarred by her marriage to Rupert, she loathed any reference to the success of his second marriage. She had now put her knife and fork together, rather like her legs, leaving her divine russet slab of pâté untouched. Hengist was tempted to ask if he could have it, but this would probably be construed as too intimate a gesture by David, who was still peering at them through the carnations.

Hengist still hadn't decided one hundred per cent between Fleetley or politics.

'We're putting your ravishing Tabitha and her horse on the front of the *Old Bagleian*,' he told Helen, 'although no one could look less like an Old Bag. We're all so proud of her silver!' Then he realized he'd goofed again. He'd forgotten how jealous Helen was of Tabitha, whom he supposed looked too like Rupert.

'You look absolutely stunning,' he murmured. 'Most heads' wives resemble overgrown tomboys, short pepper and salt hair, slim figures: senior, senior prefects. It's not homosexual, just that most heads feel easier with boys. How are you looking forward to David retiring?' he went on. Christ, he hoped they didn't move into a cottage on the Fleetley Estate.

'We've got a house in Umbria,' said Helen, 'and we're looking for somewhere in Dorset. We're both going to write. David's doing Aeschylus and I'm working on a literary memoir.'

Hengist was about to say Helen's inside story of marriage to Rupert and Rannaldini would sell much better than any translation of Aeschylus, but just stopped himself. 'We'd better get another bottle.' He tipped back his chair.

At the next-door table, two of his dearest friends, Tim Hastie-Smith, head of Dean Close, and Pete Johnson, head of Millfield, were discussing Colin Montgomerie's triumph in the Ryder Cup. As waitresses and waiters in grey silk cheongsams rushed in with the main course—large squares of roast lamb and shiny brown parsnips—Hengist turned to the lady novelist, who said she was writing about two schools and asked him to tell her about being a headmaster.

'Big egos and like this'—Hengist plunged his knife into his lamb to reveal its pink interior—'very square but tender inside.'

'I must remember that,' laughed the lady novelist. 'What else makes a great head?'

'Ability to fill the school and pick first-class staff.'

'Energy and charm?'

'Certainly.' Hengist filled up her glass.

'Intellect?'

Hengist shook his head. 'Huge self-belief is much more important.'

'Have you ever won anything at the Teaching Awards?'

'No, that's a state-school affair, even though Lord Hawkley's one of the judges. They think we have it too easy.' He noticed she was looking down at some speech notes on her lap.

'Don't be scared, we'll be a terrific audience, so used to laughing at parents' weak jokes.'

'I'm going to end by quoting from "Rugby Chapel", about heads as heroic great souls leading and inspiring others on to the city of God.'

' "Ye, like angels, appear, radiant with ardour divine!" ' quoted back Hengist. 'They'll love that.'

The lady novelist was thrilled Hengist was writing a biography of Thomas and Matthew Arnold.

'Will you send me a review copy?'

'How bad was that school, Larks something, you joined up with?' shouted old Freddie Wills across the table.

'Well, they had a geography mistress who'd never been to London,' said Hengist, howling with laughter, so everyone else joined in.

Anyone could charm the birds off the trees,

reflected David enviously, with a packet of Swoop, but Hengist could charm the birds away from a loaded bird table on the coldest of winter days, because it was so much more fun to be in his presence.

He, Freddie and the lady novelist, who'd probably end up in bed with him later, were discussing a collective noun for heads.

'You've got a pride of lions, a gaggle of geese,' said Freddie.

'How about a hurrah of heads?' suggested the lady novelist.

'Or a "Hail, fellow, well met" of heads?' volunteered Hengist.

Aware that Hengist was having far more fun with the plump lady novelist with the loud laugh and shiny face, Helen knew she had been crabby. She had always found him disturbingly attractive. With his sallow skin, laughing slit eyes, dark curls rising from his smooth forehead and spilling over the collar of his dinner jacket, he looked like some Renaissance grandee. His height, strength, merriment and overwhelming vitality made one long to be in bed with him.

'How's my ex-stepson, Cosmo?' she asked. 'As obnoxious as ever?'

'Probably,' said Hengist, 'but he's very clever. I'm afraid he makes me laugh.'

With no Sally to drag him home, Hengist had a lovely end to the evening, drinking the minibar dry in his suite and playing bears round the furniture with his friends.

'Are you going into politics, Hengist?'

'No, no, I could never leave teaching.'

122

Next morning, Hengist had a frightful hangover and didn't get away as early as he'd hoped. This was the way to travel though, flying over magenta ploughed fields flecked with gulls, like waves on a wine-dark sea. Down below was St Andrews, with its ancient university and town hall built of big, proud, yellow stone, the colour of the turning trees. What a lovely place for Sally and him to retire to. A seat of learning, where he could at last write his books. Perhaps he didn't want Fleetley *or* politics.

At midday, the helicopter dropped him at Bagley, sending the leaves flying upwards, then whizzed off to take Rupert racing.

Dropping little bottles of shampoo and body lotion on Miss Painswick's desk, although her body was not somewhere he wished to go, Hengist asked if anything interesting had happened.

'Only these.' She handed him two letters marked 'private and confidential', one presumably offering him Shadow Education, the other asking him to take over Fleetley in the Michaelmas Term of 2005. Hengist pocketed them.

'How was the trip? asked Miss Painswick. 'You were awfully good at Bournemouth.'

'And awfully bad at St Andrews. Could you get me a vast Fernet-Branca?'

'Mr Bruce is in your office, by the way, says it's urgent.'

Bounding up the stairs, Hengist was amazed to find Alex sitting in his archbishop's chair, flipping disapprovingly through his mountainous in-tray. Alex's blackcurrant eyes glittered behind his spectacles with the same air of excitement as when Theo was arrested.

Feeling even more in need of a hair of the dog, Hengist edged towards the whisky decanter, then, dropping a St Andrews Bay Hotel bath cap on the big oak table in front of Alex:

'I've brought you a present. I know how you like transparency.'

Alex didn't smile.

'You'd better sit down. Something very serious has occurred.'

Not Sally? Hengist felt a lurch of terror, but Painswick wouldn't have been looking so cheerful.

' "Lay on, Macduff," ' he said lightly.

'I'd like you to explain this.' Alex chucked an exam script down on the table. 'This was handed in as Paris Alvaston's second history paper.'

Hengist picked it up and went cold to his bones. His heart stopped, then began to crash out of control. 'So what?'

'That is not Paris's writing. Only four people knew the combination to the safe: the exam officer, Ian Cartwright—who as Paris's foster father was not a disinterested party—Miss Painswick and yourself.'

'Course it's not Cartwright. I can't imagine Painswick achieving an A star either.'

'We've checked with a graphologist'—although he'd have recognized anywhere that arrogant, flamboyant scrawl seen so often on praise postcards—'it was your writing, headmaster.'

There was a crash of cut glass on glass as Hengist poured himself a large whisky. For Paris's sake, he

475

mustn't give in without a fight and prepare a defence, which of course was non-existent.

In a flash, he realized he would lose his school, Shadow Education and Fleetley, and Paris would lose his A star. It might have been better if Sally had died. She was so straight and true, the disgrace that would submerge him would kill her anyway.

It was a few moments before he realized Alex was saying, 'I suppose you couldn't bear your little guinea pig to fail.'

Then he backed away as Hengist turned on him, like a raging lion:

'It was your bloody fault. If you hadn't shopped Theo in the middle of GCSEs, Paris would never have screwed up. He was knocked sideways by Theo leaving.'

Hearing a thud, they both jumped.

'We're busy,' called out Alex.

The door flew open and in bounded Elaine, hurling herself on her master with joyful squeaks, then racing round the room knocking over a side table, a waste-paper basket and a vase of scarlet dahlias with her thwacking tail, before jumping on the window seat to indulge in some scrabbling running on the spot.

'Get that beast out of here,' screamed Alex. In no way could he more have asserted his new ascendancy.

Elaine was followed by Sally. Devastated by the Oriana saga, she had been looking tired and drained for some time. Now, with highlighted, newly washed hair softening her sweet face and a pale blue cashmere jersey caressing her breasts, she looked utterly ravishing.

'Darling, when did you get back? How lovely.

476

The Bishop's caught up in traffic, but he'll be here in half an hour.' Time for sex, her eyes smiled. 'And some prospective parents have turned up.' Then, noticing a muscle bounding in Hengist's jaw and Alex's face longer than a tomb stone: 'What on earth's going on?'

'I regret our Senior Team Leader has been caught cheating,' said Alex heavily.

In the distance, Hengist could see spirals of mist, the ghost of his career, curling up from Badger's Retreat. ' "O! the fierce wretchedness that glory brings," ' he said bleakly.

'Hengist wouldn't cheat,' cried Sally in outrage. 'He's the most honourable man.'

Hengist turned back, stroking Elaine, who, wagging her tail gently and joyfully, was gazing up from the ripped window seat.

'I'm afraid it's true.' He tried to meet Sally's eyes. 'Paris found out Theo'd been arrested and made such a cock-up of his paper, I wrote it instead.'

'Oh, Hengist,' Sally clung on to the back of the sofa, 'how could you? Poor Paris could have retaken it! He'll be mortified, the press will crucify him after all the crowing about A stars.'

'Paris Alvaston, in fact, suspected foul play,' intoned Alex. 'Joan Johnson overheard him saying he couldn't possibly have got an A star, as he'd trashed his second history paper.'

Loathing herself, Sally turned to Alex: 'Does this have to get out?'

'My duty is to the other students,' said Alex primly, 'and I must immediately inform the chair of governors.'

There goes politics and Fleetley, thought Hengist. His heart was thumping relentlessly, his knees shuddering together.

'As I'm not prepared to be an accessory to a crime'—Alex cracked his knuckles—'I have also alerted the police.'

'Oh dear,' sighed Hengist, draining his whisky, 'such a bad effect on recruitment. To have one master arrested looks like misfortune, but two, definitely carelessness.'

'Don't be so bloody flippant,' yelled Sally.

Elaine vanished under the sofa.

'Theo's was a lapse, motivated by lust,' said Alex sanctimoniously. 'This is a far greater crime. Who knows how many papers Hengist tampered with? Our entire year's GCSE marks could be declared null and void. I'm sure Fleetley will appeal.'

A smell of moussaka was drifting from the kitchens. In two neighbouring practice rooms, pupils could be heard hammering out pieces for the Queen's visit.

Alex sat back in Hengist's chair. Perceptibly, he was shrugging on the mantle of power. I hope he gets it better cut than his suits, thought Hengist irrationally.

As Sally slumped on the sofa, he could see the line of her suspender belt through her grey skirt and that she was wearing sheer black stockings and high heels.

'It's a sad way to end your career, Hengist, but I have to think of Bagley,' sighed Alex. Then, seeing a Panda car emerging from the Memorial Arch: 'Here come the police.'

As he opened the door, Miss Painswick nearly fell into the room.

'The new parents will be old parents if they're kept waiting much longer,' she said tartly, 'and the

478

Bishop's arrived.'

Alex smoothed his beard. 'I will entertain his lordship.'

'Mrs Cox has made celeriac purée,' said Sally in a high voice, 'the Bishop liked it so much last time.' Turning to Alex, she stammered, 'Hengist only did it for Paris's sake.'

'No, I didn't, I did it for myself, said Hengist. 'I'd invested so much in Paris, I couldn't bear him to fail.'

'You have brought independent schools and the entire exam system into disrepute,' said Alex, no longer feeling the need to conceal the extent of his loathing. 'You could get five years.'

What a dreadful combination, thought Hengist, Alex and ruin staring one in the face.

*   *   *

After lunch, in a frenzy of righteousness, Alex rang his chair of governors, not only to tell him about the cheating, but that Hengist had been knocking off a member of the governing body.

'Good God, not the Bishop of Larkminster?' said Jupiter in alarm.

'No, and a parent too, I'm talking about Ruth Walton.'

Jupiter said, 'Good God,' a second time. He'd always fancied Mrs Walton. One of his favourite sayings was: 'That man's the true conservative Who lops the moulder'd branch away.' There was no way Hengist was going to get Education now.

Putting down the telephone, Jupiter was about to dial Fleetley, then, remembering Lord Hawkley would be still at the Headmasters' Conference, he called the St Andrews Bay Hotel.

123

Hengist was arrested, taken down to the station for questioning and kept overnight. Dora, dying to find out what was going on, in overalls, wig and the guise of smartening up the general office for the Queen's visit, was so shocked as she assimilated the terrible truth that she managed to paint Miss Painswick's coat, as well as an entire wall, vicarage green.

Sally retreated to Head House, sat on the bed in which she'd been looking forward to Hengist making love to her, and cried. She'd never dumped on others. She'd been too busy listening to other people's problems and, unlike the clubbable Hengist, had always kept her distance. So she was now intensely alone.

What would happen to them? Hengist would never get another job in teaching. Nor would the New Reform Party look at him and—apart from the terrible disgrace—what would they live on? They had always spent a fortune on entertaining, on pictures, books and the garden, but never bothered to buy a house or save any money. When he had gone abroad on school or political business, Hengist had invariably picked up the bill. And how would such a free spirit ever survive in prison?

Randal Stancombe, who loved hospital cases, decided as night fell to call on Sally. The humiliating amount of coverage over Rupert getting his GCSE, abetted by Hengist and Janna, had increased his detestation of all three. He'd zapped Janna by moving the bulldozers in on

Larks; now he was overjoyed to learn, from a very over-excited Poppet Bruce, of Hengist's arrest.

'How's Sally?'

'In shock. I took round some organic hot cross buns and offered her counselling, but she insisted on being on her own. I'm sure she's hurting.'

Randal had always fancied Sally. What sweet revenge to take her off Hengist. Champagne might be too celebratory a gesture, so he settled for a huge bunch of bronze chrysanths.

He didn't tell Anthea of his plan, even though she'd been delighted by the turn of events. Sally and Hengist had always shown their preference for Anthea's late husband, Sir Raymond, and constantly displayed favouritism towards Dicky and particularly Dora. Anthea didn't feel Sally deserved any sympathy, so Randal decided to make a mission of mercy on his own.

Showering in his penthouse at Cavendish Plaza, he drenched himself and the blue spotted handkerchief with which he had so often wiped away ladies' tears in lavender water rather than Lynx. Lynx would come later. If there were people with Sally, he'd just leave the flowers with a caring message: 'Thinking of you, Randal', which would soften her up for a later pounce.

Nice property, Head House, thought Randal as he pressed the doorbell. How long would Alex let her stay on?

Sally had clearly been crying a great deal; her face was blotchy and swollen, bloodshot veins intensifying the blue of her eyes. Upset by her mistress's tears, Elaine rushed to the door hoping Randal might be Hengist to make her better.

At first Sally didn't recognize Stancombe. With

his mahogany tan and huge circular shield of bronze chrysanthemums, he resembled a Zulu warrior.

'I only popped in, Sal, to offer my condolences,' and he was over the threshold.

He could tell she was in a state. She was shuddering uncontrollably, the fire had not been lit, none of the sidelights had been turned on and she had obviously been trying to persuade that bloody dog to eat. An untouched bowl of chicken curled and dried on the carpet.

'You shouldn't be on your own.'

'It's awfully kind, but I'm better that way. Rupert thinks Hengist will be bailed first thing tomorrow, unless he comes up before Anthea Belvedon. Oh, I'm sorry, Randal, it's Rupert's way of joking.'

'I know,' said Randal bleakly, 'only too well.'

Sally started frantically plumping cushions. 'I don't mind for me, but Hengist was so excited about the future. He would never have touched Paris's paper if Paris hadn't been so devastated by Theo's arrest. Hengist wasn't there to reassure him and came back to find Paris had put in a completely dud paper, just signed his name and a few incomprehensible sentences. So Hengist answered the paper for him.'

'No wonder Paris got an A star,' said Randal coldly. 'I don't approve of cheating, Sally.'

'Neither do I, but Hengist has lost everything.' She started to cry. 'Please go.'

'I'm not leaving you like this.'

Randal had changed his hair, Sally noticed mindlessly, it was shorter and gelled upwards like an oiled, black pincushion. Turned upside down, he could be used to spike up the leaves littering the lawns outside. He was now telling her she was a fine woman.

'Look at that dog, Sal, asleep on its back, taking up nine-tenths of the settee, leaving you no space. Hengist is the same, taking up nine-tenths of your life. You've devoted yourself to a taker who wasn't worth it.'

'That's not true.'

'Hengist broke my heart.'

'Your heart?' Sally stopped plumping a silver wedding cushion in which the embroidered initials H and S had been entwined.

'I cared very deeply for Ruth, then discovered she and Hengist were having a relationship.'

'Ruth's a great friend of both of us!'

'Hengist is a persuasive guy. He also had a relationship with Janna Curtis. Sorry to be brutal, Sal, but you're too straight and sincere not to know the truth.'

Sally gazed at him bewildered. 'But Janna's such a dear.'

'Stands to reason.' Randal paced the room turning on radiators. 'If ladies are sweet to you, you'll invite them to your posh dos and they'll have a chance to pop upstairs for a quickie with Hengist.'

'Don't be revolting. How dare you? Hengist is such a super chap and so kind, mothers, pupils, schoolmistresses are always falling in love with him.'

Stancombe produced a trump card. 'Here's a love letter he wrote Ruth and a picture of them in Paris. She left it under the lining paper in my penthouse apartment.'

Sally glanced at a very loving photograph in some

484

nightclub and a letter which began: 'Ah love, let us be true To one another!' in Hengist's writing, and threw it aside. Randal had his blue spotted handkerchief at the ready.

'Get out, you revolting sneak,' yelled Sally.

'I could make you happy'—a squirt of Gold Spot—'I can't bear to see you so alone,' and Randal had grabbed her, tugging her towards him, burying his full, cruel lips in hers, pressing his muscular body against her.

'You b-b-bastard,' screamed Sally.

'My, you're a foxy lady,' panted Stancombe as under her discreet cashmere jumper, he'd discovered splendid breasts, supported by a pale blue lacy bra. Putting his other hand up her tweed skirt, he encountered stockings and suspenders but no panties; remembering Hengist on the answerphone to Ruth: 'Darling, don't wear any knickers,' he added, 'You know you want it, Sally.' He would have taken her on the sofa if it hadn't been for Elaine.

'I don't,' shouted Sally. 'If you don't get out I'll call the police,' and gathering up Volume One of the *Shorter Oxford Dictionary*, she clipped him round the ears, sending him reeling backwards, splintering an occasional table.

'Why, you vicious cow . . .'

Rushing to her mistress's defence, Elaine nipped Randal on the back of his thigh, then darted off as the doorbell rang.

'GET OUT,' sobbed Sally.

Randal, in his haste, had not shut the front door properly. Next minute Paris, clutching a half-bottle of Ian's brandy, marched in. 'I wanted to see you were OK. Oh, sorry.'

485

Elaine accompanied Paris, snaking her long nose into his hand, whacking his jeans with her tail.

'Randal was leaving,' gasped Sally, hastily reloading her bra and pulling down her jersey.

'Good,' said Paris, noticing a trickle of blood flowing from Randal's forehead.

'You'll regret it, Mrs Brett-Taylor. I came offering support,' shouted Randal, banging the front door behind him.

Paris went to the kitchen and poured Sally a large brandy, which she choked on but which warmed her.

'What did he want?'

'To gloat. He brought some hideous flowers.'

'Bin them.'

'Not the flowers' fault, must give them the chance of a few more days of life.'

Sally slumped, shivering, on the sofa. Both Ruth and Janna . . . Oh, Hengist. And he'd sworn after Pippa: never again. Wretchedness was sinking in as his laughing, open, reassuring face looked down at her from Daisy France-Lynch's charming little portrait on the right of the fireplace . . . Paris, having topped up her glass, was meanwhile consumed with his own concerns.

'I'm sorry, but no one will tell me the truth. Did Mr Brett-Taylor switch my and Boffin's papers?'

'No, he wrote yours. It was a very wrong thing to do. But he knew how brilliant you were and couldn't bear you not to produce the goods.'

'So Boffin really did only get a B.'

Paris's satisfaction, however, was short-lived.

'According to Dora, who's been hanging around Painswick's office, Hengist will be fired if he doesn't resign, so both Theo and Hengist lost their jobs because of me.'

Paris was deathly white now, trembling in horror.

'It's not your fault.'

'And if Hengist goes, Artie will be next and Ian and Patience will be turfed out.'

'Theo may well get off.'

'But Hengist's career's ruined.'

'No, no, there are thousands of things he can do—write his books ... Oh, God.' Tears were pouring down Sally's face; shock was taking over as she knelt by the fire, sweeping up non-existent ashes.

'What did Stancombe really want?'

'To badmouth Hengist. Oh, Paris ...' Sally wiped her eyes with a sooty hand, 'I shouldn't be telling you, but Randal said Hengist had been ... been ... having an affaire with Ruth Walton. I didn't want to believe it, but he produced such a happy photo of Hengist and Janna in Paris.' She clutched her head. 'I mean Ruth.'

'Janna?' said Paris unthinkingly. 'That was in Wales.'

'Then it's true.' Picking up the lovely little Staffordshire dog, which had fallen off the occasional table during Randal's descent, Sally promptly dropped it on the fender where it smashed in a dozen pieces. 'Oh no, watch out for Elaine's paws, that was a wedding present.'

'I'm sorry.' Clumsily Paris swept up the pieces. 'I never told anyone. I caught them on the geography field trip. He was at her bedroom window.'

'So that was why you never came and saw us?'

'Sort of. Fuck, I never meant to tell you.' He tipped the fragments into the waste-paper basket.

Sally couldn't stop crying. Paris wasn't

487

embarrassed; people had always been crying in the children's home. He put his arms round her. 'I'll look after you. I'm sure they were one-night stands and one thing is certain: Mr Brett-Taylor adores you. Like Brutus, you are his true and honourable wife, as dear to him as the ruddy drops that visit his sad heart.'

'Oh P-p-p-p-paris.'

He was stroking her hair; Elaine snuggled up on the other end of the sofa, so he stroked her too.

'You ought to go,' gulped Sally.

'Have you got a best friend I can ring?'

'Not really, Hengist was my best friend.'

Paris felt so sorry for her. He gave her another top-up of brandy, then kissed her juddering mouth very tentatively.

'Hush, please don't cry.'

Sally struggled like a captured bird, then went still.

Paris was amazed by the voluptuousness of her body. Sliding his hand up her silken black legs, he encountered shaved pubes, or did women her age go bald down there? It felt smooth, then sticky. Her legs were long and slim and there was only a tiny roll of fat round her waist.

Sally gave a moan as his hand slipped between her legs and slowly, caressingly, moved upwards. The other hand unhooked her bra; out tumbled beautiful, high breasts, still darkened by the Tuscany sun.

'I always dress up for Hengist when he's been away,' she muttered.

For thirty years, only Hengist in his heavyweight strength had made love to her. Paris was Narcissus, Adonis, Endymion, a slender Greek youth with a body and a cock as hard and white as marble. He didn't give her time to think, because it was the only way he knew of lessening both their anguish. It was quick and, because of his kindness, extraordinarily cathartic.

Afterwards, as if she were Little Dulcie, he removed the rest of her clothes, dressed her in a white cotton nightgown and put her to bed.

'Got to do my teeth.'

'Do them in the morning, they won't fall out.'

Then he filled up a hot-water bottle and found her a sleeping pill in the bathroom cupboard.

'I don't take them,' protested Sally. 'Hengist tries to cram too much in and has bouts of insomnia.'

'Take one now.'

Sitting on the bed, Paris stroked her face.

'Elaine,' she mumbled.

'I'll take her out and see she gets something to eat.'

'And the poor, hideous flowers.'

'Yeah, yeah. Don't feel guilty in the morning. I reckon Hengist owed us.'

* * *

She was woken from heavy sleep by the telephone. It was Oriana.

'Mum, it's just come over the internet. "Toff school head arrested for cheating". Is it true?'

Sally shook herself into consciousness.

'I'm afraid so.'

'What happened? How could Dad?'

Clutching the telephone, Sally wandered groggily downstairs. Paris had put Stancombe's chrysanthemums in the mauve bucket with which

Mrs Cox cleaned the kitchen floor. There was a bowl of untouched cold roast beef beside Elaine.

'You're beautiful,' Paris had written on the hall mirror in marker pen, 'all the guys fancy you.'

Oriana was still talking: 'Dad threw up his entire career for one GCSE?'

'I guess so,' said Sally, 'and we're getting a divorce.'

'That's not like you, Mum.'

'I can cope with cheating but not being cheated on.'

*   *   *

Echoing her father last Christmas, Oriana told the press that 'when one of your family does something reprehensible, you take it on the chin.'

124

Once Sally demanded a divorce, Hengist seemed to lose any interest in fighting his case. Despite Rupert bringing down an ace barrister to defend him, he refused to offer any excuse. His actions had been unforgivable. He apologized unreservedly for the distress he had caused a great school and particularly his wife and Paris Alvaston. He appeared unmoved when he was subsequently sent down for three months. Life without Sally was such hell anyway, it didn't much matter whether he was locked up or not. He insisted on no visitors.

Bagley was devastated. Hengist had been hugely popular. He had raised the school's profile at the same time as his own, and any liberty he had taken with his globe-trotting he had returned in glamour, vision, kindness and fun.

' "There hath passed away a glory from the earth," ' sighed Cosmo.

Bagley also loved Sally. They knew how tirelessly she had shored up Hengist, how kind she had been, particularly to the non-teaching staff, how many miserably homesick children she'd comforted, how diligently she'd rammed coronation chicken into square plastic boxes and raced up motorways to organize fundraising dinners.

Now the dream was over. She and Hengist had split up and were to be chucked out of their ravishing house because Poppet and Alex, as acting head, wanted to move 'their brood' in before Christmas. Ideally, they would have liked Sally, who'd met Her Majesty on numerous occasions, to be out before the Queen's visit, but were loath publicly to appear uncaring. Then there was the little hurdle of the next governors' meeting when, hopefully, Alex would be confirmed as head with a salary of £150,000 a year.

Poppet kept dropping in on Sally to measure up rooms and windows and offer counselling. 'I'm sure once you leave Bagley, you'll find it easier to achieve closure.'

'Should we organize a leaving present?' she asked Alex. 'After all, Sally is leaving Hengist *and* Bagley. Perhaps a small refrigerator or a Dyson; I expect she and Hengist have only one between them.'

'And who will have custody of Elaine?' sobbed Dora, who would no longer be able to boost her pocket money and pick up stories waiting at Hengist and Sally's dinner parties.

'At least Alex and Poppet won't need Pickfords to move their lack of furniture,' drawled Amber. 'They could probably get it all into Van Dyke. Joan is definitely flavour of the month. Lando's got her at ten to one to get deputy head rather than Biffo.'

Rumour and suspicion were swirling round like autumn mist. Alex was determined to scrap the school beagles before February 2005, when hunting was bound to become illegal, and close the stables, which pandered to an elitist few and was the centre of subversive activity. He had also introduced a tagging system to ensure pupils were always in the right lesson and safe in their houses by eight o'clock.

'There'll be no more shagging in Middle Field,' sighed Milly as they waited to go into chapel, 'and Theo won't be allowed back even if he's proved innocent. Stancombe's builders are pulling down the classical library and the archives as we speak. Look what I've just found in the skip: Theo's translation of *Medea*.'

Paris snatched it. 'I'll have that.'

*   *   *

The press had a field day. Ashton Douglas was interviewed at length about his 'great wegret' that, against his better judgement, he had allowed Paris Alvaston to be plucked from the security of a care home and thrust into the hothouse atmosphere of a rich decadent public school, where he had had to suffer the humiliation of being cheated for when an exam was beyond his capabilities.

Col Peters's hatchet job in the *Larkminster Gazette*: 'The Head that wasn't there', picked up by all the nationals, listed Hengist's away days, leaked by Alex. Alex, photographed very flatteringly, was quoted as saying his goal was to put Bagley back on the rails and engage with the wider community.

In the same *Gazette* there was a profile of Ashton Douglas, entitled 'Schools Saviour', with a picture of him accepting a cheque from Randal Stancombe for £25,000,000 for the sale of Larks High School, which would go towards the education of Larkshire's children. Randal was quoted as saying he had very exciting plans for the area, including health and sports centres, playgrounds, a row of shops, even a police station for the Shakespeare Estate.

Nudged by Randal, Alex had immediately axed all Hengist's plans for the Queen's visit, liaising with the Lord Lieutenant and the royal household and guaranteeing Randal as much access to Her Majesty on the day as possible.

'Engaging with the community', Alex had also invited a lot of local movers and shakers to meet the Queen, but had pointedly left out Artie, Ian and Patience and, more seriously, Biffo, who was even more upset when he saw the agenda for the next governors' meeting and discovered he was not being put forward for deputy head.

'You promised me this, Alex, when I supported you over the Theo business.'

'That was before I analysed your maths results, which could have been better,' replied Alex coldly. 'You're nearly sixty, Biffo, and not cutting it any more. Of course I want you on side, but suggesting Sally Brett-Taylor be allowed to stay on was not helpful. I'd rather you didn't make suggestions like that.'

Alex speedily assumed the role of head. He'd been running the school for the last two years anyway. Now, like a second wife, he was determined to exorcise every trace of the Brett-Taylors; for a start, ordering the digging up of Sally's glowing, subtly coloured autumn borders and replacing them with regiments of clashing bedding plants.

Alex knew nothing of the art world, but had recently been putting out feelers for the right person to paint him. At some function, Poppet had met an interesting artist called Trafford, who, responsible for some ground-breakingly obscene installations, had been nominated for the Turner. Trafford, who was coming down for a recce next week, also had some challenging ideas, according to Poppet, about a sculpture to replace General

494

Bagley and Denmark. Everyone knew of Arnold of Rugby, why not Bruce of Bagley? mused Alex.

He was gratified how many of the press were ringing him up for quotes, and now that he was appearing on the box a lot, he'd invested in contact lenses, like his icon Jack Straw, and a new wardrobe. Channel 4 was coming down for a programme entitled 'Whither Independents?'—or should it be 'Wither?' Alex had quipped to the researcher. They'd be filming outside, so Alex intended to wear a smart new raincoat in fashionable stone, belted to show off his good figure, which he'd acquired in celebratory mood the day after Hengist had been forced to resign.

The new raincoat was hanging in the general office when Dora, who was highly displeased with all Alex's pointless innovations, wandered in with cups of coffee for herself and Miss Painswick.

'Why is Tabitha Campbell-Black no longer on the front of the *Old Bagleian*?' she demanded. 'She's an icon.'

'Equestrianism is regarded as elitist,' explained Painswick sourly. 'Mr Bruce is replacing her with a picture of the Science Emporium.'

'How pants is that?' Dora was leaning forward to read the list of acceptances for the Queen's visit, which Painswick was typing out, when Alex walked in, causing her to jump and spill coffee all over his raincoat.

'Oh bugger, sorry, Mr Bruce.'

'Don't swear. Sorry isn't enough. You will take that raincoat to the dry-cleaner's, pay for it and return it by tomorrow when I need it. Why are you hanging round here anyway? You should be in . . .'
He pressed a button on the tagging computer.

'. . . French lit. Why hasn't Mr Deverell reported you?'

'Mr Deverell doesn't need the tagging system because we all love him. No one misses his lessons.' Dora glanced up at the clock. 'I'm only a minute late.' Grabbing the raincoat, she shot out of the office.

Later in the day, Dora returned sulkily to Boudicca. There was no way she was going to fork out for dry-cleaning, so she chucked Alex's mac into Joan's washing machine. Next morning, attaching safety pins and a couple of coloured tags to prove it had been dry-cleaned, Dora hung it back in the general office.

Alas, when Alex flung it on to go into the Long Walk with Channel 4, he was horrified to discover it had shrunk to mid-thigh, and wouldn't remotely button up. Alex was so thrown, he didn't get half his points across and forgot to plug *A Guide to Red Tape*. After the crew had gone, he summoned Dora in a fury.

'Those dry-cleaner's shrunk my raincoat.'

'They couldn't have. Perhaps you've put on weight.'

'Don't be ridiculous. I've weighed eleven stone two since I left Bristol.'

'You should have flung it round your shoulders like a matador.'

'Just shut up. Where's the receipt?'

'I chucked it away.'

'Well, find it then.'

'That Polly Toyboy on the phone for you, Mr Bruce,' called out Painswick.

Sidling out of the office, Dora remembered there had been a piece of paper with writing on in the

496

mac pocket, which she'd left on her bedside table.

As Cosmo was as anxious as she was to depose Alex and bring back Hengist's very benevolent despotism, Dora showed Cosmo the piece of paper later in the day. 'It's in Mr Fussy's wincy little writing and it says: ' "BC Green Dolphin, six o'clock, August 27th", plus a mobile number.'

'What's BC?' pondered Cosmo.

'Before Christ—Mr Fussy's so old; and my God, that's Stancombe's number. Engraved on my heart. My mother's always ringing it.'

Next day, while Painswick was at lunch, Dora and Cosmo checked Alex's diary.

'He should have been at an "Against Gender Bias Workshop" in Birmingham at six o'clock on the twenty-seventh.' Cosmo clicked his tongue. 'Our Senior Team Leader has been moonlighting.'

*   *   *

Cosmo was a regular of the Green Dolphin, a trendy country pub, two miles from Bagley. Hanging on the walls beside fishing nets, tridents and leaping dolphins, was a mug engraved with his name.

As Lubemir had immediately cracked Alex's tagging system, Cosmo escaped that evening to the Green Dolphin to chat up his friend Susie the barmaid. Fortunately the place was virtually empty.

'Your usual?' asked Susie, getting down his mug and filling it up with a concoction made up of black vodka, Tia Maria and Coke, entitled Black Russian. He was a one, that Cosmo, with his soulful eyes and flopping curls.

Susie remembered 27 August well, because they

were all there: 'Ashton Douglas, Alex Bruce, Rod Hyde, Col Peters (the revolting pig), Russell Lambert (the planning permission king, who allowed Stancombe's horrible expensive houses on the edge of the village here, blocking out the view from my mum and dad's cottage), Des Reynolds, smoothie pants, and his lordship, Randal Stancombe. They had a private room and drank buckets of Bolly, obviously celebrating something.'

'It's called "engaging with the wider community",' said Cosmo, making notes. 'Strange, or not so strange bedfellows: Randal, Alex and Rod perhaps, but what were Russell and Ashton doing there? I bet Stancombe handed out a few suitcases of greenbacks or Caribbean villas as going-home presents.'

As 27 August had been around the time Stancombe got his hands on the Larks land, Cosmo decided he must try and get into Stancombe's office. Difficult when he'd treated Jade in so cavalier a fashion—and when Stancombe had changed the locks after he split up with Ruth Walton. Alex Bruce had also put such a lock on his files recently, so Cosmo decided to try and gain access to those of another member of the party: Ashton Douglas at S and C.

There were advantages to having a famous mother. That very evening, Dame Hermione invited Ashton Douglas to a little supper party the following night in her beautiful house in neighbouring Rutshire. Ashton, an opera buff, was in heaven, kissing Hermione's white hands, almost too excited to eat his lobster pancakes.

Afterwards Dame Hermione sang to the guests, and during 'Where e'er you walk' gazed directly at

Ashton.

Later, over a glass of Kummel, she told him:

'My son is obsessed with citizenship, Mr Douglas. He's taking it for AS level. He has such a feeling for his fellow citizens and the work of the Borough. It would be so wonderful'—Hermione opened her big brown eyes—'if he could do a few days' work experience in your fascinating office to learn about education.'

'We'd be honoured, Dame Hermione,' said Ashton warmly, who had no idea of Cosmo's capacity for evil and thought he looked fetchingly like a Caravaggio catamite as, back home for the weekend, he sat quietly in the window seat engrossed in a book called *Know Your Town Hall*, which was actually a jacket wrapped round *L'Histoire d'O*.

'Bingo,' crowed Cosmo next day to Dora. 'I'll get access to Ashton's offices and find out exactly what's going on.'

Fortunately, most of the Lower Sixth were out on work experience and Alex was too obsessed with the Queen's visit to bother about Cosmo's destination.

'My interesting news is that my Aunt Lily and the Brigadier are planning to fight the development at Larks,' Dora told Cosmo, 'because the builders are endangering natterjack toads and loads of rare wild flowers, which aren't out at the moment, but which the Brigadier, who is a keen bottomist, recognizes by the leaves.'

'Ashton Douglas is also a keen bottomist,' said Cosmo. 'I'd better wear steel underpants. I might even write a musical called *Kiddy Fiddler on the Roof*.'

499

125

Paris was in despair, overwhelmed by the misfortune he'd brought on Bagley.

'You've created even more havoc than the Paris who started the Trojan Wars,' Boffin told him nastily as they came out of prep the following dank October evening. 'First Theo, then Hengist chucked out; both their careers ruined; Hengist's marriage wrecked. Artie, Biffo and your dear foster parents'll be next for the chop. Alex doesn't like fossils.'

Somehow Paris managed not to throttle Boffin. He'd caused enough trouble already. Bagley had completely lost its charm. Back at the Old Coach House, Ian was not sleeping and his temper grew shorter as Alex delved into every aspect of the school's finances. There was no Hengist or Emlyn for Paris to have fun with any more and every time he popped in to cheer up Sally, he found her unravelling with despair, and felt hideously responsible.

He loathed Dora and Cosmo having secrets and whispering in corners together. He liked the charming and emollient Artie, but didn't have the same bond with him that he had with Theo. Where the hell was Theo and how was his back and how was he getting on with Sophocles? And Paris had worries of his own. He'd be seventeen in January and if Patience and Ian didn't want or could no longer afford to keep him, he'd be out of care and on to the scrap heap, no doubt joining the criminal classes and the homeless, like so many care leavers.

Alone in the dusk, Paris punched the wall of the Mansion several times until his knuckles ran with blood, like Oedipus's beard after he'd pierced his eyeballs again and again with the brooch pins of his hanged wife and mother, Jocasta. A passage Theo had translated with such terrifying vividness. Paris shuddered. There was still one trail he hadn't followed up.

On his way back to Ian and Patience's for supper, having wrapped his hand in bog paper, he dropped in on Biffo to return a maths textbook. He found the old boy plastered in a thick fog of smoke, farts and drink fumes. The fire had gone out; Biffo was three-quarters down a bottle of red; another bottle lay in the waste-paper basket.

'Are you OK, sir?' Paris relit the fire, then played a sneaky trick. 'We're looking forward to you being deputy head.'

Like an old walrus confronted by an eskimo's harpoon, Biffo glowered at him. 'Not getting it.'

'Everyone thinks it's a done deal.'

'Huh, Alex says I'm not cutting it any more. Results not good enough.'

'You got me through maths, you must be a bloody genius.'

Paris waited for Biffo to nod off, then he grabbed his red leatherbound book filled with the addresses of old boys and other masters. Many entries had a diagonal through them and were marked RIP. There was only a handful of women's names.

He was half an hour late back at the Coach House. His steak pie had dried in the oven; Dulcie, expecting a goodnight kiss, had refused to go to bed. Ian and Patience were in their coats, waiting to go out.

'What's the point of a tagging system if you bloody well ignore it?' yelled Ian. 'Alex has been on, demanding where you are. It's Patience and I who get it in the neck. Have you no consideration? What the hell have you been doing?'

'Looking for my real parents,' shouted Paris, running upstairs and slamming the door.

*   *   *

The following evening, Cosmo rang Dora in triumph. He had had a brilliant first day at S and C.

'I found several references to BC at the Green Dragon and other places. It must be some kind of club. The one on the twenty-seventh of August seems to be definitely celebrating Randal finally buying Larks. They had another get-together the day Hengist was arrested. They've obviously been trying to get their hands on the Larks land for ages. There was an email from Ashton to Rod Hyde way back in November 2002 saying—listen to this: "Despite all our efforts, Janna Curtis is not failing as expected. We must also watch our step, as she is accusing us of rigging figures and results and changing boundaries and bus stops." '

There was a pause.

'Have you heard a word I said, Dora?'

Dora, who'd been holding her breath like a baby, gave an almighty bellow.

'What in hell's the matter?'

'Paris has run away. He left an envelope with twenty-five pounds in to pay Ian back for not getting history. Then he said he was sorry for all

502

the misery he'd caused and not to try and find him. And worst of all, there was no Hengist to give him a can of Coke and some sandwiches for the journey.' Dora bawled even louder.

'What an applause junky. Can't bear to be out of the limelight for a second,' sighed Cosmo, then, in a kinder voice: 'He'll come back when he's cold and hungry.'

*   *   *

Alex immediately alerted the police and the social services and, while blaming the whole experiment on Hengist, was desperate for Paris's return. The last thing he'd wanted was a crisis distracting either the governors when they met next week, or the media when they should be concentrating on the Queen's visit.

The police were very reassuring. Lads often ran away after a family row. At least he'd left a note; he'd probably be home in the morning.

But Paris did not come home. As the days crawled by, Ian and Patience sank into blacker despair. Patience wouldn't leave the house in case he returned. Dora kept bunking off classes and at night, combing the woods with Northcliffe and Cadbury.

'Where's Pawis?' cried Dulcie over and over again.

Ian couldn't concentrate on anything. How could he have shouted at Paris on that last evening? Taking a wireless into the bursar's office, he listened to every bulletin until Alex grew very sharp with him.

'It's only a foster child, after all.'

503

Pleading for help, Dora rang all her media contacts, who wanted to know if Paris was having woman trouble.

'Are you his girlfriend, Dora?'

'No, but I'd like to be. He's so beautiful, I'm sure he's been kidnapped.'

*   *   *

'We just want him home and safe,' Ian and Patience told the press.

'He might go to Feral or Emlyn,' suggested Dora. 'If he'd known where Theo was, he'd have gone to him.'

'We've checked Theo Graham,' said Chief Inspector Gablecross, 'but there's no sign.'

'And he can't go to Hengist,' sobbed Dora, 'because he's in prison.'

*   *   *

Sally felt desperately guilty. She never should have slept with Paris. They hadn't again, but he'd been so adorable, popping in most days, holding her in his arms and sending her praise postcards. Calling on the Old Coach House, Sally found Patience mucking out the horses, her mobile in the breast pocket of her tweed coat. Her face was utterly devastated by tears, her eyes huge purple craters.

'Oh Sally, we tried so hard not to crowd him; now we realize how desperately we love him. It's all our fault. Paris's last words to us were that he was going to find his real parents. Ian thought he was just trying to hurt us. We should have stayed in, but Poppet was holding some awful parenting workshop, and we felt we should go to gain brownie points.'

Patience collapsed sobbing on a hay bale.

*   *   *

Over at Wilmington, Janna had been equally devastated, not least by Hengist's arrest. Jubilee Cottage was on the market, the 'For Sale' sign creaking desolate in the east wind. As a hair shirt and to pay the mortgage, she was filling in for a head of English on maternity leave in the next county, which meant an hour's drive there and back every day, leaving poor bewildered Partner alone in the house, ripping up carpets, scrabbling at doors and biting the ankles of estate agents, who showed fewer and fewer people over the house.

Patience had called to tell her Paris had bolted.

'He so admired you, Janna. He might easily turn up.'

'Oh God, I probably won't be here, I'm working miles away and such long hours.'

'Poor Paris was devastated about Theo and Hengist. Alex is being such a brute turfing Sally out in November. She's just been here. Paris found out Ian and Artie were under threat too, poor boy. He must have felt all his security crumbling.'

As Janna switched off the telephone, she wondered if she ought to stay home, just in case Paris did turn up.

He loved me once, Atthis, long ago.

In need of comfort and the comfort of comforting, Janna rang Sally and thought she'd got the wrong number when the call was answered by a deep, lilting, utterly unforgettable voice that set

505

her heart crashing.

'Emlyn. I must have misdialled. I wanted Sally.'

'I've just driven down to see her.'

There was an interminable pause.

Oh Christ, she'd craved the sound of that voice for the longest four months of her life, now she couldn't think of anything to say.

'How's the Welsh Rugby Union?'

'Fine.'

There was another long pause.

'Emlyn, I wrote to Sally about Hengist. How is she?'

'Not great.'

He was making no effort. He was still angry with her.

'Sally didn't write back and she's usually so punctilious. Is she OK?' Janna was so frantic to see Emlyn, she added, 'Shall I pop round?'

'I wouldn't. That bastard Randal told her Hengist was having an affaire with Ruth.'

'Oh no!'

'Randal was trying to pull Sally; then he told her about Hengist and you. Paris, caught off guard, confirmed it.'

Janna gave a wail of anguish.

'I can't bear it, poor Sally. Oh my God, I'm sorry. But it was over months ago.'

'Was it?' said Emlyn bleakly.

'Truly, truly, when I found out about him and Ruth, when you marked my stupid suicide note. Oh, please tell Sally she's the only person he's ever loved.'

'I'm sure she'll find it a great comfort,' said Emlyn acidly. 'I've gotta go.'

'Please, please don't.'

506

But he'd hung up.

Sobbing wildly, Janna drove over to Bagley and parked in the hedgerow at the bottom of the drive.

After an hour, listening to the screech owls and watching the moon rise through the mist, she heard the familiar racket of Emlyn's Renault, careering and bumping down the drive. She prayed he'd turn left towards Wilmington, but she only caught a glimpse of his thick blond hair before, with a screech of tyres, he hurtled right towards Wales.

*   *   *

Patience and Ian sank deeper and deeper into despair. They had never known there were a hundred hours between each tick of the clock, and no sleep in the night, as a day became a week. There was no trace anywhere of Paris.

The police, by the increasing gravity of their demeanour, clearly felt something must have happened to him and suggested Ian and Patience appealed to the public for information at a press conference. This was absolutely packed out—the Arctic Prince being an on-going story.

The Cartwrights tried to be very stiff-upper-lipped, but they looked dreadful, hollow-eyed, trembling, their clothes falling off them and when Patience had to speak, she broke down.

'Honking away like a red-nosed reindeer,' shuddered Cosmo who was watching with Painswick and Jessica on the portable in the general office. 'Not much incentive to return.'

'We love him so much,' brayed Patience, her blotched face collapsing. 'We just want him to come home and know he's safe.'

'For God's sake, pull yourself together, woman,' hissed Ian.

'We were fostering him, but we wanted to adopt him,' struggled on Patience, 'if he'd have liked it, that is, but we never told him, we were so frightened of being pushy. We all miss him, particularly our little granddaughter Dulcie and Northcliffe our dog, who just sit waiting by the front door. Paris is such a super chap.'

'Cringe-making,' drawled Cosmo.

'Oh, shut up,' said Jessica and Painswick, who were both in tears.

After Ian and Patience, Nadine was interviewed and very indiscreetly confessed that she blamed herself: 'The placement was too middle class and Mr and Mrs Cartwright were too elderly to foster a teenage boy.'

126

When Hengist resigned so suddenly, Jupiter Belvedon, as chairman, had telephoned the rest of the governors and suggested they invite David Hawkley to attend the next meeting, to advise them on steadying the ship. This was agreed to be an excellent idea, particularly since Lord Hawkley was leaving Fleetley, and as he'd been touring schools with the Great and the Good looking for a Head of the Year for the Teaching Awards, he would have many fresh ideas.

It was also agreed that as the Queen's visit was so imminent, it would be better to have a holding meeting beforehand to discuss logistics and mull over possible candidates to take over as head, then schedule a second meeting shortly after Her Majesty's visit, when they could have a jolly post-mortem and probably confirm a shortlist for the new head.

The only person deeply displeased by this development was Alex, who wanted the matter sewn up. Gathering allies, he suggested that a previous winner of Head of the Year at the Teaching Awards, Rod Hyde of St Jimmy's, should be invited to join the meeting as an impartial adviser, as well as Joan Johnson, the favoured candidate for deputy head; also that to discuss arrangements for the Queen's visit Randal should be brought in at half-time.

As none of these three would be able to vote for anything, Jupiter and the board agreed.

The governors had all loved Hengist and were very upset by his departure. Meetings in his day had been held in London over an excellent dinner at Boodle's, or at Bagley after a luscious lunch laid on by Sally with plenty to drink. Alex intended to scrap both these procedures. They were expensive, and people couldn't think straight if they were drunk.

Poppet, however, didn't want her hospitality to compare unfavourably with Sally's, and before the meeting, which was held at three o'clock on the fourth Friday in October, laid on a light buffet and soft drinks.

As a result, General Broadstairs, the Lord Lieutenant, who'd been up since five cub hunting and was absolutely starving, helped himself to most of Poppet's quiche, imagining it was a first course, which left cheese and cress sandwiches, plain yoghurts and figs for everyone else.

Jupiter retreated to a corner with David Hawkley:

'Any more thoughts on joining us on Education?'

'I'm sixty-five,' said David firmly, 'much too old for politics and about to retire.'

'Can you resist a chance to play God with the education of this country's children? Greek and Latin in every primary school?'

They were distracted by Poppet, bringing in and insisting on breastfeeding nineteen-month-old Gandhi.

'At least the lucky little sod's got a drink,' grumbled Jupiter as, hungry, resentful and very sober, the governors filed into the boardroom next door.

Here they were further distressed to find a less faded square on the magenta damask walls, between the portraits of General Bagley and

Sabine Bottomley. This, at the last meeting, had been inhabited by Jonathan Belvedon's lovely, smiling portrait of Hengist, with his hand on Elaine's head and Sally's photograph on the bookshelf behind him.

'Beautiful picture. Hope it's been given to Sally,' chuntered the Lord Lieutenant.

Alex smiled thinly. Having learnt Jonathan's portraits went for over two hundred thousand pounds on the open market, a discreet sale could buy a lot more IT equipment.

Outside in the park, leaves were drifting downwards in free- fall. Jupiter sat at one end of the long polished table, with David Hawkley on his left and the Bishop on his right. Alex sat at the other end flanked by Joan and Rod Hyde, rigid with disapproval to be among the governing body of an independent school.

Miss Painswick, a box of Kleenex beside her, was taking the minutes and tearfully assuring Ruth Walton there was no news yet of Paris.

The Bishop kicked off with prayers, including one for Paris's safe return, then, when everyone was seated, added: 'I'd like to express the governors' universal regret at the departure of Hengist Brett-Taylor. We've all enjoyed Hengist's friendship and marvellous hospitality and felt privileged to be part of an exciting adventure in turning Bagley into a great school. The lapse that toppled him was regrettable, but understandable.'

'Hear, hear,' said everyone but Alex and Rod and Joan.

The first item on the agenda was the appointment of a new head.

'I'd like to stick my neck out,' said Joan bravely,

511

'and say that Alex has been virtually running the school for the past three years.'

Jupiter gave her a glare which said, 'You're a new girl so shut up,' and announced that it was essential to look at outside candidates.

'We always have. Several were being considered when it was rumoured that Hengist was taking over Fleetley on Lord Hawkley's retirement'—he smiled at David—'and I think we should follow these through. Not that I don't think Alex is doing an excellent job.'

'Then appoint him as head,' urged Rod Hyde. 'Schools should not be allowed to drift. A strong hand on the tiller.'

'I suggest we need more time before making a decision,' said the Lord Lieutenant, thinking what a damned attractive woman Ruth Walton was and the more meetings the better.

Ruth, in turn, was thinking that David Hawkley was utterly divine: strong, macho, brilliant and so gravely good-looking. Taking off her suit jacket, she breathed in deeply.

Alex then said he didn't wish to speak ill of the departed, but he did feel Bagley should be run more economically. So much of the land wasn't being utilized; so many bursaries had been offered to foreign pupils, particularly if the mother was, er, good-looking.

'And talking of good-looking women,' butted in the Lord Lieutenant, 'what about Sally Brett-Taylor, to whom we're all devoted? She should be allowed to stay in Head House till she finds somewhere suitable to live.'

'Hear, hear,' said all the governors, except Alex and his allies.

512

'Surely she could be lent one of the cottages off the campus,' suggested Rod Hyde, 'then Alex and Poppet, whom I see as the ideal couple to run Bagley Hall, could take over Head House immediately. It's hard even for acting heads to be constantly reminded of unfortunate past regimes. It divides loyalties.'

'I agree with Rod,' said Joan. 'Head House is a symbol of authority. The school needs strong management at once, particularly during the Queen's visit.'

Outside the window, Jupiter could see his sister Dora and Bianca Campbell-Black marching up and down brandishing placards saying: 'Bring back Hengist Brett-Taylor'.

Marching the other way, with a four-foot penis destined for the body parts zone of the Science Emporium balanced on his shoulder like a musket, came a grinning Stancombe workman, reducing Bianca and even a tear-stained Dora to fits of giggles.

'Let's leave this decision until after the Queen's visit,' said Jupiter.

One of the school cooks then came in with tea and biscuits, on which everyone fell.

Stirring Sweetex into his cup, feeling he wasn't making sufficient headway, Alex said, 'Before Randal arrives to brief us, I would like to raise the matter of Theo Graham, whose case is due to come up next month.'

'I hoped the police were dropping the charges,' said David Hawkley quickly.

'The evidence is so overwhelming. It really pains me to do this,' lied Alex, 'but you should look at these.' Walking down the table, he placed copies of

513

the poems and the photographs of Paris in front of Jupiter. 'The DVD of young boys of such a distressingly pornographic nature is still with the police.'

David Hawkley read one poem, then another and another, the hair lifting on the back of his neck. They were exquisite.

'Theo and I were at Cambridge together,' he said coldly. 'He is a man of utter integrity. I cannot believe he would ever touch a boy.'

'His base nature clearly overcame him,' intoned Rod.

'My problem'—Alex had returned to his seat—'is whether to look for a new head of classics. A Mr Margolis is filling in for Theo, but my inclination would be to phase out the dead languages at Bagley.'

'You what?' thundered David Hawkley.

'Whatever the outcome of the case,' Alex battled on, 'if we let Theo back into school, the no-smoke-without-fire brigade would never let up. Theo's only two or three years off retirement. With a small pay-off, he could enjoy exit with dignity.'

'Theo is one of the greatest classical scholars of his age,' said an outraged David. 'If there's any further chance for your scholars to be taught by him, they should take it.'

'I agree with Alex,' butted in Rod Hyde, taking two more biscuits. 'Mud sticks. Bagley has had such appalling press recently, they must prove they're serious about rooting out corruption.'

'Almost all the boys in Theo's house have been dispersed, anyway,' Joan joined in the attack.

'Not quite all of them,' said a voice, and in walked Paris.

514

In one hand he was carrying a dark blue carrier bag patterned with gold Roman emperors, in the other a furiously leaping and mewing cat basket.

What a beautiful boy, thought David. Adonis bathed in moonlight. He'd never seen anyone so pale.

Miss Painswick dropped her shorthand notebook and burst into noisy sobs. 'Oh Paris, thank God you're safe.'

'Where the hell have you been?' Alex had gone as magenta as the wallpaper. 'The entire country's looking for you. How dare you vanish like that and then barge in here? Go to my office at once. I'll deal with you later.'

'You'll deal with me now,' said Paris coolly.

'Show some manners to your headmaster,' bellowed Rod Hyde.

'Deputy head,' countered Paris. 'I've come to talk about Theo.'

'This is not the time,' screeched Alex, 'and don't let that cat out.'

But Paris had opened the basket.

'He'll pee everywhere.' Jupiter snatched up his papers in alarm.

'No, he won't, I gave him a run five minutes ago.'

Everyone watched mesmerized as Hindsight landed on the table with a thud. The Bishop proceeded to pour some milk into a saucer and was delighted when Hindsight padded over and drank the lot.

'What a fine cat. Must have been thirsty.'

'Like most of us earlier,' giggled Ruth Walton. 'It's a lovely cat.'

Alex had had enough. Marching down the table, he grabbed Paris's arm. 'Get that cat and yourself

515

out of here, at once.'

'I want to talk about Theo,' persisted Paris, prising off Alex's skinny fingers.

'As one person who has never given an account of that night,' said Jupiter, 'Paris is a crucial witness and should be heard.'

'Hear, hear,' piped up Miss Painswick, receiving a daggers look from Alex.

'This is Theo's cat,' said Paris, running his finger round and round Hindsight's plumey tail. 'He'd be an even better witness.' Then, out of the Roman-emperor-patterned bag, he produced an ivy-green leather folder filled with manuscript paper. 'Which one of you's Lord Hawkley?'

'I am.'

Paris flushed. 'Your translations of Catullus and Ovid are really cool.'

'Thank you.' David's hatchet face softened fractionally.

'Theo asked me to give you this with his love. It's Sophocles,' said Paris. 'Much better than your rotten *Guide to Red Tape*,' he added over his shoulder.

'Sophocles.' David was down the table in a flash, grabbing the folder, opening it, stopping to read bits in wonder, then flipping through to the end. 'My God, he finished it.'

'All seven plays, the night before last,' said Paris. 'I wrote out the final pages for him.'

'You were ordered not to contact Theo Graham.' Alex was spluttering, hysterical, impotent with rage. 'How dare you? This could compromise his trial.'

'Theo's dead,' said Paris flatly, seeing a flare of relief in Alex's eyes. 'He died yesterday in my

516

arms.' Then, turning like a viper on Rod: 'Make something of that, you prurient bastard.'

The Bishop crossed himself. 'Took his own life.'

'Not at all, he had an inoperable tumour on his spine, claimed it came from being stabbed in the back so often.' There was only the slightest quiver in Paris's voice. 'He's been on morphine for weeks. Dr Benson's been looking after him. He drove up to Windermere this morning and signed the death certificate. He gave me a lift here.'

'I'm very sorry,' said a shaken Ruth Walton. 'Milly was devoted to Theo.'

David Hawkley put down Sophocles, a tear running down his cheek.

'How did you know where I was, Paris?'

'I rang Fleetley. They said you were here.'

'Why didn't the police find you at Windermere?' demanded Joan.

'They were evidently sniffing around last week. I only found him on Monday. At least we had three days together. Merciful death came at last,' he said carefully, 'and a dead man knows no pain.'

Hindsight, ready to witness more drama, settled himself, purring loudly, on the Bishop's knee. Paris strolled back to Alex and stood over him. 'You broke Theo's heart,' he said softly. 'He loved Bagley and his archives. They were his life, but he knew once Hengist had resigned, you'd never let him back.'

'You were told not to go near him,' repeated Alex, clearly jolted. 'Where did you get his address?'

'From Biffo's phone book. Poor old bugger was drunk with despair that even though he'd helped you get rid of Theo, you were still going to dump

517

him: "Biffo, you're not cutting it any more." The sudden mimicry of Alex's reedy whine was so exact, the governors shivered.

'At least Biffo had the decency to make sure Hindsight was safely delivered to Theo's door in Windermere in July,' Paris told Alex contemptuously. 'You'd have put him down.'

'That is quite enough on the subject,' boomed Joan.

'I loved Theo,' said Paris softly and defiantly. ' "Forty thousand brothers Could not, with all their quantity of love, Make up my sum." '

Glancing across the table at Alex, Rod nodded knowingly.

'I know about shirt-lifters and bum bandits!' Paris snarled at them. 'Since I was three, I've defended my ass in children's homes and foster homes all round the country.'

God he's wonderful, thought Mrs Walton as Hindsight, finding the Bishop's knees a trifle bony, settled on her bosom to get a better view all round.

'Theo never laid a finger on me.' Paris's voice trembled. 'The only thing he touched was my heart. He opened my mind; he shared things with me. Yes, I loved him, but not in the way you stinking pervs would understand. The night before the second history paper, I had a nightmare. I woke and found a man in my room, and screamed until I realized it was Theo; he was just turning off my bedside light and putting my books away. He calmed me down. I was so knackered cramming for history, in which I was so desperate to please Hengist, I fell back asleep at once.'

'What about the photographs?'

'They must have been taken on the geography

518

field trip. Look at my hair now.' He shook his head so it flopped over his face.

'And the poems?' David handed them to Paris, who took a minute or so to translate the first one.

'I've never seen it before; it's beautiful.' For a moment he seemed about to lose it. 'It's a privilege to have inspired such love.'

No wonder Hengist cheated for him, thought David.

'Last night, after Theo'd died'—Paris had regained control of himself—'I went outside. It had been grey and windy all day, but suddenly every star in heaven was out: Pegasus and Aldebaran, the Pole Star and the Great Bear, who Theo told me was once Callisto. They'd all come out to welcome a new star to heaven. I felt happy he'd got a lot of fans up there.'

Paris slumped against the wall, his face in his hands. Miss Painswick and the Bishop blew their noses. Everyone jumped at the sound of slow clapping as Cosmo sauntered in.

'Very good, Paris, you should really go on the stage.'

'Get out,' howled Alex.

'This is a private meeting,' said Jupiter icily.

Ignoring them both, Cosmo helped himself to a biscuit and, murmuring, 'Hello Hindsight,' stroked the cat and briefly the splendid bosom of Mrs Walton, who had earlier tipped him off that Theo's future was on the agenda.

'I shopped Theo,' he told the flabbergasted company, 'because I was jealous of Paris. Artie, Hengist, Theo, Sally, the bursar, even Emlyn were always fussing over him. I took and then put the nude photos under the lining paper of Theo's desk.

519

I made out to Alex, who doesn't read Greek, that the poems were much dirtier. Theo asked me to get his DVD machine working, so I shoved in a pornographic DVD for a joke. When I heard screaming coming from Paris's bedroom and Theo came out, it seemed the perfect opportunity.'

'This is disgraceful,' thundered David Hawkley, who, being married to the widow of Cosmo's father, the late Roberto Rannaldini, was aware of Cosmo's capacity for transgression.

'It is,' agreed Cosmo soulfully. 'In fact, I was so ashamed when it all backfired, I confessed to Mr Bruce what I'd done and he simply wouldn't believe me, because he wanted Theo and Hengist out so badly. He's keener on new blood than Dracula. There won't be a master left at Bagley, at this rate.' He smiled lovingly at Mrs Walton.

Alex was quivering with rage:

'How dare you tell such lies!'

The governors were clearly astounded. Even Jupiter looked shocked. And where does that put my deputy headship? wondered Joan.

'You can both get out,' said Jupiter.

At that moment, Miss Painswick's assistant, the comely Jessica, knocked on the door. 'Mr Stancombe's downstairs.'

Aware he'd put in a dud performance, Alex ordered Jessica to show Randal up at once, so they could regain the ascendancy, revealing the mysteries of the Science Emporium.

The governors, however, needed a few more minutes to decide whether Cosmo was telling the truth about Theo.

'Cosmo Rannaldini is a compulsive liar,' spluttered Alex. 'Any of my colleagues will bear this out. Theo is past history. Bagley must move on.'

'I think this whole affair'd better be set aside for reflection until after Her Majesty's visit,' said Jupiter.

Joan, who was watching Paris with difficulty shoving Hindsight back in the cat basket, decided to seize the initiative.

'Where are you going, Paris? Someone must alert the authorities that you're back. Have you any idea how much police time you've wasted? What the dickens d'you think you've been doing?'

'Finding my real parents,' snapped Paris.

*   *   *

On the Mansion steps, he and Cosmo faced each other.

'Plans are afoot to oust Mr Fussy,' said Cosmo. 'I'm doing work experience at S and C this week to get dirt on him.'

Then there was a long pause as a workman passed them in the half-light, buckling under a huge gall bladder.

'Thank you for rescuing Theo's reputation,' said Paris softly, 'and that's for fucking it up in the first place,' and he hit Cosmo down the steps, before gathering up Hindsight and disappearing into the October gloom.

127

Over at the stables, Patience took the thousandth call from an increasingly frantic Dora.

'I'm so sorry, nothing I'm afraid. The police still think something might come out of our television interview. I'll ring you the moment we hear anything, and, darling, it's getting dark, don't go looking in the woods, it's not safe with just Cadbury.'

'Where's Paris?' wailed Dulcie, who was staying the night.

Patience had even greater cause for anguish. If the governors rubber-stamped Alex as head at today's meeting, she and Ian would be out of the Old Coach House by Christmas—so there would be nowhere for Paris to come home to.

A fatalistic Ian had left the office when Painswick went in to take the minutes and, in anticipation of their departure, was mindlessly sorting out drawers in the sitting room. He had discovered one of Paris's notebooks. On the first page the boy had scribbled 'Paris Cartwright' over and over again, then the initials PC, then 'politically correct', then 'Mr Wright', 'Mr Wrong', 'Paris always Wrong'. Then 'Dora Cartwright', then 'Paris Alvaston Cartwright' over and over. Out of the middle pages fluttered a picture of Theo and a piece of paper with a blob, coloured olive green, turquoise, royal blue and shaped like a peacock's feather. Perhaps there had been something between him and Theo.

Overwhelmed with despair and longing, Ian gave a sob. If only he'd been more demonstrative towards the boy. Next moment, the notebook crashed to the floor as Paris walked in, ducking nervously as though expecting blows and recriminations.

Ian just took his hand and shut his eyes for a moment, then he mumbled, 'It's very, very good to see you, Paris.'

'You're out of logs, I'll get some.'

'Would you like a gin and tonic?'

'Yes, please.'

How sweet-faced the boy was, even though he looked as if he'd been sleeping rough, and had lost a hell of a lot of weight.

By the time Paris struggled back with the logs, Patience had been alerted and came galumphing downstairs.

'Oh Paris, how lovely to see you, we've missed you.'

She longed to hug him. Little Dulcie, who came rushing in in her blue pyjamas, had no such reserve and hurled herself into Paris's arms with screams of joy. Paris hugged her back, colour suffusing his shadowed face. A minute later Northcliffe bounded in, singing at the top of his voice, dragging one of Patience's huge bras like a mini Himalayas.

'The mountains have truly come to Mahomet,' observed Ian. 'I'll get some ice.'

Outside, he made a discreet telephone call.

'It's OK, Sally, he's home.' Then, not knowing the permutations: 'Could you let Janna know? And Feral too, if you get a moment.'

If only he could ring Hengist in prison.

After that, they didn't leave Paris for a second, fearful he'd vanish. Paris couldn't stop yawning.

'Your bed's made up,' stammered Patience, 'if you'd like to spend the night.'

'Please,' said Paris. 'There just one problem.' Patience's heart stopped. 'I acquired a cat on my travels; he's outside.'

Patience laughed in relief.

'That's wonderful, we've got far too many mice and Northcliffe loves cats.'

They were just feeding Hindsight a tin of tuna when Dora rang.

'Bloody cow, bloody tagging system, Joan won't let me out. Is he really back?'

'Have a word,' said Patience, going off to fill a hot-water bottle. Paris was already in bed when she knocked on the door, an equally weary Hindsight curled into the back of his legs.

'I'm really sorry,' he said. 'Until I saw you and Ian on TV, I didn't realize.'

Patience sat down on the bed and took his hand.

'Doesn't matter; you're home. Ian is so pleased. He just loves having another chap around the house.' She tucked the hot-water bottle in beside him. 'Sorry there aren't any flowers.'

'That's OK—flowers are for guests. What really pissed me off was Nadine saying we were wrong for each other. You know I said that about running away to find my real mother and father?'

Patience nodded, quite unable to speak.

'Well'—Paris's hand tightened on hers—'I guess being away taught me, if it's all right with you, that I did find them—that you and Ian *are* my real parents.'

Patience still couldn't speak, but she nodded frantically.

'I don't need to call you Mum and Dad, I'm just

524

grateful I've found people I love, who, however horrible I am, seem to love me, so I can start again.'

'Oh, Paris.'

A tear splashed on to his hand.

Paris's eyelids were drooping.

'You're tired, shall I read to you?'

Paris nodded, but still clung to her hand.

Taking down Hans Andersen's fairy tales, Patience turned to 'The Snow Queen', and began: ' "Attend! We are now at the beginning. When we get to the end of our story, we shall know more than we do now," ' but by the time she'd finished the first paragraph, Paris was asleep.

128

It was time for the high noon of the school year, the National Teaching Awards, in which hundreds of teachers, including all the regional winners and their partners, are invited for a splendid weekend in London. Activities included a grand ball on Saturday night, seminars, and sightseeing. The climax, however, was the televising of the national winners receiving their awards at the Palace Theatre on Sunday afternoon, followed by a riotous party and no teaching the following week, because it was half-term.

The winners in the ten different categories had been originally nominated by two members of their school community. Their schools were then visited by regional judges and later by a team of national judges, amongst whom was Lord Hawkley.

'The Awards are an amazing celebration of teaching,' he told the *Observer*, 'although, of the six hundred people crammed into the Palace Theatre on Sunday, I will be one of the only public-school voices. No member of an independent has ever won an award.'

This year Alex Bruce, because of his clean-out at Bagley and his brilliant (except for Lando and Jack) science results and, of course, his *Guide to Red Tape*, was hoping to be the first. Rod Hyde, who'd formerly won Head of the Year, was hoping to score again.

A thousand years ago, it seemed, when Janna had been teaching English at Redfords, Stew Wilby had talked about putting her forward for an award.

Now it would never happen. She no longer had a school to nominate her.

It was half-term Sunday, and she had reached rock bottom. The head of English on maternity leave for whom Janna was covering had brought in her adorable baby last week, and Janna had been overwhelmed with despair that she would never have Emlyn and his babies and the family life for which she so desperately longed.

In a bleak week, Stancombe, after a few hiccups—like the Brigadier pointing out the presence of fritillaries and natterjack toads in the grounds—had obtained a compulsory purchase order on both Larks buildings, to make way for—he'd finally come clean—a supermarket development.

The *Sunday Express* had rung for Janna's comments:

'Why don't you write us a piece about your battle to save Larks?'

'And call it Tesco of the D'Urbervilles,' screamed Janna.

She had been to the gym earlier, pounding out her hatred of Randal and Ashton on the machines. She ought to spend the rest of the day painting the kitchen some enticing pastel shade, as no buyer had yet come forward. Instead, she turned listlessly to the lonely hearts ads in the *TES*.

'Beautiful female,' she read, 'thirty, five foot seven, slim, brown hair, green eyes, enjoys long walks, reading, keeping fit, good wine.'

How bloody conceited to describe oneself as 'beautiful'.

'Eighteen-year-old woman, enjoys power boating, weightlifting, GSOH,' said the next ad, 'seeks female for friendship, possibly more.'

Janna supposed GSOH stood for good sense of humour—that was bloody conceited too.

How would she advertise herself? she wondered.

'Titchy carrot-haired loudmouth, failed head, near alkie, lousy SOH, seeks'—Oh God—'Emlyn Davies for infinitely more than friendship.'

The Brigadier was revving up for his new series bringing epic poems to life. He and Lily were so dottily in love, Janna didn't want to be a dampener, and it was almost a relief they were in Rome recceing the first programme about Horatius keeping the bridge.

Still fatally drawn to Larks, Janna decided to go for a walk there and see the trees, probably for the last time. At least on a Sunday afternoon the bulldozers would be still.

Leaping out of the car, Partner immediately found a stick three times as big as himself and kept tripping over molehills as he lugged it round. The place looked desolate: great craters filled with rain, huge trees knocked over, bottles rammed into the tennis-court wire, the bird table still on its side in the playground. Catching sight of her, a robin shot forward hopefully.

The door to Appletree was open. As she wandered the corridors, she could hear the ghost voices of children. On the staff room wall, someone had scribbled: 'School's out for summer.' Underneath someone else had written: 'School's out for ever.'

'You will go through a time when everything hurts,' murmured Janna.

Still trying to negotiate his huge stick through the doorways, Partner dropped it and went into a

528

flurry of barking, then scampered on ahead. Following him into the gym, Janna discovered the back view of a blond man in a navy blue jersey, so tall he could gaze out of the high window at the town. His hands were shoved deep into the pockets of his dark grey trousers, showing off a high, tight, beautiful bottom.

Janna lost her temper. 'Stop gloating, you bloody developer,' she shouted, then, as he turned round, she gasped, 'Emlyn!'

'I thought I'd find you here. Hello, boyo.' He stooped to gather up Partner, who, squeaking with delight, frantically licked his square blushing face, giving both humans a moment to collect themselves.

'I've got an invite for two for the Teaching Awards,' Emlyn said ultra-casually. 'Wondered if you'd like to come. We'd be home by ten. Artie, as well as Alex, has been nominated for an award. The first independent teachers ever.'

In panic, Janna grabbed back Partner. 'I can't leave him. He's terribly depressed. I have to abandon him during the day; Lily and the Brigadier are away.'

'They're back,' said Emlyn. 'They said they'd love to dogsit.'

Janna was confused. When they'd last spoken, Emlyn had been so antagonistic.

'I've got too much to do. I've got to paint the kitchen.'

'Paint the town red instead. It's a grand do.'

Then she noticed he was wearing a white frilled evening shirt under his blue jersey.

'This is a set-up.'

'Sure it is.' The warm, wide, unrepentant smile

529

transformed his square, heavy face. 'Pearl's even waiting at home to do your make-up.'

After a lot of persuading, Janna went back and changed into the bronze-speckled Little Mermaid dress she'd worn to the geography field trip party in Wales. Full of chat, Pearl was determined to make Janna look beautiful rather than outlandish and straightened her hair so it fell in a sleek russet cascade to her collar bones.

'Knowing what a blubber you are, I'm not giving you any mascara on your lower lashes. Emlyn says it's a box-of-tissues evening, miss.' Then, as Janna pestered her for news of the children: 'Feral got two goals for the Rovers yesterday; Johnnie and Kitten have split up again; Kylie's up the duff again—no, maybe she ain't.'

The Brigadier and the new Mrs Woodford applauded when Janna came downstairs wrapped in her bracken-brown pashmina.

'What an incredibly pretty girl you are,' said Lily. 'Don't worry about Partner, he can have the extra piece of steak I'd bought in case you felt like having supper with us.'

'Here's a little something for the journey,' said the Brigadier, handing Janna a silver flask of vodka and tonic.

The sky was brilliant blue and the sun set behind them like a huge blood orange. Torrential rain nearly turned them back at Windsor. Emlyn wanted an update on the Larks children and regaled her with Bagley gossip gleaned from Artie. Poor Dora was evidently outraged because her bitch of a mother had had even poor Cadbury castrated. Cosmo, on the other hand, had been delighted to receive a red Ferrari for his GCSE

530

results.

Emlyn's muddy Renault Estate as usual looked as though he lived in it. Books, newspapers, CDs, laptops were piled high and amid the chaos were a half-empty crate of beer, a midnight-blue velvet jacket in cellophane back from the cleaner's, clean shirts, new socks and underpants still in their packaging. The Christmas Scottie, she noticed, still bounced from his car keys—probably as a wistful reminder of Oriana.

Janna was even more confused. Why was Emlyn being so nice when he'd been so angry before? She ached to put a hand on his great chunky thigh or stroke his big strong hand on the wheel. He'd lost more weight, was muscled up and was clearly revelling in the new job.

'The boys are beginning to express themselves and play in their Welsh way, lots of attack and guile, and we've got a brilliant new centre called Gavin Henson.'

He even had cautious hopes of the Six Nations in 2005.

'What will it be like tonight?' asked Janna.

'Lots of on-message celebs handing out awards and attributing their entire success to some inspirational teacher; lots of winners attributing their success to everything from the school gerbil to the site manager; constant emphasis on the team effort rather than the individual, belied when rival heads are discovered throttling each other in the bog.' Emlyn's huge shoulders shook with laughter.

In London, the trees had hung on to their leaves; rain-soaked, shining gold, they softened every building.

531

'This city now doth like a garment wear the beauty of the afternoon,' sighed Janna, gazing in vodka-aided ecstasy at the gleaming river beneath glittering bridges and the London Eye, a silver halo tossed aside by some falling angel.

Teachers were decanting from buses and milling round outside the theatre as they arrived.

'Janna Curtis,' cried a pretty blonde, 'you did so well for your Year Elevens. Look, it's Janna, you know, from Larks High,' she called out to her friends, who all gathered round to praise Janna.

'You're much prettier than your picture.' 'Is that your partner?' 'Isn't he lush?' 'You put up such a good fight.'

'They've read every word about me,' squeaked Janna. 'So up yours, Ashton.'

As Emlyn, who'd been shrugging himself into the dark blue velvet jacket, shepherded her firmly through the crowd into the Green Room, large glasses of champagne were thrust into their hands.

'Oh look, there's Ted Wragg, he's so funny.' Janna took a huge gulp. 'And there's Lord Hawkley, and that redhead with him is Rupert's ex-wife. Taggie's much prettier,' she added defensively.

'Better have some blotting paper.' Emlyn beckoned a waitress bearing a basket full of chicken and prawns on long-pointed sticks.

'God, they look delicious'—Janna grabbed four—'and those sticks are perfect for pricking bubbles as a "critical friend"—and talk of the devil, here come Rod and Alex.'

'What's going on in your neck of the woods?' a BBC minion was asking them solicitously.

'The Queen's opening our new Science

Emporium on Wednesday week,' Alex was boasting.

'Goodness, it'll be Sir Alex soon,' said the minion admiringly. 'The other Sir Alex better look to his laurels.'

The smug smile was then wiped off Alex's face. 'What are you doing here, Janna Curtis? You can hardly qualify as a past winner or a nominee this evening.'

'Nominees up, Mother Brown,' sang Janna, doing a little dance. 'I came with Emlyn,' she announced happily, then, thrusting out her glass to a passing waitress, 'I'd love another one.'

The BBC minion, who had shiny dark hair streaked with scarlet and caramel, introduced herself as 'Bea from the Beeb' and said, 'Janna Curtis, I so admire your stand in Larkshire. We're so delighted you could make it.'

'Have you had a great weekend?' asked Janna.

'Amazing! Last night's dance was fabulous, and teachers are such lovely people, so modest and self-effacing; they hate being singled out from their colleagues for praise.'

'Alex and Rod are just like that,' enthused Janna.

Emlyn choked on his drink.

'Although one headmaster,' admitted Bea from the Beeb, 'who didn't win last year, was so furious he had a nervous breakdown.'

'There are the warning bells, we'd better go in,' said Rod frostily.

'Is that gorgeous guy your partner?' whispered Bea.

'I wish,' sighed Janna.

Not wanting to let her spirits droop a millimetre, she managed to secrete a three-quarters-full bottle

533

of champagne under her pashmina as she and Emlyn flowed with the laughing, excited tide into the auditorium.

It was a lovely little theatre, with cherry-red velvet seats and cherry-red boxes, like the drawers Janna hadn't pushed in before she left: those spilling over with rejected clothes, these with teachers, or with technicians manning a huge overhead camera like a pterodactyl to capture the Great and the Good in the audience.

'Oh hell,' said Janna, 'Rod Hyde and his admired wife and Alex and Poppet are just across the aisle.'

Poppet, in an extraordinary white broderie anglaise mob cap and a milkmaid's dress, was flushed with success from delivering her first TROT workshop.

'TROT stands for Total Recognition of Transpersons,' she was eagerly telling the Education Secretary. 'So enriching to exchange views with other caring professionals.'

'Silly bitch,' muttered Janna; then, as a female bruiser in the row in front swung round disapprovingly, 'You could use that one in your back row.'

'Hush, or we'll get thrown out,' warned Emlyn. He caught sight of Janna's bottle: 'What have you got there?'

'Petrol,' said Janna.

Emlyn tried and failed to look reproving.

They were in wonderful seats about ten rows from the front. Technicians, checking camera angles and locating possible winners, scuttled around in pairs, one carrying the camera, the other the wires, as though he was holding up the long tail of a mouse.

534

The beautiful set was hung with panels in Three Wise Men colours: glowing scarlet, amethyst, turquoise, and sapphire blue. A midnight-blue canopy overhead glittered with little stars. On the red and gold podium awaiting the first winner, was one of the awards. Named a Plato, it was a gold curved oblong with one end fashioned into the profile of a Greek god.

'He's got Rupert Campbell-Black's nose,' observed Janna. 'What a lovely party,' she added to Emlyn. 'There's David Miliband. He looks as though he's still in Year Ten.'

Emlyn had temporarily found room for his long legs in the gangway. 'You will tuck them inside when we begin?' begged a returning Bea admiringly.

Emlyn was so broad-shouldered, Janna also found it impossible not to brush against him as he leant in to avoid technicians racing past. There is not room in this theatre, nor in all the world, to contain my love for him, she thought helplessly as she took another slug of champagne.

A handsome organizer was now telling the audience they were here to celebrate excellence in education. 'To ensure maximum media exposure for the profession we all love, we want you to shout and clap as much as possible.'

'Hurrah,' yelled Janna, clapping like mad.

'I've been used and abused by the BBC,' grumbled an old trout in the row behind. 'I will not clap to order.'

There were so many shining bald heads and spectacles in the stalls reflecting the television lights that no other lighting was needed. Gales of hearty laughter, no doubt to show off their GSOH, greeted every joke from the warm-up man.

'All round the theatre, you'll find teachers seated in areas. There's Northern Ireland to the left in the dress circle and Wales over on the right.' Emlyn raised a hand to two young women teachers. 'And right over there are the Larkshire contingent. Look, they're waving at you.'

Janna waved back. 'Where's Yorkshire?'

'In the gallery.'

'Oh my God, there's Stew,' gasped Janna.

'Who?' Emlyn swung round sharply.

'My old boss.' He's put on weight, she thought.

She was brought back to earth by a roll of drums.

'Pray silence for your head boy of the evening,' said a voice, and on came Eamonn Holmes, who, despite a sombre dark suit and red spotted tie, looked, with his sweet little face and naughty grin, much more like the terror of Year Seven.

'Welcome to the Oscars of the teaching profession,' he said, looking round at the audience. 'Now you'll know what it's like to be in assembly.'

'He can't say that,' gasped a hovering BBC minion, 'it'll diminish them.'

'You're not allowed to make jokes about gowns and mortarboards, or about Whacko and canes,' whispered Emlyn.

There was another roll of drums, and actor Bill Nighy ambled somewhat nervously on to the stage to present the award to the Primary Teacher of the Year. As a photograph of him as a dear little boy appeared on the screen above the podium, he talked charmingly and deprecatingly about his school days, then announced the winner, who, from the gasp of joyful surprise, turned out to be a charming brunette sitting in the row opposite

536

Emlyn.

As she ran down the aisle and mounted the steps to the platform, Janna cheered and cheered. The clips of her brilliant rapport with the children were so touching that the tears spilling down Janna's cheeks became a cascade when she glanced sideways and saw the winner's incredibly proud husband also crying his eyes out.

From then onwards, Janna worked her way through her box of tissues and her bottle. All the winners—from Best New Teacher, the Teacher Who Used IT Most Imaginatively, to the Teaching Assistant of the Year—were so brilliant, innovative and imaginative, and the children so sweet, and the celebrities so exciting. Janna loved Sanjeev Bhaskar and had always been a fan of Imogen Stubbs, beautiful, clever, posh, but also a true socialist.

129

Rupert arrived at the Palace Theatre alone and in a foul temper. The last time he could remember being in London on a Sunday, except for the Countryside March, was when he'd taken his ex-wife Helen out on a first date—and look what trouble that had got him into.

He'd only agreed to give away an award because Jupiter had insisted it would be good for his image and that of the New Reform Party to get in with the lefties. Except for Janna and Hengist, who'd both lost their schools, he loathed the teaching profession. They'd been so bloody patronizing about his GCSE and got so uptight if you mentioned their long holidays.

Now, still in his dark blue overcoat so he could make a quick get-away, Rupert stood in the Green Room drinking whisky, watching the whole thing on a monitor and thinking he'd never seen so many ghastly beards in his life, nor so many old boots built like semis in Croydon and with Tim Henman hair. Rupert loathed very short hair on women, even more than beards, particularly when it showed off hulking great necks. Talk about the planet of the napes. Rupert was so fed up, he couldn't be bothered to laugh at his own joke.

He'd been listening to the big match on the car wireless. Feral would shoot himself if Man U broke Arsenal's run of 49 wins. It was a measure of Rupert's increasing fondness for Bianca's boyfriend (whom he'd watched scoring two goals for the Rovers yesterday) that he'd started taking

an interest in soccer as well as English literature—
any minute he'd be taking up Morris dancing.

There in the audience was that stuffed shirt
David Hawkley, married to Helen, stepfather to
Tabitha and Marcus. How small the world was.
Muttering about gravitas, Jupiter was determined
to give Education to David in place of Hengist,
who'd been so much more amusing. Rory Bremner
had done over Jupiter last night—bloody funny.

'Isn't it a fun evening?' Bea from the Beeb broke
into his thoughts with a plate of smoked salmon
sandwiches. 'You should have seen all those major
civil servants, not known for their frivolity, bopping
on the dance floor last night.'

'Letting their lack of hair down,' said Rupert
sourly.

He loathed civil servants even more than
teachers.

On the other hand, the blonde now accepting a
Plato for school and community involvement was
very pretty. He could happily have got involved
with her. Lovely legs too; perhaps teachers weren't
such boots.

*   *   *

Again and again the camera crews ran backwards
down the gangway, as though they were filming
royalty, and the little stars in the indigo firmament
brightened as each winner, the real stars of the
evening, mounted the stage.

'When's Artie going to get his award?' asked
Janna.

'I'm afraid it's gone to that head of science, two
categories back,' whispered Emlyn.

539

'Artie should have won,' protested Janna noisily, and was shushed. As her big gold programme kept sliding off her knees, rather than bury her head in Emlyn's lap when she retrieved it, she leant down to the left, which gave her the chance to take another slug from her bottle.

Emlyn was half laughing, but she wished he'd loosen up and get into party mode. He still seemed tense and watchful as the lights turned his face glowing ruby, then sapphire, then aquamarine, then Lenten purple, each time more gorgeous. I love him, thought Janna helplessly. I just adore him.

'I know it's going to be Rod Hyde,' she cried in despair, then cheered and cheered, because the winner of the Lifetime Achievement Award wasn't Rod, but a darling old duck from a London primary who let the children run all over her office in the lunch hour.

'Please be quiet,' hissed the horrified Number Eight in the row in front.

Janna would have raised two fingers, if Emlyn hadn't held grimly on to her hands.

'You've got to behave yourself.'

'That's it for the evening,' said Janna, then nearly fell off her chair with excitement as a blow-up of a beautiful sulky little boy appeared on the screen, and a grinning Eamonn Holmes announced one last award to be presented by someone often described as 'the handsomest man in England', an owner/trainer, ex-showjumper and Minister for Sport, who'd called himself 'the most immature mature student' when he recently gained a 'B' in GCSE English literature.

And on stalked Rupert to a frenzy of wolf

540

whistles and catcalls. He still had his overcoat on, but smiled slightly when Eamonn asked him the Arsenal/Man U result.

'Rooney scored in extra time,' replied Rupert. 'It's his birthday. He's a Scorpio like me.

'I was so useless at school,' he went on, in his clipped, flat drawl, 'that I normally don't like schoolmasters or -mistresses one bit, but I have to confess, watching the television in the Green Room, I have seen some fantastic examples of teaching that might have galvanized even myself.

'I'm here to hand out a special new award: the People's Prize, to the teacher whom the most pupils, parents, teachers and members of the public all round the country felt had done the best and most heroic job, and in the winner's case, pulled in five times as many votes as the rest put together.

'This was a head who fought against all odds for their school,' went on Rupert, 'and kept it open under remarkable circumstances, who inspired confidence in children who believed they were worthless, who inspired the staff into believing every teacher can teach and every child achieve, and who never gave up on a child.'

Tears rushing down Janna's cheeks took away the rest of Pearl's make-up. 'What a wonderful person she must be,' she murmured and, turning, seeing tears in Emlyn's eyes, added, 'Don't be sad.'

As she stroked his cheek, he trapped her hand.

The cameras were slowly creeping up the aisle.

'And the winner . . .' As, utterly deadpan, Rupert slowly opened the gold envelope, Alex Bruce, halfway out of his seat and deliriously punching the air, was sent flying by the overhead camera.

541

'The winner . . .' repeated Rupert with a triumphant smirk, 'is one of the few schoolmistresses I like: Janna Curtis of Larkminster High School.'

An explosion of cheering rocked the theatre, particularly from the South-West and from Yorkshire up in the gallery.

'I don't believe it,' gasped Janna, turning to a tearful, beaming Emlyn.

'Well done, lovely, you did it, just watch these clips.'

Among the television crews who'd been doorstepping Larks for the past year had been one from the BBC. Now they showed clips of Janna racing round hugging all the team when they beat Bagley at rugby; yelling, 'You're worse looters than the Iraqis,' at Searston Abbey staff when they arrived prematurely to remove earmarked books and computers; crawling across the park, waving branches of swamp cypress, bringing Birnam Wood to Dunsinane; and finally of her praising or comforting her children on Results Day.

Glowing testimonials followed from Stormin' Norman and Chantal Peck, who said Janna was just like a 'Citizen's Advaice Bureau,' and the Mayor of Larkminster, who said she was a 'cracker'. Even the Bishop described her as a 'very live wire'.

Then there were clips from children all round the country who'd followed Larks's progress on the news.

'Janna seems so nice, we'd love to go to her school.'

Finally, Dora appeared saying how much they'd all liked her at Bagley.

542

'I cannot believe this,' muttered Janna as the film came to an end.

'Yes, you can.' Standing up to let her out, Emlyn steadied her, before setting her off on her tottering path.

Utterly shell-shocked and extremely drunk, she staggered up on to the stage, where Rupert caught her, enveloping her for a second inside the blue silk lining of his overcoat.

'Bloody marvellous, darling. Can you manage a few words?'

Turning, Janna reached out for and nearly missed the microphone. Freckles were the only colour in her face. As her speckled Little Mermaid dress, damp with champagne and tears, clung to her, people could see how thin she was.

'It's been a wonderful evening,' she began. 'I've never been so proud of my profession.' Then, pulling her thoughts together: 'I'd like to thank everyone who voted for me, and all the Larks teachers and children who worked so hard, and the parents, and particularly the anonymous donor who gave us a hundred and twenty thousand pounds so we could keep Larks open for another year, although S and C Services and the county council did eff-all to help us,' she added to equal laughter and gasps of disapproval.

'Rather a looshe cannon,' murmured a grinning Rupert, thinking there was something infinitely touching about Janna's little bitten nails clutching the mike.

'And we'd never have done it without the help of the staff and children from Bagley Hall,' she went on defiantly, adding, over a storm of booing, 'particularly without Hengist Brett-Taylor.'

'Hear, hear,' shouted Rupert.

'Cheat!' yelled the audience.

'Hear me out,' yelled back Janna. 'We must stop demonizing the independents as they demonize us. We've got to work together for all children. Hengist gave so many of our pupils a chance. He enabled Paris Alvaston, for example, to learn Latin and Greek. This is a Plato'—she brandished her award—'but how many of you can quote a single line Plato wrote?'

There was a long pause.

'Plato said democracy leads to despotism, which is happening in this country today, when schools are closed down just because the powers-that-be want to make a fat profit selling off the land.'

The horror and alarm on the faces of the majority of the audience turned to sympathy as Janna burst into tears.

'But what does it matter? How can I be a great head if I lost my school? All I want is my children back.'

Emlyn was on his feet about to vault on to the stage. Rupert and Eamonn were moving forward when a dirty violet and yellow football rolled across the stage towards Janna's feet, followed by Cameron Peck, followed by his mother, carrying Ganymede.

'I'm training as a nursery nurse,' Kylie Rose told the audience, 'and taking singing lessons.'

She was followed by Aysha and Xavier, hand in hand, who were going to the same FE college. Graffi, waving a paintbrush, unrolled a scroll showing a draft of the mural he was painting for the long room at Penscombe. Kitten, looking breathtaking, was modelling and back in love with

544

Johnnie, who was working in a racing car garage. Danijela was altering clothes at Harriet's Boutique. Monster had got a job working as a bouncer in a nightclub and, despite Rooney scoring in extra time, a beaming Feral came bouncing on, like Tigger, in Larkminster Rovers orange and black colours, leading a giggling Bianca, who was in turn leading Rocky, who was working on the Penscombe Estate as a chippy, until miraculously, every Larks High pupil was crowding the stage.

Pearl came last strutting around with her royal-blue rooster hair.

'I did Miss's make-up earlier,' she announced, then, turning to Janna: 'Looks as though you could do wiv a touchup, miss. Miss didn't have a clue we was all coming up, or she was getting an award. Mr Davies organized the whole fing. I'm working wiv Trinny and Susannah now, so I get paid for telling people they look gross. And if anyone wants my card . . . ?'

The audience smiled fondly, particularly when Pearl took Janna's hand: 'Larks didn't die, miss. Honest. We just want to say it lives on in us and in all our memories, so thank you for everything you did.'

Great were the cheers and the rejoicing as they were all swept off the stage to make way for Lords Puttnam and Attenborough.

*   *   *

Afterwards it passed in a dream. Dazed and amazed, all Janna wanted to do was get stuck back into the champagne and talk to the children and

545

find out about Graffi's dad and Feral's mum. But once Pearl had redone her face, everyone, particularly the press and the photographers, wanted a piece of her.

Overwhelmingly important at the back of her mind was what was Emlyn's part in it? Had he come over to Larks merely to lure her up to London? Had he persuaded all the children to vote for her because he cared for her or was it the altruism of a colleague wanting justice and recognition for a colleague?

She must ask him. She was just taking another slug of champagne to give herself courage, when Stew, her old head from Redfords, hove into sight and kissed her on both cheeks.

'Well done. I couldn't be more proud. Good, you stuck up for Hengist Brett-Taylor. Nice man, if misguided. I must have trained you jolly well. It's a crime you're doing supply,' he continued, lowering his normally loud commanding voice. 'How'd you like to be deputy head at a city academy I'm taking over in Lancashire?'

'Oh Stew, it's good to see you. You haven't met Emlyn Davies.'

The two men shook hands without enthusiasm.

'You must have been planning this for weeks,' said Stew, then, turning back to Janna: 'Mike Pitts has been telling me that everyone decided Emlyn would be the best person to hijack you, darling.'

Janna was hazily wondering why she loved Rupert calling her 'darling', but bitterly resented it from Stew. He was also too old for that trendy short hair at the front, as though a rat'd been nibbling it all night. Then she looked up at Emlyn, who didn't have a millimetre of meanness or weakness in his big kind face.

'What happened to Artie's award?'

Emlyn looked sheepish. 'I made that bit up.'

She was now seeing him through swirling black clouds.

Next moment Bea from the Beeb was asking, 'Could you bear to have your photograph taken with the rest of the winners?'

'All right, but don't go away,' Janna begged Emlyn. 'I want to ask you something. Oh look, there's David Puttnam, my hero. Oh dear, I don't feel very well.' She suddenly buckled, stumbled and flopped to the ground.

'She's fainted, give her some air,' shouted Stew.

'I think you'll find she's passed out,' said Emlyn. 'I'll take her home.'

Janna's children, quite used to bringing parents back from the pub, hoisted her aloft and carried her out of the theatre.

' "Go, bid the soldiers shoot",' said a grinning Rupert.

'Utterly deplorable,' chuntered the Bruces and Hydes.

'So unnecessary to bring up Hengist. She only won that award because of all the publicity,' grumbled Poppet.

'Shut up, you jealous old bitch,' shouted Aysha to everyone's utter amazement.

*   *   *

Emlyn wrapped Janna in her bracken-brown pashmina and his jacket and drove her back to Larkshire with the winter stars, Castor and Pollux and the big and little Dog Stars, accompanying him

547

all the way home.

Janna was a winter star, he thought wistfully. The darker the night and things had got at Larks, the more brightly and cheerfully she had rallied everyone. She looked about fifteen; occasionally she muttered in her sleep, but as he took her little hand in his, she slept on.

She had been so reluctant to accompany him earlier and so defensive until she got pissed. Was she still keen on that asshole Stew, or on Hengist, whom she'd defended so fiercely this evening?

Using her keys to let himself into her cottage, he put her down in the hall while he switched off the burglar alarm. Next moment Partner hurtled in from next door, but even when he barked joyfully and rushed up and down hurling all his toys in the air, Janna didn't stir.

'I hoped I'd carry you over the threshold a different way,' Emlyn told her as he took off her shoes and put her to bed in her clothes, then, dropping a kiss on her lips and switching off her mobile, he left her Plato in her arms.

130

Janna was woken by *Newsnight* on the landline, congratulating her and asking her to come on the programme that evening. Clutching her head, wincing at white sky glaring through the window, noticing the time, she gave a screech of horror. She'd be fatally late for work.

'Can I call you back?'

But, as she started scrabbling for clean pants and tights, she caught sight of herself still in her bronze speckled party dress and then of the Plato gleaming in the dark folds of the bedspread, and, attempting to piece last night together, she remembered it was half-term.

Having splashed her face with cold water, scraped moss off her tongue and cleaned her teeth, she tottered downstairs. There was no note anywhere. What had been Emlyn's part in all this?

She was simultaneously reassuring Partner she'd feed him in a second and groping for Alka-Seltzer when a hammering on the door made her clutch her head again.

Outside Lily was looking distraught.

'You were wonderful last night, Christian and I were so proud, but, darling, I've done something dreadful.'

'You've never done anything dreadful.'

But Lily, it seemed, had been having a tidy-out, prior to moving into a new house, and had discovered a recorded delivery she'd taken in for Janna two days after the Prom.

'I was so excited to be marrying Christian, I must

have shoved it to one side and forgotten to give it to you.'

'Couldn't matter less. The only thing that matters at the moment is finding the Alka-Seltzer. It's probably a final reminder from the Gas Board . . .' Janna's voice trailed off. 'Goodness, it's Emlyn's writing.'

'Oh dear, that's even worse, I'm so sorry.' Janna hadn't seen Lily so upset since her mower broke down.

'Truly doesn't matter.'

'Come and have a drink at lunchtime and tell us all about the awards.'

'Sure, thanks.' Ripping open the envelope, Janna wandered back into the kitchen.

Darling Janna [she read incredulously]

I'm so sorry I was such a complete shit last night. I lost my temper because I wanted you to myself so badly and quite rightly you put the kids or rather Monster first. You probably won't want to but could we start again? You may be still crazy about Hengist and I had so much to work through with Oriana. But suddenly the prospect of not seeing you every day for the rest of my life fills me with such utter despair. I know you're busy winding up Larks, but why don't you come up to Wales next weekend? My mother longs to meet you, and there's a good head's job coming up in a school near here.

Janna couldn't read any more. She was blushing too much and reeled into the garden, collapsing on to the old garden bench surrounded by rotting apples, oblivious of guzzling wasps wooed out of hiding by such a warm windless day.

Emlyn had written this letter on the day after the prom, recording it to make sure it reached her, and she'd never replied. That's why he'd ducked out of Results Day, been so curt on the telephone when she'd rung him at Sally's and so tense and guarded yesterday.

'The prospect of not seeing you every day for the rest of my life fills me with such utter despair . . .' Oh Emlyn.

It broke her heart to think of him, waiting for the post and by the telephone, convincing himself she didn't care.

Then panic gripped her—perhaps he'd moved on, and found some Blodwyn to love. She didn't remember any emotions betrayed yesterday. He hadn't even bothered to leave a note. Looking up for guidance, she found the glaring white sky dalmatianed with liver spots. Midges shifted around like footballers adjusting before a corner.

She had to call Emlyn at once. Racing into the house, she switched on her mobile, which rang instantly, and she swooned with disappointment to hear a light, patrician, rather patronizing voice. It was Oriana, who'd seen the Teaching Awards.

'Well done getting a Plato, and thank you for sticking up for Dad.'

'Did I?' wondered Janna. The whole thing was such a haze.

'It was very brave of you,' continued Oriana, 'I'm so pleased they didn't edit it out.'

'I haven't watched the tape yet.' Janna sat down on a kitchen chair on top of a pair of trainers, feeling defensive.

Perhaps Oriana wanted Emlyn back.

'Was it really OK?'

'Fabulous. Charlie and I both cried.'

'How's the baby?' asked Janna, feeling more cheerful.

'Due in a month, thank God.'

Partner was pointedly shoving his empty bowl round the floor. As Janna reached for a tin of Butcher's Tripe, Oriana asked:

'Have you been to see Dad in prison?'

'He doesn't want any visitors,' sighed Janna.

'You're not still in love with him?'

'Oh goodness no,' stammered Janna.

'You deserved that award,' went on Oriana briskly, 'but frankly Emlyn orchestrated the whole thing. He got cramp writing all the kids' nominations and transcribing the tapes of the parents who couldn't write. Theoretically you shouldn't have won because you don't have a school any more, but Emlyn kept on at them.'

Oriana's awfully upfront, thought Janna, and how does she know so much about what Emlyn's been up to?

'Why did he make such an effort?' she asked sulkily, then felt utterly deflated at Oriana's reply.

'Because he has an innate sense of justice.'

'So did Pontius Pilate,' grumbled Janna.

'I'm now going to break a confidence,' announced Oriana.

Janna, who had been trying to rotate the tin-opener handle with the same hand that was holding her mobile, let go of the tin, which crashed to the floor as Oriana added:

'It's high time you realized it was Emlyn who gave you that hundred and twenty grand to save

Larks.'

'Emlyn?' whispered Janna. 'Oh God, he couldn't have! And I spent so many hours banging on to him about Randal, and how Randal couldn't be all villain if he was capable of such generosity. I even speculated whether it could be Hengist or Rupert. Emlyn never said a word. Oh, how heroically kind of him—' Her voice broke. 'I never dreamt. Where did he get the money from?'

'He was saving up to buy himself and me a really nice house,' said Oriana reprovingly.

'This is terrible,' groaned Janna. 'That was why he was always so poor, not able to fly out to see you in Iraq, not flying out to watch England and Wales in the World Cup, refusing to go Dutch to the opera. Oh God, why didn't he tell me?' Her brain was reeling all over the place, as though its steering had packed up on a mountain road.

'And why me?'

'Because he loves you,' said Oriana.

'What did you say?' whispered Janna.

'Because he loves you. Look how he's given and given and given to you, ferrying your children and their parents to public meetings, organizing entire productions of *Romeo and Juliet*, even coming to teach at Larks, which must have been a helluva culture shock. Making sure of your career by getting you a Plato. What have you ever done for him?'

'Listened ad nauseam when he rabbited on and on about you,' snapped Janna. 'And you're one to talk after the revoltingly contemptuous way you treated him. I've never seen anything so horribly cruel and humiliating and in your face as you and Charlie last Christmas.'

To her amazement, Oriana laughed.

'Good—now I'm convinced you love him too. Well, it's payback time, so go and find him.'

'Are you sure he loves me? He didn't say anything last night.'

'You've got to make the first move.'

'Where is he?' gasped Janna.

'Training with the Welsh squad at the Vale Hotel in Glamorgan, just the other side of Cardiff,' rattled off Oriana. 'Exit thirty-four on the M4. Should take you an hour and a quarter. It's known as the Lucky Hotel, because entire teams hole up there before big matches and really bond and thrive—I'm sure you and Emlyn will do the same. And you can jolly well ask Charlie and me to your wedding.'

As she rang off, the purr of the telephone sounded like a great contented cat. Looking down, Janna saw Partner had the tin between his paws. 'Sorry, darling.' In a daze, she emptied the contents into his bowl. Then she wandered round the room, warming her hands on her burning face, trying to take in the enormity of Emlyn's colossal sacrifice. And bloody Randal had let her believe he'd given her the money, and let everyone else think so too. She'd murder him. But what did Randal matter? She must get to Emlyn.

All shaking fingers and thumbs, she tried to dial his mobile, but it was switched off. It was twenty to one now. He might only be training in the morning.

Gathering up Partner and her car keys, she ran out barefooted and still in her party dress to her green Polo. Never had the little car hurtled so fast, rattling poor Partner from side to side in the back.

554

Respite came for him twice. First at the Severn Bridge, rising like huge palest green Aeolian harps over the shining levels of the Bristol Channel and needing a £4.60 toll. Janna, however, had forgotten to bring any money. In his booth, the toll-keeper, who had 'Carpe Diem' tattooed on his brawny arm, was utterly intransigent: no £4.60, no Wales. Fortunately a man in the fast-growing, hooting queue behind a sobbing, pleading Janna had last night seen the Teaching Awards and said it would be a privilege to pay her toll.

Gibbering her thanks, scribbling his address to return the money, Janna scorched on even faster. Partner's second respite came when his mistress was flagged down by a traffic cop as she was passing Cardiff. Fortunately the traffic cop had also seen the Teaching Awards and on learning Janna was trying to reach Emlyn Davies, who was a local hero, put on his blue flashing lights and gave her a police escort. This was a good thing, because she'd reached a state when she was muttering, 'M34, exit four', and would never have reached the Lucky Hotel without help.

But gradually the turning trees grew thicker, thronging the edge of the motorway like rugby crowds cheering her home. And there was the Vale Hotel in its lovely green valley, a beautiful Palladian house with red roses still flowering behind little box hedges and flags hanging limp in the windless air.

And there, even lovelier—she gave a shriek of joy and relief—was Emlyn's Renault, easily the dirtiest, scruffiest, most overloaded car in the place. Two women in white towelling dressing gowns, on their way to the spa, directed her to the

555

Indoor Training Arena.

Tearing up a little hill to a big green building hidden by trees, Janna barged inside, past a big sepia photograph of Emlyn's hero, Gareth Edwards, through a glass door and found herself in a vast enclosed area, half the size of a rugby pitch and carpeted with artificial grass. It was so like a huge hangar, she half expected Kenneth More to roll up or a Hercules to taxi in after a hard night's work.

Instead, twenty odd members of the Welsh national squad, mostly pale-faced, black-haired, black-eyed and gloriously hunky, were running about practising back moves, set line-outs and tackling great red rubber bollards; and there, towering over them, shouting, encouraging, advising but not as sharp or focused as usual, in a grey tracksuit adorned with the three Welsh feathers, was her own golden-haired, ruddy-faced Hercules down from the skies.

'Emlyn,' screamed Janna, 'oh Emlyn.'

'Janna,' gasped Emlyn as, lovely as the Olympic torch approaching its final destination, still in her party dress, bare-armed and barefooted, she hurtled across the bouncy green grass towards him.

Six feet away, she halted, panting for breath, fighting back the tears.

'Oh Emlyn,' she gasped, 'I only got the letter you sent me back in June after the prom this morning. Lily signed for it, but she was so excited about Christian proposing, she shoved it in a drawer.'

Then seeing his face lighten in incredulous hope and bewilderment, she stumbled on:

'It's been the most miserable time of my life for me too. At first I blamed it on losing Larks, but

556

now I realize I said goodbye to that months ago, and it was only you I was missing. I just love you to bits. I don't care where I live as long as it's with you.'

As she edged towards him, they were both oblivious of the flower of Welsh rugby also gathering round, transfixed with interest to see one of their normally roaringly articulate coaches utterly lost for words.

'And what is more'—Janna brushed away the tears—'Oriana told me about the money. Emlyn, it was all your savings for her and your future and you never let on. I can't even begin to thank you and for all the other things you've done for me.'

'A lot of that money was left me by Dad,' mumbled Emlyn. 'Nothing would have pleased him more than it being spent on Larks. Oriana ought to be shot.'

'So ought Randal,' admitted Janna, but she was not to be deflected.

She was so close now she could feel the heat of his body and, looking up, see the dark underside of his blond curls, his massive torso heaving and his square jaw gritted in an attempt not to break down.

'D'you remember once asking me what I'd most like in the world?' she asked.

'You said a waiting list.'

'Well, I've changed my mind,' sobbed Janna. 'I want a wedding ring, and the chance to spend the rest of my life loving you and paying you back for all the kindness.'

When Emlyn just gazed at her and said nothing, she stammered, 'But only if you haven't changed your mind and still feel those wonderful things you said in your letter.'

It is difficult even in a fast lift to rise from darkest hell to heaven so quickly. Emlyn still couldn't bring the words out. Below him Janna's flaming red hair seemed to fan out as cheerfully as a bonfire on a grey winter day, and her love seemed as true and real as the grass beneath her little feet was artificial.

'If I still feel like that?' asked Emlyn slowly as, softly as a falling leaf, his hand touched her soaked cheek. 'Oh God, lovely, if only you knew.'

Wiping his eyes, pulling her into his arms, enfolding her in a great bear hug, looking down into her adorable face, where every freckle seemed to be declaring its love, he kissed her on and on and on until the ecstatic Welsh rugby squad gave them a standing ovation.

'With breath control like that, Emlyn,' shouted one of the forwards, 'you should be teaching underwater swimming.'

'Aren't you going to introduce the lady?' shouted a back.

The fast lift had clearly reached heaven. With a huge smile and an arm about a dazed but beaming Janna, Emlyn glanced round at the squad. 'I'd like you to welcome the future Mrs Davies to Wales,' he said proudly.

Instantly there was a patter of tiny feet as Partner, having wriggled out of the Polo window and conned his way to the training area, happily took up his position beside them.

131

Two days before the Queen's visit, Dora, utterly outraged that Alex Bruce had banned all dogs from the campus and wearing a 'Ban the Ban' badge on each lapel, accompanied Artie Deverell and his two Jack Russells, Verlaine and Rimbaud, round Bagley village.

Dora loved Artie because in his languor, sensitivity, extreme kindness and slight air of helplessness, he reminded her so much of her late father, Raymond. Artie, in turn, was devoted to Dora. When his feckless, totally unsuitable chef boyfriend had finally walked out two years ago, it had been Dora who'd mounted a relief operation, which resulted in every member of the Upper Fourth bringing round their cod in cheese sauce, cooked in food technology, for his supper that evening.

Today she was in full flood. 'It's so pants of Alex changing everything,' she stormed. 'The eventing and polo teams and the beagles were going to meet the Queen at the gate and act as outriders up to the Mansion. You know how she loves horses and dogs. And Paris was going to recite a beautiful poem he'd written.

'Instead the poor dear's got to listen to an IT lesson, watch Poppet teach RE and then tour that stupid Science Emporium and witness Boffin perform some stupid experiment, splitting the atom or finding a cure for bird flu. Although Mr Fussy's flapping around so much, he'll give us bird flu anyway.'

Passing the charming cottage where Cosmo had installed Mrs Walton, reaching the White Lion, they wistfully breathed in the smell of lamb braising in red wine, parsley and garlic. School food had deteriorated depressingly since Poppet's lentil-loaded, salt-free regime had taken over.

'If we turn left here, down Stream Lane,' Dora told Artie, 'we can sneak the dogs back to your house undercover via Badger's Retreat and the golf course. I've done it often enough with Cadbury.'

It was a mild, windless day; gold leaves clogged the dark waters of the stream. Birds sang sweetly in the rain-soaked air. The path was strewn with tawny willow spears.

' "Yellow, and black and pale, and hectic red," ' quoted Artie, as the Jack Russells bounded ahead, stopping to fight and snuffle down rabbit holes.

'Hengist wanted the Queen to watch a history lesson,' said Dora crossly.

'Might have been tricky,' mused Artie, wondering nervously, as he lit a cigarette, how far Poppet's no smoking ban extended. 'The Upper Fifth are doing the Russian Revolution, the Middle Fifth, the English Civil War.'

'And we're doing the French Revolution,' giggled Dora, chucking a stick for the dogs. 'Might have been a bit tactless, all those kings and queens having their heads chopped off. But she'd have seen some terrific teaching. Hengist's lessons were wonderful. We were making a guillotine and tumbrels when he was arrested. The acting head of history Mr Fussy's roped in promptly put them on the skip. He keeps groping Bianca; we call him the Randy Republican.

'Emlyn was a terrific teacher too,' Dora sighed, as they crossed over a wooden bridge back on to Bagley land. 'Exciting about him and Janna getting married; I hope they ask me to the wedding. And wasn't it lovely her getting that Teaching Award and not Mr Fussy, and all the Larks pupils coming on to the stage. I think Paris was upset not to be part of it, he was very fond of Janna,' Dora added wistfully, 'and he's terribly upset about the bursar being booted out at Christmas. I do wish Hengist would come back.'

Oh, so do I, thought Artie.

Ahead, after a night of downpour, serpents of opal blue mist were writhing out of Badger's Retreat.

Artie let Dora run on. Since Hengist, his real, never-confessed love, had left, Bagley had lost its lustre. Artie had already had numerous approaches from other schools. Even Fleetley was putting out feelers. But he had loved Bagley so much and, like Theo, so longed to end his days here, he couldn't rouse himself to go to interviews.

In his breast pocket was a letter from Hengist.

'Dear Artie, I'm so sorry I let you down. If I'd made you deputy head as you deserved, none of this sorry business would have happened. Please look after Sally and the school if you can. Yours ever.'

Yours never, thought Artie sadly.

'Couldn't you be head?' Dora's shrill voice broke into his reverie.

'I don't think Mr Bruce would like that.'

'Everyone loathes him.'

'That's enough,' said Artie firmly, dodging to avoid a stick which Dora in her rage had thrown

561

straight up in the air.

'My God,' he exploded as they reached Badger's Retreat, 'they've daubed red spots on everything, even Hengist's Family Tree.'

'Mr Fussy must be going to chop them down. He thinks woods are pointless. And he's banished Cadbury so the Queen won't meet him, which will be a great disappointment to her. Instead she'll have to listen to Alex's boring speech. Poor Painswick has to keep on retyping it when she's not ringing the Met. Office to check the weather: "Oh, it's you again, Miss Painswick, it's going to bloody chuck it down."'

'And what's more . . .' Dora retrieved the stick, teasing the Jack Russells, who launched into a frenzy of yapping.

'For God's sake,' hissed Artie in alarm, 'they'll get arrested.'

'And what's more'—Dora chucked the stick—'I was in the general office and quite by chance caught sight of the agenda for the next governors' meeting, and I promise you General Bagley and Denmark are for the chop. Because the General was an imperialist who kicked ass after the Black Hole of Calcutta, Poppet wants him toppled like Saddam Hussein and replaced, I would think, by some manky statue of Mr Fussy brandishing a test tube and a copy of *Red Tape*.'

Artie was appalled. 'They can't pull down General Bagley. It's a beautiful sculpture.'

'And Denmark's so realistic, I always want to give him an apple.'

'And the General was a most civilized old boy,' protested Artie, 'who took copies of Racine and the *Iliad* to India with him, kept springers, was an excellent watercolourist, then left all his land and his house to found this school.'

'Well, I do know'—Dora glanced furtively round—'that Mr Fussy, who knows eff all about art, has asked an artist called Trafford to come up with alternative suggestions. I bet he doesn't realize Trafford, who is a best friend of my brother Jonathan, is wildly expensive and often charges twenty thousand for a maquette.'

Despite his horror at the threat to the General, Artie laughed. 'Trafford has certainly made a convert of Poppet,' he said. 'She much admired his latest installation: *Tranny by Gaslight: The Story of a Sex Change.*'

'Working title: *From Willy to Womb.* It's absolutely disgusting,' thundered Dora, 'and cost half a million pounds. And I bet she hasn't seen *Sister Hoodie*, Trafford's video of a teenage girl beating up an old woman.'

'How can Poppet accuse our beloved General of colonialism,' said Artie indignantly, 'when her new best friend Randal Stancombe is busy colonizing Larkshire?'

As they neared Bagley and Artie hid both Jack Russells under his coat, they passed Theo's old house, now the home of the Randy Republican, who'd put a picture of Trotsky in the window.

'I'm determined to plant an oak tree in Theo's memory,' said Artie, 'but Alex is resolutely against it.'

'He's also banned school fireworks tonight for the first time in twenty years,' raged Dora, 'because they leave even more mess than dogs.'

563

132

Twenty-four hours to go. To the excitement of the female pupils, Bagley swarmed with hunky security men and sniffer dogs checking everywhere for weapons and explosives.

The red carpet couldn't be laid yet because the white gloss on the corridor wainscots was still wet. The sea-blue curtain covering the plaque on the Science Emporium wall, which the Queen would unveil to commemorate her visit, had fallen off when Joan Johnson jerked it back in rehearsal, but was now firmly secured. The splendid lavatory, specially built for the royal visit and nicknamed the 'Roylet', had been equipped with pot pourri and Bluebell, allegedly the Queen's favourite soap and toilet water. The framed print of *The Laughing Cavalier* had been replaced by a more neutral field of poppies and relocated in the dressing room of Dame Hermione Harefield, who, with her demands for vintage champagne, four dozen yellow roses and her own private loo, was causing far more hassle than the dear Queen.

There was good news however. The forecast was fine, if chilly, and Alex's bible the *New Scientist* had accepted, alongside a huge turnout of press and television who didn't realize all the celebs, including the Russian Minister of Affaires and Rupert Campbell-Black, had cancelled out of loyalty to Hengist.

'What story do you want to tell the Queen about the school?' General Broadstairs, the Lord Lieutenant, who was a governor anyway, had asked

Alex on their first meeting after Hengist's departure, and Alex had replied that he wished to 'showcase Bagley's scientific and technological achievements in an emporium which would be the envy of scientists the world over'.

What Alex really wanted was to nail the top job and for people to love him more than Hengist. He was furious Janna had won an award and had finally got together with that Welsh gorilla who'd tried to drown Poppet, but he supposed they deserved each other.

Alex didn't find diplomacy easy. He had failed to thwart Poppet's plan to serve vegetable curry for everyone after the Queen had gone. Randal Stancombe too, once he'd learnt Boffin was performing some ground-breaking experiment in front of the Queen, had insisted that his Jade must present the Queen with her bouquet. Alex didn't dare say he'd promised that role to Little Dulcie who, with her wheelbarrow, had laboured harder on the emporium than any of the workforce. He didn't need to appease Patience and Ian, quite the reverse, but he must buy Dulcie a teddy bear. Randal had also insisted that Dora, who, as Jade's potential stepsister, might be jealous, must present Her Majesty with some dog she'd made specially in pottery. Alex hated kow-towing to Randal and Poppet. Once he was head, he'd call the shots.

*   *   *

The Queen had several other engagements on the same day in Larkshire. It was essential none of them overran. She was due to reach Bagley at 11.30 and must, on pain of guillotine, leave by

565

12.30 to reach a hospital on the outskirts of Larkminster at 12.50.

After endless telephone calls and meetings with local police and members of the royal household protection team and the route being rewalked and the itinerary reworked to the final second, an increasingly uptight Alex insisted on one more, school only, rehearsal after lunch.

Biffo, acutely aware his job was on the line, had been given a stopwatch and put in charge of operations. Searching for a stand-in for the Queen, he promptly roped in Trafford, the louche artist invited down by Alex and Poppet to provide an alternative to General Bagley, whom he found eating a doughnut and reading a porn mag in the staffroom.

'And since you're so good at acting,' Biffo added bossily to Paris, 'you can double up as Lord Lieutenant and headmaster until Alex gets here. Anyone involved in events the Queen is going to witness can take up their positions around the route.'

Dora should have been standing by General Bagley's statue waiting to hand over her pottery dog immediately after Jade had presented the Queen with her bouquet. Reluctant to miss anything, however, Dora had managed to lose herself among a group of Lower Fifths, including Bianca, whom Biffo had grabbed as they came out of the dining room to act as press. After all, no one is more qualified than me, rationalized Dora.

Trafford, meanwhile, attempting to appear more royal, had topped his shaved head, designer stubble and pig-like features with the large rose-trimmed mauve felt hat Miss Painswick had bought specially for the big day, reducing everyone to fits of giggles. Thus encouraged, Trafford pretended to jump out of a limo outside the Mansion steps, saying in a high voice:

'My husband and I, what a beautiful school, we haven't been here before.'

'Stop being silly, Trafford,' snapped Biffo, consulting his notes. 'Now, as Lord Lieutenant, Paris, you present Jupiter Belvedon as chair of governors and MP for Larkminster to Her Majesty.'

'Who will try and flog her a picture,' quipped Trafford, 'and take eighty per cent.'

'Shuddup,' said Biffo through gritted brown teeth. 'And now Paris presents Alex to Her Majesty and now you, Poppet.'

'And Poppet will give me a nice curtsey,' said Trafford.

'I will *not*,' squawked Poppet, 'I don't bend my knee to anyone.'

'Right,' said Trafford.

'Then, as headmaster, I present Mr Randal Stancombe, who's donated this wonderful building to Bagley for the furtherance of science,' said Paris, getting into the swing of things.

'And then his wife,' prompted Biffo.

'Mrs Hyacinth Bouquet,' muttered Dora.

'Who said that? That's not funny,' roared Biffo.

'Push orf,' announced Paris. 'One says that every five seconds to the press: "Push orf." '

'Then you present Mr Ashton Douglas,' said Biffo.

Everything went comparatively smoothly until they reached the Science Emporium.

'We're now touring these splendid zones.'

Trafford was getting more regal by the second. 'My word, Mr Randal Stinkbomb, this is awesome, particularly this.' Trafford peeled a 'Bring back Hengist' sticker off a vast replica of the pancreas. 'How long have you been building this, Mr Stinkbomb? Push orf, press, although not if you're as ravishing as you are,' he added to Bianca.

Paris meanwhile was watching Dora, who was laughing so much she could hardly write in her reporter's notebook. He remembered her showing him how to make that peacock feather: 'Would you like to take part in an experiment?'

'How truly interesting,' trilled Trafford as the royal party entered the Zone of Chemical Investigative Science. 'My husband and I simply dote on chemistry.'

'Wake up, Paris,' snapped Alex, 'as headmaster you should be presenting Boffin.'

'As what?' drawled Paris sarcastically.

'Like this. I'm here, I'll do it,' said Alex, striding up. 'Your Majesty, may I present Bernard Brooks, the son of Sir Gordon and Lady Brooks, one of Bagley's most gifted and talented pupils, who's going to perform a ground-breaking experiment.'

Alex turned lovingly to Boffin who, dressed in white coat and goggles, his sparse light brown hair tied back, an expression on his shiny, spotty face of a priest preparing communion wine, was pestling silver and reddish powders together in a mortar.

'In this invention,' said Boffin pompously, 'I'm combining iron oxide and aluminium in order to weld railway tracks together.'

'You must patent it and sell it to British Rail,' gushed Trafford, pushing Painswick's hat to the back of his head, 'and our royal train will rattle

568

more safely over it.'

'Boffin is so pants,' muttered Dora as Boffin carried on mixing, gazing round to see he had everyone's attention.

'Buck up, Boffin,' said Biffo curtly, 'we're ten seconds behind schedule.'

'Would anyone thus have hurried Archimedes?' reproached Poppet.

'Such procedures must not be rushed,' agreed Alex.

Next moment the Zone of Chemical Investigative Science was rocked by a mighty explosion that showered the floor with glass as the windows blew in and bottles and containers of chemicals flew off the shelves and everyone was blown six feet across the room.

'It's a bomb, it's a bomb.'

'Clear the building,' yelled Biffo as, amid shouting, screaming and sobbing, people fell over themselves to escape.

Paris, however, had only one thought. Grabbing Dora, he pulled her under the nearest table, shielding her with his body. As black smoke engulfed the room to a crescendo of choking and coughing, he became aware of delicious softness.

'Get out of here, everyone out!' bellowed Biffo.

Paris stayed put and, as the smoke cleared, he looked down and saw Dora, blond eyelashes mascaraed with soot, face blackened, but her eyes still duck-egg blue, widening as they gazed up at him. In them and in her sweet, pink, trembling mouth he saw no fear, only love.

Oblivious of the chaos around them, with a feeling of utter rightness and coming home, he dropped his head and kissed her, feeling her breastbone rise as she gasped in wonder, her mouth opening and her tongue creeping out tentatively to meet his. Paris put his hands on either side of her sooty face, stroking back her hair, smiling slowly, joyfully: 'It's happened,' he whispered, 'at last I can love you,' and he kissed her again.

'And I love you.' Dora choked slightly. 'I always have.'

'Paris Alvaston,' thundered Joan, whose red tie had been blown off, 'come out from under that table at once. You're unaccounted for outside. Watch out for broken glass. Who's that with you? Dora Belvedon, I might have guessed. What do you think you're doing?'

'Covering the visit for the school mag,' said Dora faintly.

Scrabbling up, pulling Dora to her feet, Paris brushed soot and glass off her blue jersey and pleated skirt as reverently as if he'd unearthed a hitherto unread play by Euripides. Unaware of everyone sobbing and shouting around them, he looked down at her in wonder:

'You and I were the chemical reaction that triggered off that explosion.'

'We were?' stammered Dora.

'What just happened to us could have blasted a man on to Venus, or broken the light barrier, or proved that God needn't exist because we do. Not even the universe began with a bigger bang, oh, darling Dora,' and he buried his lips in hers a second time.

'Paris!' thundered Joan.

'I cannot understand what happened,' Boffin's voice curled petulantly through the smoke.

570

'Perhaps too much aluminium?'

'What were you trying to achieve?' asked an ashen protection officer.

'A revolution in railway safety. It'll work next time. Ouch!' Boffin gave a furious squawk as Lando emptied a fire bucket into his face.

'You're an asshole, Boffin.'

'Thank God no one's been hurt.' Joan Johnson was comforting a shaken Poppet, who quavered that everyone was going to need counselling.

'Except those two,' giggled Bianca and everyone turned to see Dora, both feet off the ground in excitement, locked in Paris's arms.

133

The sight of Paris in a clinch with Dora proved the last straw for Stancombe, who'd just rolled up and taken stock of his ransacked emporium.

'You've got less than twenty-four hours to repair this building,' he howled at Teddy Murray. 'You can work all through the night. I want every man in Larkshire on the job.'

Such was his determination that even Graffi's father Dafydd was dragged out of the Ghost and Castle to help. Fortunately the damage was mostly confined to the one chemistry zone, which would need the windows mended, the walls replastered and repainted and all the flasks and containers replaced and refilled.

Boffin inevitably received an earful from Stancombe:

'Of all the fucking stupid, criminal things to do!'

To Boffin's fury, even Alex agreed with the royal household protection team and the local police that even if the building were declared safe in the morning, the Queen would open and tour the emporium and speak to the students but witness absolutely no experiments.

'Dad will not be pleased,' said Boffin ominously.

Despite unearthing splendid skulduggery at S and C Services, Cosmo and the rest of the Lower Sixth, returning from work experience, were gutted to have missed the fun. Cosmo was further irritated to find the ladder outside his room had yet again been removed by the protection officers. How could he ever escape to pleasure Mrs

Walton? Replacing it, he leant a Randal Stancombe board across the bottom rung.

Although heavy frost was forecast, the lawn behind the Mansion, on which stood General Bagley and Denmark, was shielded from an icy north wind howling down the Long Walk by the vast, if temporarily damaged, bulk of the Science Emporium. Although the General was oblivious to cold, the pupils lugging four hundred chairs for the not so Great nor Good through the dusk and placing them under a blue striped awning were grateful for the shelter.

'Ha, ha, ha, my mother's twenty-two rows back, next to Rod Hyde,' crowed Dora, examining the seating plan. 'She will go ballistic.'

The pupils dispersed wearily to supper and prep, but Dora lingered and was discovered by Alex Bruce hosing down General Bagley and Denmark and chatting to security men and their dogs.

'So many pigeons have dumped on the poor old boy,' explained Dora, aiming the hose at the General's bristling moustache, 'we must wash it off. After all, he is our founder.'

Not for much longer, thought Alex, then ordered Dora to buck up and get back to Boudicca.

The moment he'd bustled off to urge on the frantic activity in the Zone of Chemical Investigative Science, a lurking Paris emerged from the shadows carrying gin and tonic in two paper cups. Balancing them on Denmark's quarters, he stood back to admire the big horse, gleaming like jet, in the lights from the emporium.

'Looks much better. Sure you're warm enough? I like winter, you can see so many more stars now the leaves have gone.' Running his hand in wonder

573

over her little, cold face: ' "and thou art fairer than the evening's air Clad in the beauty of a thousand stars".'

'Oh Paris,' said Dora, gruff with embarrassment and delight, 'that is so poetic.'

'Marlowe said it first,' Paris admitted; then, in bewilderment: 'I just feel a great Niagara of love has been released from inside me.'

'How heavenly is that?' Dropping the hose, Dora wriggled into his arms. 'How did it happen?' she asked, gasping for breath a minute later. 'I wanted it for so long.'

'I suddenly remembered you giving me the peacock feather. Bad things happened in the past, which made me bad at loving and at letting people get close.'

'Not any more.' Dora hugged him so tightly, he groaned. 'I'm here for you now,' and she kissed him again.

It was only when the abandoned hose started snaking around, soaking their legs, that she looked down and squeaked in excitement, 'I've got a brilliant plan.'

As Graffi's father Dafydd wandered past with a tool kit, she called out that they needed his help. Dafydd was only too happy. The entire workforce, he said, was on the verge of going on strike because Little Dulcie wasn't presenting the bouquet.

*   *   *

Much later, having downed two bottles of red to calm his nerves after the explosion, Biffo Rudge thought he'd seen a ghost, then realized it was

574

Dora Belvedon astride Denmark, training a hose on the General's hat.

'What on earth are you doing?' he bellowed.

'I miss my pony so much'—Dora pretended to cry—'Mr Bruce kindly allowed me to spruce up Denmark and the General. I'm just washing behind the General's ears.'

'Horse must have Arab blood'—Biffo patted Denmark—'with those curved ears and wide eyes and that lovely dish face. Bagley was a good fellow too, not your usual military bonehead.'

'Isn't it tragic Mr and Mrs Bruce want to melt him down?' said Dora innocently.

'First I've heard of it,' exploded Biffo. 'Talk about the old order being ripped away.'

'Our founder flounders,' sighed Dora, 'and after he gave us our lovely school. But if he looks nice and clean tomorrow, more people will want to keep him. I've only got a bit more pigeon crap to get off, Mr Rudge, and then I'll race back to Boudicca.'

*   *   *

Fortunately, Alex Bruce was distracted during the evening by a crisis. The protection teams refused to allow in any more chemicals before the Queen's visit, so all the glass vessels being replaced in the Zone of Chemical Investigative Science had to be filled up with coloured water, by which time it was nearly ten o'clock.

'No longer Dirty Denmark,' said Dora, finally handing the hosepipe back to Dafydd. 'Do you want me to roll it up?'

'No, you get home, lovely. We'll be working all

night. Shame Hengist's left, he wanted all the Larks kids to collect their GCSE certificates from the Queen, then bloody Bruce killed the idea. Chantal Peck had already bought her hat and been practising her curtsey all round the estate.'

'That's really sad,' said Dora. 'How's Graffi?'

'Triffic. He and Rupert are thick as thieves. Rupert's tickled pink with his muriel and I'm getting some triffic winners.'

*   *   *

Over in his minimalist living room, soon to be abandoned for the vast splendour of Head House, Alex was yet again going through his speech with Vicky Fairchild. The explosion in the emporium had removed his eyebrows so he could no longer raise them quizzically to make a point.

'Just a little more warmth in the words "Your Majesty",' cooed Vicky. 'I know how shy you are, Alex, but let the caring persona shine through.'

Upstairs, Poppet slept soundly. Tomorrow's outfit, a crimson, yellow and green bandanna and a warm wool ketchup-red smock, was already folded on a chair. Little Cranberry Germaine was yelling her head off, but let Alex deal.

Alex plugged Cranberry on to Poppet's left breast and reflected that if tomorrow went well, he'd be voted head by the governors on Friday and could have mistresses like Hengist. He'd always admired Vicky Fairchild.

*   *   *

Sally Brett-Taylor turned over a sodden pillow.

Tomorrow, so no one would be embarrassed and because she couldn't bear to look at the butchered school gardens, she'd make herself scarce. She must also pull herself together and find somewhere to live. In the old days, Elaine had slept, often on her back, on the chaise longue at the bottom of the bed. Now she kept vigil in the hall, painful for her bony legs and elbows, always facing the front door, pining, not eating, hoping Hengist would walk in. How do you explain to a dog that Master has gone to kennels?

Sally was pleased to learn from Patience, on the Bagley bush telegraph, that Paris and Dora had finally got it together and yet she was sad. Paris had comforted her during the bleakest time of her life. Like the Marschallin, she must let him go with both hands.

*　　　　*　　　　*

Post-Mrs Walton, Cosmo crept back into Bagley very happy. Work experience had been equally rewarding. He had found the initials BP in Ashton's diary for tomorrow night, after the Queen's visit. Amber, at work experience at the *Gazette*, had found BP on the same date in Col Peters's diary. Dora had found it in Mr Fussy's.

Cosmo had also discovered, when a card arrived in a mauve envelope from the egregious Crispin Thomas, that it was Ashton's birthday tomorrow. Cosmo had therefore arranged for Dame Hermione, when she serenaded the Queen, to slip in a 'Happy Birthday to Ashton'.

Cosmo, who went every which way to gain what he wanted, even promising Ashton a blow job for

577

his birthday, had introduced Lubemir into S and C's offices as a comely bit of rough trade.

Tomorrow, he and Ashton would spend all morning at Bagley, he to conduct his mother and the school orchestra, Ashton to be presented to the Queen. This would leave the office unguarded for Lubemir, who had already unearthed the shadow of an email from Alex to Ashton on 6 October: 'HB-T resigned. BR ours.'

What the hell was BR? Was it a typo for BC or BP? After a lot of thought, Cosmo decided it must be Badger's Retreat, so Stancombe could chop down Hengist's beloved trees, which had since been daubed with red plague spots, and, with Russell fiddling planning permission, slap desirable residences with a view all over the area.

Lubemir had also dug up so much shit on the bringing down of Janna and BC was looking increasingly like Birthday Club and BP like Birthday Party.

Russell had a planning office in County Hall and Milly Walton, working as a clerk in another department, had found a BP in his diary for tomorrow night. A good day's work.

On his way back to his cell, Cosmo called Milly's mother:

'Angel, can you do one thing for me? Suck up to Stancombe tomorrow, pretend it might be on again and see if you can wheedle your keys back. I desperately need to get into his files. I love you.'

Going upstairs Cosmo found Paris in his own cell, wrapped against the cold in a Black Watch tartan duvet, reading John Donne and looking happier than ever before.

' "She is all States, and all Princes, I, Nothing

else is",' mocked Cosmo.

Paris flushed slightly. 'Whatever.'

Cosmo then debriefed him on the day's findings. 'Nasty little den of thieves going to that party tomorrow night,' he said finally. 'None of them has written down the address, so we may have to trail one of them.'

'Not in anything as obvious as your Ferrari,' chided Paris, but when Cosmo added that it was Ashton's birthday tomorrow, all the luminous happiness drained out of Paris's face.

'The third of November,' he said bleakly, 'that means he's forty-five tomorrow.'

'How d'you know?'

'Does he have a lisp, can't say his Rs, and have a big watch on the inside of his wrist and stink of asphyxiatingly sweet aftershave like poison gas?'

'That's the one.'

Paris shut his eyes, remembering the blindfolding, so every other sense was heightened, the holding down, the soft caressing hands, the laughter. The terrible pain and indignity going on and on, the grunting and heavy breathing: 'Shut up, you little wat or we'll weally hurt you.' The suffocating scent he could now smell on Cosmo.

As Paris glanced up, Cosmo was shocked by the depths of suffering in his face. He was shaking violently.

'How d'you know him?'

'I was the birthday present at his fortieth birthday party,' Paris said flatly. 'Not a bweeze, being gang waped.'

'My God, where was this?'

'In Oaktree Court, in a back room. I never saw any of them; they blindfolded me and tied my

579

hands. God knows how many of them had me, I lost count. I don't know if Blenchley, the care manager, was one of them. Next day he told me I was imagining things. If I said anything, he'd move me on or have me taken out.'

Cosmo shook his head in bewildered admiration. 'And you never grassed?'

'I was only eleven, I was too ashamed, I felt so dirty. Who would have believed me? I was terrified of losing my friends. Ben Longstaff, who ran away from the home after threatening to grass them up, died in a very suspicious fire.'

If Paris had looked up, he would have found genuine compassion on Cosmo's face. 'I'm truly sorry. Was that why you screamed when Theo came into your room?'

'Yes.'

'Christ, I'm sorry,' repeated Cosmo. 'We'll nail them. Can you handle Ashton being here tomorrow?'

'It's OK.' Paris wandered towards the window. Through the newly bare trees he could see Dora's window in Boudicca. 'I can handle anything now.'

134

Bagley Hall was still in shock and in a growing state of mutiny over Hengist's departure. Both staff and pupils missed his warmth and genuine interest, his great laugh, even his bellows of rage. All they could think was how much he would have enjoyed welcoming the Queen, bounding down the Mansion steps, rubbing his big hands in joy, sweeping her off on a magical mystery tour of the school.

Instead they had to suffer Mr Fussy as powerless as Canute to keep back the great gold tidal wave of leaves unleashed by last night's frost, which now covered pitch, path and, mercifully, most of the hideously clashing flowerbeds. Mr Fussy was doing his nut and blaming every leaf on the bursar and his groundsmen.

Tension had also gripped Boudicca.

'Who's used all the hot water?' screamed Jade Stancombe. 'I'm handing the Queen her bouquet, I ought to have priority.'

Joan in a pinstripe suit was inspecting nails, hair, even breath for alcohol and that everyone was wearing the regulation on-the-knee sea-blue coat and beige skirt, with sufficiently polished shoes.

'And you're all to leave your mobiles behind.'

In the Science Emporium, the brightest pupils, their hair tied back, wearing white coats and goggles, nervously waited at their benches, ignoring the 'Bring back Hengist' stickers attached to the liver, the colon and the interactive whiteboards.

In the RE suite, the Lower Fifth played pass the parcel with a gurgling baby Cranberry and awaited Poppet to give them a lesson on birth as a rite of passage.

Outside, beneath a bright blue sky, crowds lining the route and gathered on the battlements shivered in the icy east wind. Inside the warmth of the Mansion, as the welcome party paced the black and white checked hall floor, Jupiter, Poppet and the Lord Lieutenant's wife, who'd arrived early because she'd driven down from London, were the only people not nervous.

Sweat crystalled Alex's forehead and was beading Ashton Douglas's discreet beige make-up. Stancombe's estranged wife, Lorraine, wheeled in for the occasion to present a united front, had disappeared yet again to powder her rebuilt nose. Stancombe constantly readjusted his gelled black spikes and his new, dark blue suit in the big gilt mirror. Jupiter was being gratifyingly friendly for once, and by chatting up Lorraine had freed Stancombe to rebond with Ruth Walton. Looking particularly sumptuous in an old rose velvet suit, Mrs Walton was clearly delighted to ignite an old flame.

Jupiter wanted Stancombe's billions for New Reform. But would this entail asking him to join the party executive, which might mean losing Rupert and Lord Hawkley, who had both formed an antipathy towards Stancombe? Bugger Hengist for letting them down.

'The Principal is within a quarter of a mile,' the Officer in Command, having received the message on his radio mike, told the welcome party and other relevant security units around the school grounds.

'I cannot think why you're all so nervous, she's only a senior citizen,' said Poppet as Ashton and Lorraine discreetly repowdered their noses. Even with a respray, Ashton's cloying aftershave was fighting a losing battle with the stench of vegetable curry drifting from the kitchens.

'Wise of the Queen to move on to lunch at Larkminster Hospital,' murmured Jupiter.

'Sally Brett-Taylor always provided the most delicious luncheon and the most beautiful flowers,' grumbled the Lord Lieutenant's wife, not known for her diplomacy. 'Garden's gorn off dreadfully, might be in a municipal park. Sweet thing, Sally. Is she here?'

'Sadly not invited.'

Nor were the bursar, Patience and Little Dulcie, as they forlornly lined the lower drive, waving flags alongside villagers and children from the local primary, only catching the briefest glimpse of the Queen as her car with its cavalcade of cars and motorbike outriders sailed past.

Oblivious of a demo of pupils waving 'Bring back Hengist' placards and Trafford and the Randy Republican on the battlements brandishing red flags and crying, 'Down with the Monarchy', the Queen stepped out of her car. Accompanying her were her personal protection officer, a lady-in-waiting, who had potted biographies of everyone the Queen was going to meet in her handbag, and the Lord Lieutenant in his splendid uniform with its epaulettes, medals and stars.

Anthea Belvedon, twenty-two rows back, swamped by the 399 dignitaries, was absolutely hopping that no one could see how lovely she

583

looked. On a big screen, she could see the crowds ringing Mansion Lawn and Randal bending over Her Majesty like a street lamp and his ghastly common wife being presented as well. There was Ruth Walton, laughing away, when Randal had sworn it was over between them, and Poppet looking ridiculous in that fearful bandanna and ghastly red smock to disguise the fact she hadn't got her figure back. Now she was refusing to bob to the Queen. So rude.

I should be over there, thought Anthea darkly, I'm supposed to be a close friend of Randal and Poppet.

Beside Anthea, Rod Hyde and Gillian Grimston of Searston Abbey were equally unhappy. Why had they been confined to very hard seats under an awning with 398 nonentities and not been introduced to Her Majesty like Ashton and Russell Lambert?

Any deficiencies in Poppet's bob were more than made up for by Dame Hermione's curtsey, more regal than any queen, as she sank to the floor in her Parma violet Chanel suit, a saintly expression in her wide brown eyes.

This distribution of largesse was cut short when her son Cosmo leapt on to the rostrum, sharply tapped the lectern and swept the school orchestra into the National Anthem, involving his mother in an undignified scramble to her feet. All four verses were sung fortissimo, rattling the Mansion windows and dislodging more leaves, followed by 'Here's a Health Unto Your Majesty' and Randal's Largo, as it was now known.

Everyone was heaving a sigh of relief and preparing for the Queen to move on to the RE and

584

IT suites, when Hermione clapped her hands and announced: 'Somebody here, Ashton Douglas, head of education in Larkshire, has a birthday today. I'm sure Your Majesty would like to join me in wishing Ashton many happy returns.'

Ashton looked as though he'd been kissed under the mistletoe. Paris, round the other side of the school, watching him on the same big screen as Anthea Belvedon, fingered his knife.

And Dame Hermione was off: 'Happy birthday to You-hoo!'

Randal, Alex and the Lord Lieutenant were as purple or red as the polyanthus clashing in a nearby flowerbed. Finally Hermione swept off.

'My mother's kind of hard to stop,' sighed Cosmo.

Her Majesty was just moving on when Hermione's dresser, who'd been bunged a tenner, cried out, 'Encore,' and, whisking out of her dressing room, Dame Hermione obliged.

Alex was about to have a coronary. There were still two students taking Duke of Edinburgh Awards to be presented and they now had only half an hour left and had to whiz through the lesson in the IT suite with no time to look at the pupils' work.

'We'll have to switch to plan B and cut the RE lesson,' said the Officer in Command.

Alex turned pale. 'We can't, my wife . . .'

Dora, waiting beside General Bagley's statue to make her presentation and also watching events on the big screen, put down her blue box and wrote in her notebook: 'Her Majesty is running behind in her tight schedule.'

Everyone was commenting on how tiny and

pretty the Queen was. How kind her blue eyes; how genuinely warm and radiant her smile; how becoming her amethyst hat trimmed with palest green feathers and how even a colour as harsh as the purple of her coat couldn't diminish her flawless pink and white complexion.

On to the Randal Stancombe Science Emporium, where the royal party toured the different zones and exclaimed in wonder at the giant tree you could walk inside and the huge ear that could be taken apart and the echo chambers, giant fibre-optics and heavenly light displays. On to the Zone of Chemical Investigative Science, which, although miraculously restored with coloured water in all the containers, seemed rather dull after yesterday's excitement.

'The Queen has the ability to make everyone feel special. Even republicans become monarchists in her presence,' wrote Dora.

Not so Poppet Bruce, who, white-faced, tight-lipped, was determined to divert the Queen back in the direction of RE, rites of passage and little Cranberry.

'I am of course known as the Queen of Arts,' Dame Hermione was telling everyone, 'and why isn't my very good friend Rupert Campbell-Black here?'

Even without Rupert, however, the media were agreeing that the Randal Stancombe Science Emporium was a triumph, that Randal would be assured his handle and Alex Bruce the headship of Bagley.

As the Queen finally emerged from this futuristic Nirvana, it was at last the turn of Anthea and the 399 very cold other dignitaries on their hard seats to hear Alex's speech of welcome in front of General Bagley's statue with the Science Emporium towering in the background. Afterwards, Randal would say a few words about his part in the great endeavour. Jade and Dora had taken up their positions beside Denmark's hindquarters.

Paris was crowded together behind the barricade with the rest of the Lower Sixth to watch the ceremony. Gazing across at Dora clutching her blue box, wishing it was his hand rather than the east wind ruffling her pale blonde hair, Paris was overwhelmed with love. The knife was to protect Dora from harm as much as to stab Ashton. He hated to leave her to carry out their great plan, but her official position beside Denmark made it possible.

Having practised a little bob, Dora turned round and smiled at him. Witnessing this exchange, Randal Stancombe, even at his finest hour, felt a skewer dipped in acid plunged in his heart. His great speech, his knighthood, Ruth Walton were as nothing to his lust for Dora Belvedon. He could see the gap of pink flesh between her skirt and her rolled-over brown socks. He was brought back to earth by the Queen's gloved hand patting Denmark:

'What a splendid animal.'

Alex in turn patted the mike, cleared his throat, raised his head self-importantly and began very, very warmly: 'Your Majesty, on behalf of students, teachers, parents, governors and supporters of Bagley Hall, I would like to thank you very much for visiting us today. It is a huge honour and marks an historical moment of our development.'

Nothing's going to stop him taking over now, thought a despairing Artie, gazing down from a staffroom window.

'On this momentous day for Bagley Hall and for science . . .' Alex was getting into his stride.

Goodness, the Queen's good at looking interested, thought Dora. As her eyes flickered towards Paris, he nodded. Imperceptibly, Dora's hand slipped between Denmark's back legs.

At first, people thought the heavens had opened; then, as there was no rattle of rain on the blue striped awning, they decided it must be a burst pipe. There was a gasp of consternation as the splatter continued and a great gush of water was located, splashing on General Bagley's plinth and spilling on to the grass.

Bewilderment, rage, horror, shock and broad grins could be seen on individual faces as it struck home that the torrent of very yellow liquid was pouring out of Denmark's cock.

'Quick, quick, he's staling,' yelled Amber. 'Stand up in your stirrups, General.'

There was a rumble of laughter. For a second, Her Majesty's face twitched. The photographers were going berserk, snapping Denmark and his gushing yellow cascade from all angles.

'The Empire Strikes Back,' murmured Artie in ecstasy.

For once, the Lord Lieutenant, the personal protection officer and the Officer in Command were at a loss.

'Stop it,' howled Randal. 'For Christ's sake, someone stop it.'

'Try one of Sweetie's condoms,' suggested Dora.

Then, to distance herself from blame, she rushed

forward, trying to stem the flow with her notebook, but the torrent swept it aside like driftwood. A proffered bucket overflowed in a few seconds, a policeman's helmet met the same fate, as did the end of Miss Painswick's parasol rammed up as a catheter.

'Try a tourniquet,' said Dora.

But no one was around to solve the problem. Alex had not issued any invitations to the bursar's team of maintenance men. Randal was casting furiously about for one of his plumbers, but after twenty-four hours on, and having been ordered to 'bloody well hop it,' they had understandably done so. None of his workforce had been inclined to stay anyway after the snubbing of Little Dulcie.

'What a pity Graffi and Rocky were uninvited,' piped up Dora, 'they'd have stopped it.'

Like Don Giovanni's Commandatore, impervious to the Victoria Falls beneath him, General Bagley gazed fiercely at the Science Emporium: 'Serve you right, Mr Bruce, for trying to melt me down.'

'Can't stop it, sir,' a drenched security man muttered to the Lord Lieutenant. 'Better move on.'

Alex, meanwhile, had lost it, trying with rolling eyes to blurt out his last two crucial paragraphs about a breeding ground for the Hawkings and Einsteins of the future and thanking Randal for his historic contribution, but Denmark peed on.

The pupils and most of the audience were by now quite unable to contain their laughter. Rod Hyde and Gillian Grimston, even Ashton and Russell, were not displeased: Poppet and Alex had got a fraction above themselves recently.

Most of the school just thought: Hengist would have known how to handle it, turning the whole thing into an enormous joke. The gold hands of the school clock had edged round to 12.25. No time for Randal's speech.

'I would like to ask Your Majesty to mark your visit by unveiling a commemorative plaque,' mumbled Alex.

At least the sea-blue curtain didn't come away in Her Majesty's hand and the dark blue Parker pen worked when she signed the visitors' book. Joan, standing like a retired Guards officer in her pinstripe suit, tugged down Jade's skirt to just above her knees before she shimmied forward to present a big bunch of orange lilies and chrysanthemums, which the Queen passed on to her lady-in-waiting. Jade then managed to redress the balance a fraction by explaining it was her father, Randal Stancombe, who had bankrolled and masterminded the Science Emporium.

Then it was Dora's turn. Aware of so many of her media contacts watching, she once again turned and smiled quickly at an impossibly proud Paris, before executing a beautiful curtsey.

The Queen said she remembered Dora's father and how sorry she'd been when he died. Dora in turn said she was very sorry when the Queen had lost one of her corgis in a fight, but that she'd obtained a photograph of Pharos.

'You must miss her, so I've made you a model.'

Peering into the box at Pharos sitting on a royal blue satin bed, for a second the Queen bit her lip and Dora was afraid she was angry. Then she said Dora's version was lovely and very like Pharos and thanked her very much.

590

She was about to move on, the wind lifting the green feathers in her hat, when something in her kind face made Dora take a deep breath: 'As the most powerful person in the land, could Your Majesty possibly bring back our headmaster Hengist Brett-Taylor? We feel the heart has been torn out of our school since he left and we'd like him back.'

'That's enough,' exploded Alex as the Queen smiled and, handing the blue box to her lady-in-waiting, moved on. Alex was so livid, he forgot to present her with a copy of *A Guide to Red Tape*.

Many pupils and staff positioned on the other side of the Mansion didn't think they'd get a chance to see the Queen close up, but she left from a different side, passing Trafford high up in the battlements, who grabbed Miss Painswick's Union Jack and cheered his head off. On the way down the drive, Her Majesty was near the window and able to wave and smile at Little Dulcie.

135

Meanwhile, like the far-distant Oxus, a steady yellow stream of liquid still flowed out of Denmark's cock.

'Heads will roll,' screamed Alex. 'Who filled up that horse with water and how dare Dora Belvedon ask the Queen to bring back Hengist? It was probably her that filled up the horse, she was hanging round it long enough last night.'

The day couldn't have gone worse. He would now have to cope with Poppet's rage, because the Queen never reached RE. Not to mention Gordon Brooks, apoplectic because he'd driven all the way down from Manchester to find Boffin's experiment had ended up on the cutting-room floor. Stancombe was understandably angriest of all. All the press would concentrate on General Bagley's horse, no doubt already writing tomorrow's headlines about the Royal Wee, and hardly mention his heroic and historic contribution. And he'd just seen that white devil Paris Alvaston kissing Dora yet again.

Alex then had to host vegetable curry for nearly eight hundred, without any drink.

The day couldn't get worse, but it did when Dame Hermione slipped a bill for fifty thousand pounds into his top pocket.

'What is this?'

'My fee, Alex. I've given it to you at half-price for Cosmo's sake and of course there'll be ten per cent off if you pay cash, which I know you can,' she added roguishly.

Alex was jolted. How could she know any such thing?

'There was no question of a fee,' he spluttered.

'Indeed there was. I never give my services for nothing, even if it's a fee for charity. A performance like today's takes so much preparation—like you, I am a true professional.'

How dare she? It was Cartwright's fault, he'd obviously agreed a fee with her. Cartwright could get out before Christmas.

*   *   *

The vegetable curry lunch in the great hall without any alcohol was not a prolonged affair, but it gave Ruth Walton time to commiserate with Randal Stancombe.

'The Science Emporium is awesome; posterity will always remember you for it.' Then, lowering her voice: 'I've missed you so much, Randal, why don't you pop round for supper tonight?'

'I'd like that, Ruth,' said Stancombe.

Rod Hyde, meanwhile, was sitting in a window seat with Anthea Belvedon, whom he regarded as a very pretty lady and an excellent JP.

'Why don't you pop round later for a jar?' he asked. 'I could show you over St Jimmy's. I'm sure our school could sort out your Dora. We're thinking of starting a boarding house for challenging students.'

'I'd like that,' said Anthea, who wanted to pay back Randal for bringing Lorraine and flirting with Ruth Walton. She was fascinated to hear about Rod's new villa in the Seychelles and thought he was rather excitingly masterful.

Poppet, determined to regain the ascendancy, insisted after lunch that Trafford unveil his ground-breaking maquette of a sculpture to replace General Bagley. The royal party had gone, but there were plenty of dignitaries and press still around. Trafford, creator of *Shagpile*, *Tranny by Gaslight* and *Sister Hoodie*, was always good copy.

Poppet, requesting quiet with a cymbal clash of bracelets, pointed to the maquette in front of her on the table, but hidden by a tarpaulin. She then introduced Trafford: 'One of our most exciting Young British Artists, who'd like to introduce his concept of a new work of art to replace General Bagley, whose image many of us strongly feel to be outdated.'

A great rumble of disapproval at her words turned to envy as the artist in question was seen to be holding a large glass of whisky.

'General Bagley's like, male, imperialistic, aggressive,' Trafford told his now very hostile audience. 'I wanted to create something like female, tender, loving and of the age.'

Poppet was in ecstasy, nodding in agreement as Trafford drained his whisky and whipped off the tarpaulin to reveal a maquette of two very stocky women going down on each other.

Alex turned green; his wife was made of sterner stuff.

'How apt—an act of reciprocal love,' she cried. 'Do we have a title?'

'It's called *Minge-drinking*,' said Trafford.

*   *   *

Hengist would have given everyone the rest of the

day off. Alex, true to his puritan ethic, insisted afternoon lessons went on as usual. Stancombe then joined him in the head's office, where, judging by the shouting, the battle of Randal's Handle was joined. After twenty minutes, Randal stormed out and Alex went on the rampage.

He had never been so humiliated in his life. He was determined to track down the ringleaders responsible for the General Bagley fiasco. Denmark was still peeing merrily and to top it, some joker had leant a sign saying 'Flood Warning' against the General's plinth.

136

At dusk, a very tired Dora ran back to Boudicca to change out of her school suit. Trying to absorb the enormity of the last two days' events and the miracle of Paris loving her, she was suddenly racked with terror.

Up to now she had led a charmed life at Bagley. Hengist had adored her and after he'd gone to prison she'd been protected because her mother was a great friend of Alex and Poppet. But if Anthea had been relegated to row twenty-two under the awning, her mother had clearly lost caste and there would be nothing to stop Alex expelling her for begging the Queen to bring back Hengist.

If, in addition, she were expelled for the General Bagley escapade, Paris as her accomplice might get chucked out too and she'd never see him again, or Patience and Ian, who'd been so lovely, or Cosmo, Bianca or Artie or all her friends.

Paris had just texted her to ask where she was and she'd texted back to say she'd see him at supper. Cosmo, who'd managed to infiltrate himself into the unveiling of Trafford's sculpture, had also texted her that he'd overheard horrible Rod Hyde asking her mother for a drink at St Jimmy's later. Dora shivered as she remembered how well Anthea and Rod seemed to be getting on, on their hard seats. Her mother would love St Jimmy's because it was free. And how dare the old bitch not pop back to Foxglove Cottage to feed and let out Cadbury, then smack him if he made a puddle?

Dora had reached her dormitory and just taken off her suit jacket, when Joan barged in, bellowing:

'You were hanging round General Bagley's statue last night, Dora Belvedon, and you're no doubt behind that disgusting act of sabotage. Well, you're for the high jump. Mr Bruce wants to see you in his office at once.'

'OK, OK.' Dora raced out of Boudicca towards the Mansion, but the moment she was out of sight, she turned right instead of left, belted down the drive and didn't stop running until she reached Foxglove Cottage.

She was just being knocked sideways by an ecstatic Cadbury when her mobile rang. It was Stancombe. He'd tracked down an event horse called Kerfuffle, advertised in *Horse & Hound*, in which Dora had expressed an interest on her last leave-out.

'Lots of people are after him. Want to come and see him this evening?'

Looking at a horse was much better than being expelled and, out of the corner of her eye, Dora noticed Cadbury had chewed up one of Anthea's new silver sandals.

'Yes, please,' she said.

'Where are you?' asked Stancombe.

'At Foxglove Cottage.'

'Where's Mummy?'

'Having a drink with Rod Hyde.'

'Good. Don't tell her anything until we've bought the horse. She'll say I'm spoiling you. I'm tied up as we speak. I'll send a car to fetch you. See you in a bit.'

Dora was not pleased when creepy Uncle Harley rolled up ten minutes later. She'd only taken

597

Cadbury into the garden, fed him and chucked the remains of her mother's sandals in next door's dustbin; she'd had no time to ring Paris to tell him where she was going or change out of school uniform into jodhpurs.

Uncle Harley was not pleased when Dora insisted on bringing Cadbury and sitting in the back with him.

'Who's going to guard your mum's house?'

'Who's going to guard me?' snapped Dora.

Outside, night had fallen like a shroud. No stars or moon pierced the sooty gloom as they left Bagley village and sped out of reach of street lamps, lighted windows or even chinks of light under doors, deep into thickly wooded country where trees writhed under the rising wind's lash, down by-roads carpeted with red and orange leaves, which danced in the headlights like the flames of hell. Even Uncle Harley's jewellery didn't lighten the dark. In horror Dora realized she'd forgotten her mobile.

'Can I borrow your telephone to ring my boyfriend?'

'There's no signal here.'

Dora clutched Cadbury tighter. Kerfuffle had better be good.

As Uncle Harley turned through pillars topped by winged monsters, with eagles' heads and lions' bodies, and drove up a long, pitted, bumpy drive, Dora couldn't see any horses beyond the rusty broken railings. As the car rattled over a sheep grid, she thought she must be careful of Cadbury's legs if they had to make a run for it. Ahead towered a house, shaggy with leafless creeper, which fell over the windows like too-long fringes.

'Where are we?' she asked nervously.

'Here,' said Uncle Harley.

*   *   *

Meanwhile, over the border in Rutshire, Mags Gablecross, avid to hear details of the Queen's visit to Bagley, was awaiting her husband the Chief Inspector's return for supper, when the telephone rang. It was Debbie, Larks's former cook, asking if Mags knew of Janna's whereabouts.

'She's in Wales with Emlyn. They're getting married, isn't it lovely?' Then, when Debbie didn't react: 'Are you OK, Debs?'

'Yes—no. I'm worried, Mags. I've handed in my notice here. Janna was right all along about Ashton. He's vile and he never stops watching my boys. I think he's put a two-way mirror in the shower.'

Mags shuddered. 'How horrible.'

'It may sound stupid, but I think something evil's going on. Russell Lambert had a birthday party here at Ashton's place back in August and instead of wanting me to help out, Ashton insisted I looked tired, and packed me and the boys off to the seaside for the weekend.

'Anyway, it's Ashton's birthday today. Stancombe called him first thing about some party this evening. I picked up the phone by mistake and got the impression'—Debbie's voice shook—'Randal was lining up some little girl "for dessert"—those were his words—then Ashton laughed and said he'd be bringing something much more to his own taste.'

'You don't know where this party's going to be?'

'No idea.' Debbie started to cry. 'I thought I was

599

imagining things but Brad went to his dad for the day, and when I got back from Tesco's this evening, there was no one home. When I phoned Brad's dad, he said he'd dropped Brad off an hour ago and Ashton had insisted on minding Brad until I got back.'

'There was no note?'

'Nothing. Oh Mags, I'm so worried Ashton has kidnapped him.'

'I'll get on to Tim at once,' said Mags.

*   *   *

Over at Bagley, Paris was equally demented. Dora hadn't returned to supper and she wasn't answering her mobile. There was no sign of her at Boudicca when he dropped in and when he raced down to Foxglove Cottage, the place was in darkness.

'Randal's always had the hots for her. I know the bastard's going to serve her up at Ashton's birthday party and dispose of her afterwards. I can't handle it, Cosmo. I love her so much.'

'Randal's safe with Ruth,' said Cosmo soothingly, 'she asked him over to supper.'

'Well, fucking ring and check if he's there.'

'Bit early. I don't want to rouse his suspicions. Oh, OK then.'

Mrs Walton answered immediately: 'Randal? Oh, it's you, Cosmo darling, any chance of you popping over later? I seem to have been stood up by Randal. Cosmo! Cosmo!'

But Cosmo had hung up.

137

Stancombe must have been looking out because the moment the car drew up, the heavy studded oak front door creaked open and he pulled Dora in out of the bitter cold. Inside it was tropical, which had given him the excuse to wear nothing but a very white, mostly unbuttoned shirt, black velvet trousers and a great deal of Lynx—hardly horse-buying kit, reflected Dora. The sort of soppy music her mother liked was belching out of speakers.

There was no furniture in the high vaulted hall, but Stancombe led her into a large drawing room with flames leaping in a big fireplace, walls lined with mirrors and leather sofas, fur cushions and a floor covered in thick, dark shagpile. In one corner, four-legged and big as a Welsh cob, stood a vast television. In another was a table covered in glasses and a trolley groaning with every kind of drink. In the centre of the room stood a strange padded leather table about three feet off the ground. Twigs and rose thorns clawed and scrabbled at the windows, like the buried-alive trying to escape from their coffins. At least the windows had handles in case she wanted to make a quick getaway.

Cadbury's hackles had gone straight up, his pink lip curled, his normally genial yellow eyes were hard and reptilian. He had no use for Stancombe, who in turn was furious Dora had brought a chaperon, but decided not to make a fuss. She looked so adorable in her school tie with her chubby little legs sticking out from underneath her beige pleated skirt and flesh visible in the gaps between the buttons of her white shirt.

Anthea was too mean to buy Dora new uniform until she was absolutely bursting out of it, and would have been appalled if she'd realized how additionally seductive this made her daughter look. Stancombe, who'd just taken the brake off any inhibitions with a vast line of coke, felt himself boiling over with lust.

As Dora plonked herself down on a brown leather sofa, Cadbury wandered off to explore, which suited Stancombe. It would enable him to shut the bloody dog away in another room.

'What would you like to drink?'

'A crème de menthe frappé,' said Dora airily, 'but shouldn't we see Kerfuffle? Another buyer might get there first.'

'He's in the stables, only five minutes from here.' Stancombe waved vaguely in the direction of the window behind her.

'I want to try him out.'

'Of course. They've got an indoor school.' Hell, he'd forgotten how to frappé ice. He was so on fire, he'd melt anything he touched.

'Wasn't the Queen lovely?' said Dora brightly. 'I thought it went so well.'

Stancombe picked up a steel hammer. 'It was a cock-up from start to finish. Whatever one's reservations about Hengist B-T, he'd have known how to run a show like that. Alex couldn't run a piss-up in a brewery.' Bash, bash, bash! The ice was going everywhere.

'It's awfully hot,' said Dora, 'can we open the window?'

'Take off your cardi, then I can admire your sexy

602

figure. You get tastier every time I see you. Said I ought to put you down like a fine wine but I think you're grown-up enough for love now.' As he handed her her drink, his fingers caressed hers.

'I am too,' beamed Dora as he sat beside her. 'I've got a boyfriend. I've wanted him to be my boyfriend for nearly three years, since he played Romeo.' She took a gulp of crème de menthe. 'That's lovely, rather like mouthwash, but I don't want to be drunk in charge of an event horse. I've always fancied older men,' she went on dreamily. Stancombe preened, then scowled as she added, 'Paris is two years older than me.'

If I bang on about Paris, it'll put him off, thought Dora hopefully. He won't dare try anything if he's Mummy's boyfriend.

'Would you like a tour of the house?' murmured Stancombe.

Suddenly aware of his burning thigh pressed against hers, Dora jumped to her feet. 'I'd rather see Kerfuffle—and where's Cadbury? I bet he's found the kitchen.'

She ran out into the hall and, turning left, discovered herself in a room with a vast double bed and walls lined with more mirrors. On the bedside table was a pair of handcuffs, some manacles and an evil-looking black whip with a long lash, which was certainly not intended to be used on Kerfuffle.

Dora froze, increasingly aware she was in the presence of evil.

' "The Good Life",' sang Sacha Distel sforzando. No one would hear screams over that.

Next moment, Stancombe had grabbed her, hands going everywhere, like the sinewy tentacles of a mad, starved octopus. 'Little Dora,' he whispered, crashing his horrible, hot, full lips down on hers, ramming his great, hard, fat tongue between her teeth.

'Don't,' squealed Dora, 'let me go, you disgusting old man, or I'll bite your tongue off. I'll guillotine your willy. I trusted you because you're Mummy's boyfriend. She's a JP and I'm under age. She'll bang you up for this. Stop it. STOP it!' She tried to knee him in the groin as shirt buttons under siege were pinging everywhere.

'You know you want me,' taunted Stancombe, as wildly excited by her antagonism as by her plump, young flesh.

'I bloody don't, I've got a boyfriend.'

'That's where you're wrong.' Stancombe was tearing off her shirt, scrabbling for the hook of her pink gingham bra, about to rip it off in his frustration. 'You need a real man, not that little wimp.'

'I don't, he isn't, I love Paris.' Dora aimed a kick at Stancombe's shins.

'Stop it, you snotty little bitch.' As he pinned her against a mirrored wall, she was impaled by an erection big as a rounder's bat. 'Can't you get it into your fucking head, Paris is gay.'

'Don't be stupid,' panted Dora. 'He wasn't gay with my friend Bianca, or Amber, or your stuck-up daughter. You're just as green with jealousy as that crème de menthe.'

'Paris is a little tart,' hissed Stancombe. 'Look at the way he flashed his ass at Theo and Hengist and Artie and Biffo, all eating out of his hand.'

He was foaming at the mouth, veins like snakes writhing on his forehead. Dora had never seen anyone so angry and would have been scared witless if she hadn't been so furious.

'Come and look at this.' Grabbing her hand, Stancombe dragged her back into the living room where he pushed her down on the leather sofa. Then he took a video from the shelf and rammed it into the television.

Dora took a gulp of crème de menthe. She must get out and where the hell was Cadbury? Next moment, ridiculous, jiggy music flooded the room and despite everything, she burst out laughing at the sight of a lot of fat, naked old men dancing round, whooping and drinking out of champagne bottles. It was like the Elephants in 'Carnival of the Animals', except they had waggling willies instead of trunks.

'Oh yuk, yuk, yuk cubed,' cried Dora as they started groping each other, fondling and slapping each other's bottoms. Then she gave a gasp.

'My God, that fat one's Russell someone, Mummy knows him, he's the planning officer. And there's revolting Ashton Douglas who Dame Hermione sang happy birthday to. He's got his socks on too; expect he's frightened of getting verrucas. God, how gross—and there's Col Peters, vile pig and Rod Hyde'—Dora couldn't help giggling—'with a wincy little willy.'

But when Stancombe fast-forwarded the tape, Dora shrieked in real anguish to see that Russell Someone was humping away—'Oh God, no!'—on top of a thin, very young girl, lying on her front on the same leather table that was in the centre of the room, with her face concealed by flopping white-blonde hair. Although her hands were tightly tied together in front and Rod Hyde and Col Peters were laughing and holding her down, she was

605

putting up a hell of a struggle.

'My God, poor little girl,' screamed Dora, 'he's raping her. How can you allow something so terrible? Turn it off, I can't look.'

'Yes, you can,' hissed Stancombe, yanking her head back towards the screen as the camera zoomed in. 'Look at the Eiffel Tower on his shoulder. That's your little rent boy.'

'My turn, my turn,' Ashton was now yelling, prising off Russell and taking over, to whoops of excitement from the others, and shafting away with unparalleled viciousness.

'Just watch,' gloated Stancombe as, in close-up again, the camera captured below the blindfold a long nose, lips curled back in agony, and teeth plunged into the black leather. The exquisite bone structure could only belong to Paris.

'You revolting pervert,' screamed Dora, hammering her fists against Stancombe's chest, 'you were raping him, that's what the Upper Sixth threatened to do to my brother Dicky. How dare you hurt Paris when he was a little boy in a children's home with no parents to protect him? That is the most disgusting, horrible thing I've ever seen.'

Rushing towards the television, Dora pressed the eject button, grabbed the video and, yanking open a window, hurled it out into the bushes.

'You stupid bitch,' howled Stancombe, 'you'll pay for it.'

'How could you film something so sick?' howled back Dora. 'So you could blackmail Ashton and Rod Hyde if they stepped out of line?'

'That's enough, it's your turn now, no one knows you're here.'

606

But as Stancombe lunged at her, they were both distracted by excited squeaking. Shoving Stancombe off balance with all her might, Dora ran to yet another room, a sort of study with a big desk. Here she found Cadbury, his pink nose deep in a wardrobe, his tail going like a windscreen wiper on speed.

'Drop!' yelled Stancombe, hurtling forward and kicking Cadbury viciously in the ribs.

'Don't hurt him,' screamed Dora, grabbing a steel lamp.

But Cadbury had been living at home with Anthea and shut in the kitchen and kicked in the ribs once too often. Next moment he'd thrown himself at Stancombe, knocking him to the floor, standing over him, growling furiously.

'Bastard dog.' Stancombe tried and failed to grab Cadbury by the balls.

'Ha, ha, ha,' panted Dora, 'serves you right for persuading Mummy to have him castrated. Pity she didn't have you done at the same time.'

When she first peered into the wardrobe, she thought she'd stumbled on a linen cupboard, then slowly realized Cadbury had sniffed out pillows and pillows of white powder.

'Good boy, good, clever Cadbury, keep him there.' Dora rushed next door and seized the handcuffs. Wrenching a terrified Stancombe's hands behind his back, she clicked them shut. Then she bound his ankles very tightly with her Boudicca house tie.

'That's a reef knot—only thing I learnt in the Brownies. You won't get out of that, nor would Joan approve of such disgusting language,' she added, pulling his green silk handkerchief out of

607

his pocket and shoving it in his raging mouth.

'Let's see what else you've got in here.' Returning to the wardrobe, Dora found several briefcases bulging with notes and, at the back, a sleek, black gun, which she laid on the desk.

'You evil man . . .' Then, horror and revulsion taking over from a sense of achievement: 'How dare you do that to my boyfriend?'

Picking up the house telephone she dialled 999.

'I want to speak to Chief Inspector Gablecross, it's very urgent.' Then, after a pause during which Stancombe wriggled like a netted tuna to free himself: 'Hello, Chief Inspector, this is Dora Belvedon, could you come at once? I've just conducted a citizen's arrest on Randal Stancombe. He's in big trouble. He's got a lot of white stuff in his cupboard that doesn't look like baby powder.

'My dog, Cadbury, deserves a medal, he's been so brave. I've tied Stancombe up but he's not in carnival mood, so please hurry. I've no idea where I am, but it's quite grand with pillars at the bottom of the drive topped with monsters . . . now I remember, Mr Brett-Taylor's got one on his crest: they're griffins. The park railings are all broken and could never keep a horse in and it's a very shaggy old house with high ceilings. There's the doorbell, it might be Uncle Harley back, so please hurry.'

As the bell rang more insistently, Cadbury barked, uncertain whether he ought to rush to the door or guard Stancombe, who mumbled furiously through his handkerchief that Dora would now be for the high jump.

The doorbell rang again. Grabbing the gun, holding it behind her back, Dora tugged open the

608

door to find Ashton Douglas, with his arm round a beautiful fair-haired little boy, cooing, 'Come on, Bwad, you'll love this wonderful house. Good evening,' he added with his thin smile. Then, clocking Dora's ripped, undone shirt, paused, unsure what game she might be playing. 'I've got an appointment with Mr Stancombe.'

'He's not here.'

There was a crash from next door.

'It's a man mending the boiler,' squeaked Dora.

Ignoring her, Ashton ushered Brad into the study.

'What the hell?'

Cadbury growled, but with more uncertainty. He needed another line of coke.

'Don't untie him, Mr Douglas,' ordered Dora, whipping out the gun, 'or I'll fill you full of lead. The police are on their way and this gun is loaded.'

'Don't be silly, little girl,' said Ashton, hastily shielding himself with a terrified Brad.

Oh help, thought Dora as the doorbell rang yet again.

'You wouldn't dare fire that gun, put it down.' Ashton, setting Brad aside, was about to untie Stancombe's feet.

'Oh yes I would.' Aiming above Brad, Dora shut her eyes and pulled the trigger. As a bullet shattered the mirror above his head, Ashton dropped Stancombe's ankles. 'And next time you go kiddy-fiddling,' she added furiously, 'take your socks off.'

'What are you talking about?' spluttered Ashton.

'A disgusting film of you gang-raping Paris.'

Ashton's face turned as green as his suddenly panic-stricken eyes. Next moment, Brad made a bolt for it. Catching him with her left hand, Dora drew him close: 'It's OK, you're safe now.'

Someone was leaning on the bell. Backing towards the front door, keeping her eyes on Ashton, Dora put on a deep voice and cried: 'Who's there?'

'Open up,' said a familiar, reedy voice.

'Mr Fussy,' exploded Dora as she opened the door.

Alex was disguised by a false beard, a deerstalker and dark glasses; his open-neck shirt, however, revealed his wobbling Adam's apple.

'Your friends are in there, you disgusting old man.'

Seeing the gun and Nemesis in the form of a Middle Fifth student with her clothes torn off, Alex turned and bolted slap into the arms of PC Cuthbert, who'd been working out with Gloria and who had no difficulty arresting Alex and slapping him into handcuffs.

PC Cuthbert was accompanied by a policewoman, into whose arms Dora thrust a sobbing Brad. Rushing back to Stancombe's telephone, punching out numbers, she was deep in conversation as Paris erupted into the room, fists clenched, eyes blazing, snarling like a snow leopard about to spring.

'Where's Dora, what the fuck's going on?'

Cadbury thumped his tail as Paris took in Stancombe flailing on the ground, Ashton cringing in the corner and Dora with all her buttons ripped off, putting back a receiver. Completely losing it, Paris leapt forward, enfolding her in his arms, clinging to her like a drowning man to driftwood, frantically kissing her over and over again.

610

'Are you OK? Omigod, what did that bastard do to you? Did he hurt you?'

'I'm fine, honest. I was just ringing Paul Dacre to ask him to hold the front page.'

For a moment Paris gazed down at her in disbelief, exasperation and then love.

'For fuck's sake, I've been through every hell in the world worrying about you. No one knew where you were. I thought I'd never see you again.' Paris's voice broke as, trembling violently, he clutched her tight. 'And don't watch, you bastard,' he added, giving Stancombe a big kick.

'I left my mobile behind, I wanted to ring you but I couldn't,' gasped Dora who, as reality reasserted itself, had started trembling far worse than Paris. 'I had to be brave for Cadbury and because I was so desperate to see you again.'

Tears were trickling down Paris's cheeks.

'I imagined such terrible things happening to you, I can't tell you . . . They're like . . . so terrible.' Having furiously wiped his eyes with his sleeve, still clutching Dora, he turned towards Ashton.

'Many happy weturns, Mr Douglas, wemember me?'

His voice was so filled with contempt and loathing that Dora shivered, Cadbury dropped his ears and Ashton backed terrified into the cupboard.

'We've never met,' he gibbered.

'Yeah, we did. On your fortieth birthday, remember, at a waif-swapping party at Oaktree Court,' spat Paris. 'I don't figure this birthday's going to end quite so well for you.'

For a second his fingers tightened convulsively on Dora's arms, then, as she said shakily, 'It's OK, I'm

611

here for you, I love you,' police poured into the house.

'Break it up, you two,' said Cosmo, tapping them on the shoulder a few minutes later. 'Well done, Cadbury. Christ! Look at that Charlie.' He snorted a pinch from a claws-punctured bag. 'It's very good; I suppose we can't have the odd kilo for rounding up this gang of thieves?'

'How did you ever find me?' asked Dora, still keeping the firmest hold on Paris.

'We followed Mr Fussy,' said Cosmo, nodding at Alex who was remonstrating with PC Cuthbert.

'I can explain everything, officer.'

'And I can tell you, Alex, baby,' called out Cosmo chattily, 'that like Trafford's minge-drinkers, you're going down for a long, long time.'

*   *   *

While Col Peters, Russell Lambert, Des Res and Rod Hyde were being rounded up, all on their way to the party, Dora had a brief private word with Chief Inspector Gablecross.

'There was this hideous video in the machine which could send this lot to the electric chair. Could Paris possibly not see it? I chucked it out of that window into some bushes in the direction of the stables.'

'There aren't any stables,' said Chief Inspector Gablecross grimly. 'You've been very lucky; Stancombe's a very dangerous man. You must have been frightened.'

'I had Cadbury,' said Dora fondly, 'and, frankly, when a true writer gets on to a good story, they feel no fear.'

138

The police proceeded to fillet Stancombe's various properties and unearth every kind of skulduggery, more drugs and arms in other deserted warehouses and evidence that he had massively bribed Ashton, Rod Hyde, Alex Bruce, Russell, Desmond Reynolds and Col Peters with villas in hot countries and huge dollops of cash.

For these rewards, they had been instrumental in stitching up Janna and ousting Hengist from power, so Stancombe could get his hands on both the Larks land and Badger's Retreat, with, eventually, his eyes set on the water meadows and razing the Shakespeare Estate to the ground.

Stancombe and Uncle Harley were also convicted for importing and dealing in millions of pounds' worth of Class A drugs. In addition, Stancombe's inability to resist a chance to blackmail or keep in line the others by filming every birthday party had provided enough evidence to send the entire gang to prison for many years.

As there were at least a dozen other incriminating videos, Chief Inspector Gablecross managed to retrieve the one Dora had chucked in the bushes and never used it in evidence.

'Now Mr Fussy's gone, Hengist can have his job back,' said Dora happily.

Fussygate, however, was the third scandal to rock Bagley and, at the governors' meeting in mid November, it was unanimously decided, at Jupiter's instigation, to appoint Artie Deverell as headmaster.

Hengist wasn't due out till after Christmas and nobody knew if he'd even want to come back. Better to root out all corruption.

Ian and Patience were asked to stay on and Wally and Miss Cambola invited to join the staff. Artie would also have liked to have invited his friend Emlyn Davies back as deputy head, but Emlyn was finding both his marriage and his job with the Welsh Rugby Union far too exciting.

The photograph of Tabitha Campbell-Black and her horse was restored to the front of the *Old Bagleian* magazine. Aided by Artie, Lord Hawkley set about clearing Theo's name and overseeing the publication of his epic translation of Sophocles. A new classical library, large enough to contain the archives, was also commissioned. Randal Stancombe, it was noted, didn't tender for the job.

Other excitements included Dora and Cadbury getting their faces in all the national press and Cadbury getting his chance to meet the Queen after all, when he won an award for gallantry.

Just after Christmas, Artie Deverell was faced with his first challenge: a letter from Joan Johnson, saying in future she would like to be known as Mr John Johnson.

'She can take over Artie's old house,' observed Cosmo, 'and at least she won't be hassled to address the Talks Society.'

139

Hengist was released from prison in January, to the sorrow of his fellow inmates. He had written their letters, sorted out their financial and emotional problems and, when pressed, regaled them with hilarious anecdotes of the great and famous.

None of them felt he had committed a crime.

'When we took SATs at school, Henge, our 'ead gave us the answers.'

Despite his cheerful exterior, they were aware too of a heartbreak no prison doctor could cure.

Whilst inside, Hengist had kept up with the outside world, reading with pride of Jack Waterlane, Lando and Amber scuffling with the police over the hunting ban, with huge pleasure of Janna and Emlyn's marriage, noting without surprise the increasing closeness of Jupiter and David Hawkley, and, with amazement, the rounding-up of the Birthday Party club.

Being in prison, no one could ring him up for quotes.

'We'll sort out the nonces, Henge, if any of 'em end up 'ere,' promised his friends.

Artie Deverell was now at the helm, but in no hurry to desert his exquisite Regency house, so there was no longer any pressure on Sally to leave Head House. But she was so unhappy she wanted to escape as soon as possible. It was just the mental paralysis induced by having to dispose of twenty thousand books, innumerable works of art and beautiful cherished furniture; it was as harrowing as distributing beloved animals if you're forced to close down a zoo.

Since she'd demanded a divorce, Sally hadn't seen or spoken to Hengist. He had refused to allow her or anyone else to visit him in prison. Anxious not to embarrass pupils or staff, he returned to Bagley to pick up some books and clothes on the Sunday before the start of the spring term. Sally therefore said she'd make herself scarce.

Hengist arrived in a blue van lent him by Rupert and, before going into Head House, wandered up the pitches to Badger's Retreat. At least this had been saved from Randal's bulldozers. It was bitterly cold and had been trying to snow, but only with the coming of night was it starting to settle. Flakes swirling against a dark yew reminded him of a bottle-green polka-dotted dress with a full skirt that Sally had worn on their first date.

How he had missed his trees in prison, and his stars, only a few of which at a time could be seen through his cell window, and most of all, his white dog, whom he kept thinking he saw in the snow shadows.

The tall ash that had taken the huge side branch off the Family Tree when it fell the night Charlie visited Bagley and Oriana came out had been sawn into logs. These had been neatly stacked, as had the logs from the branches off the Family Tree. Two men were making a bonfire out of the brushwood. All our life tidied away, thought Hengist. On other trees, where branches had been sawn off, the circular scars had not closed up at the top, like horseshoes nailed to the trunk.

I could do with some luck, reflected Hengist.

Oriana coming out had been such a tiny thing

616

compared to losing Bagley, Fleetley and Education. Although Education would have been a two-edged sword, now he fully appreciated the ruthlessness of Jupiter, who had scuppered any hope of his return to Bagley. It was some comfort that Rupert had resigned from the New Reform Party.

But none of this mattered a jot compared to losing Sally and the desolation of stretching out in bed and finding her no longer by his side and having no one to share and recapture the tragedies and triumphs and laughter of thirty years.

Above, the snow now lining the limbs of the trees was like the body lotion Sally had rubbed into her arms every day, always making herself soft and beautiful for him. He had thrown away a pearl far richer than his tribe.

The three figures of the Family Tree, although battered, were still locked together. This year's riveted olive-green buds were already formed; Hengist picked up one of the curling sepia leaves with its cherry-red stem and put it in his pocket.

‘ "I have lived long enough," ’ he quoted wearily:

'And that which should accompany old age,
As honour, love, obedience, troops of friends,
I must not hope to have.'

Oh, he'd loved his troops of friends, but they were as nothing, again, compared with losing Sally. He had let her down, taken her for granted, betrayed her. For the first time in years, in prison, he'd had time to think.

He passed a young oak tree, planted 'In loving memory of that great scholar and schoolmaster,

617

Theo Graham'. Hengist wished him well, free of pain in the Elysian Fields.

That must be Artie's work. The earth, although frozen, was newly dug. Artie would make a strong, wise and compassionate head.

Hengist had sent ahead a list of the books he particularly wanted and, arriving at the house, found them awaiting him in packing chests in the hall. On the hall table was a huge pile of post, including an emerald-green carrier bag with an envelope attached.

Recognizing the spiky handwriting, Hengist opened it:

Dear Mr Brett-Taylor [Paris had written],

I wanted to thank you for everything. I've just retaken history, and it was dead easy. I should get an A star, so a middle finger to Boffin Brooks. I'm staying on now that Mr Deverell's head and I'm going to work really hard to go to your old college at Cambridge. I won't have any problem with top-up fees as Theo left me everything.

I'm sorry for all the trouble I caused you and Mrs B-T. Please don't take this wrong, but it meant a lot that you cared enough to cheat for me.

Love from Paris

PS Dora sends her love too.

PPS These are for the journey.

Opening the carrier bag, Hengist found a can of Coke and some tomato sandwiches with the crusts cut off, and broke down and wept for the first time since he'd been arrested. Finally, deciding he must

618

pull himself together, he opened a second letter, also recognizing the flashy, green scrawl.

'Dear Hengist,' Cosmo had written, 'I wonder if I could interview you for a programme I'm making for Channel 4 called *Cheating Heads.*'

And Hengist laughed until he cried, and this was how Sally found him as she tiptoed into the hall: once again the radiant, handsome, happy man she'd married. But when he turned, starting violently, she could see the deep lines of grief etching his face and that his thick, dark hair had gone completely grey.

'I didn't know you were going to be here,' he began.

'I wanted to see that everything was...' stammered Sally, clutching on to the front door handle for support.

Next moment the lights went out and the whole campus was plunged in darkness.

'Oh sugar, I lent the torch to Dora. She and Paris have taken Elaine for a walk.'

Jumping every time they bumped into each other, aching with longing, they found some candles in the kitchen and lit them from the gas cooker. Taking a lit candle into the drawing room to light more candles, Hengist could dimly see the snow outside tumbling down, blanketing everything in whiteness, making the ugliest shapes beautiful. Thinking sadly that he would never have cause to read it again, Hengist spread the pages of the *TES* on the remains of last night's fire. To his amazement, after few seconds, the pages leapt into flame. From the ashes, thought Hengist.

Sally brought down thick jerseys for them both. Hengist noticed her hair had been newly washed—

probably not for him—and her faint, familiar scent of red roses made his senses reel as it mingled with the smell of white hyacinths in the peacock-blue bowl on the low centre table. Sally had always staggered her planting of bulbs so they brought joy throughout the dark winter.

Hengist poured them both large Armagnacs and they sat on the carpet in front of the fire, separately pondering on the impossibility of dividing up their possessions or their lives.

Take what you want, they had both written to each other. But as the firelight flickered over the room, Sally noticed the bronze greyhound Hengist had given her to celebrate Cheerful Reply's victory, which had sealed their engagement. Then all the wedding presents, the little Sickert from her father and mother, the green Victorian paperweight from David Hawkley, the Rockingham Dalmatian from Rupert Campbell-Black and his then wife, Helen. How could you cut Sickerts and greyhounds in half? Or that lovely photograph of Oriana on graduation day or of Mungo on his first day at prep school?

On the piano—had Sally been playing it? wondered Hengist—was the music for the entrance of the priests in *The Magic Flute*, which had been played at their wedding. Next to it was a wedding photograph of Sally looking ecstatically happy. After a second glass of Armagnac and with the warmth of the fire bringing colour to her blanched cheeks, she looked just as young and pretty as on their first date.

'I feel guilty about taking so long, when Artie must want to move in,' she said helplessly, 'but I just don't know how to divide things up.'

'I'll cut out my heart and give it to you, it's yours anyway,' said Hengist in a low voice. 'I never wanted to leave, but I'd destroyed our marriage. I'd let you down irrevocably. It was the only option. You were right to tell me to go.'

'What are you going to do?' asked Sally.

'Write, I suppose. There's Tom and Matt to finish and I might have a crack at the novel on the Fronde. I'm sure it would sell more than Alex's apparatchik lit. I got a nice letter from Transworld saying they'd be interested in my memoirs.' Then, with difficulty: 'How's Elaine?'

'She misses you appallingly, she really pined.' Sally's voice trembled. 'In her gentle way, she never complained, but I think she should go with you.'

Then the lights flickered and went on. Both Hengist and Sally scrambled to their feet, gazing at each other, both aged as though blasted by lightning, but frantic to reach out.

'Fuck, fuck, fuck,' howled Hengist as the doorbell rang.

There was a pause, followed by quick steps, then a dark head came round the door. The skin was so smooth, the big eyes so large, clear and purple-shadowed, Hengist thought at first it was a pupil returned early.

'Hello, Mum,' said Oriana, then her face lit up:

'Dad, I didn't know you were here.'

'Just going,' mumbled Hengist.

A wail from the hall made them all jump.

'I've brought Wilfred, if that's all right.'

Going out into the hall, Oriana returned with the most adorable baby, strong, deep-blue-eyed, chubby-faced, with already a down of dark hair.

Sally took him in ecstasy.

'What a splendid little chap.' She gazed at him in amazement that something so wholesome and beautifully formed should emerge from such a strange, unpropitious union.

'Look at his sweet hands and his lovely skin, and I love that track suit, it must be American, they make such fun clothes. Oh Oriana, he's heavenly.'

After a minute she handed him on to Hengist.

'I hope you don't mind us giving him Hengist as a second name, Dad,' stammered Oriana.

'Not at all. Very gratifying; he's beautiful,' said Hengist in a choked voice as he gazed in wonder at his grandson.

'We chose a fantastic guy as a donor,' said Oriana, 'a baseball champion, a summa cum laude at Harvard, so Wilfie'll probably end up playing rugger for England after all.'

Profoundly relieved that her parents were taking it so well, Oriana then asked them if they'd like to come to New York for the christening next month.

'Charlie's parents are utterly spooked by the whole me and Charlie scenario,' she went on. 'You two would add a wonderful normality to the whole thing and be brilliant for my street cred.'

'Not me, surely,' said Hengist quickly.

'Hush,' said Oriana, reaching up to kiss his rigid cheek.

'Where is Charlie?' asked Sally.

'In the car.'

'She must be frozen, go and get her.'

'Only if you'll agree to come to the christening and stay on for a week or two. You both need a holiday.'

Sally didn't answer. The grandfather clock

continued its jerky tick.

Outside Hengist could just make out Elaine hurtling home through the snow, kicking up a white spray like a downhill racer. But still, for him, the chasm loomed. Still Sally didn't speak; then her hand slipped into his.

'Yes, we will,' she cried joyfully, 'that would be grand, Daddy and I would simply love to be there.'

The end

ACKNOWLEDGEMENTS

During the four years I have been writing *Wicked!*, so many people from both the maintained and independent sectors helped me, that a list of them all would be longer than the book. Most of them were insanely overworked, which made their generosity with their time and ideas all the kinder.

I should add that all were in some way experts in their field, but because *Wicked!* is a work of fiction I only took their advice in so far as it suited my plot. The end product is no reflection on their expertise.

I must start by thanking two inspired heads from the maintained sector: Virginia Frayer and Katherine Eckersley, to whom *Wicked!* is dedicated, because of their devotion to their pupils and the heroic attempts both made to save two wonderful schools, the Angel, Islington, and Village High School, Derby, from closing down.

Both Virginia and Katherine are happily now in other jobs, but at the time they talked to me for hours with great courage and allowed me access to their schools. I was also lucky to receive similar help from another inspiring head, Gill Pyatt of Barnwood Park, Gloucester. This school met a happier fate in 2005, when the Tories snatched control of Gloucestershire and with an hour to spare dramatically reversed an inexplicable decision by the County Council to close it down. To prove the point, Barnwood Park was later in the year declared the fourth most improved school in the country.

I was also made hugely welcome by two other brilliant local heads, Jo Grills of Stroud High and Vivienne Warren of Archway, who let me rove round their schools talking to pupils and witnessing inspirational teaching. Other great heads included Nigel Griffiths of John Kyrle School, Ross-on-Wye, Paul Eckersley of Selby High, Aydin Onac of Tewkesbury School, Jan Thompson of Cranham C. of E. Primary, Chris Steer of Sir Thomas Keble. I am also grateful for the shared wisdom of an awesome trio of former heads, Anthony Edkins, Jill Clough and Marie Stubbs.

The independent sector was equally helpful and I owe a massive debt of gratitude to two most humane and charming headmasters: Martin Stephen of St Paul's and Tim Hastie-Smith of Dean Close. They were always there when I needed help and gave me wise and witty advice on everything from royal visits to the endless speeches that bedevil a head at the beginning of term. In Tim's case, because Dean Close is indeed geographically close, I was allowed frequent access to his lovely school and enchanting staff and pupils.

I was also uniquely privileged to be able to pick the very considerable brains of two charismatic former heads, Dennis Silk of Radley and Ian Beer of Harrow, and to enjoy the beguiling company of Tom Weare of Bryanston, Peter Johnson of Millfield, Angus McPhail of Radley and Jennie Stephen of South Hampstead High School.

An incredibly valuable slant on school life was provided by headmasters' wives, who included Diana Silk, Angela Beer, Joanne Hastie-Smith,

626

Joanna Seldon, by a headmistress's husband John Thompson and masters' wives Dee Brown and Emily Clark.

I would like to thank Hamish Aird, our son's Social Tutor and former Sub-Warden of Radley, for his wisdom over the years. Special gratitude is due to Colin Belford, Deputy Head of Archway, for his advice on everything and for being an absolute charmer, to Tony Marchand, Deputy Head (Academic) at Dean Close, for his help on exam procedure, and to Simon Smith, Deputy Head of Brighton College, who invited me down to his school to witness a most successful partnership scheme between the College and Falmer, a local comprehensive, which was crucial to the plot of *Wicked!* Martin Green from Brighton College, Norma Smith and Rose Styman from Falmer and both sets of pupils were also marvellously eloquent on the subject.

The teaching I witnessed on numerous occasions made me long to be back at school again. From Stroud High, Kathryn Loveridge was inspirational on the *Odes* of Horace, and Andy Webb on *Romeo and Juliet*, as was Guy Burge from the Angel, Islington, on English grammar, Steve and Ray Jones from Village High School on all aspects of GCSE history, Paul Davies from Dean Close on the Russian Revolution, Claire Matthews and John Evans from Archway respectively on *Macbeth* and football, while from Barnwood Park, Ursula Jeakins excelled in French, Gill Moseley on music and Beverley Atkinson, Head of Science, was particularly brilliant on explosions.

I also had most rewarding input from other wonderful teachers: Veronica Rock, Colin Dodds,

627

Judith Drury, Di Medland, Dominic Hayne, Jose Hellet, Vanessa Macmillan, Anita Bradnum, Suzy Hearn, Sue Dean, who wrote a wonderful pantomime, Jill Barrow, Bob and Fran Peel, Andrew Cleary, Andrew Robinson, Vaughan Clark, Justin Nolan, Ailsa Chapman, Corinne Pierre, Trish Hillier, Carole Roome and Josephine Sutton.

In order to experience the terrors of teaching, I did give a two-hour lesson at Barnwood Park, in which I tried to explain to different groups the mysteries of writing a book and seeing it through to publication. As homework I set a task of designing a book jacket for *Wicked!* The results were fabulous and the children delightful. Nevertheless I needed to sleep for three days afterwards and was, as a result, even more overwhelmed with admiration as to how teachers can go so cheerfully through the same process day in, day out, thirty-nine weeks of the year—partly because they get such fantastic support from the non-teaching staff. On this front I'd like to thank Naomi McMahon, Marian Shergold, Margaret Turner, Clare Walsh, Brenda Dew, Ann Cave, Ali Sim and Jane Harrington for the support they in turn gave me.

I'm also grateful to those unsung heroes, the governors, who put in hours of unpaid work supporting their respective schools, and who were particularly patient in explaining the role they play. They include Peter Nesbitt, David Corbett, Deborah Priestley, Mark Westbrook and Mark Barty-King.

The true heroes of *Wicked!*, however, are the pupils. It is impossible for me to express my appreciation of those who helped me and the enthusiasm with which they entered into the whole adventure. Not a day passed without letters decorated with Pooh and Eeyore or Wallace and Gromit winging their way from Bryanston or Queen Anne's, Caversham, cataloguing the latest high jinks whilst stressing how hard everyone was working!

A stars must go to Tom Barber of Dean Close, for his marvellous run-down on life at a public school, to Carl Pearson, whose beautiful essay *My Dream* is reproduced on page 708, to Mabel McKeown and Anastasia Jennings for such entertaining dispatches from the front and to Karina Clutterbuck, who showed me how to turn an ink blob into a peacock feather.

Other pupils, who regaled me with riotous anecdotes and painstakingly initiated me into the mysteries of mocks and modules, include Henrietta Abel-Smith, Phoebe Adler, Jenny Frings, Alana Nash, Sam Muskett, Georgia Morgan, Georgie Klein, Jessica Seldon, Kit Cooper, Frankie Hildick-Smith, Ned Wyndham, Max Morgan, Teddy Chadd, Theo Hodson, Freddie Miles, Robbie McColl, Sarah Kilmister, James Bowler, Harriet Manners, Georgie Clarkson-Webb, Leo Robson, James Merry, Michael Dhenin, Sam Rogerson, Dean Monahan, Charmaine Moss, Michelle Pickering, Lauren Doble, Harry Flinder, Natalie Torr, Carmelita Winslow, Anthony Scott and many others.

I cannot emphasize too strongly how genuinely bright and good-hearted these children were and would like to stress that although pupils, teachers, parents and supporting cast behave by turns

629

heroically and simply dreadfully in *Wicked!*, no character is based on anyone living. Any coincidence is accidental, unless they are as eminent as Her Majesty the Queen or Lord Puttnam and appear as themselves.

I was lucky enough to be invited on four occasions by Lord Puttnam to one of the happiest events in the school calendar, the National Teaching Awards. Here I enjoyed great teaching, was beautifully looked after by Carolyn Taylor and Sarah Davey and revelled in the company of the Awards' irrepressible anchorman Eamonn Holmes and BBC producer, Kate Shiers. I hope I will be forgiven for inserting an extra category into the 2004 Awards.

A hugely enjoyable event in the independent calendar was the 2004 Headmasters' Conference in St Andrews, where I stayed at the lovely St Andrews Bay Hotel and found myself in the company of Titans. Here I would like to thank Martin Stephen for inviting me and Roger Peel and Chris Addy for their wonderful organization.

A large section of *Wicked!* is taken up with all aspects of GCSE, which I found unbelievably complicated, particularly when I introduced a mature student. I must thank Helen Claridge, Moira Gage, the exam officer of Stroud High, Cathie Shovlin of OCR, Madeleine Fowler and Yvonne Hutchinson-Ruff of Stroud College. They were all heroic in their attempts to explain things. I hope the liberties I've taken aren't too flagrant.

Education has many luminaries supporting it from the outside, so I am equally grateful to Margaret Davies of Capita, who came in like Red Adair in a skirt to galvanize the LEA in

Gloucestershire, to Andrew Flack, Director of Education at Derby City Council, to Dr Judy Coultars, Human Centre Technology Group, University of Sussex, to Jonquil Dodd, Senior Research Officer (Performance) Gloucestershire Education; and from Gloucestershire Social Services: Margaret Sheather, Executive Director, Alan Barton, Complaints Manager and Cathie Shea, Looked-After-Children Manager of Gloucestershire Social Services, Pat Gifford, Education Liaison Officer, Gloucestershire Children and Young People's Services, and to the staff of the former Causeway Care Home, Stroud. All nobly gave me their time.

I also had wonderful advice from Anne Clark, Lib Dem Councillor for Cotswold District Council and from Tory Councillors Jackie Hall and Andrew Gravells of Gloucestershire County Council who were both hugely instrumental in saving Barnwood Park School from closure in the nick of time.

My characters, both human and animal, sometimes fall ill and make miraculous recoveries, so I was lucky to be able to consult Dr Laurence Fielder and Dr Tim Crouch at Frithwood Surgery and John Hunter and his team at Bowbridge Veterinary Surgery. Carole Lee and Judy Zatonski from Greyhound Rescue, West of England and the Celia Cross Trust inspired me on Greyhounds.

I needed an exciting team-building activity in *Wicked!* to unite my two schools when they first meet. Hazel Heron of Roedean suggested I spoke to Ian Davies of Pinnacle Training, who in turn suggested a brilliant competition when groups of pupils compete to be the first to build and fly a hot air balloon.

There is a lot of rugger in *Wicked!* Here I got wonderful assistance from Matthew Evans of BBC Cardiff, David and Justine Pickering, Ralph Bucknell, Phil Butler and in particular from Stephanie Metson, Marketing Manager of the beautiful Vale Hotel, Glamorgan, known as the Lucky Hotel, because subsequently successful teams so often hole up there before big games. Stephanie showed me the vast indoor arena and entertained me royally.

On the sartorial front Robert Hartop of Grooms Formal Hire, Andoversford, initiated me into the latest fashion in men's evening wear, while Mariska Kay and Lindka Cierach advised me on lovely women's clothes. Duncan Armstrong, my bank manager at Coutts, and Stephen Foakes, my former bank manager, were brilliant on money. Dear Stephen Simpson of Hatchards is again to be hugely thanked for tenaciously tracking down any books I needed. Sounds Good of Cheltenham did the same for CDs. I am extremely grateful too to the resourceful and unflappable Phil Bradley of Cornerstones for driving me from school to school.

I am also indebted to Diane Law at Manchester United, Andrew Yeatman at the Met Office, Marc Stevens at the LSO for answering complicated queries and to Mike Zealey of ISIS, Lyn Sweeney and Sarah Hutchens for checking facts.

Gloucestershire police, as always, have been marvellous, answering my endless questions with patience, humour and imagination. I'd particularly like to thank Inspector Chris Hill for his advice on royal visits, Marie Watton, DC Liz Smith and Child Protection Officer DC Ian Bennett.

Last year saw the tragic, untimely death of Gil Martin, horse and lurcher lover and ex-super sleuth of Gloucestershire CID, who for fifteen years had advised me on all matters criminal. Gil was a brilliant, kind, enchanting man, whose loss to his family and legion of friends is immeasurable.

One of my heroes in *Wicked!* spends twelve years in care. On a train to Swindon, I was therefore very lucky to meet Josephine Cook, who told me most movingly about her experiences as a foster child. I am also grateful to Phil Frampton and Paolo Hewitt who each survived heartbreakingly harrowing childhoods in care to produce marvellous memoirs: *The Golly in the Cupboard* and *The Looked After Kid* respectively. Both books were an inspiration and both men, I'm proud to think, have become friends.

I am also beholden to the authors of the following books which provided both enlightenment and factual background: *Ahead of the Class* by Marie Stubbs, *Handsworth Revolution* by David Winkley, *But Headmaster!* by Ian Beer, *Why Schools Fail* by Jill Clough, *Special* by Bella Bathurst and the invaluable *Good Neighbours* by the Independent Schools Council.

Journalists do not automatically expect kindness from their own profession. Few, however, could have been more charming and helpful than Sarah Bayliss, editor of *The Times Educational Supplement*'s *Friday Magazine*, Rachel Johnson, Julie Henry, Amelia Hill, Geraldine Hackett, Quentin Letts, Chris Bunting, Will Woodward, Jo Scriven and Fay Millar of the Brighton *Argus*. I must also thank *The Times Educational Supplement*, who produce enough good stories

633

every week to furnish a hundred novels, for keeping me up with events. Our local press were also an endless support. Ian Mean of *The Citizen*, Anita Syvret of the *Gloucestershire Echo*, Skip Walker, former editor, and Sue Smith, present editor of the *Stroud News & Journal*, so often paved the way for me with local schools.

Gold stars must especially go to *Guardian* writer Jonathan Freedland and Wendy Wallace of *Friday Magazine* whose moving pieces on the imminent closing of the Angel, Islington, and the rejuvenation of Village High School, Derby, sowed the seeds of so much of *Wicked!*

My friends, as usual, deserve straight As. Caterina Krucker, a lecturer in modern languages, was a shining example of the passion and effort that goes into preparing and delivering a great lesson. Edward Thring was magisterial on bursars, Marcus Clapham great on Greece, Pete Hendy on Ofsted and anything scientific, Andrew Parker Bowles on racing and Bill Holland on music. Peter Clarkson, Associate Lecturer on Art History at the Open University, lent me endless books and his marvellous thesis on the concept of chivalry and mediaevalism in Cheltenham public school architecture, and Paul Morrison was illuminating on developers. John and Anne Cooper valiantly tried to untangle the red tape of education law. Jo Xuereb-Brennan was dazzling on acronyms. My brother Timothy Sallitt and his wife Angela were funny as ever on everything. Other friends who came up with great ideas include Shona Williams, Jill Reay, David Fyfe-Jamieson, Derick Davin, Jane Workman, Peregrine Hodson, Marion Carver, Tim Griffiths, Susannah and Bill Franklyn,

Sue Lauzier, Jane Farrow, Bill Holland, Liz and Michael Flint, Rosemary Nunneley, William and Caroline Nunneley, Marjorie Dent, Heather Ross, Anna Gibbs-Kennet, Rupert Miles, Roz Murray-Smith, Anna Wing, Janetta Lee, Joyce Ball and Karina Gabner.

I must also apologize to all the people who helped me who I have forgotten to include.

My marvellous publishers Transworld are a constant joy to deal with and I was particularly touched that Gail Rebuck, Larry Finlay and Patrick Janson-Smith kept in touch during the long haul, and never chided me for delivering late.

At the risk of adjectival overkill, I am convinced I have the sweetest, most encouraging editor in Linda Evans, the nicest, most charismatic publicity directors in Nicky Henderson and Patsy Irwin and the kindest, wisest, most cheering-up agent in Vivienne Schuster of Curtis Brown. No author is so blessed. Nor should Laura Gammell, Anneliese Bridges and Stephanie Thwaites who assist them, be forgotten. Nor Richenda Todd, my brilliant copy-editor, and Deborah Adams, who gave splendid help at proof stage.

On the home front, it is hard to describe my gratitude to my PA Pam Dhenin for masterminding the production of such a vast ungainly manuscript. I thank her for her tolerance, huge encouragement and for never complaining about my appallingly indecipherable writing as draft after endless draft was followed by interminable corrections and checking. Great chunks of the manuscript were also typed equally brilliantly and heroically by Annette Xuereb-Brennan, Mandy Williams, Pippa Birch and Zoë Dhenin, who all deserved A stars

635

for pitching in with suggestions, and producing the most beautiful typescript at phenomenal speed. Zoë Dhenin is also to be thanked for checking endless facts and tracking down everything from hotels in Baghdad to Croatian Christian names.

Other A stars should be awarded to my wonderful housekeeper Ann Mills and to dear Moira Hatherall, who restore order out of chaos, prevent the house disappearing under a tidal wave of paper and provide so much comfort and laughter.

Most of all I must thank my sweet family for putting up with force ten sighs and utter neglect for months on end. My husband Leo, our son Felix and his wife Edwina, our daughter Emily and her husband Adam Tarrant, our grandson Jago, and five excellent cats, all provide an essential mix of love, fantastic copy and endless good cheer.

CHIVERS
LARGE PRINT
–direct–

If you have enjoyed this Large Print book and would like to build up your own collection of Large Print books, please contact

Chivers Large Print Direct

Chivers Large Print Direct offers you a full service:

• Prompt mail order service

• Easy-to-read type

• The very best authors

• Special low prices

For further details either call Customer Services on (01225) 336552 or write to us at Chivers Large Print Direct, **FREEPOST**, Bath BA1 3ZZ

Telephone Orders:
FREEPHONE 08081 72 74 75